# the
# Couple

## Sarah
## Mitchell

Published by Bookouture in 2019

An imprint of StoryFire Ltd.

Carmelite House
50 Victoria Embankment
London EC4Y 0DZ

www.bookouture.com

ISBN: 978-1-78681-790-7
eBook ISBN: 978-1-78681-789-1

# CHAPTER ONE

*Now*

A voice.

It floats over the shoulder of the woman in front of me, words never intended for my ears. My brother's girlfriend is speaking to my mother, the milk-soft nape of her neck exposed by the overhead lights as she leans in close. Her tone may be low and confidential but I'm standing just behind them hearing it all, unwatched, unnoticed, until a maternal sixth sense makes my mother spin abruptly on her heel.

'Claire!' My mother's expression encapsulates shock masked by a hasty screen of pretence. I see the momentary panic as she scrabbles around for something to say, the alien lipstick, put on for me, for this, my special celebration, bleeding into the tiny lines around her mouth. 'Elsa was just saying… we were both telling each other… how wonderful you're looking tonight.'

This is not, as well she knows, an accurate summary of Elsa's remarks, and as if to compensate my mother throws her left hand towards me, finds my fingers and squeezes hard. 'What we really meant to say was how beautiful you're looking tonight. Just beautiful.' She smiles, eyes bright with sudden sincerity, although nobody else, not even, it occurs to me, my own, cellophane-packet new fiancé, has called me beautiful this evening. She presses my hand again, gazes first at me and then at Elsa, as if checking there is no trail of explosive between us that is about to ignite in her absence. 'I'd better go and find your stepfather,' she says, and is gone.

Elsa won't meet my eyes. She's staring into her drink, as if she wishes it were a lake that would swallow us up in a gulp of champagne. Her neck and face are reddened by a mottled flush that has nothing to do with alcohol – neither she nor my mother have dared to touch a drop – from fear, I think, of letting down their guard so far away from home. Around us, the room is thrumming; almost two hours into the evening and the energy levels have notched upwards. Strands of conversation weave a steady tapestry of noise while the army of young waiting staff – shirts, ties and hair all beginning to unravel in the heat – persist with the final few canapés, the cocktail sticks and tiny pink serviettes.

My own hands are empty. As soon as the party started I drank two large glasses of fizz, knocking back one straight after the other like shots, but stopped when Angus caught my eye and very slightly shook his head. Angus rarely touches alcohol. I think he wants to set me an example, as if anxious to quell any of my old student habits that might accentuate the modest age gap between us. I've told him more than once that I was the model student, too worried about my debt, which grew like ivy, wild and untrammelled, however much I lived on Co-op vouchers and charity shop clothes, to binge-drink in nightclubs or the student bar, but I'm not sure he believes me. Tonight, I like to think, is an exception; the bubbles are an effective and necessary fix for the knots that are cramping my stomach. After all, doesn't everyone get a little nervy at their own engagement party?

'Claire?' Elsa's voice is hesitant. 'I'm sorry… I didn't mean…' The words fail on her tongue.

'It's OK,' I say. 'I'm fine about it. Honestly.' And since neither of us can think of anything to say next we drop into a conversational hole.

Out of this room of sixty people, Elsa only knows my family. She is not here for me, why would she be? I am a competitor for Rob's attention, I hear her elfin presence in the disengagement of his voice and the abruptness of his answers whenever – rarely, now – I call him. No, Elsa is here for Rob, and for my mother and stepfather whom she adores for being loving and stable, unlike her own relatives who she left in Poland years ago. We've played down, of course, our family history of the errant, absent parent – as far as Elsa is concerned my actual father might never have existed. Now, the fabric of her blue satin dress hangs gracelessly from her slender frame, pulled out of shape by an oversized bow that reminds me of an election candidate's party rosette. I imagine she bought the outfit especially for the occasion but it looks garish and out of place amongst the understated charcoals and greys of Angus's friends.

I suspect I look out of place too, though since my presence is central to the occasion nobody would be rude enough to say it, or possibly even to think it. Normally I can make myself attractive, even, to adopt my mother's acclamation, beautiful. But my beauty is the kind that is painted in thick brushstrokes, the type that can be dialled up or down with the presence or absence of make-up and good clothes, that can let you slink unnoticed through a crowd one day and make an entrance, steal a scene the next. I am not someone who turns heads in an airport terminal at 5 a.m., yet give me red lipstick and a fitted shirt, let me shake loose my hair, undo an extra button and clasp my hands behind my back to inch my chest forwards, and I can wield the power as well as anyone.

Tonight however, my efforts have fallen short. Although my dress is outrageously expensive, it is also black and short and plain and it happens to bear a striking similarity to the uniform of the waiting staff, add a white apron and I could vanish into the background altogether. Not that I would object if I were asked to pick up a plate and hand around some canapés. I have to keep reminding myself that Angus is *my* fiancé, that this is *our* party, that these are *our* friends – because that's not really the whole picture. It's true, of course, that Angus is my fiancé; it's true we sent out cards with gold embossed lettering inviting these people to celebrate our engagement; and it's also true that some of the guests I, personally, chose to be here. Yet nevertheless, I can't shake off the sense that something is amiss. I want someone to clap their hands and stop the show – a film director, perhaps, with a black-and-white clapperboard. He could rush through the door that leads to the hallway, and beyond to a West London street, and with a wave of his arms and a shake of his head insist the scene is cut and we must all start again.

Back to Elsa. The colour is subsiding from her cheeks and eventually she stops contemplating her pale pond of un-sipped Moet. 'Honestly, Claire, I'm so pleased for you and how it has all worked out. After everything you went through with Daniel. That's all I was trying to say.' To my astonishment she takes a step towards me and plants the lightest butterfly kiss on my right cheek. She turns away before I can react and all at once I want to pull her back and ask her, beg her, not to leave me on my own, but already she's melting into the knots and clusters of bodies, in search, I imagine, of my brother. As I watch her silky blue back recede, her voice, the words I overheard her say, are so loud in my head I'm surprised the whole room is not stopping to listen to them.

'It's such a relief, isn't it,' was what I heard her murmur to my mother, 'to know that Claire is finally over Daniel? You must have been so worried about her, but now nobody would guess anything like that had ever happened.'


'Claire! There you are! We've only been engaged ten days and I thought you'd run out on me already!' Angus takes my elbow.

The noises in my head subside; the world gives itself a little shake and settles back into its groove. My husband-to-be is regarding me with his steady, grey-eyed gaze. 'Come on, Claire. There's a friend of mine I want to introduce you to.'

As he leads me over, I realise how obvious it is that Angus's friends are occupying one half of the room, and my friends, the rather less crowded, opposite half. It's not surprising, I suppose, since this is the only opportunity they've had to meet. This is the first party we've thrown, the first time that most of the guests here have seen us together, which is the almost-inevitable result of the fact that Angus and I have known each other for less than four months.

*

We met at a low-budget conference on the future direction of immigration policy. I was with a work colleague who recognised Angus as we arrived together at the registration point. Although it was clear they knew each other, a moment of awkward hesitation ensued before, as if by way of last resort, Angus and I were introduced. After the formalities were over we were each handed a clip-on plastic name badge and a white china cup of coffee that was so strong everyone later joked the caterers must have been tipped off about the quality of the speakers and wanted to ensure we all stayed awake. I suppose Angus made an instant impression because he was tall and attractive, but his good looks were tidy, almost formal – sharply cut, blondish hair, polished shoes and a tailored twill blazer – and the impression was only the fleeting, tangential kind. Then at the midday break, on the way to the side room where a plated cold lunch was being served, he appeared by my side, took hold of my elbow – much as he is doing now – and steered me towards an empty table. It didn't feel so much like a sexual move, more a proprietary one, as if he was collecting a piece of his luggage he'd left temporarily in the hallway.

'So *Claire*,' he said, when we'd sat down, making a point of reading from my name badge. 'What do you do?'

I liked the way he spoke. A noticeable northern burr called to mind peat fires and whisky, though later I learned his parents had left Edinburgh when he was just a child. I poked at the rather tired lettuce that accompanied a piece of quiche before I replied, the intensity of his gaze reminding me that I was wearing a well-cut suit and my hair had been brushed into a smooth, thick waterfall over my right shoulder. 'The Home Office,' I said eventually. 'I work for the Immigration Service.' The description always appears grander than I want it to, or maybe it has been ruined for me by the tone my mother adopts whenever she describes my role to one of her friends – a breathy mix of deference and pride that sabotages her attempts to sound casual about the fact that her daughter, raised in a terraced house in Ipswich, now works at a Government address in SW1. I suppose the job conjures images of heavy wooden desks and leather chairs, of neat shelves of files, and civil servants beavering away within a library-like hush. The truth is rather different: modern, modular furniture whose plastic surfaces overflow with stack upon stack of beige folders stuffed with papers, all of which are months old and required attention yesterday. If things had worked out differently it wouldn't have been my first choice of career, but at the time it seemed to be a way of being closer to Daniel.

'Are you a lawyer?' Angus asked. There was a subtle emphasis on the word lawyer. *Distrust or respect? Disdain or interest?* I couldn't tell.

'Not technically. But I have to know about immigration law and keep up to date with policy changes because I represent the Home Office when their decisions are appealed.'

His fork hung in mid-air, as if struck with awe by my not-so-lofty position, or awaiting further explanation.

'Think of all the claims that get refused,' I volunteered. 'I have to defend the Home Office if an appeal is brought.'

'Even if you think the decision was wrong?' His eyebrows lifted as the fork moved towards his mouth.

'Yeah… well,' I sighed. Shrugged. Gave the standard answer I've learned to give whenever anyone asks that question, which is all the time and always as if they're the first person ever to think of it. 'It's how the system works, but sometimes it's pretty obvious the decision was wrong and there's not much I can say.'

'Well, it sounds like interesting work.'

I wasn't sure whether he was asking a question, but after a moment he began to eat again. I thought of the waiting rooms full of desperation: fear of being sent home, fear of death, of hunger, fear of being found out; lies in every kind of language and terrible, unspeakable truths from the bleakest corners of the world. And the task of sorting one from the other in the space of a two-hour hearing. Interesting hardly covered it. I decided to assume there was no question.

I studied his serious features, the squarish jut of his chin and I found I wanted to hear the earthy tones of his voice again. Putting my elbow on the table I cupped my chin prettily in my hand and turned up the dial, 'What do you do?'

'I run a chain of hotels.'

'Really?'

His mouth broke into a slow smile, as if smiling was an activity only to be undertaken with forethought and deliberation. There was something very attractive about it, that level of self-awareness; it seemed to be a sign of someone truly adult, although as I studied his face I realised he was not as old as I had first assumed. There was probably no more than five years between us.

'The properties aren't enormous but we are gradually acquiring a foothold in most of the major towns across the UK.' Angus told me about the business of hotel management. How his firm identified suitable small buildings in up-and-coming locations with good transport links and developed them into places where someone travelling on business or leisure could spend a night or two without breaking the bank.

'Boutique hotels?' I suggested. He nodded, pleased, and gave me his card with the name of the company, MPC, printed in black inter-locking letters. No unnecessary frills, but comfortable places to stay at far less cost than the exorbitant prices charged by other city chains.

He kept eating while he talked, pausing every so often to check I was following. When I asked what he was doing here, learning about the potential effects of Brexit on the immigration rules in a third-rate west London conference centre, he blinked at the dumbness of my question and told me the impact of Brexit on immigration was crucial to the economy, something anyone who was serious about business had to understand to be able to assess the sectors of the market likely to suffer most. Besides, a lot of his employees were from mainland Europe. Then he reached into the top left-hand pocket of his jacket and pulled out an old-fashioned black leather diary.

'When can I see you again, Claire?'

As I hesitated, he smiled once more in that careful, slow-burn way, and I found myself saying that I was free on Friday; this Friday evening, as it happened.

Was ours a whirlwind romance? That's the term, they give, don't they, to a love affair that moves so quickly? But that's not the phrase I'd use to describe our relationship. Whirlwind suggests gusts and eddies, overnight storms of passion, followed by mornings of sweet, spent calm. If wind strength is the analogy here, I'd say that Angus was an unrelenting force six, a steady press of energy that propelled me ever forward to this, the occasion of our engagement party.

*

Stepping around several of our guests Angus steers me purposefully towards a man who is standing with his back to us. I have time to clock the lack of jacket and paisley shirt before the sound of a teaspoon on glass slices through the chatter. We look up to see my stepfather standing beside the drinks table, the crowd pulling back to a respectful distance. Somebody must have given him something to stand on because his face is visible over the crowd and it wears a stunned, quite horrified expression as the trickle of murmuring fades and then stills completely. This must be my mother's doing, I have never in my life heard my stepfather speak in public and I wonder how she can possibly believe it is a good idea for him to start now.

He gulps and after a moment unfolds a piece of paper that he proceeds to hold in front of his eyes as if to block out our presence. For too long there's a ghastly hush as he teeters like a high-board diver staring down at a postage stamp of water. I count to three... four... five. The tension in the room gathers and dilates, and then, just when I think my grip will snap, any second, the stem of my wine glass, he begins, and everyone in the room breathes out at the same time.

At first it's fine. He says the usual stuff that people always say at these occasions: the thank yous – to me and Angus for holding the party, to everyone for coming, to the caterers. After that he describes how happy everyone is for us – him and my mother, all our guests, and how happy he knows we are too – and finishes with a weak joke about his impending wedding speech. I'm sure that was supposed to be the end because his hand holding the script drops, he catches my gaze and smiles. I smile back. It was that small moment, I think, that must have given him a gust of confidence, the sudden inspiration to go off-piste.

'Finally,' he says, and my heart lurches in panic, anticipating, somehow, that he is about to wreck everything. 'I just want to add that Brenda and I are tremendously pleased Claire has such a wonderful new start with Angus, how delighted we are she can now put everything that has happened behind her.' He beams at his audience as if expecting an outburst of cheers and whooping. Instead, the temperature of the room plunges by several degrees. Angus's friends exchange glances; mine, on the other hand, avoid looking at anyone at all. My cheeks ignite while Angus's face is bright with questions so stark they could be scrawled across his forehead in black marker pen.

Although it's obvious my stepfather realises something is wrong, he seems bewildered, as if he doesn't understand what it is, exactly, that he's said amiss. Maybe he believes that because my family know about Daniel, all our guests must do as well; maybe he thinks that because of social media we – *the young* – don't have secrets from each other any more; maybe he assumes, and this, I suppose, would not be unreasonable, that I must have told Angus – the man I will marry in a few months' time, the man I surely love – about Daniel. Locked into bringing the thing to its proper end my poor stepfather pushes his spectacles further up the bridge of his nose and swallows so hard I can see the convulsion move his throat. 'So,' he says, unhappily, 'it just remains for me to ask you to raise your glass to toast the happy couple.' He raises his glass, as does my mother, who has appeared, for the sake of solidarity, at his elbow.

'Claire and Daniel!'

There is a hesitation before the answering echo, as our confused guests adjust to this unexpected detour in the script.

'Claire and Daniel!'

Angus says it too, tilting his glass in my direction. I copy him, but my own hand stops at shoulder height, paralysed. Although I'll have to come up with something to tell him later I'm pretty certain I won't be required to provide an explanation here; Angus couldn't bear to admit anywhere so visible that he has no idea what my stepfather is talking about.

The instant the toast is over, my stepfather steps off whatever he has been standing on. There is a disjointed pause before, to my relief, Angus starts to clap, and gradually the rest of the room follows his lead until the applause reaches a respectable level, a level that might, if I'm lucky, bury my stepfather's faux pas under its hail of bullet-like noise.

I am impressed by the self-restraint that prevents Angus demanding answers the second the taxi door slams. We are halfway home before he swivels towards me, allowing the oncoming traffic to illuminate his strong, regular profile. What was it, is the gist of his questioning, spoken with a hand on my knee and an unhurried, almost kindly curiosity, I had put behind me? *And who is Daniel?*

I have had more than an hour to prepare and I am ready.

'A boyfriend. An old boyfriend,' I tell him. 'He used to get a bit out of hand, that's all.' I laugh, but lightly, gossamer-feather light.

'Out of hand?'

'Unpredictable. Unreliable.' I turn away from Angus to look out of the window at an altercation happening on the pavement right beside us in front of a restaurant. A man and a woman are screaming at each other. The woman tries to leave but the man grabs her handbag. It falls from her shoulder and he hauls on the leather strap as she strains against it, shouting into her face.

I could have used another word about Daniel. Angry, I might have said. Daniel sometimes got a bit angry.

'Look! Look what's happening over there.' I point towards the scene that resembles a *Crimewatch* re-enactment rather than real people arguing. People who will have to contend with each other long after our taxi has left them in its wake; who will have to face each other tomorrow, perhaps even the following week or the following year; perhaps when nobody else is there to see how far they can be pushed.

# CHAPTER TWO

All the seats in the waiting area of Ellerton House are occupied. There are adults leaning against walls, and children huddled on the nylon carpet at the feet of women dressed in brightly coloured saris, black and brown abayas and blue denim jeans. Conversations swirl in languages and dialects I don't recognise, the names of which I probably wouldn't even be able to place on the right continent. Until I started this job I had no idea there were so many different countries in Africa, places you have to escape from rather than leave, where the opportunity to travel across Europe for weeks in the back of a stinking truck is regarded as a life chance and not a life sentence. One man is curled in a corner, with his head against the wall and his feet drawn up: tucked into a foetal position. His skin is a deep, dense black and his hair a scrub of grey; an ancient Manchester United football shirt with Beckham printed across the back hangs loose over his trousers. By the chair sits a Lidl carrier bag, papers spilling out of the top; some of the groups are talking with lawyers, but he seems to be entirely alone.

I wonder if his case is one of mine. I have three today, all listed in front of the same judge. My files bulge with clumps of tattered documents held together by elastic bands: interview notes, payslips, telephone records, and most importantly of all the decision of the immigration service that has stopped somebody coming into the country, or required them to leave. I make my way to the special room that is allocated to people like me, the happy band of brothers that represent the Home Office. There's scarcely more room in here than in the waiting area. Most of my colleagues are reading, bent over the files spread on their laps, or on their mobiles taking last-minute instructions.

'No, that can't be right!' one of my co-workers sighs, rolling her eyes at nobody in particular. 'I'm certain it's not there. Some of the papers are definitely missing, and the judge won't adjourn the case again. It's already been adjourned twice before. The decision being appealed was made in 2016.'

I find an empty space, park the enormous black wheelie bag that contains my papers and dig out the folders from the third case. I should have looked at it last night, but I didn't get allocated my list for today until I was leaving work and by the time I got to this file it was so late that the tedious ink of the paragraphs and subparagraphs of immigration rules had begun to swim into an incomprehensible jumble. To my surprise, when I examine it now the case appears quite straightforward. An Indian man is seeking permission to enter the UK to join his wife. His application was refused because the Home Office official thought his wife didn't earn enough to support him, but now she has provided payslips, and copies of her bank statement to show the money being paid in. It seems to me they satisfy the income rules quite easily.

Just before ten o'clock I gather my files and head into the court where my cases will be heard. It is exactly the same as all the other nineteen courts in this building; a raised dais at one end for the judge, with a desk that spans the entire width of the room in front of tables and chairs that have designated slots for the person whose appeal is being heard and the home office reps like me. The room is bright and modern with windows high above the thrum of central London. There is no wood panelling, no red-robed judge or wig-adorned barrister, no sense of history – but the present is here in spades, reproachful and urgent, and it presses in on us from every corner of the globe.

The man in the Beckham shirt springs to his feet as I go in but sinks back down when he realises I'm not the judge. All the applicants in court eighteen are huddled against the back wall. Beside Beckham is a family: a mother, a father and four sons with exactly the same molten-brown eyes, all of which are fixed with desperation on their barrister. The final member of the cast is a young woman from India. I guess that she's the wife in my just-read file. Dressed in skirt, shirt, heels and tights, she might be interviewing for a secretarial post. She seems determined to catch my eye and smiles so brightly when she does that a sudden splinter of doubt makes me wonder if her case is quite so strong after all.

While I'm still trying to recall if there was anything at all suspicious in her paperwork, the door to the court reverberates with a medieval thumping. 'Court rise!' The judge's clerk enters followed by a female judge I haven't seen before. The judge makes waves to the assembled crowd to sit, the gesture is vague yet there's an intensity, a watchfulness, to her manner coupled with a tendency for her gaze to stray towards the clerk, as if checking for a prompt. I guess she must be new. She takes a pen from a pencil case, which is the zipped, transparent kind that students take into exams.

The judge wants to take the file with the family first, but is told by the barrister an interpreter may be needed and he is busy in another court.

'All right,' she says, 'I'll take your case at 11 o'clock and the asylum matter now. Who is representing Mr Nasimi?'

The man in the football shirt lifts his gaze from his knees. The judge looks hopefully at the barrister, but he is shuffling out of court with his family and shakes his head apologetically.

She turns back to Beckham, 'Do you know where your solicitor is?' There is no reply. The judge consults the papers. 'An interpreter is needed in this case too,' she says, although it's not clear whom she's informing of this fact. I can see her wondering what the hell she is supposed to do. 'I'll take the third matter first,' she decides, indicates for the Indian woman to come forward and is rewarded with a beaming smile.

I question the woman in the normal way; I ask her about her husband briefly and then about her job. She tells me she works in a new digital marketing firm as an administrator, she answers the phone and books the client companies into meetings. Her answers are clear and convincing and soon I nod to the judge to tell her that I've finished my cross-examination. The woman begins to rise from the witness table, but the judge intervenes. 'Wait,' she says. 'I've got a few queries of my own.'

Twenty minutes later the judge is still interrogating, rooting amongst the papers like a bloodhound. 'So these are your payslips?'

The woman nods and smiles the same bright, brittle smile, although this is the second time the judge has returned to the stack of standard-form payslips.

'And these are your bank account details?'

The woman nods again.

The judge flicks between the two clips of documents, saying nothing.

I am beginning to feel impatient. I'm certain now that there is nothing suspicious about this case, and I want to move on to the next. Otherwise we won't finish the list until late this afternoon and I'll have to spend yet another evening preparing the case papers for tomorrow. I look up as the barrister comes back into court with the family; he glances at the clock on the wall and then at me. I shrug.

'Where is your employment contract?' the judge asks.

'It's here, Madam, on page 32.' The Indian woman points to a document in front of her and the judge turns the pages of her bundle.

'And where is the covering letter?'

The Indian woman doesn't reply. I think that she can't have heard the question.

'Where is the covering letter?' the judge repeats.

Fractionally, the air in the room tightens.

'What do you mean, covering letter?'

'An employer wouldn't send you an employment contract, without a covering letter.' The judge's voice is steady and focused.

For some reason I, the barrister, the family with the four children, even the asylum man, appear to be listening intently now, but I don't really understand why the exchange is so enthralling. The Indian woman probably didn't bother to keep the letter and I can't see why that matters. To my surprise that's not what she says.

'The contract wasn't sent to me by post. It was sent as an attachment to a message on my mobile.'

'Do you have your phone with you? Can you find the message?'

The woman takes it from her bag with the air of someone hypnotised and begins to search; her fingers stumble over the screen while we all sit, waiting. Eventually she finds what she was looking for and holds out her hand; she's not nearly close enough to the judge to pass her the phone but she can't seem to move. After a moment the barrister clears his throat, stands up, slips the mobile from the woman's grasp and takes it to the judge, careful not to look at it himself.

Seconds pass, and nobody says a word. The Indian woman is staring straight ahead, handbag on lap, immobile. There's a baby crying somewhere in the building, but none of us in court eighteen are the least bit interested in the baby. We are all concentrating on the judge. Eventually she lifts her head.

'I'm going to read out the message,' she says pleasantly, far too pleasantly, 'and then I'm going to ask you some questions about it.'

The woman nods. In fact we all nod, like children spellbound by the prospect of a story.

'Your job,' the judge begins, eyes back on the mobile, 'is an administrative assistant in a digital marketing firm. There are four people in the office apart from you, and your boss is called Maria. Your duties are to arrange meetings between potential clients and the website designers, and deal with the paperwork. The address where you work is on your employment contract, which you must memorise because you will probably be asked about it at the hearing.'

'You see' – the judge is speaking directly to the woman now, her voice fraying with anger – 'what this message suggests is that somebody is telling you about a job, a job that you don't really do, so that you can pretend to this tribunal you earn enough money to bring your husband into this country!'

'No…' The single word is barely audible.

The judge's attention is directed back at the screen. She appears to have scrolled further through the messages. A moment later she starts to read again, 'If you need further details say the client base is within the M25. The contract states you work an eight-hour day Monday to Friday and alternate Saturdays.' She pauses, 'You have replied to this message with a smiley face and some text which says, "*thank you so much*".'

'It was about a different job.' The woman swallows. 'A job I thought I might apply for within the same company, which is why I had to be told everything about it.'

'Then why was the employment contact for the job you are doing now – the job you have told this tribunal you are doing now – attached to these messages?'

There is no reply.

'Well?' The judge is writing now, the efficient glint of her ballpoint skims over the paper.

As though she can't bear the interrogation a second longer the woman's head drops as suddenly as if her neck had snapped. She is gazing at the handbag on her lap with wide, defeated eyes. I remind myself she has lied to the court, attempted to defraud my employer, the Home Office, but I can no longer hold her in my sight. I think it is her shame I cannot bear, but at this very second I am not entirely certain.

'I will reserve my decision and my judgment will be sent to you in two or three weeks' time.' The judge is going through the formalities although there is no doubt what the outcome will be. She picks up a different file. 'Now, do we have an interpreter for the asylum matter yet?'

'Excuse me.' The Indian woman hasn't yet stood up, although the man in the Beckham shirt is hovering just behind her shoulder. 'What will happen now?'

The judge takes a short, impatient breath. 'As I said a moment ago, you will get my judgment in about three weeks.'

The woman still doesn't move, although her right hand is fiddling with the clasp of her handbag, opening and shutting it over again. 'But the people who gave me these papers, who sent the messages, what will happen to them?'

The judge blinks at her in naked astonishment. 'I really couldn't say. Why?' she adds. 'Is it any concern of yours?'

The woman doesn't answer, but the raw flick of panic in her eyes as she leaves the room makes me wonder if it might be.

# CHAPTER THREE

After the hearings finish I head straight for West London, but I misread the directions that Angus sent me, get off at Acton Town instead of East Acton, and then spend a fruitless ten minutes trying to work out where I am on Google Maps before I notice my mistake. By the time I arrive at the property Angus wants me to view in Ealing, the heels I bought on Oxford Street at the weekend have rubbed a blister into my left ankle and I feel like shoving my hideous wheelie bag straight into the path of an oncoming lorry.

The house, however, stops me in my tracks. For a start, it's an actual house, rather than a flat, and it's end of terrace too, boasting wide sash windows and woodwork that has been painted recently and with care. In this sort of location, close to the tube, close to shops, with a nice leafy park just around the corner, the parking slots are full of Audis and BMWs and properties like this normally cost close to a million.

I double-check the address, which I noted on my phone. I am still adjusting to life with Angus, more precisely to life with Angus's money. When my father exited our family to shack up with an American wannabe actress, my mother, Rob and seven-year-old me swiftly plummeted from a four-bed house in a cul-de-sac boasting child-friendly road bumps to a hovel above a newsagent. The arrival on to the scene of Andy, my kindly stepfather, saved us from complete penury but our circumstances remained modest to say the least – for ages I kept an old Boden catalogue under my pillow to let me pretend I still belonged with those shiny little girls playing on a beach in a pretty dress and matching cardigan.

It goes without saying that when I moved to London neither my mother nor stepfather was able to write me a big fat cheque, *just to get you started on the housing ladder, darling,*' and without a job in banking I assumed I was destined to the non-existent joys of the long-term rental market: a dodgy shared house in a dodgy neighbourhood an equally dodgy bus ride from the nearest train station. Angus, however, changed all that when his arm locked on to mine at the immigration conference. As soon as we began to house-hunt it became clear that he had in mind a quick purchase of the kind of place – a two-bedroom apartment, in a nice, privately owned block – which previously I could only have dreamed of. And if ever I wonder about Angus, about the speed of the relationship, the depth of the romance – if doubt ever sidles in – a two-minute conversation with my mother, her blatant delight that at least one of her children has not been held back by her inability to hang on to their father, can dispel those qualms pretty quickly.

The notion of an actual house, however, in London W5, is not only a dream of a different order but also an unexpected one, because we have already agreed to buy another property. Angus was insistent, however. Apparently, the estate agent had hinted, rather bluntly, that the owner has money problems and is very keen to sell. As Angus relayed this information his voice flashed with the excitement of a man with a bargain in his sights, a killing to be made.

I ring the bell and wait. Eventually the door opens, but not to an estate agent. The man behind it is quite old, mid-forties, I guess. He has, dark hair with threads of grey that flatter rather than age, brown eyes and a lean, tanned face suggestive of travel and money – and instantly more compelling than the pasty complexions of my civil service colleagues. He is average height and wearing jeans with a white, immaculately laundered shirt that looks like it belongs behind a suit but is unbuttoned at the neck, and he is cradling a large glass of red wine. We consider each other for a long, unnerving second.

'I suppose it's safe to let you come in?' he says, eventually.

The words are sardonic, of course, spoken with humour, but flecked, I come to realise later, with vigilance.

My face must register shock or anxiety, or possibly both, because the man's shoulders immediately drop, he laughs and pushes the door further open so that a mechanical drone from a radio or television spills on to the pavement.

'I'm sorry. A joke. A bad one. Come in.'

Although it is summer, the city dusk has already fallen. An invisible sun is slipping beneath the earth, the air turning mauve as the classy cars and buildings light up like fairground rides. A few doors further up the street a couple is leaving one of those ubiquitous pasta places. A conversation drifts over their retreating footsteps; the man is jovial, slotting his arm around the woman's waist.

'I'm Mark,' he says, because I haven't moved. 'Mark Tyler.' And he holds out his hand.

I can't help but stare at him.

'The estate agent had to leave, but it doesn't matter because I got back from a business trip earlier than I was expecting. Really,' he adds, 'I don't bite.' He gestures at the wine. 'I opened this a while ago. I got a little bored waiting for you.' He smiles again, but when another moment passes a frown begins to crease the space above his nose. Actually, I'm not reacting to what he's said. At the time, I barely register the oddity of his opening remark. The reason I am paralysed, rooted to a spot between the bins and a tub of shabby geraniums, is because he looks exactly like an older, more intriguing version of Daniel. Finally, I shake myself, mutter an apology – something about work and getting lost – and then I step over the threshold.

Inside the place is striking, just as Angus promised on the telephone. He's gutted the entire ground floor to make it one big space, the kitchen at the far end with white cupboards and grey tiles, the front all taupe carpet and magnolia woodwork. Bookshelves have been fitted either side of the fireplace. One has been modified to accommodate a flat-screen television and somewhere on the far side of the world racing cars are screaming around in tarmac circles. It looks to me like a room from a magazine that only lacks a celebrity sprawled over a sofa.

Mark walks over to the television, switches it off, and we are stranded suddenly in the middle of an awkward silence.

'A glass of wine?' He angles the bottle over an empty glass, pauses and cocks his head to one side. 'Or perhaps you're the type who doesn't drink during the week?' He is teasing me already, his voice a singer's baritone with an accent that slices square the end of his words. I should feel uncomfortable or patronised, instead, absurdly, I am flattered at his familiarity. I take the glass and let him lead me towards the back of the house.

He maintains a steady chatter, describing where he sourced this fabric, why he used Romo rather than Sanderson, or Ross rather than Conran. The labels trip from his tongue like the names of family members. I open cupboard doors, run my hand along the breakfast bar, and ask the usual questions about how long he's lived here and whether the roof is OK and are there any damp problems, but by the time I follow him upstairs I already want to buy the house so badly I am formulating phrases I can use with the estate agent as to why we are pulling out of the purchase Angus and I settled upon two weeks ago, and ignoring the stabs of guilt that are needling the insides of my stomach.

Four doors lead from the landing. First, at the front, he shows me the main bedroom, awash with creams and pale yellow. Next a room that is perfect for a cot – though instinctively I choose not to draw attention to the ring on my finger, my soon-to-be wedding.

The third door he opens with a flourish. Inside is a bathroom. The bath, the size of a bed, is sunk into black marble, the shower has a vertical line of body-jets and a floor-length mirror along the inside wall. Standing in the doorway I find I am blushing and whether it is association, premonition, or simply the effects of alcohol on an empty stomach, is impossible to tell. In any case, Mark has already moved towards the other, fourth, room. Here the door is slightly ajar, the darkness inside diluted by the soft gleam of a night light. He holds it a little further open to a single bed and a child-size form nestled under the duvet. Without him doing anything, I understand that I am not to go in.

'Normally my ex-wife has custody of him during the week,' he says. And shuts the door.

Back downstairs, he tops up our glasses and sits on a beige leather sofa. He gestures at the other, facing him.

'So, Claire, what do you think?'

I take another mouthful of wine, buying time, but I cannot see a reason not to tell him. I explain that my fiancé and I have agreed to buy a flat already, from an elderly woman who is moving in with her son; that all has been agreed and solicitors instructed; that I only came to view the house because Angus was so insistent. I hear my words, earnest and concerned – and empty. I stop and he smiles, clearly amused.

'But you did come didn't you, Claire?'

When I say nothing, he raises his eyebrows encouragingly, as if he is prompting a child in a nativity play. I nod slowly, caught moth-like by his gaze. I think this is how Daniel would have looked in fifteen years' time.

'And you have no legal obligation to buy the other property?' Mark continues.

I shake my head obediently.

'Well then...' He shrugs dismissively, reaches for the bottle, and begins to ask me questions about my work.

An hour later, I am still talking. We have covered the Department – its external and internal politics – my home, even Angus. Curled within a golden pool of meticulous lighting, the hateful shoes kicked beneath the sofa, I am feeling quite loquacious. There is no stopping me, although my enunciation, thickened by wine, requires increasing attention. Mark seems enthralled by the minutiae of my job and I am still in full flow when he glances, rather suddenly, at his watch.

'Goodness,' he says.

I look at my watch too. 'Goodness,' I repeat. I gather my things in a clumsy rush. At the door there is a large rectangular mirror set within an ornately carved frame. I see my face, flushed along the cheekbones, my mahogany-coloured hair, flattened by the earlier walk, like wings against my face, my eyes which are green, and the brown, rather rumpled, cloth of my suit.

'Beautiful, don't you think?'

For a wild split second I think he is referring to me.

Then he says, 'It's Spanish. From before the civil war.' He runs a reverential finger around the edge of a pale walnut rose petal.

'Yes,' I say, feeling stupid. I touch the mirror too, my heart pounding unaccountably. And then, because he seems to expect something more, 'How lovely to own something so special.'

There is a small pause before his fingers slip from the wooden frame and onto the sleeve of my jacket. 'You must give me your phone number,' Mark says. 'Just in case' – finding my eyes, he holds them captive – 'we need to speak some more about the house.'

Back in our rented apartment, Angus is standing in the kitchen, still in his suit. He seems to be watching the entrance, waiting for me.

'What did you think?' he asks, the moment I close it behind me.

'I like it,' I say carefully. 'I like it a lot, but can we afford it? It must be much more expensive than the apartment on Warrington Road?'

Angus turns his head away from me to loosen his tie, pulling at the knot with the fingers of his left hand. 'It's not actually been formally put on the market yet but the estate agent is sure we'd get it at a knockdown price because the owner needs to move in a hurry.'

'We've agreed to buy Warrington Road,' I persist. 'Do you think we can really pull out now? Won't the seller be terribly upset?' I hope my protest is because I am a nice, ethical person who considers it important to keep her promises whether or not I am legally obliged to do so, but I suspect it might be because of Mark, an animal-sharp instinct that is telling me to stay away from him. I wonder if my plea sounds as half-hearted to Angus as it does to me.

A cloud appears to cross Angus's face but it clears so quickly I immediately doubt whether I saw anything at all. Instead he smiles, crosses the kitchen and cups my chin between both his hands. 'Dear, sweet Claire, I really do think you would buy an apartment you didn't want, just because of what you'd told some old lady.' His mouth touches mine, but his eyes stay open, our gaze locked. Then his hands fall and already he's moving away from me, towards the bedroom, which is no distance from our sitting room, which is no distance at all from our kitchen. I think of the space in Mark's house. I imagine my mother's reaction when she sees it.

'I'll call the estate agent in the morning,' Angus says. 'Tell them we're withdrawing our offer on Warrington Road and making an offer on a different property.' I see him take off his jacket, dust the back of it with the flat of his hand, and reach into the wardrobe for a coat-hanger; he is a tidy man, all of the debris in the bedroom, the heap of worn-once clothes, the random, discarded knickers, a half-empty packet of Oreos, is mine.

'What about Mark?' I say in a rush.

'Mark?'

'Mark Tyler. The man who's selling the house. *Mr* Tyler,' I correct myself quickly, refer to him as an estate agent might have done when speaking to me. As the words spill out of me, I realise that I've been wanting to say Mark's name since the moment I got home.

'What about him?' Angus is standing very still, dangling his jacket.

'Nothing,' I say and contemplate my hands, the solitaire diamond pressing on the third finger of my left hand. I consider telling Angus that I have met Mr Tyler and decide, intuitively, against it. 'I suppose he'll be pleased, that's all, since we're buying the house.'

When I look up Angus hasn't moved. He is wearing a strange, searching expression, the expression of somebody peering into shadows at someone they might, or might not, recognise. Since my stepfather's indiscretion at our party I've noticed that Angus looks at me that way quite often. Eventually he slots his jacket into the wardrobe. 'Yes, I imagine he will be pleased' – he appears to mirror my choice of words deliberately – 'if he really needs to get rid of it that badly.'

'Do you think,' I say, 'we should see if he accepts our offer before we withdraw our one on Warrington Road?'

Angus shakes his head. 'There's no need. Not from what the estate agent told me.'

'Do you know,' I persist, 'why he is so desperate to sell?'

Angus shrugs and mumbles something non-committal and indecipherable, his voice muffled by the soft folds of his suit. I wait for his head to turn back towards me, so he can reply properly, but he is entirely preoccupied with the arrangement of his jackets as if to make clear he has no further interest in the financial predicament of a stranger.

After a second I go to the bathroom, slide the comforting bolt and splash water on my face. I tell myself it is irrelevant why Mark needs to sell the house so quickly, and it is irrelevant that he looks like Daniel, the only thing that matters to us is that Angus and I can buy a beautiful house for a bargain price, but my stomach is two, maybe three steps ahead of me, and it is jumping with nerves.

When I reappear Angus is talking on his mobile. 'A large bunch,' he's saying. 'To be sent to a Mrs Foxley at 14 Warrington Road, W13.' Then, after a moment, 'I don't know. Whatever you think best. Roses? Or lilies perhaps?' He catches my gaze and raises his eyebrows, making it a question for me as well.

My mother always says that lilies are for funerals but it doesn't seem appropriate to mention this now. Roses, I tell him. Roses would be best.


Later that evening I call my mother to give her the news. She answers after two rings and immediately puts the handset on speakerphone so that my stepfather can hear too. I picture the pair of them perched on the sofa in front of the lounge fire, which consists of a plastic replica of a pile of logs lit by a constant syrupy red glow. They always sit close together. I expect my mother retains a lingering dread that Andy might one day walk out of the house and buy a one-way ticket to the other side of the world like my father did. Not that my stepfather has ever shown the slightest inclination to rove further or longer from home than the local dominoes club on a Thursday night. Now my disembodied voice speaks, so I imagine, from the cushion propped between them.

'And how is the Home Office?' my mother asks.

'Busy,' I say.

'But not too busy?' She always likes to monitor the price of my success, to check I am not becoming strained or unbalanced by the demands of my working life; to reassure herself there is nothing, any more, to worry about.

'No,' I lie, and glance towards the door, where my suitcase-sized briefcase is waiting. I was supposed to have started work by now but I know tonight my thoughts are too distracted to focus on the labyrinth complexity of the immigration rules. I'll have to get up early instead. Glad to have a reason to change the subject, I tell them about the house. The new house I saw today.

'I thought you and Angus had already bought a flat?'

'We didn't buy one, Mum. We just agreed to. But we can still change our minds. This is an actual house, and much nicer.' As I'm speaking, the memory of the taupe-and-cream sitting room, and of Mark's face – his Daniel-like eyes and his Daniel-like smile – is like incense, sweet and heady.

'Oh…' my mother is saying doubtfully. 'Are you really allowed to do that? It doesn't sound very fair to the poor seller of the first place you liked. I thought you told me she was an old lady.'

'People do it all the time, Mum,' I snap. 'Anyway, we're sending her some flowers. To make up for the disappointment.'

'Oh…' my mother repeats. She is not convinced, and I can see why. Flowers are nice, but they are only a gesture, a sop, a derisory plaster, that don't really compensate for anything at all.

# CHAPTER FOUR

Three weeks later I come back from lunch to find Agatha bent over my desk, peering at something through black-rimmed glasses. She steps smartly to one side as I approach.

'Your phone has been bleeping, Claire.'

It's lying on top of a document entitled 'Assessing the Credibility of Asylum Seekers', but I know it was left underneath the file, which is why I didn't see it when I gathered my things. Now, miraculously freed from its papery covers, a text message is pasted in the middle of the screen.

*Claire – call me. Mark*

The words are a crackle of static, a brush of flesh against an electric fence. Agatha watches as I zip the phone into the side pocket of my bag. She has the desk opposite mine; they butt on to each other and are divided only by a low Perspex screen. If my eyes stray from my computer I sometimes find myself looking straight into Agatha's round, pale blue ones, and when my telephone rings I become aware of the sudden hush, the fixed set of Agatha's shoulders, and the gentle fingering of her papers so that not a word is missed. Recently I have taken to conducting my personal telephone conversations in the toilets.

*Go on*, I dare her silently, *ask me who Mark is.* But she won't have the nerve. Agatha is in her thirties, single, and wears A-line skirts from Marks and Spencer that fall a good inch below her knees.

I suspect that underneath we are not so far apart, she and I; the difference is mainly show, and a finger's width of fine wool cloth.

After about forty-five minutes, I pick up my bag and head for the ladies. The building where I work when I am not conducting cases in the tribunal is in the heart of London. It boasts an elegant stone facade and overlooks a backstreet near Tottenham Court Road. But it, too, has been gutted. The work areas surround the central lift shaft and are arranged into a series of open-plan stations separated by full-height partitions. When I first arrived I would often circumnavigate the entire floor without managing to identify my desk amid the maze of wood veneer. This time I find my way without incident, passing, en route, a meeting room, though possibly 'room' is inapt to describe the transparent, box-like structure in question. Inside, I can see my colleagues; one is jabbing his pen at the points on a graph of rising numbers. The others have the glazed expression of passengers on a long-haul flight. One of them, Lucy, catches my eye and briefly taps three fingers to her lips. I pull a sympathetic face.

I tell myself the call is about something tedious, possibly the Land Registry or the seller's questionnaire. Nevertheless, I can feel my heart quickening in anticipation of the conversation, the fact he has chosen to call me and not Angus. The ladies' room is empty. Absurdly, I check my hair in the mirror before I stand at the window and locate his number, the traffic a silent, metallic river below. He answers just as I am steeling myself for the disappointment of voicemail. There is a fraction of a second where he is still speaking with someone else.

'Claire!' he says, and I get a warm feeling in my stomach, as if I have swallowed a mouthful of brandy. 'Can you come round to the house tonight? After work?' His voice is light but has surprising urgency.

'I suppose so,' I say. 'Why?'

'Remember the mirror? The Spanish mirror by the door?'

'Yes,' I say doubtfully.

'I think you should buy it.'

'Buy it?' I repeat, slightly dazed.

'It looks so good where it is, it would be a shame to move it. And you liked it, didn't you?'

*Did I?* I think of the curling petals, someone crouching with a knife in front of a slab of wood, sunburned hands focused on their work, before anyone had heard of Franco or Cabanellas or Mola.

'You said it was expensive,' I say slowly. This isn't quite true but I am thinking of Angus, his possible reaction to a spontaneous purchase of an antique mirror. The last time I splashed out on something for our soon-to-be new home he chided me for not consulting him first – '*It's our house, Claire, I thought we would enjoy furnishing it together…*' – although all I had bought was a forty-quid vase from Fenwicks.

'Think of it as an investment,' Mark prompts. 'Like art.'

'How much are you asking?'

'We'll see. You can make me an offer.' He is teasing again.

'Does it have to be today? I should talk to Angus first.'

Mark sighs so heavily it seems like the air itself is oozing through the telephone wires. 'I'm afraid it does. I fly to Poland tomorrow. Business trip.'

'What about when you get back?'

'Come on Claire, *Carpe Diem*. I might have sold it by then.' Now he sounds slightly impatient, as if I am being more difficult than he expected. But he changes gear with the smoothness of melted chocolate. 'Besides, there might be other things – other pieces – you might like.' He hovers, for just a second. 'And, of course, it would be nice to see you, Claire.' The way he says *Claire* is like a touch or caress. Daniel rarely called me by my name, I was '*babe*' or '*sugar*' and dull with imprecision.

I swallow. 'All right,' I say. 'I'll be there about eight.'

'Wonderful,' he says, as though it really is.

Later that afternoon, my phone trills again. Another text from Mark.

*Claire – don't forget to bring cash*

I stop at the bank on my way to the tube station. At first I withdraw three hundred pounds from my own account. Normally, I take out fifty pounds, sometimes seventy, occasionally a hundred, but never as much as three hundred. Even so, I wonder if it is enough. I have no idea how much the mirror is worth. I imagine Mark's reaction if I get it wrong; see him shake his head; hear him say, *'That's a shame, Claire. I thought you would realise how valuable it is.'*

I hesitate only a moment before I remove another three hundred. This time I use our joint account: the one Angus and I set up to pay for the wedding, the honeymoon and, of course, the mortgage. It is substantially more joint in name than it is in nature. Although we both put in the same proportion of our wages, Angus's income from the hotel chain consists of a different number of digits from the one I am paid by Her Majesty's Treasury.

Holding that much money, I find my heart is racing. The novelty of the amount makes it feel like a windfall, like it's come from somewhere else. Since the wedge of notes is too thick to fit in my wallet I buy a cheap birthday card – a Labrador being pushed in a wheelbarrow – and use the envelope from that instead. I tell myself I can pay some of it back into the bank the following day; I don't have to spend it. I tell myself I mustn't let myself be talked into anything. But, of course, I do. And I am.

The mirror is beautiful. Mark stands close behind me, pointing out the intricate details of leaves and vines along the edges. I can feel his breath on my hair, the brush of his sleeve on my ribs. The mirror, he tells me, is worth a great deal, considerably more than the six hundred pounds I tell him, foolishly, that I have brought with me. But since we are buying the house, he could let us have it for that. And, he adds, as though it is an afterthought, something merely to clinch the deal and illustrate his generosity, he will even throw in another item – a small oak chest, banded in iron – for free. He opens champagne to celebrate, letting the cork shoot over the room and the froth spill down the side of the bottle.

As I am about to go, my phone rings. It is Angus.

'Where are you?' he says.

'I…' – I hesitate, it's the wrong time to try and explain – 'I got delayed.' Mark is watching me carefully. He catches my eye, raises his eyebrows. I have to turn my back on him to stop myself from laughing.

'I've cooked dinner,' Angus says, from far away. 'You didn't tell me you would be late back tonight.' He sounds like a petulant child about to throw a strop in a supermarket.

'I'm sorry,' I say and try to mean it. I remind myself that Angus is someone who knows what he wants and expects to get it. That I am lucky to be included on his wish list and an occasional sulk is only to be expected of a person so driven, that it is a small price to pay. 'I ran into Julia, an old friend from university, and we went for a drink. I should have called you.' I haven't actually laid eyes on Julia for five years and am unlikely to see her anytime soon – neither of us, I think, would want the awkwardness of that encounter. But Angus isn't to know this and since I am sure he will never meet her, my little white lie will go unnoticed.

'Well,' he says, sounding partially mollified. 'I suppose I'll have to eat on my own.' Then he adds, 'Another time you must remember to tell me if your plans change.'

As I shut my phone Mark is smirking. 'It sounds as if you'd better go, Claire.'

I feel awful, but it is a pretend kind of awfulness that is nearly excitement, as if a little bit of me has broken loose.

At the doorway we pause, Mark dips his head and for an astonishing second I think we might kiss. Instead, he places his lips in the middle of my right cheek and they linger a moment before he draws them away. 'Good night, lovely Claire,' he murmurs and it sounds closer than a paper's width to *come upstairs*. In that moment I am back five years earlier. I am standing outside the lightless windows of my student halls. It is three in the morning, the night I first went out with Daniel. He says, '*Good night, beautiful Claire,*' touches my cheek and walks away into the dark, leaving my skin aflame.

# CHAPTER FIVE

It is the transition between summer and autumn, when the weather tempts with a day of glorious sunshine before issuing a stern reminder of the months of wind and rain ahead. It is also two weeks and three days after Angus and I moved in. I am standing at the bottom of the stairs, wearing a work shirt over my underwear, but not yet a suit – instead a dressing gown is slouched over my shoulders, the collar damp from the ends of my showered hair – and carrying two mugs of tea. Already it has become hard for me to think of the house as the same place that Mark lived. The open-plan rooms are cluttered with packing cases and hastily bought, ill-judged furniture that has required mind-numbing trips to stores on the North Circular and painful hours of self-assembly, while the soft, shimmering paintwork now appears duller, almost drab. It seems that Mark must have taken something of the allure of the place with him when he left. Maybe it's just that dreams never do actually materialise, the best you can hope for is a rough approximation.

To my surprise, my reckless purchase of the Spanish mirror didn't appear to bother Angus at all. To the contrary, he looked quite pleased when I finally took the plunge and confessed. I bent the truth a little, invented a visit to the house to consider what extra furniture we might need after we moved in, how the seller – '*Mr Tyler*', I managed to say – talked me into buying his mirror, how lovely it looked on the wall, how hard it was to resist. 'Well, I hope you got it for a good price, Claire,' was all Angus said. When

I told him the amount, his face twisted, as if with the effort of a piece of mental arithmetic, and then he nodded. 'It sounds like you did. Good.' And he never mentioned my indulgence again.

I glance at the mirror now, as I place my foot on the first step, not at the glass – I would rather avoid the sight of my bare complexion and morning shadows – but at the golden, walnut frame. Beauty, they say, is in the eye of the beholder, but they don't tell you how fickle the beholder can be; the carving is still beautiful, of course, but not as beautiful as it was when I stood beside it with Mark, drinking his champagne.

At that second the sound of a mobile reverberates. Angus's work phone – he tries to separate his business from his personal calls. I see the screen flash from our dining table, the casing shudder with the energy of the vibration. I hesitate but then hurry towards the noise as quickly as I am able to without spilling the tea. Inevitably, just as I arrive the sound stops, but like an echo or a footprint the identity of the missed call is displayed for all to see. It's only a number, not a name, but it looks familiar. Not very familiar, but nevertheless a number I might, at one time, have used myself. I wonder, briefly, who would want to call Angus before seven in the morning, but a phone call is not such a remarkable occurrence that I give it any more thought.

Upstairs at least our bedroom is tidy, the clothes unpacked, the packing crates banished to the landing. I step over Angus's slippers – which are appropriately tartan and placed very precisely, as they always are, next to his bedside table – put down one of the mugs and touch his shoulder. 'Wakey, wakey!'

His eyelids flicker and then open completely; one of the things I noticed about Angus the first time we spent the night together was his ability to move from sleep to total wakefulness almost instantaneously. That and the fact he slumbers in near total silence; no snores, no grunts, unless I really listen I can barely hear him breathe.

'Have I overslept?' The sweep of Angus's gaze is taking in my partially dressed state, my wet hair.

'No, don't worry, the alarm hasn't gone off yet.'

'But' – he is gazing at the mugs – 'you've already made the tea!'

'Something woke me early. Probably the bins being collected. I thought I might as well get up.'

'But that's my job Claire. You know I always make the tea.' Angus has a fixation for little rituals. I guess it might be to do with the fact that his parents split up when he was sixteen. The affair – his mother – the divorce and the house sale all happened while he was away at school. It must have felt like a scene change in a theatre, by the time he came back on stage all of his familiar landmarks had disappeared. I know he is still in contact with them – his parents – but neither of them made an appearance at our engagement party and they never feature in his conversation. Even so, it's an oddly stern response to a cup of tea.

I assume he is joking and perch on the edge of the mattress. The bedroom is cold – Angus likes to sleep with the window open at least six inches regardless of the weather – and my wet hair and bare feet are making my body temperature plummet. I think how nice it would be to slide back inside and curl myself around his sleep-warm torso.

'So? This morning it's my turn to be the tea lady.' I put down my mug next to his, shrug off the dressing gown and begin to peel back the duvet.

'What are you doing?'

'What does it look like I'm doing? I'm cold!' I pull the duvet a little further and wriggle into the space between the bedside table and Angus. The gap is so small I have to tilt myself sideways, hooking my left leg over his, so that I'm almost lying on top of him. The heat is meltingly sudden. I touch his calf with my toe, and when he doesn't respond I slide my hand under his T-shirt and over the smooth gleam of stomach. Lying so still, so inanimate, he reminds me of a mannequin that has been polished with a duster ready for display in a department store.

'Claire…' His voice is a brake, but I don't want to hear it.

'Come on, Angus. You surely can't be cross I usurped your tea-making role!' I shift position so that I am straddling him, remove my hand from his T-shirt and undo the buttons of my blouse with showy deliberateness. As the cotton falls open I lean forward, letting the rich sweep of my hair fall across his ribcage. Although his expression remains blank I am smiling into his eyes because he normally finds an offer like this irresistible. It's not actually until I'm reaching behind my back to unclasp my bra that he finally stops me. All at once his fingers close around my wrist and he sits up.

'Not now, I can't be late for work this morning. I've got an early meeting.' He pushes me away, lightly but firmly, and heads for the shower. For a moment I lie back against the pillows in stunned stillness. I am no longer cold, but hot, too hot, and my emotions are a muddy mess of every kind of colour. A second later I fling back the covers, dress rapidly and give my hair a cursory blast with the dryer. By the time I hear the water stop in the bathroom I am already downstairs with my coat on.

I am about to leave when Angus's mobile bleats again. This time I am quick enough across the room to answer it, but instead I simply let it ring. The number blazing on the screen is, I think, the same one as before. I have a repeated sensation of familiarity although it is only a vague, unreliable notion. For a moment I rack my brains, wondering who it might be, but since no candidates come to mind I assume I must be mistaken.

I head for the door then at the last moment my resolve weakens, I stop and double back. As children we were always advised never to go to bed on an argument and I suppose the same principle should apply about leaving for work. Not, I tell myself, that Angus and I have had an argument.

I pick up the phone and take it upstairs. 'You've had two missed calls on your work phone this morning.'

Angus is knotting a thick silk tie. He spins at the sound of my voice; he probably assumed I'd already left the house, but if he's pleased to see me it doesn't show. 'Thanks,' he says, 'just leave it on the bed.'

I turn to go.

Then, 'Claire?'

'What is it?'

All at once his features relax, the light returns to his eyes. 'Have a good day!'

I smile back, but as I leave the bedroom I see that his mug of tea is still sitting on the bedside table, untouched and stone cold.


That afternoon I am sitting in a meeting when I begin to feel that telltale tickle in my hands and feet. When I lost Daniel – temporarily at first, and then definitively – my body used to fragment like this, a symptom, perhaps, of post-traumatic stress. It hasn't happened for a long while now, but sure enough within minutes the writing on the paper, the features of my colleagues, the lines and contours of the room, begin to blur and soften as if we have all been plunged underwater. I look at my watch but the numbers are jumping and popping. A discussion is swirling around me about a proposal to make a small but significant change to the immigration category known as Highly Skilled Migrants. Maggie, our new manager, is leading it and everyone is anxious to demonstrate that they have read the hefty pack of reports and statistical data.

A colleague called Nigel – my work buddy from the immigration conference – has grabbed an opportunity to speak, 'I agree with the reasoning,' he says, pushing his glasses further up his nose, 'but I wonder if the penultimate paragraph on page 5 might be better placed after the current Shortage Occupations List on page 7?'

There is an outbreak of rustling as everyone turns to page five and I am thinking that I cannot possibly make it to the end of the meeting when Maggie's voice cuts across the fog, 'Claire, you're very quiet. Is there anything you want to say?'

I am the most junior person in the room. Maggie, kind and conscientious, is anxious to ensure I am feeling valued, but I cannot now recall my carefully prepared contribution, let alone articulate it. A silence with army-blanket weight settles on our laps, and then, from a distance, I hear Maggie's voice again.

'Goodness, Claire, you've gone a very funny colour! Are you feeling all right?'

I murmur something about a migraine, an easier explanation than the more complicated real one. There's a collective intake of breath, a scraping of chairs, someone dials reception, someone else escorts me downstairs and before I know it I am in the back of an Uber weaving through the unremitting West End traffic, courtesy of the taxpayer.

When we pull up outside the house I notice that the downstairs curtains have not been drawn. They are long and heavy, indented with a pale fawn stripe. I try to remember if I opened them this morning when I made the tea but it feels as if a pendulum is repeatedly striking my right temple and all I can think about is climbing into bed. I thank the driver and root for my key amongst a wad of crusty tissues and supermarket receipts. When I open the door, I am confronted by semi-darkness; it seems the curtains over the French doors that lead out from the kitchen are drawn too. At the same time I can hear the light squeak of footsteps on a tiled floor. Instinctively my hand reaches for the light.

'Don't, Claire!'

In the split second that follows I see a man at the entrance to the kitchen. I think *Daniel*, then realise it is Mark, but my primal instincts react more quickly than my brain can process the fact of recognition and I jump nonetheless, making a noise somewhere between a gasp and a scream. Mark raises a finger to his lips and comes quickly towards me. He is wearing the same combination of white shirt and jeans, but the shirt has worked loose and his breaths are ragged. He pushes back his hair from a damp forehead.

'Mark! What are you doing here?' I gaze around the sitting room as if an explanation might be found, wrapped in newspaper, amongst the half-empty packing cases.

'Claire,' he says, and he is whispering, 'I can explain, if you could just…'

At that moment there is a rap of knuckles on the front door. I jump again. Mark takes hold of my arm.

'Don't answer it.' His hand closes around my wrist.

'What do you mean?' I say. 'Who is it?' I am whispering too. There is more knocking, which turns quickly to pounding. I can hear voices outside: angry, foreign voices.

Someone opens the letterbox and shouts, 'Open the door, or we break window.'

I stare at Mark; his face is rigid. I glance down and see that my wrist is turning white. 'We must call the police,' I say. I reach into my bag with my free hand, scrabbling for my phone.

'No!' Mark shakes his head and jerks my shoulder. It hurts. A second later there is a grating sound, a raking of something sharp between the glass and the window frame.

'We have to open the door,' I hiss. 'The glass will smash.'

'If you open the door,' he says, looking straight into my eyes, 'I'm not here.'

'Why don't you go out the back?'

His fingers tighten. 'Somebody will be watching the back.' He smiles, and I realise he is asking me to take his side. 'Remember Claire. Not here.'

I nod, and then he lets go of my arm. My mouth is dry and my stomach is pitching like a theme-park roller coaster. As I walk forwards Mark slips back into the kitchen.

I open the door keeping one hand firmly on the handle and the other braced against the wall. There are two men. One is tall, bald and bulky, although his weight appears to consist of more fat than muscle. The other is shorter and quite wiry. His long white hair is held in a ponytail and he has pale, almost colourless, eyes. Both are wearing poor-imitation leather jackets, grubby jeans and trainers.

'What the fuck are you doing to my house?'

They are surprised at my initiative, but recover quickly.

'Where is Mark Tyler?' It is the white-haired man who speaks. His accent is from Eastern Europe – Russia or the Ukraine, perhaps.

'Mark Tyler?' I repeat. 'He moved a fortnight ago. I live here now, with my fiancé.'

'We think he is here,' the bald one says, simply.

I glare at them. 'No, I told you. He left. We moved in.' I open the door just wide enough to show them a few of the packing crates.

'We think we see him here.' The disconcerting eyes of the man with white hair are watching me intently. He is not interested in the packing crates.

'You think he forgot to move out?'

The bald one flicks his head towards the window. 'Why are curtains shut?'

'Because I have a headache. A bad headache. The light hurts my eyes.' I realise with a sense of wonder that this part is actually true. I do indeed have a headache. 'I had to come home from work. And now you are making it worse.' I speak with the righteous force of someone wronged and when they flinch I take the opportunity to slam the door and the noise of it reverberates around my skull like cymbals clashing. I sink onto the carpet against the wall, tuck my arms around my knees and close my eyes. I can hear a thudding in my ears and from outside agitated, incomprehensible conversation and shuffling feet. Suddenly there is stillness, and then a louder voice punctuated by silence; one of them is talking on a mobile. An eternity later, the sweet sound of retreating footsteps.

I become aware of Mark beside me. He is sitting so near that his upper arm and thigh are pressed against mine.

'You were marvellous, Claire.' He is still whispering. I open my eyes and see that he is buoyant now; all his poise returned.

I rub my forehead. 'Who are they?' I ask. 'What did they want?'

'Oh, money. They just wanted money.' He sounds nonchalant, as if the whole thing has been a bit of a laugh.

'How much money? What do they want it for?'

'Doesn't everybody owe someone money?' Though his tone is light his lips purse in a *'don't be naive'* sort of a way. But I don't owe anyone money, not unless you count our newly acquired mortgage; the mortgage that has occupied several of our evenings with long, sober discussions and ten-year projections of income and interest rates. I am a girl with only one credit card, paid off each month without fail, who was taught to avoid debt by my angst-ridden, penny-counting mother with the same intensity children are taught to avoid sweet-bearing strangers.

Mark gives a little shake of his head as though closing the subject and jumps to his feet. Immediately I miss his body heat. I am trembling a little and feel sick, perhaps it is shock, now the adrenaline has subsided, or perhaps it is the almost-migraine. Mark leans over the top of me and puts his left eye to a tiny, unobtrusive peephole that I've never spotted beneath the letter flap. Is it normal, I wonder vaguely, to be able to spy out of your own front door? From my foetal position I glimpse his chest under the gaping shirt – black whorls of hair on a tough, functional torso – before he straightens and turns his attention to me.

'Come on, Claire, up you get!' He holds out his right hand and I notice the neatly clipped nails, the signet ring on his little finger. I let him pull me to my feet and we stand facing each other, as if waiting for a waltz to strike up. My eyes are fixed on the space between the starched white of his collar and the dip of his neck, and I can smell his sweat beneath the spiced scent of cologne. Outside,

I know, the pavements are full of mothers pushing buggies, dog-walkers and pensioners buying milk; all the ordinary business of the early afternoon, but in the sepia light of this shuttered room they seem as distant as palm trees in a travel brochure. I wonder if the highly skilled migrants meeting is still going on, whether Nigel is proposing a revision to the final paragraph on page 30; Maggie, stoical, reaching for her pen again.

Mark hasn't let go of my hand. Now he begins to knead my knuckles and rub his thumb into the flesh my palm. I freeze, and he lowers his head, closes the wet warmth of his mouth over my forefinger and slowly begins to suck, swirling his tongue the length of the bone and over the joints, all the way to the tip of the nail. He pauses to breathe, studying my face, waiting, and when I say nothing, when I fail to retract my hand, or tell him to stop, he does the very same thing to my middle finger and, after that, the finger so lovingly adorned with diamonds, and finally my poor, ravenous, little finger. I shut my eyes and Daniel is there, naked in bed. It's a Sunday morning, chapel bells. Daniel: who loved me once but won't ever love me again. The pain and nausea tiptoe away and I tilt increasingly forwards until Mark slides his hand under my skirt and presses me into him.

Later, as I wait for Angus to come home, I try to make myself face up to the awfulness of what I've done, but I can't seem to concentrate. My brain is like a hacked computer and my attempt at accountability keeps swerving onto a different track entirely. Although, of course, I'm perfectly aware that Angus and I are engaged, it feels like a fact I know about somebody else – a cousin, for example. Someone to whom I might send a card, say, '*how nice, I do hope you'll be happy*' and never give them another thought. Instead of Angus, *my fiancé*, my head is full of Mark; full of the Daniel-like bronze of his irises, the Daniel-like curve of his lower lip. Instead of worrying how easily I went astray I spend the whole time before the front door opens reliving the seconds Mark took to unbutton my blouse, recalling the arc of his shoulders over my own, hearing his voice, soft and persistent, *'How is your headache, Claire...? What about now, Claire...? Is it better now?'*

# CHAPTER SIX

## *Five years earlier*

I am lying with my head on Daniel's stomach. The air is sweet with the smell of June, of plants in flower, of trees in bloom, of sun-touched skin. And alcohol, of course. This afternoon the leitmotif is Pimm's and lemonade; if I open my eyes I can see my glass lurched sideways in the grass, the last dregs of amber aglow with the same lengthening summer light that is soaking into our coupled bodies. Above, the sky is the lavish green of a chestnut. Around us the soporific soundtrack of murmured conversations, of giggles and kisses, the end of a party when the ending has no consequence because another will begin as soon the first one stops, a blurry pageant of carefree, careless hedonism.

Our exams finished twelve days ago. During the weeks beforehand the dial swung steadily from warm to hot, and from there to scorching hot, the library windows wedged open to the drone of normality from the street below, testing my endurance as I fought to memorise the particulars of contract law and tort, of international treaties and human rights. My head ached with list upon list of cases, each like a miniature painting, a bite-sized story framed by man-made rules and judge-made precedent. Slowly I learned how they slotted together as precisely as Lego, the big foundation stones of principle dividing into smaller rooms of category and subcategory, and then upwards into chimney pots and roof tiles of nuance and clarification, all combining to make one titanic structure, an entire architecture of rights and wrongs. Soon the days bled into night, the world reduced to plastic boxes of revision cards crammed with bullet points in coloured inks. When I closed my eyes I could see only the blue and the black, the magenta and the green, my handwriting a diaphanous, unrelenting beacon leading towards the final twelve hours of my degree.

We thought the weather would never last, my fellow students and I. Day after day when we chanced upon another pale sufferer taking the same five-minute cigarette break we would curse the luck that corralled us inside while the rest of the country was busy acquiring suntans. Yet when exam week arrived the temperatures remained sky-high. As I wrote and wrote under the unremitting gaze of the clock I had to pause every so often to wipe my hands on my skirt, vaguely aware of the dark half-moons under my armpits, the glue-like burn that was holding me to the chair as my hand scurried back and forth, back and forth, across the page.

And still the weather holds. While Facebook and Twitter are full of moaners who have had their fill of heat and are now complaining about their inability to sleep, or the threatened hosepipe ban, we students – we ex-students – can't believe our luck. Tripping from one party to the next, none of us are bothered about sleeping or hosepipes. Released from our desks like animals from a zoo, we are wild with the novelty of a freedom that feels earned, and the heatwave is our friend, making a midnight playground of the parks and riverbanks.

Daniel's fingers find my hair and embed themselves within its strands. 'I don't want to move, do you?'

I merely shake my head against the warmth of his belly.

'We're supposed to be going to Mike and Lucy's party.'

I pretend I haven't heard. I roll onto my stomach, but rotate on the same spot of lawn so that my face, my cheek, is lying on his stomach. Somewhere close there is a bee, flower-filled and industrious. My limbs are molten and too heavy to move; I can't feel any boundary between me and Daniel and the ground. Everybody else – our friends, our families – is superfluous. This, I think, *this* is the second I would still the sand in the hourglass and halt the orbit of the earth.

'Daniel?' I murmur, but before he can answer, his phone starts to buzz and my head is so close to the noise that it seems like an act of aggression. Daniel's hand reaches into the pocket of his shorts as the phone falls silent. He sighs and we settle back to how we were, although I'm aware now that the lawn is hard from lack of rain and that the edge of Daniel's right hip is jabbing into my shoulder. Almost immediately the mobile trills again. This time Daniel is quicker, but still it dies before he can quite raise it to his ear.

'Fuck! What's going on?' He shifts on to his elbows, cupping a hand over the casing to shield it from the sun as he tries to make out the number.

'Who is it?'

'I can't see…'

We settle again, close our eyes, but we are tense now, poised, as if perching on a ledge.

Waiting for *Her* to call again.

I knew Daniel before we started going out together. He studied law like me and I'd seen him from afar, not so much in terms of distance, but as if he was untouchable, an expensive item in a shop window I might gaze on with desire but never dream of purchasing myself. He was always with a girl. She was pretty, sometimes in quite a spectacular way, so when he turned up to a lecture on his own it seemed at first surprising, newsworthy even, then very quickly not surprising at all. After that it was only natural to wonder who of us would be the next.

The first time we spoke he appeared behind me as I was getting a brackish-coloured coffee from the vending machine in the library, shortly after the countdown to exams had begun in earnest. 'So you're finally taking a break,' was all he murmured, but the way he spoke made it an observation, not a question, and revealed both that he'd been watching me and that the encounter was a deliberate one. After that it – we – moved so quickly it felt like stepping off a cliff, mistaking the path in the dark or fog and falling before I had a chance to get my bearings or catch my breath.

Now we are an item, a couple, already careless invitations get issued to the pair of us, and yet even while I revel in the intoxicating status of Daniel's girlfriend, I'm aware that it will never last. I remember his solitary arrival that day in the lecture hall, how everyone pretended not to notice and I worry, constantly, how long my turn on the carousel will last. Unable to stop myself I chase him for words of commitment, searching them out as if they are pledges, promises I can enforce; anything to quiet the little voice that whispers that I too will soon be old news. I know the tighter I cling the more certain he is to slip from my grasp, but it makes no difference. He has the power and I have none, and the only way to pretend otherwise is to lay his declarations of love over the chasm at my feet like branches concealing an elephant trap.

Last night we weaved our way across town after an evening at a pub where we had lingered late and long. The moon was thick and white, spilling like paint on to the surface of the Cam and gilding the vista of rooftops and church towers. As we crossed one of the bridges, our arms wrapped around each other's waists, I made him stop. There was nobody about, only the perfection of the silvered light and the water. A clock chimed three, slowly, lazily; each strike sounding like it might be the last. For some reason – maybe I sensed, in the way you might sense a ghost, what was to come – a trickle of dread made me suddenly shudder.

I nudged Daniel so that his back was against the stonework and I was in front of him. Our gaze locked. 'Do you love me?' I whispered. 'Do you really love me?'

'Of course I love you, babe.' He touched my cheek, his thumb stroking it gently.

I stared into his eyes. 'If you could stop everything right now and freeze this moment – us – here – forever – would you do it?'

'What?' His brow furrowed. Then he laughed, uncertainly, and drew his hand an inch from my cheek. 'What do you mean? Why would I do that?'

'*If* you love me, then how could it get better than this?' I waved my arm loosely in the direction of the river, but kept my eyes fixed on his face. 'If time were to stop right now, we wouldn't ever have to get ill or old. We wouldn't ever argue or take each other for granted. We would never love each other less than we love each other this very second.' I was trying to sound romantic, poetic even, but my voice came out breathy and intense.

He shook his head and laughed again. 'I think you must be drunk!' He kissed me. 'Don't be so serious. You're talking nonsense!'

I pulled my head back, dramatically. 'I am serious,' I said. 'I want to know. Maybe you don't love me at all. Maybe you think you could do better?'

'Oh, is this what it's about?' His features relaxed but the force of his gaze deepened with exaggerated showiness. 'Then here's my answer. If time had stopped just now' – he held up his left forearm so we could both see his wristwatch and the second hand crawl a quarter way around the dial – 'then this would never have happened.' He kissed me again, but hard and long, my mouth melting so deep into his that I could taste, beyond the wine and the whisky, the uniqueness of him, and our hands began to reach for the skin beneath each other's clothes.

His phone rings again.

'Jesus!' We both sit up and Daniel stabs the screen. 'Hello?'

There is silence. At least I think there is silence, but I must be wrong because Daniel is listening, and as he listens his expression solidifies. After a moment he twists around so I can't see his face at all and then he says quietly, 'Don't, please don't cry. Not again.'

And I know for certain exactly who it is.

I touch his arm, but he still won't look at me, and a second later he gets up and moves completely out of earshot.

When he finally returns he squats beside where I am sitting with my arms wrapped around my knees.

'I thought you said it was all over now?' It's my turn not to look at him.

'I hadn't heard from her in a while. I just assumed she was better, but she's still very upset. She's moved out of her college accommodation and is renting a room in the north of the town.'

'And I'm supposed to care?' I begin to rip the grass into an angry little pile.

'She didn't manage to do her exams…'

'… I know.'

'She may not even get her degree.'

'*I know*.' This is old news, but Daniel always brings it up. I guess he feels guilty.

Daniel's hand closes over mine. 'Don't be like that, babe. It's not easy for her to see us together.'

'Well, in that case she should go home.'

Daniel doesn't reply.

I toss the last of the limp blades to one side and lean against him. Through his T-shirt the baseline thump of his heart is directly next to mine. I know what losing him will feel like; I don't suppose I will be rational about it either. I breathe out, slowly. 'Sorry.'

'That's OK.'

But it's not OK. I can tell there's something else he needs to say. There's a pause that scratches like fibreglass before he brings himself to add, 'Look, I won't be long.'

The sentence takes a second to register. 'What do you mean?' Although I have worked out what he means I want him to say it out loud. I want him to admit that he's spoiling our perfect day to meet his crazy ex-girlfriend and dry her tears – again.

Daniel straightens up; I notice that he's still clutching the phone as though expecting it to sound again at any moment. 'I'll be back,' he says, 'in time for Mike and Lucy's party. Wait here. I'll be half an hour, an hour, at most.' He is moving already, stepping back away from me as though I might suddenly grab at him.

'You'll make it worse.'

He's shaking with head. With guilt? Regret? I really can't tell. 'I have to go talk to her. She's so unhappy, babe.'

'And what about you, Daniel?' My throat is too knotty and sore to speak properly, I practically have to spit the words out. 'How happy are you?'

'Hey, babe' – he makes an effort at levity, holds his arms out wide in an embrace to the world – 'I'm happier than I've ever been.'


He's gone less than an hour. I see him returning through the gateway into the garden as I'm chatting with Myla and Barney, two medics I've known since my first term when we were thrown together in the same flat and had to navigate the demands of the enforced intimacy that is part of a drunken fresher's week. They managed it pretty well by hooking up with each other on the first night and staying together ever since.

As Daniel approaches I see his fists are in his pockets and his gaze keeps flicking down towards the ground.

'Myla and Barney were telling me about their plans for the summer,' I tell him. I am determined not to show how pleased I am to see him back so soon or ask him any questions, but the effort is wasted.

'She wasn't there,' he says shortly. 'I waited thirty fucking minutes at the Starbucks in the Grand Arcade and she didn't fucking show.'

Myla touches Barney's arm and they melt away, making some convoluted excuse that neither Daniel nor I bother to take on board.

'Well, you went to meet her, you couldn't do more than that,' I shrug. My tone is carefully nonchalant although my heart is cheering and mentally I've already chalked it up as a victory.

'What a fucking waste of time.'

'Forget it. Forget *her*.' I put the flat of my hands against his cheeks and kiss his mouth. He kisses me back, pliable and contrite.

'It's ruined the afternoon.'

'No,' I say. 'It didn't. I've had a lovely time.' It's lucky he didn't come back twenty minutes earlier, when I was still sitting where he left me, tearing up the grass. I like this sudden reversal of my role, no longer the clingy, ungracious girlfriend, instead the generous, supportive girlfriend. For a moment I allow myself to believe I am someone that Daniel will want to stay with, that we have a future just like Myla and Barney. The feeling lasts all through the rest of the afternoon and into the evening. It lasts during our lazy meander to Mike and Lucy's party, stopping to kiss in doorways, brazen and shameless; it lasts as we join the heaving jam of bodies in a tiny flat downing vodka martinis to a backbeat of indie and jazz; it lasts during the long stagger home through the blue night air, oblivious to anyone but each other. It lasts, even as we ascend the twisting staircase to Daniel's room, hanging onto each other for balance, our footsteps loud against the stone, our whispers raucous and jubilant.

It lasts until I see the heap of clothes huddled beside Daniel's door. The clothes stir, a head lifts, and the light from the overhead bulb catches the glass of a gin bottle and face smeared with so much lipstick she resembles a pissed clown.

'For fuck's sake!' But he says it gently, more in shock than anger.

'Daniel…' The voice is slurred – which is inevitable, given that the gin bottle is empty. 'I'm so sorry… I'm really so sorry…'

Daniel steps forward, but I stay rooted at the top of the steps and all at once Daniel and I are no longer a couple, instead there are three of us, three separate individuals: him, her and me. The heap of clothes attempts to get a purchase on the door handle and stand up but immediately she loses her balance and sits down again hard. Her chest convulses, I think she's about to cry but instead she starts to puke and a stream of vomit runs down her light-blue cardigan and makes pools in the folds of her skirt. I try to look away although I am transfixed with the horror of it. The sour, fermented stench filling the corridor makes me want to retch myself.

'Oh God… Oh Daniel. I'm sorry. I'm so sorry…' Her stomach heaves again to produce a final drool of sick, and then she begins to weep.

Daniel kneels down beside her, looking at me over his shoulder. I think the look means just wait, be patient, I'll get rid of her.

I'm wrong.

'I'm going to have to deal with this,' he murmurs, his voice low and not with intimacy, it's more as though he's speaking quietly to me to spare her blushes, 'so I think you'll have to go back to your own room tonight. Sorry, babe.' For a split second I wonder if I can have heard him right, in my confusion I assume for a moment he must surely have meant to direct that last part of the sentence to her, that stinking mess of a person collapsed like a homeless wino on the floor. I hover, uncertain what to do, but when Daniel's gaze doesn't waver, I realise he was speaking unmistakably to me. I understand that he, that both of them, are waiting for me to leave. Instantly my celebrated, chalked-up victory evaporates, like a mirage that vanishes just as soon as it floats within touching distance.

# CHAPTER SEVEN

## *Now*

I have my arms full of dirty washing when the telephone rings. It's the landline, not my mobile, which means the caller is either somebody in India offering to fix my computer, or my mother, neither of whom I particularly want to have a conversation with right at this moment because I have finally begun to clean the house.

Angus has been away all weekend – a conference in Frankfurt, dull, apparently, and not worth the claustrophobia of an overcrowded departure lounge and the crawl through passport control that is already snail-like even pre-Brexit. I think he is coming home tomorrow rather than tonight. I hope this is the case because while, in his absence, I have not exactly trashed our home, the living space presents very differently from how it did forty-eight hours ago when he kissed me as he left and told me in a tone that sounded surprisingly directive to '*be good*'.

It seems his entreaty was not entirely misplaced. Left to my own devices, free of Angus's routines and standards, I find I have not moved on quite so far from my student habits as I might have believed. Plates sticky with half-eaten meals and mugs of cold tea now perch by the side of the bath and on the sitting room carpet, while a wine glass, an empty bottle of New World Chardonnay and a saucer full of cigarette butts litter our bedroom – I'll have to sleep with the window open tonight to get rid of the telltale reek.

The bed itself is strewn with the contents of my wardrobe, the result of my attempt the previous evening to clear out some old clothes for charity – an exercise I abandoned after I finished the wine. The alcohol was enough to unleash the thoughts of Mark that had been hovering on the sidelines, ready to claim the centre stage; the way he led me unequivocally up the stairs, the path his fingers took as they prised apart my shirt and slipped inside the cup of my bra. The touch that felt like Daniel – that was Daniel as long as I didn't open my eyes. As the bedroom grew dark I sat for an hour, perhaps longer, smoking and not bothering to switch on the light. Remembering that afternoon I felt guilt, of course, a feeble stir somewhere in my stomach, but my need for him, the want of him was so strong the wine and cigarettes exacerbated rather than dulled my desire. Instead of sorting through my fashion failures, I fell asleep amidst the fluffy fragrance of old sweaters, my hand deep inside the waistband of my jeans.

This afternoon, gazing at the debris of the weekend – *my* debris of *my* weekend – I was strangely reluctant to clear it away. Instead of shame I felt an odd sense of comfort. I suppose the house felt more mine than it had ever done before, like a dog denoting its territory with a trail of pee, the fusion of sweet and acrid odours, the clutter of untidy possessions, was the mark – the smell – of me, asserting a little independence beyond the swim lanes of my newly ordered and coupled life.

I wait for five rings, six, but when the phone continues to yelp I finally drop the laundry onto the kitchen floor and step over a Boots carrier bag to pick up the receiver.

'Claire, is that you?' My mother's standard opening line takes no account of the fact she knows Angus is away and save for the possibility of an overconfident burglar, I am her only option.

'Hello, Mum.' I sink onto the floor beneath the Spanish mirror – the armchair is crowded with shopping from Zara and the sofa has my coat strewn across it. I prepare myself for one of her Sunday chats about my work, Angus and the wedding. She rings often these days, any excuse to revel in my acquisition of a handsome fiancé and my sudden, reassuring affluence nicely visible in bricks and mortar. To be honest, normally I enjoy basking in my change of fortune with her – nobody wants to be the child whose family makes an effort not to pity. Besides, the memory of that tiny flat above the newsagent – the damp that meant the washing never dried, the light bulb on the stairs that never worked – has been burned forever into the bones of us both.

This time, however, I soon realise my mother doesn't want to talk about Angus and me at all. After a couple of perfunctory questions she gets straight to the point.

'We've got some news. Or rather your brother has some news.'

'Oh?' I hear her intake of breath over the rain that has started to fall, striking the windows in gravel-like gusts.

'You're not the only one who will be getting married. Robert and Elsa have got engaged.'

'Really? That's wonderful!' Even as I make the correct noises my brain is processing the fact that something doesn't sound quite right. My mother's voice is not transparent with pleasure in quite the way I would expect. Why hasn't Rob called me himself? Despite the arrival of Elsa in our lives I like to think we are still close, bonded by all those times we walked home from school together, better able, with the other by our side, to stare down the bullies and the dope-pushers from the council estate. When Daniel and I fell apart, Rob was the only person I could bear to talk to me.

'I think they would have waited until after your wedding, they didn't want to steal the limelight, only...' The sentence stops abruptly.

'Only what?'

'Only Elsa is pregnant.'

'Oh,' I say. I remember how she didn't drink at my engagement party, how I thought it was because she was afraid of letting her hair down in front of my friends when in fact she had her own, far more precious, reason for abstaining. I wonder if my mother has discussed with Rob who should break the news to me and know immediately they must have done.

'Claire?'

'What?'

'You're not saying anything, are you all right? About Elsa, I mean. It hasn't upset you too much has it, that she's pregnant? I don't imagine it was, you know, *deliberate*. I expect it just happened without them really meaning to…' My mother's voice tails away with the embarrassment of discussing Rob and Elsa's sex life; if right now she could resort to stories of storks and the delivery of babies in little white bundles I'm certain that she would.

'I'm fine,' I say. 'I'm very pleased for them.' I pick a piece of fluff off the floor, although my clearing-up operation has some way to go before a scrap of fuzz on the carpet would be noticeable.

'That's good,' my mother says. She doesn't sound entirely convinced.

'I'll give Rob a call later,' I tell her, injecting more conviction into my voice, 'to congratulate them.'

'Will you? That would be marvellous. I think they will be at home tonight because they don't go out much at the moment. Apparently Elsa's feeling very sick. I've told them it's perfectly normal, still Rob can't help but worry and Elsa doesn't feel like eating or drinking so there doesn't seem much point in—'

'Mum,' I cut through her babble, 'I have to go. I need to tidy the house before Angus gets back, it's a bit of a tip.'

'Is it?' She laughs, although I don't think she would if she could see the place. 'Well, in that case I'd better let you get on with it!'

After I put the phone down I head to the kitchen and fill the kettle. Tea, I decide, in preparation for the big house clean, but my head is full of babies. Babies – and now, of course, Daniel. And Daniel makes me think of Mark. Which brings me back to

Daniel again. A not-so-perfect circle. The water is almost at boiling point when I realise that tea is the last thing I feel like drinking. My little brother is going to be a father. Taking another bottle of white wine out of the fridge, I kill the power to the kettle and listen as the life drains out of it almost instantaneously.

Later that evening I discover we have run out of milk, bread and coffee, the staples of any well-managed kitchen. Still, there is a Seven Eleven less than a mile away and, I tell myself, a brisk walk will do me good. If I run the errand now then not only will I seem considerate and organised should Angus pop home tomorrow before heading to the office, I also have a proper reason not to call Rob; it is nine o'clock already – it has taken me that long to make the house presentable again – and by the time I get back he and Elsa are likely to be in bed. After all, being pregnant is exhausting. Given the unsettled nature of the weather, I fetch my mac and belt it tight around my waist.

The Seven Eleven is busier than I expected, the checkout queue moving slowly. Idling in a semi-soporific state, clutching my modest collection of shopping I wonder what each of the customers is doing here; what does it reveal about us and our inadequacies that we have chosen to spend the last dregs of our weekend under the glare of strip lighting that makes us resemble characters from another tedious vampire movie? The man in front of me is holding a wire basket heavy with eight large tins of dog food. Is that truly an emergency purchase or just an excuse to get out of the house? He is short with thinning, curly hair and has a small man's hunch to his shoulders. It is easy to imagine him beleaguered by his wife, driven to temporary escapes, little freedoms. But perhaps he is just besotted with his dog. Or lonely, maybe the Seven Eleven is the closest he gets to a night out.

I am so busy inventing lives for the man with the dog food it is at least a minute before I notice the long white ponytail dangling from the head of the male customer who is standing in front of him. For a moment I stare transfixed, both certain it is the same man who came to my door searching for Mark and equally sure my mind is playing tricks, conjuring him up because I have spent so much of the afternoon, of the whole weekend, in fact, thinking about Mark.

While I am watching the queue shuffles forwards. The dog food man moves up a place and his basket collides, very slightly, with the thigh of the customer ahead of him. As the white-haired man turns around, a glimpse of his unusual, almost translucent irises, a snap of recognition, activates my fight-or-flight response like a panic button.

Spinning on my heels, I hurry to the exit not daring to look back in case I make contact with those startling eyes. Only once I am on the pavement do I realise that I am still clutching my basket. I risk a peek towards the shop, but thankfully neither a man with a white ponytail nor a security guard materialise in the doorway. At this precise moment I'm not certain which of them would be the most terrifying. Hands trembling, I quickly decant my intended purchases into the rolled-up plastic bag I keep in my handbag, dump the basket next to a rubbish bin and head towards home.

The streets appear unusually and eerily quiet. It is dark, or as dark as it gets in the city, and the headlights of the traffic dazzle on the lacquered surface of the road still wet from the earlier deluge. At one point I pass a communal garden, a scrub of green with a hedge surround, and I half expect a moon-bleached face to float out from the dense black foliage. Mark said he owed the man with white hair and the fat guy money. More precisely, he said he owed *somebody* money – perhaps ponytail and lardy arse were merely tasked with the job of debt collecting. Whatever their particular job title might be I have no desire to run into either of them again. During the last few weeks it has occurred to me that despite my Oscar-worthy performance they might not have left the vicinity when I assumed they did, they may have stayed to watch the front door and could well have seen Mark depart an hour or so later. Not only might they know I lied, they might also assume Mark and I are together, a couple; they could believe I am their best chance of finding him.

I am so preoccupied with listening for footsteps, twisting occasionally to look over my shoulder at who might be following, that I walk straight into the open car door that is blocking two thirds of the walkway. It takes me a moment to realise the collision is not entirely due to my carelessness but also the fact that the lights of the vehicle, both inside and out, are switched off.

'Jesus! What the hell…?' I am rubbing my knee, still trying to squint back along the road when a familiar voice says, 'Get inside the car, Claire!'

My heart does a lazy somersault and then explodes with shock, 'What the hell…?' I say again.

'Get inside!' Mark is leaning across from the driver's side, his left arm extended along the inside of the passenger door that he pulls sharply shut as soon as I am sitting next to him.

There is a second when neither of us speak before I blurt out, 'I've just seen one of those Eastern European guys that came to the door. He was in the queue at the Seven Eleven.' I'm processing the fact it's one hell of a coincidence that I've now run – quite literally – into Mark during the space of the same ten minutes, when the transitory illumination of a passing car reveals the lack of surprise on his features and the penny drops. 'You knew he was somewhere around here, didn't you?'

'I've been keeping an eye on him from time to time. I wanted to see where he went, if he ever went back to the house.'

'*The house*' obviously means his house. *My house*. My stomach lurches. 'And does he?'

Mark shrugs. 'I think so, occasionally, just to see if he can spot me. I don't suppose he has given up on finding me just yet.'

I nod, as though this is normal, to be expected, but I also glance out of the window along the night-soaked street. 'Did you realise he was in the Seven Eleven?'

'No. I lost him tonight. However, luckily for me you've filled in the gap nicely.' Mark's left hand moves across my thigh and its heat burns into my mac, through my jeans and scores into the skin as if he is branding me. 'Did he see you?'

I shake my head. A rabbit snared in headlights. 'I don't think so. I left the shop very quickly, without paying in fact' – I glance guiltily at my plastic bag – 'but I can't be sure.' I swallow, my eyes directed at the place where Mark's face is lit at periodic intervals before disappearing into the void again. 'Do you think it matters? Would he follow me?'

'Only if he thought you could lead him to me. What do you think? Would you do that, Claire?'

I shake my head, although the gesture is probably invisible. I am distracted by Mark's hand, by the force he is exerting on my leg. I am wondering what will happen next, knowing what I want – but shouldn't want – to happen next, when he releases his grip and switches on the ignition and the sudden beam of the headlamps destroys the mood. 'Best not hang about here. We don't want our little friend to stumble upon us when he returns from his shopping trip.'

We move off into the traffic, heading further away from the house. I am about to ask where we are going, but decide against it. Mark is staring straight ahead, expression unreadable. His profile could be Daniel's. I try to remember if we ever drove anywhere together, Daniel and I. The closest I get is a patchy recollection of a taxi journey back to my college. It was the same evening he told me that he didn't want to go out with me any more, when the air was so toxic with the wine and the whisky we had drunk you could have exploded it with a match. I can just about recall how the cabbie refused to take me without Daniel, because of the state I was in, how I made him kiss me one last time, how I felt him tilting, tempted, on that back seat. How he finally pulled away and bundled me out of the cab on my own.

I realise Mark has driven around to the parking area on the far side of Walpole Park, an expanse of cultivated lawn with paths for roller skates and buggies, swings and slides, and even a small animal enclosure where small children push fingers full of grass and cabbage leaves through the wire fencing. I have been known to take a book and sit on one of the benches there. I've watched the pregnant women and young mothers enjoy their special club, their sense of belonging and identity, seen them take it all for granted. After all nobody ever appreciates what they have until it's taken away from them. The gates of the park are locked now, the iron struts rising out of the gloom like the bars of a prison.

Mark cuts both the engine and the lights, engulfing us in a private black cocoon. My heart is skittering with the expectation of his touch, my skin tingling. Instead, he says, 'So, Claire, how are you enjoying the house?' It is a banal question, one an acquaintance might ask at a drinks party, but his tone is oddly serious.

'I like it,' I say. 'I like it very much.' The parking area is deserted but across the other side of the road is a traditional-looking pub, clumps of people going in and out, noise and movement obvious through the mullioned window. It is like gazing through a one-way mirror, seeing them yet remaining invisible.

Mark nods, appearing to digest my answer carefully. Then he says, 'I was wondering if you could use a cleaner?'

'A cleaner?' I can't believe I've heard him properly. I turn away from the pub to look at him, although it is so dark I can smell him better than I can see, the mingled scent of aftershave and skin, musk and animal, intensified by the trapped confines of the car.

'A girl used to come and clean for me two mornings a week. I know she's looking for work at the moment and it wouldn't cost you much.'

I wonder if there is a whole subtext to this exchange I am missing, or whether Mark intends merely to chat about the house and broker an employment contract before he delivers back me home. At the same time, the thought occurs that had such a girl been available this afternoon I would happily have paid her twenty quid or more to sort the mess to which I've just devoted a large proportion of my Sunday both making and clearing up.

'I suppose she could be useful,' I say carefully, guessing that Angus probably wouldn't object to having a cleaner, given his increasingly barbed comments about our differing attitudes to tidiness and housework.

'Great,' Mark says. 'I'll tell her to call you.' Then he adds, 'By the way her name is Victoria.'

'OK.' I'm not expecting that either; Victoria sounds like somebody with a sharp blond bob who works in advertising.

A second or two passes before, with a change of register, Mark says lightly, teasingly, 'Have you missed me?'

Immediately my pulse quickens; I badly want to reach out and touch him. I grasp my left wrist with my right hand and after a long pause, I manage to ignore the question and say, 'Why did you stop me on the pavement? You could have let me walk past?'

Mark hesitates, as if considering his answer. 'You looked frightened, vulnerable. I wanted to help.'

'You could have got my attention some other way than making me walk into the door.' I bend forward and flex my knee, more to make the point than because it is actually hurting.

'I didn't want to draw attention to the car. In case you were being followed. Hey' – he leans over and pulls me towards him – 'I don't think it turned out so badly, do you?' And then he finds my mouth with his mouth and both my willpower and my annoyance evaporate to nothing. I am conscious only of the sensation of his lips, his tongue, his fingers at the back of my skull working into the roots of my hair, pressing me closer, our kissing a fusion of possession and total surrender. When we draw apart, I am panting.

'Claire?'

I only murmur a reply, busy with the buttons of his shirt. His hand closes over mine.

'Have you set a date yet, for the wedding?'

The question shocks me into silence. I have never mentioned my engagement, but I suppose the diamond ring speaks for itself. It is too dark to see Mark's expression, whether he is angry or jealous, there is only his breath and the bulk of him less than a hair's width away. I wonder if I want him to be jealous, what I would do if he asked me to break the engagement, and know in that instant I wouldn't leave Angus. It has taken me so long to throw off the past, get somewhere to be proud of, to reach dry land breathing and alive, that I'm not going to abandon that security anytime soon.

'No date yet,' I offer, finally. 'Do you mind?'

'Mind?'

'About Angus, my fiancé?'

There is silence and for a second I believe that he does actually care. I am processing this thought with a heady mix of pleasure and concern when I feel a tugging at my waist and realise he is undoing the belt of my mac. He has already pulled the coat open and found the zipper of my jeans before he bothers to reply. 'No, Claire,' he says quietly, 'I don't mind at all.'


Later, after we have prised ourselves apart, he pulls up in a side street just around the corner from home. I ask him – I can't help myself – to come back with me, but Mark refuses. Just in case, he says, the white-haired man is watching the house. When he sees my hand hover on the door handle as this thought sinks in, he tells me he will wait ten minutes and then call; if I don't answer he will come to check I am OK. Emboldened by his chivalry I get out of the car.

As I approach our tiny front garden I notice the downstairs lights are glowing behind the sitting room curtains although I'm pretty sure I didn't leave them switched on. I glance over my shoulder but Mark is parked out of sight. For a moment I hesitate, key poised in the lock, before I tell myself not to be paranoid and march straight inside.

Angus's suit carrier is sitting by the bottom of the stairs. The shock is worse, somehow, for being a completely different threat to the one I had anticipated. It is not simply guilt but the awareness of how close I came to being discovered, saved only by the spectre of a long white ponytail spying from the bushes. The scenario that so nearly was, of Angus walking in and finding me with Mark, begins to unspool inside my mind like a third-rate movie. The track gets as far as Angus filling the frame of the bedroom door, roaring with fury, before my brain fuses with horror and the story derails completely. It would have been an end to the relationship, to the engagement, to living in the house, and where would that have left me, the reformed black sheep? Instead of planning a happy summer wedding I would have been everyone's fool again, pretending not to notice the shame and pity in their voices.

I look at myself in the walnut-framed mirror. My cheeks are bright, my hair tousled, my eyes gleaming green. Although I am shaking there is nothing in my appearance incompatible with a fast walk to the supermarket and back. Plus I have all the evidence I need. I take a deep breath, 'Hello!' I call up the stairs. 'How nice you're back so early!'

Overhead I hear the creak of footsteps on the landing and then Angus appears at the top of the steps. 'Where have you been?'

I hold up my environmentally friendly, reusable plastic bag, as if it is a trophy or a prize fish. 'We'd run out of a few basics. I thought I'd stock up in case you came home before going into work tomorrow. Lucky really, since you're back now.' As I don't know when Angus arrived, I realise I am taking a risk. If he returned shortly after I left for the Seven Eleven then the fruits of my unintended shoplifting are hardly going to account for an absence of well over an hour. To my relief, however, he smiles.

'That's great, Claire. I noticed we were out of coffee when I came in. Shall I make us some now?'

'Yes, do.' I run up the stairs and kiss him lightly on the mouth as I hurry by. I'd forgotten how good-looking he is – and how different from Daniel. I am jittery with the luck of my undeserved escape and I need to learn my lesson fast. The only possible place for Daniel is the past, and from now on that has to be where Mark stays too. 'I'm just going to take a shower, to freshen up, and then I'll be right with you.' Dipping into our bedroom I open the window to blast away the last trace of smoke, before selecting my prettiest, sexiest nightie and heading to the bathroom. The best form of defence is surely distraction.

As I drop my clothes on the bathroom floor my mobile begins to ring from my jeans pocket. I answer it quickly. I'm about to say to Mark, *I'm fine*. I'm about to say, *Angus is back*. I'm honestly about to say, *stay away from me*. My fingers are so close to my face I can smell Mark on my skin, but as I open my mouth to speak I see the call is actually from Vodafone.

# CHAPTER EIGHT

A week later I am sitting in the foyer of a hotel in central London. The young woman sitting opposite me and Angus pushes a square of card across the polished surface of the coffee table. She's wearing a navy trouser suit with a badge pinned on the jacket label that reads *Kerry*. *Events Manager* is written underneath her name.

'The finger buffet is one of our most popular choices,' she says, her eyes darting between us as she tries to gauge our reaction to her sell of the hotel's wedding reception packages. Whatever expression she finds in our faces causes a faint trace of uncertainty to wash across her features before she ploughs gamely onwards.

'Now with this option we provide three different types of bruschetta, three additional savoury options, such as watermelon, feta and mint skewers, chicken salad tartlets, and honey-drizzled chipolatas' – she ticks off her fingers as she speaks, presumably to be sure not to leave out the chipolatas – 'followed by our signature finger desserts, miniature chocolate éclairs and strawberry tarts. It's ideal if you intend to have more than sixty guests because it avoids the cost of a sit-down meal, which would also mean having to use one of our bigger, more expensive function rooms.'

This little speech has obviously been rehearsed many times before and she delivers it faultlessly. Kerry is about my age and she has a wide, uncomplicated face that is enhanced by a pepper-shake of freckles over the bridge of her nose and pair of rather trendy, black-rimmed glasses.

I dutifully pick up the proffered card on which is printed a suggested menu. Several similar ones litter the tabletop, as if we have all been playing a children's game of some kind. Snap, perhaps, or Go Fish. The latest recommendation comes with the title: *Finger buffet: Option A.* Kerry is still gripping a number of others in a fan arrangement, like an alternative hand she has yet to play.

I gaze at the list of suggested sandwich fillings; the references to additional extras such as coffee and truffle chocolates; the text that informs me the wedding cake can be cut and served as part of the buffet, if the bride and groom so desire. My head is spinning, though in a useless, non-engaged way, like the pedals on a bike set in a gear that is too high to achieve any proper traction. It's not yet nine o'clock in the morning, and already we have been sat here in the bar area of the hotel discussing menus with Kerry for over an hour.

Although this is supposed to be a breakfast meeting – we have drunk coffee and sipped freshly squeezed orange juice – the basket of croissants remains untouched. I have no appetite, only a queasiness that is a messy combination of chronic guilt and lack of sleep, and Angus never eats anything in the morning. He timed this appointment because the hotel is very close to the Immigration Tribunal, which is where I need to be in thirty minutes' time. To tell the truth, I would rather be there now, concentrating on somebody else's problems. I am exhausted with the effort of maintaining the pretence – as much to myself as to Angus – that nothing has changed; that what happened with Mark was no more than a blip, like snow in July, or rain in the Sahara; that I am excited to be sitting here in this handsome hotel with my handsome fiancé planning our wedding when actually thinking about anyone other than Mark is a struggle that most of the time I seem to be losing.

'Well, what do you think?' Angus's voice is tense with impatience and I realise I have no idea how long I've been studying the details of *Finger Buffet: Option A.*

'I'm not sure.' I put the menu back down on the table, careful not to look at him or at Kerry. 'There's lot to think about. We don't need to make a decision this morning, do we?'

'No, we don't *have* to make a decision' – Angus picks up the card himself, although he only holds it at a distance, not bothering to read it – 'but I imagine the hotel gets very booked up for wedding receptions.'

'Absolutely' – Kerry leans forward to emphasise her approval – 'and the availability of the rose garden makes us a very popular choice in the summer.'

We were given a tour of the rose garden before we sat down, 'tour' being Kerry's word, not mine, since Angus and I were merely required to step outside into a modest, rectangular piece of lawn surrounded on all sides by cliffs of concrete the eight o'clock sun stood no earthly chance of scaling. It's true a bed of rose bushes occupied the very centre of the grass but most of them were bare and the few blooms that remained were dead, speckled with sparse, limp petals nobody had bothered to remove.

'Well, perhaps we should make a provisional decision now. I'm sure if we changed our minds in a few weeks' time the hotel wouldn't object. Isn't that right, Kerry?' Angus also leans forward, closing the distance between his charcoal jacket and Kerry's name badge, and she flushes so suddenly, so prettily, it occurs to me that she probably fancies him. Instinctively I slide my hand on to Angus's thigh. This surge of possessiveness feels odd yet at the same time pleasantly familiar, like an almost-forgotten friend making an unexpected reappearance. If I feel jealous, I wonder, does that make my infidelity worse or better?

'The hotel certainly wouldn't object' – Kerry continues, obviously anxious to nail a booking – 'once an event is reserved in the diary we can accommodate menu variations up until four weeks beforehand. So long as the change doesn't require a room alteration.' Her eyelids bat behind her glasses as she returns Angus's TV presenter smile.

'I don't think that's what Angus was saying,' I tell her. 'If we make a provisional commitment now and change our minds later we would want to be able to cancel the reservation completely, not just the menu.'

Angus frowns and shifts fractionally further away from me. The movement is enough to dislodge my hand. 'No, Claire, that's not what I meant. I realise if we pay a deposit we wouldn't be able to cancel the whole thing.'

There is a tricky silence during which Kerry's gaze resumes its uncertain flicking between us. After a second she says, 'Why don't I leave you to chat for a few minutes? While you're doing that I'll go and fetch the events diary, just in case we need to put you in it!'

As she sidles away, Angus's jaw stiffens. 'I don't see any reason not to make a provisional booking today. A hotel in central London would be ideal, and these reception packages are very reasonable.'

'Like the one for '*Finger Buffet: Option A*'?' I don't try to keep the sarcasm out of my voice.

Angus stares at me. 'I can't understand why you're being so difficult.'

'We might' – I hesitate – 'want to consider other venues.' At this moment I have no idea if it's my fixation with Mark that is making me drag my heels so hard I can feel them burning on the plush blue carpet of the hotel, or whether it is Angus who is in the wrong, forcing a pace that is unreasonably fast. It's in his nature, of course, to steam ahead without considering alternatives, to identify an objective, a goal, and then pursue it relentlessly. It is probably why we came to be engaged so quickly.

As if he has read my mind, Angus says very suddenly, very quietly, 'Is it the venue that's really the problem, Claire?'

The question is so unexpected that my thoughts disintegrate. 'What do you mean?' I make an effort to keep my hands still and my breathing even.

'Sometimes you seem so distant, so distracted. Lately I've found it difficult to talk to you. And now you seem reluctant to book a venue for our wedding reception. I'm beginning to wonder if there's something wrong, something you're not telling me.' A granite-like edge is just detectable within the mellow register of his voice and the gaze of his eyes is sharp, sharper than it was only a moment before.

'Have I? I didn't realise. I didn't think… I've just been busy at work, that's all.' I imagine my culpability blazing through the hopelessly flimsy cover of my words, like the disgrace of a scarlet bra flaring beneath the thin white cotton of a shirt.

'Don't you want to plan our wedding?'

'Yes, of course I do. I'm just not certain I want it to be in London.' I pause and flail and somehow manage to locate a firmer foothold. 'Isn't it traditional for the bride to get married in her home town?'

'You can't want the wedding to be in Ipswich?'

'Well…'

'And we've already talked about this.'

'Have we?'

'You said your mother would understand about the wedding taking place in London, since we would be the ones paying for it. Have you forgotten?'

'I…' I do vaguely recall a conversation late one night about the cost of the reception, about my stepfather wanting to contribute something to the day – flowers or my dress, I think – although I don't remember it being linked to the choice of venue. However, I am still too shaken by how close to the truth Angus has sailed to be able to articulate this protest. A last-gasp thought occurs to me. 'What about one of your hotels? Why don't we hold the reception in one of those?'

Angus's expression alters to one of patient incredulity. 'They're *small* hotels, Claire, remember. None of them have reception rooms big enough to host the kind of wedding we have in mind. Look' – he touches my arm – 'I'll go and speak to Kerry now and make a provisional booking. There's no need for you to wait, I know you're anxious to get to the tribunal.' His tone has softened completely and as he stands up his eyes begin to sweep the room for Kerry. A second later I feel the brush of lips on my hair and when I turn his face is only inches from my own. 'I'm sorry for what I said earlier, about you acting like there's something wrong. I can see how hard the department is pushing you these days, how tired you get. I ought to be more understanding.'

I realise he has misinterpreted my response to his barely veiled accusation; he has put my shocked reaction down to being upset. I gather my belongings with relief. I know his comments should be treated like a warning bell, a well-timed reminder to stay back from the brink, yet I am so longing to check my mobile it's all I can do to restrain myself from checking it. Nevertheless, I manage to stride out of the lobby without stopping to unzip the inner pouch, even when I am completely out of sight of Angus. I have found that often it is better not to consult the phone at all than suffer the lead-weight disappointment of seeing there are no missed calls.

I haven't spoken to Mark since the evening of the Seven Eleven visit – seven whole days ago. I have combed through that encounter with the thoroughness of a psychologist, searching for crumbs of optimism, any words or phrases indicating a desire to meet me again, but there are none. He didn't even phone when he said he would, ten minutes after I left his car, to make sure I was all right. The brutality of that truth remains the same no matter how many times I check my log of missed calls. While I walk I recite the refrain I have been telling myself a hundred or, perhaps a thousand, times an hour, from the instant I saw Angus's bag on the sitting room carpet, that I can never be with Mark again.

I know it's bad enough that I've already cheated on Angus, but errors can be forgiven, can't they? One or two slips don't make me a bad person. People falter, people fail; people are human after all. The important thing is not to repeat past mistakes and to appreciate what I have. And yet the endless repetition of that tiresome mantra doesn't stop me jumping every time my mobile rings or, when it doesn't, staring at the screen and willing it to stir from its sullen, uncooperative slumber on my desk. Just the thought of speaking to Mark and my skin pricks with anticipation. I tell myself that *if* he were to call, I must refuse to see him. I am committed to Angus, who deserves better than to be betrayed. As the tribunal comes into view I twist the glitter-ball diamond around my finger to remind myself where my loyalties lie, but the ring is not a perfect fit and the flesh of my knuckle catches and bunches underneath the gold.

Outside the building a few of the security guards are having a smoke. Although it isn't cold they are grouped in a collegiate huddle with their shoulders hunched and they nod to me as I use my security pass to go through the gate. Their faces are as familiar to me as, I suppose, mine must be to them; we are just as much part of the system as the edifice of courts and waiting rooms, and the intricate network of laws and procedure. It is only the identity of the customers that change, revolving in and out of the public entrance day after day. If every person bringing an appeal were to stand in a row, how far across London would the line snake? I imagine them queuing behind one another, weaving through the sophisticated bustle of Exmouth Market, fighting for standing room between the shoppers on Oxford Street, and curling around the perimeter of secure, leafy Hyde Park; all waiting patiently and invisibly amidst the self-absorption of the city.

My working day passes uneventfully until the final case on my list. A boy from Afghanistan has claimed asylum. Apparently he is fourteen but this is hard to believe because although his body has the slight build of a young child, the burned-out expression on his face belongs to somebody much older. He says his father was a commander in the mujahideen and only came back to the family home for a few days each month in order to avoid being captured by government forces. One day, soldiers or police with guns came looking for his father. They shot his brother but he escaped over a low wall at the back of his house and some family friends took him and his mother to Tehran. From there agents helped him travel to the UK in the back of a truck.

He gives his evidence through an interpreter without any sign of emotion, even when I question him about his family. 'What happened to your mother?' I probe.

'I don't know.'

'Did she stay in Tehran?'

The boy shrugs. His eyes are a closed door.

'Why didn't she come with you?'

The boy speaks so quietly the interpreter has to ask him to repeat himself before he can tell us the answer to my question.

'There was only enough money to pay the agent for one person,' the interpreter says at last. 'His mother wanted him to go. He had a mobile phone which contained a telephone number for his mother but it was stolen during the journey across Europe.'

'So how does he get in touch with his mother now?'

The boy's answer is delivered in the same flat tone.

'He doesn't know how to get in touch with his mother,' the interpreter translates. 'He hasn't spoken to her since he left Tehran.'

I gaze at the boy and he stares back at me. I don't know whether to believe his story or not, none of the witnesses who could support his account of events are living in the UK or are even contactable; he is completely on his own. I tell the judge I have finished my cross-examination. He is an elderly man who has recorded the evidence faithfully and been scrupulously polite to everyone in court, but it is hard to imagine him rolling up his sleeves to intervene, descending into the fray so to speak, and sure enough he says he doesn't have any questions. Whenever this happens I like to think it is because I have done my job so well there is nothing left to ask, but it is more likely to be a question of style. Judges vary in their approach, which is natural, I suppose, but still unnerving when you think about it. I wonder if this judge would have believed the Indian woman with the fake employment documents.

Just as we are gathering up the case papers, the boy mumbles a few sentences and the interpreter interjects. 'He wants to add something.'

The judge hesitates before opening his file and picking up his pen. 'Very well, what does he want to say?'

'He says that if he goes back to Afghanistan he will be killed. The soldiers who shot his brother will come back and look for him also. It is the punishment for his father being in the mujahideen.'

The statement is delivered in the same matter-of-fact tone, but a sliver of fear shows in the boy's face, like cold blue light seeping under a door. I think the judge spots the change too, because when he speaks to the interpreter his voice is noticeably gentler. 'Tell him I'll take that evidence into account when I come to make my decision.'

By the time I leave Ellerton House the pavements are beginning to swell with impatient commuters and the traffic has thickened to a heavy crawl. As I bend down to check I have packed all my papers into my wheelie bag somebody brushes past. Glancing up, I realise in a stomach-churning split second that I recognise the symmetrical line of the profile, the willowy posture, and the narrow curving shoulders that are now moving rapidly away. Without it being a conscious decision I snap shut the case and plunge into the crowd. It is only as I am approaching her back that I see she is not who I thought she was, the hair is different – too short and the shade of blond too dark – and I am engulfed with a flood of disappointed relief.

At the next junction the traffic lights are green and the traffic oozes past, pinning the pedestrians to the curb. I crack and take out my mobile to search for messages from Mark, but there is only one from my mother asking if I have given any thought to bridesmaids because my cousin Gina's daughter is nearly four and would absolutely love to be a flower girl. I am putting my phone away, trying to visualise myself processing down the aisle with a train of picture-book bridesmaids, when a voice – her voice – says at my elbow,

'Claire?'

My illusory scene disintegrates.

'Julia,' I say.

We look at each other for a long, considered moment. I imagine that she is studying my face as much I am studying hers; the new hairstyle, the thinner cheeks, the very beginning of lines – the faintest fork marks – around her eyes, but still the same effortless, artless beauty I always envied. And I guess, like me, she is probably remembering the last time we saw each other and then I know for certain that she is because I see her lips press together and a shadow fall like a curtain across her face.

'How are you, Claire?' she asks.

'I'm fine,' I say. 'I'm well.' I hesitate and then extend my left hand. 'I'm about to get married.' Naturally I don't add that I was just, at that moment, checking for messages from another man.

She makes a brief pretence of examining the diamond. 'How beautiful. Congratulations.' She doesn't bother to ask me who the lucky man is and after a moment I drop my arm.

'What about you?' I say. 'Are you well?'

'Yes,' she says. 'I'm very well.'

'Are *you* married?' I ask, 'Engaged?' I honestly don't intend to sound competitive, but I suppose the question might come across that way – given our history.

'No,' she says shortly. 'I'm not.'

'Seeing anyone?' I shouldn't persist like this, but then she did ruin the best, the most important, relationship of my life, even if she paid for it, as we both did, in the end. Besides, I am curious to know if – *how* – she has moved on. Both of us appear so normal and yet what we have in common, what we both want so much to forget is – I have to admit – less so.

She shakes her head and I change tack. 'So what are you doing now? Where do you work?'

'Oh' – she blinks – 'in the city, near Bank.'

I wait for details, but she doesn't elaborate. I realise she doesn't want me to know any more; she doesn't want to give me an address; she doesn't, in fact, want to risk running into me again. I can't blame her for that; I would probably rather not see her again either. She is wearing a tailored suit, a silk shirt and heels – a successful working woman's attire – yet the images I can't shake off are the ones from five years earlier: her wretched face, the red stain soaking through the dirty jeans, the shocking, sticky gush of liquid. I remember her desperate, choked plea, 'I can't stop the bleeding, Claire! I don't know what to do.' And the way she shouted into the deserted stairwell, until finally, eventually, aid arrived. 'Help! Somebody help us! Please!'

Bizarrely, I have an almost overwhelming urge to ask her about Daniel. '*Have you seen him?*' I want to say. '*How is he doing?*' Even if he doesn't contact me any more, it is hard to believe he no longer talks to her, that he wouldn't make some effort to get in touch. I realise now how much he loved her, I was always the dispensable, disposable one: use, spoil and throw away. But my mind is playing tricks, dreadful, outrageous tricks. Here with Julia beside the relentless London traffic, I am being absurd. Daniel won't speak to her, he won't speak to anyone. However much we might want to ask him questions, or talk, in a rational, grown-up way, about the apportionment of blame, we can't, because Daniel has been dead for nearly five years.

# CHAPTER NINE

A watched pot… as they say, so it is typical that Mark calls the first occasion I answer my phone without giving any thought as to who might be on the other end. It's about 8.30 a.m. on a cold November Wednesday and already I'm in the office, trying to figure out why so much time appears to have elapsed between the date a Nigerian woman made an application to stay in the UK after her student visa expired and the decision of the Home Office rejecting the claim. In the meantime she has got married, had a child and become the assistant manager of a care home – only, of course, none of this has been taken account of in the decision because it hadn't happened when she filled in the necessary paperwork.

'Yes?' I say, without even looking at the screen, wondering if the date typed at the start of the decision can possibly be a typo.

'You don't sound very pleased to hear from me, Claire,' Mark says, and there is a lost second while the page I am holding swims out of focus and my voice shuts down completely.

When words eventually arrive on my tongue they are not what I expect them to be. 'You were supposed to call, to check I hadn't encountered any problems from the man with the white ponytail.' I don't like how I sound, the childish blurting out of hurt and disappointment over something he has probably long forgotten, but I can't help it.

There is a fractional pause, then, 'I drove to the corner of your road. I could see the lights were already on before you got home and guessed that Angus had come back.' He laughs lightly. 'I didn't think it would be a good idea to call you.'

I swallow, wrong-footed and also ridiculously pleased, although I try to stay angry. 'Well you took your time. I wondered if I was ever going to hear from you again.'

'I've been away. Business abroad.' His tone is gentle, mollifying, and he adds, 'A call to you was top of my list for when I got back. In fact I haven't yet left the airport, I'm still waiting for my luggage.'

'What a shame you aren't aware that mobile phones now have this remarkable ability to make international calls.' Although my voice is laced with sarcasm I am relenting already, an ice cube pooling at speed under the glare of a lamp. Of course he can sense it.

'How about lunch, somewhere nice, to make it up to you?'

'When?'

'Why not today?'

'I'm busy. I have a team meeting that begins at two o'clock.' It is a poor effort to make good my conviction not to see him again. The timing of his call seems judged to perfection, a long enough wait for my guard to have dropped, my resolve to have weakened, but not such a gap that my want of him is any less acute.

'In that case we'll start early. I'll book a table at twelve.'

I don't reply. The bones of me know that our date is not suddenly so pressing because he is eager to see me; I realise he must have an alternative motive, but it is the kind of knowledge to which you close your eyes and exist, quite happily, in willful ignorance. Often, we choose to see only what we want – until the final denouement leaves us no other alternative.

'Claire?'

A restaurant is public and therefore harmless, surely?

'Where shall I meet you?'

'It's called La Mezza. The address is on Old Jamaica Road in Bermondsey.'

'Bermondsey?' That's across the river in southeast London. Unless I splash out on a cab the journey could take me an hour. 'Why are we going all the way over there?'

'I know the restaurant. It's very good and not as far as you think. I'll see you there as soon after twelve as you can make it.' He says goodbye and hangs up before I can protest any more.

When I look up I realise Agatha has come in while I was mid-conversation. She has a file spread open on her desk but is staring at it with the forced concentration of somebody whose attention is elsewhere. At about eleven o'clock I pick up my handbag, hoping Agatha will assume I am slipping to the loo, but as I stand up she fixes me with her pale blue gaze. 'Going out, Claire?'

I consider lying but suspect she has heard too much of my dialogue with Mark for that to be a plausible option. I select the almost-truth, which, as a tactic, has served me well in the past. 'I'm meeting a friend for lunch. She works in Bermondsey. I'm taking a longer lunch break than normal but I came in early this morning to make up for it.'

Agatha nods. I am halfway through our open-plan office, heading towards the lifts, before she calls after me, 'Team meeting at two. Don't forget, will you?'


La Mezza turns out to be a Lebanese restaurant. I step from the sterile shapes of newly regenerated Bermondsey into a lavish candlelit room that is hung with rugs and smells of garlic, nuts and lemons. The decor comprises reds and ochre with dark wooden furniture and lots of black-and-white photographs of olive trees and mosques. It is the perfect setting for a debauched evening, rowdy laughter and the clatter of cutlery and clinking glasses, but in the middle of the day it is like stumbling into the wrong country or a different time zone.

When my sight adjusts sufficiently to the gloom to pick out Mark, I see he has chosen a back corner – although his discretion seems unnecessary since none of the other tables are occupied – and also that he has been watching me since the moment I came through the door. As I approach he gets to his feet and I am wondering how to greet him before it is too late to worry because we are so close the leather-like notes of his cologne are a taste on my tongue. He kisses my cheek, prolonging the contact, whispering my name into my ear and murmuring how nice it is to see me again. By the time we sit down my body is craving the touch of his fingers and the press of his mouth. The pretence that I might have come here for food, for conversation, is exposed for the lie I should have known it to be from the instant I agreed to see him again.

He picks up the menu and looks at me over the top of it. 'How long do you have?'

It crosses my mind that his motivation for asking might be because there are bedrooms above the restaurant and I immediately feel heat spread to my cheeks. 'If I book a cab I can stay until one thirty,' I say far too quickly, but he only nods and drops his gaze to study the menu.

'What do you want to eat?' he asks a moment later.

I force myself to consider the list of dishes, although I have never heard of most of them. As I am reading a middle-aged waiter – or perhaps he is the owner – arrives at our table and hands Mark a wine list. A very erect man, his cropped black hair makes an unbroken line from his scalp to his chin then stretches over his upper lip to form a neat moustache. They obviously know each other because Mark enquires about someone called Marissa, whether she is better now, if the problems have been resolved. I assume Marissa must be the waiter's wife or daughter but when I glance upwards, to indicate that I am with Mark and I, too, am interested in the answer, the man's reply is spoken without affection and the gaze of his lamp-black eyes is hostile; it suggests he would rather I kept my eyes on the laminated paper and minded my own business.

A few minutes later a very young waitress brings a bottle of red wine, pours us both a generous glass, then pulls a notebook from a skirt pocket to take our order. When I tell her I'll have hummus followed by chicken, Mark shakes his head and laughs, 'No you won't, you must try something different, something unknown. Live a little, Claire. Variety is the spice of life. Now you've experimented with *shoplifting*' – he widens his eyes to emphasise the euphemism – 'you should have no trouble pushing a few culinary boundaries.' His voice has acquired the familiar flirtatious shade I remember, and now I know precisely where it leads my stomach clenches with expectation.

'She'll start with the *baba ganoush* and I will start with the *hindbeh* and then we'll both have the *rosto*,' he says, appearing to revel in his mastery of the exotic names. Then he slaps the menu shut in an exaggerated gesture of flamboyance and hands it to the waitress without so much as glancing at her.

Immediately after she has gone his gaze tightens. 'Did Victoria call you?'

'Yes – well, no. Actually she just turned up on the step.' About ten days after my Seven Eleven adventure the doorbell had rung at 7.30 a.m., Angus had already left for work and I was on my way out. The girl who stood there looked like a child wearing an older sibling's coat: pale skin, fair hair scraped into a listless ponytail and tremulous blue-grey eyes. When she handed me a cluster of references I saw that her name was actually spelt Viktoria, although by that stage it was already obvious that she wasn't English.

'So what arrangement did you make?'

'She comes round twice a week. At first it was just Mondays but she did such a good job I asked her to do Fridays as well.' Thirty quid for two mornings is a bargain, the place is now immaculate and she's also willing to run small errands like picking up milk or collecting our dry cleaning. Now I can't imagine how we managed without her.

'Great.' Mark nods as if ticking an item off a list. 'I'm glad to hear you're taking such good care of my house.' He reaches for my fingers, pins them flat against the tablecloth and begins to stroke the back of my hand with his thumb.

'Your house?' I raise my eyebrows at his presumptiveness.

He shrugs. 'Not legally, perhaps, not any more, but it's still mine in spirit. I did all the renovations, designed the layout, picked the colour schemes.' His tone harbours a surprising intensity and sense of grievance.

I remember the pride with which he regaled me with his choice of fabrics and brands of furniture and it crosses my mind whether sleeping with me had something to do with possession, asserting control over a space he thinks of as his own. The thought, however, dissolves before I can engage with it properly, the notion rubbed to nothing by the constant rhythmic pressure of his thumb on my skin.

'Why did you sell?' I ask instead, 'If you loved it so much.'

'Because I had to.' He scowls. 'Besides' – he lifts his palm away from mine in a sudden, deliberate gesture – 'we can't always have what we want, can we, Claire?'

The flagrant innuendo sends my gaze plummeting to the swirls of embroidery adorning the white damask tablecloth. I am about to return my hand to my lap but before I can move Mark traps it again with his own, as if he is cupping a spider or a fly.

'You look extremely attractive when you blush. Unbelievably sexy; however, you probably know that already.' He dips close and brushes a piece of hair away from my face.

I realise he is playing with me, manipulating me like a puppet vulnerable to every tweak and jerk of its strings, nevertheless I can't help but smile and lift my eyes to meet the potent brown of his own. I attempt to turn the conversation towards a different subject.

'Have you seen the guy with the ponytail again? Or the other man?'

Mark settles back in his chair and looks at me. 'No,' he says slowly, 'but I've been away, remember.' Then he adds, 'Does it worry you? The thought they might come back?'

I shrug, make an attempt at nonchalance. 'A little perhaps, not much. It's not as if I could help them since I don't know where you live.' My last sentence dangles like a loose thread, but Mark ignores the blatant hint. After a second or two I give up and ask, 'Is that why you had to sell the house, because you owed those men money?'

'No. They had nothing to do with the sale of the house. There was a misunderstanding between us, that's all.'

'Misunderstanding?'

'About a business deal. They were too greedy. They misunderstood how much money they would make.' His voice drops as if he is closing a lid. He drinks a large draught of the red wine and I follow his example. A moment later the young waitress arrives with our food, the dishes vying for space on an ornate silver platter beneath a pungent hood of spices.

As we eat we talk about my work. Whenever I try to explain my job to my mother and Andy I find myself giving them the barest, most basic description – the struggle required to convey the nuances of the immigration rules and the peculiar brand of everyday desperation that fills the tribunal is too much effort on a weekday evening when tomorrow's files are stacked in the hall. Besides, despite the stream of well-intentioned questions, my family don't really care about the details of my work; the purpose of their calls is for reassurance I am fine, that there is no new cause for worry, and to refresh their sense of pride in their government-worthy daughter. Yet with Mark the facts of the cases slip out of me as easily as if I am recounting the plot of a favourite film or book, just like the first time I met him, when I went to view the house, and I poured out the minutiae of my job from the comfort of his sofa. I scoop up the creamy paste of the *baba ganoush* with chunks of bread and devour the tender meat of the *rosto* while I tell him about the woman with the fraudulent records.

'Are you certain the documents were fake?' Mark asks.

I nod, cradling my wine glass. It is full-bodied with a velvety blackberry taste and it complements the oily aromas of the food and the autumnal chill outside perfectly. 'You would never have known it from the papers themselves, but it was obvious from the answers she gave to the judge and the message on her phone.' I think of that splintery smile, the flash of distress in the woman's face as the hearing finished and I feel a twinge of guilt for exploiting her story like this, turning her shame into lunchtime entertainment.

'Can you remember her name?'

'Her name? No, why does that matter?'

Mark ignores the question. 'But it would be on the court records?'

'Yes, she gave a witness statement which means her name and address would be in the file.'

'So the police could look if they wanted? They could bring criminal proceedings against her for lying to the tribunal?'

'I suppose so.' I blink at him, perplexed at the level of his interest. 'But I don't think they would do that. They don't have the time to trawl through cases searching for people to prosecute. An awful lot of witnesses lie in court. They must do when you think about it because they frequently contradict each other.' I drain my glass, tipping back my head to catch the last silky drips. Then I sit up again suddenly. 'Oh my God, what is the time?'

Mark consults his watch. 'Ten to two.'

'Shit! I have to go.' I begin to push back my chair, but once the initial adrenaline shot subsides my movements slow as my brain begins to process the fact that it's already too late to get back to the office in time for the team meeting, even if I'm lucky enough to find a cab out in the wilds of SE16 immediately. It's probably better to miss the briefing altogether and invent an excuse – another headache, bad news from home, a dentist's appointment – then arrive thirty minutes late, breathless and smelling of blackberry wine. Besides, I don't want to leave. I have no objection to leaving the restaurant, but I don't want to leave Mark. What I want is for us to go somewhere else, a place he can undo my shirt, button by button, slide my bra straps over my shoulders and bury his lips in the curve of my neck. Slowly, I sit down again. 'It's only a meeting. It's not very important.' I smile to make it clear I am choosing him over my work – and over my fiancé.

Mark raises his eyebrows. 'Dear me, you're becoming quite the rebel.' But I can tell he is pleased because the honey-like glaze has returned to his voice. 'Since you're not in a rush,' he says, catching my gaze and holding it still, 'we must have some arak.'

He signals to the waitress and a couple of minutes later she brings across a tray containing a magnificent long-spouted brass jug and two cups filled with ice. The liquid pours from the spout in a lofty, transparent arc but the moment it hits the ice becomes milky and opaque, like something in a chemistry experiment or a magic show. Mark hands me a drink and takes one himself. 'Don't sip. It tastes better if you gulp it straight. Now…' He clinks his cup against mine and tips the contents down his throat.

After a second I follow suit. It's like swallowing liquid fire. At first I can't taste anything at all, only the rush of heat swan-diving down my throat and engulfing my stomach. Gagging, I stretch for the carafe of water that has been sitting on our table all through the meal, but which neither of us has yet bothered to touch. Mark moves it out of my reach, laughing, and I begin to laugh too. The flames recede and I taste aniseed, a curled, warm ball of it lodged in my gut.

I don't remember exactly how many more times the waitress performs the water-to-milk trick, but by the time Mark stands up and says, 'Time to go, Claire,' I'm drunk enough to have lost my sense of time, to assume we are heading together somewhere upstairs, or even outside; I wouldn't care if it happened down an alley or in a park. I have forgotten work, abandoned Angus, my thoughts can only process what I desire, and what I desire is Mark.

As we leave the restaurant the cold air feels shocking, almost hostile, and I lean against him, trying to sustain the sense of intimacy. A section of his shirt has become untucked from the waistband of his jeans. I slide my right hand within the folds of his coat and slip it beneath the cotton, electrified by the roasting surface of his skin. It is then, I think, something in that moment, a stiffening of his back, a slight increase in his walking pace, which alerts to me to the possibility that our minds are following different tracks, he wants something from me again, but today it is not sex.

Beyond the restaurant Mark turns left. The street is a cul-de-sac with terraced houses on either side interspersed by occasional shards of commercial life. I spot a shabby newsagent, and then a launderette that has a fruit machine in the window where a woman is standing with a rucksack full of clothes at her feet. We appear to be heading towards the end of the road and a low-rise office block, which by my calculation blocks a view of the river. In my befuddled state I assume Mark must have some kind of appointment but at the last moment he veers to one side, guiding me down a narrow passage that snakes between the grey stone of the offices and the dirty brick of the houses. A short distance ahead I can see a patch of grass littered with a bottles and plastic carrier bags.

I stop. 'Where are we going?'

'Somewhere private, that's all.' Mark takes a step forward and when I stay motionless he tugs at my arm. 'Come on.'

I don't move. A primal, animal instinct is waking up somewhere deep beneath the chalky surface of the arak.

'Really, Claire! You're not scared of me, surely?' Although his voice is infused with joking sarcasm, his tone is strained. I am not scared exactly, I am wary rather than frightened and I don't understand the reasons for my feelings, but I sense that Mark does and that he is doing his best to disguise them. He makes another effort. 'I want to do you a favour. I've got something you might find useful, but we need to be somewhere private before I can tell you what it is.' His grasp moves from my arm to my hand, his fingers play with mine, lightly and without force. I watch the pale light catching the silver of his signet ring. Even now, when all my ancient genes are focused on self-preservation, the binary choice of fight or flight, his fluctuating touch is like an electric current, a pulsing strobe of distraction. 'Please, Claire. I'm trying to help you. Don't make it so difficult.' That final descent to entreaty, that hint of vulnerability is enough to unfreeze my feet, and I allow myself to be led slowly through the alley and into the open space beyond.

The area in which we arrive is not much bigger than a couple of tennis courts. The river borders one side. It stretches, lank and grey, behind concrete and railings towards a bank of city infrastructure that is too distant to decipher in any detail. High walls surround the other three sides although none of them have windows, only an expanse of blank, implacable masonry. It appears that the focus of the buildings is elsewhere, some place much more pleasant; they have all turned their backs on this patch of scrubby green.

I see the grass is actually struggling to grow between slabs of cement and guess that perhaps some kind of waste plant or electrical generator used to be located here: an eyesore that nobody wanted to look at. Close up the ground is peppered with grot – needles, cigarette butts, condoms and the kind of tiny plastic tubes that are used for snorting. I touch one of the bottles with my toe and it rolls away to expose a scrap of blackened aluminium foil.

The grimness of the place makes me shiver. That and the pigeon-grey canopy of sky, which seems to have drained the colour from our surroundings. Mark misinterprets. 'Are you cold?'

I shake my head and the arak sloshes around my skull. I feel both drunk and sober at the same time. I am fully aware of our strange location; I assume something is about to be required of me, yet nevertheless I have a sense of liberation, of stepping outside myself. The weak afternoon light makes Mark look older; it saps the tan from his skin and whitens the silver veins in his hair.

Despite this, I know that if he began to touch me, pressed me up against a wall and reached under my skirt, I wouldn't possess the willpower to object.

Instead, he swings on to the front of his stomach a soft black briefcase he has been carrying on his shoulder. I noticed the bag while we were eating and thought nothing of it, now I remember the care he took to move it out of the way of the waitress's feet, the precious, pernickety way he settled the carrying strap across his chest as we left the restaurant.

'I'm going to give you something,' he says. 'You need to look after it carefully.' I have an instantaneous, laughable notion he is about to produce a living thing, a rabbit or a guinea pig perhaps, but the thought vanishes abruptly. I realise that whatever he has in mind is nothing like that. His hand hovers on the zip. I think he's expecting me to ask him what's inside, hoping I will play along and add to the drama.

I stay silent and wait.

He reaches into the inner pocket and begins to draw something out. The afternoon light snags a black, metallic, betraying glint, but he stops before the object is fully visible. 'I want you to take this, Claire, and keep it at the house.'

'What is it?' I ask, although I must know already because when he tells me there is no surprise, only a twisting, aching kind of thrill.

'A gun.'

I stare at the briefcase, at the barrel projecting from its interior. 'I can't do that,' I manage to say after a moment or two. 'I don't have a licence for a gun; it would be illegal. If somebody found it, I would lose my job, maybe even go to prison—'

Marks interrupts me. 'It's a replica, Claire. A good one, but only a dummy. It's not against the law to own one of these.'

We stand in silence for a second. His attention flicks around the sightless walls before settling back on me.

'Why do you want me to have it?' I still can't drag my eyes away from the open flap of the briefcase.

'You're clearly worried about those men returning, and to be honest I don't think either of them will give up on me easily. If they do come back you can wave this at them.'

'I don't know how to fire a gun.'

'You won't have to fire it. You won't have to do anything other than show them you've got it. If they see you with it they'll know you mean business. I doubt they'd ever bother you again.'

'But—'

'Claire,' stepping very close Mark cups my chin in his left hand and impales me with his eyes, 'it's not just you I'm thinking of. The sooner they give up on you the sooner they'll forget about me as well. The only link to me that they have is the house.'

I am within breathing distance of the shapes and planes of his face, the indefinable likeness to Daniel that makes him so entirely irresistible. It dimly occurs to me that neither the white-haired man nor the chubby guy has actually bothered me since they first came to the house, yet all I can think of is how badly I want Mark to kiss me.

'Where shall I keep it?' I don't say the word gun.

'In the wooden chest, the one I gave you with the mirror. You still have it don't you?'

I nod.

'Good. The key is in the bag.'

I remember my futile earlier attempts to open the box, the rattle of the metal lock as I jerked the lid in frustration.

'Of course,' he continues, 'you mustn't leave the key where somebody could see it.'

'So where…?'

'Beneath the mirror. Attach it to the underside of the frame. OK?'

I don't reply.

'Is that all right, Claire?' Mark prompts after my silence has hovered in the afternoon air a fraction too long. When I still don't say anything, when I don't protest, he eases the black strap free of his shoulder and steps forward to place it over my neck as if presenting me with a victory medal or a garland of flowers.

'What about the security at my work? They scan every bag going into a government building.'

'You're not going back to work, are you? It's too late now.' He doesn't add that I'm in no fit state to sit at a desk and assess somebody's right to a future. I watch as he takes his wallet from an inside jacket pocket and peels off four twenties. 'Get a cab. Go straight home and sort this out before your boyfriend gets back.'

I stuff the notes into my purse, my movements made awkward by the fiddle of two straps, two bags: my handbag holding my purse, my Oyster card, my make-up pouch and the finer points of *Finger Buffet: Option A*. And the other containing the gun. The briefcase is heavier than I anticipated but the way its weight hangs against my chest is oddly reassuring, empowering even.

'When will I see you again?' I ask; perhaps the most pathetic question in the whole of human history.

'Soon,' he says. 'I have to go away again for a few days, but it won't be long. I'll get in touch next week, I promise.'

'I don't even have a number for you.'

He smiles at me. 'Yes, you do, I rang you this morning. And I also phoned you about the mirror, remember? Before you moved into the house. My number must be on your mobile twice now.'

I think back to the conversation in the female toilets at work, and it seems such a long time ago. I can't believe I had forgotten about that call, and its ability to trace me to Mark, but in some ways I'm pleased about the memory lapse, I don't think I would have been able to resist the lure of those eleven digits. I would have made a greater fool of myself than I have done already.

'Look' – Mark is reaching into his inside jacket pocket – 'I'll even give you my number again, in case you can't find it for some reason.' He takes out a pen and scribbles on the back of an old receipt, using the palm of his left hand for support. As I put the scrap of paper in my coat pocket, I see the ink is a bright, navy blue and the zero is scored with a diagonal line: the handwriting of a true showman.

He turns towards the passageway where we came in. 'Shall we go?'

I shake my head. 'I'm going to stay here for a little while.' Partly I want to get my head straight, sober up a little: adjust to what has happened in the last few minutes. Partly I want the kind of parting he might not want to provide in public.

'Are you OK?'

'Yes,' I tell him. 'Say goodbye here.' I tilt back my face, and after a second he obliges, kissing me long and deep and hard, as though we are long-term lovers, Bermondsey's answer to Bonnie and Clyde. I want to ask if I will see him next week, however he is leaving already, walking quickly towards the narrow alleyway without looking back.

I decide to wait ten minutes to avoid running into Mark in the street and appear as though I'm chasing after him. Alone, I pace for a while beside the railings. Beyond them the surly river flows on but the surrounding windowless walls feel as attentive as a stand of spectators. Eventually, I come to a halt, unzip the bag and slip my right palm inside. My fingers make contact with the casing, tentative at first, barely daring to touch it, then slowly they enclose the sleek curve of the handle.

Somewhere across the water a hooter sounds, a ship, probably, blasting notice of imminent arrival or departure. It is enough to make me jump, to whip my hand from the briefcase and look around with horror. Nobody is here, of course, in this forgotten pocket of impropriety. I shiver once – an uncontrollable, violent shudder – then consult my watch, to see if the requisite ten minutes have passed, before I head for the street.

# CHAPTER TEN

## *Five years earlier*

'Why don't you contact the police?'

'The police?' Daniel sounds horrified, as if I've suggested hiring a hitman. 'She's not a criminal.'

'The amount she calls you, the number of texts and messages, I think it amounts to harassment. That *is* a crime.'

We are both in his college bedsit, the light is draining from the day but so far neither of us has bothered to get up from the floor and resort to electricity, so the room has the appearance of a black-and-white photograph; an arty take on Cambridge university life: the view of spires and rooftops through the mullioned window, the jumbled duvet, the surplus of books and wine glasses, and two real, stressed-out students.

Daniel sighs, leans back against the bedframe and shuts his eyes. It makes me impatient, this attitude of his, which seems to fluctuate between laziness and something I can't quite put my finger on. Whatever it is, he seems to be willing to bury his head in the sand and wait for the storm to pass. I wonder if perhaps he is secretly enjoying the situation, the thrill of being an object of obsession, the focus of a mania that places him incontrovertibly and irreplaceably in the centre of our universe. Perhaps it is more than that. Maybe he is keeping his options open, ready to ditch me as quickly as he dumped her.

I tell myself I am being unfair, that the situation is more stressful for him than it is for me. After all, I can tell he has lost weight and occasionally I glimpse lines etching into the skin around his eyes and mouth, a preview of the man he will be in fifteen years' time. Still, I can't shake the sense I should be cautious, the belief that I am the one balanced on the tightrope, with the fall into blackness beneath.

I touch the toe of his outstretched trainer. The littered remnants of an impromptu meal surround us: coffee cups, plates dirty with toast crumbs, a tub of butter with a knife balanced across the middle and a large jar of Marmite pasted with the thought-provoking slogan, '*Love it or Hate it*'.

There is a ping as Daniel's phone takes delivery of another message. 'Jesus fucking Christ.' He lifts his head with undisguised weariness and reaches for his mobile. There is no urgency in his actions any more. We are beyond that. I wait for the explosion, the bitter retort, but this time his mouth twists into a relieved, sardonic smile. 'It's Ned,' he says, referring to a friend of his. 'He's asking if we want to meet in the bar later.'

I shrug. 'Do you want to?'

'Not really.' Then he adds as though we have been following the previous thread of conversation without a break, 'I can't go to the police.' He picks up the mug of coffee by his thigh, although I can see from where I'm sitting that it's stone cold and the milk has retracted into a fatty, leaf-shaped puddle.

'Why not?'

'Because it's not like she's a stranger. She's my ex-girlfriend and I ought to be able to sort it out myself. I know who she is, what kind of person. She might be a bit of a nutcase, but she's not dangerous. I can deal with her. It's just fucking irritating, that's all.'

I let his words sit for a moment and expand within the sepia tones of the room. It's more than *fucking irritating* and I want her out of our lives.

Eventually I ask, 'How many texts today?'

'I don't know. I haven't counted.'

'Roughly.'

'A dozen. Maybe fifteen.'

This isn't as bad as I was expecting, but his gaze dips into his coffee and I can tell it's not the whole story.

'What about yesterday?'

'Day or night?'

'For God's sake! Either. Both. How many texts did she send yesterday?'

He looks up. His eyes are closed. 'Two hundred and fifty-eight.'

'What? Two hundred—'

'... and fifty-eight. Yup.'

The image of her hunched fanatically, permanently, over a screen, stops me in my tracks and the arrival of a still, shocked silence makes me want to turn on a lamp or light a candle to give chase to the shadows.

'Daniel, you really should go to the police—'

He cuts across me. 'She says she'll wait. That's the latest thing.' His tone is conversational yet its very normality somehow adds to the sense of disquiet.

'What on earth do you mean?'

'In these recent texts she says she realises I didn't appreciate what I was doing when we split up, that the stress of exams obviously made me irrational and unpredictable. She understands it's just a matter of time until I recognise my mistake and she wants me to know that she'll wait. And that she'll forgive me.'

'She's crazy.' I don't sound as adamant as I would like and I try again. 'She's really crazy.' After a pause I add, before I can help myself, my words tentative and badly lacking in humour, 'I guess if she keeps it up long enough she'll eventually get what she wants. Maybe you will go back to her?'

'Of course I won't go back to her!' Daniel slams his cup down and glares at me. 'For God's sake, babe! We've both just agreed she's behaving like a fucking lunatic.' His eyes jump, suddenly, to the door. 'What was that?'

'What?'

'I thought I heard something outside.'

We both freeze. I even hold my breath, ears straining to catch the slightest noise, but there is nothing, only a backdrop of traffic, the muted thud of a road drill, a distant car alarm; the constant soundtrack we block out from habit until we need to stop and really listen.

After a second, Daniel lets go of his cold coffee and says, 'I'm going for a shower.' His statement is one of practical intent, made without any hint of invitation. He is still dressed in cycling shorts and a red Lycra T-shirt that has sweat stains under the arms and across the top of his back.

His bike is a new passion. Most days he heads out for at least an hour, although recently I've noticed his rides have been getting even longer. When, a week or so ago, I asked him where he went he merely shrugged. 'Nowhere. Anywhere. At least when I'm moving I can't hear my phone all the fucking time.' Yesterday, I was browsing the shops on the edge of town when a figure shot by, head down, knees pumping against the easterly breeze. It took me a second to realise who it was before I found myself shouting rather uselessly at his retreating back. He hadn't seen me of course. I don't think he could see anyone at the speed he was travelling.

As he walks past me now I catch hold of his calf. 'Don't leave.'

He looks perplexed. 'I'm only going to the bathroom.'

'I realise that.' My grip tightens around the muscle of his calf. I don't know how to say what I want to say. That these calls, these texts are like an unchecked tumour; that I'm scared the poison will spread through the roots of our relationship and upwards to engulf every green shoot, every last bud. That it will extinguish us completely.

He extracts his leg from my grip, touches the top of my head. 'It'll be all right, babe. I'll sort it out.'

When I hear the shower start I move onto the bed and lie down. He stays under the spray a long time and the steady hiss of the indoor rain becomes wadding that muffles and dampens my thoughts. I must have dozed off because I'm aware of waking suddenly, as if someone has shaken my arm or yelled in my ear. The first thing I notice is the silence, louder and more acute than the monotony of the water. The next is the smell. Acrid. Smokey. Something, somewhere is burning.

'Daniel?' I yell for him as I sit up. The room is empty but it appears completely normal, there are no flames licking the curtains, no peeling of paint on the walls, no threat of heat on my skin. 'Daniel?'

He comes out of the small adjoining bathroom with a towel around his waist. 'What is it?'

'Can you smell anything?'

He stares at me. 'Can I… what?'

Although I swing my legs over the bed, my eyes are darting feverishly around the room. 'There's a fire. I can smell burning. Can't you?'

He opens his mouth, eyes wide with incredulity, and then his expression abruptly changes. 'For fuck's sake!' He points to the door that leads to the staircase, where thin, grey tendrils are curling beneath the wooden panelling. 'Jesus! It must be on the landing!'

We both stare transfixed at the trails of vapour. My pulse is hammering in my throat. 'How many floors up are we?' I ought to know, I've been here often enough but the connections in my brain won't work, fragments of memory are retrieved and immediately forgotten.

'Three,' Daniel replies.

I go to the window. There is nothing below but sheer brick leading to a concrete surface lined with bike stands.

'I'm going to open the door.'

'No, don't do that!' I shout. I can't help myself. 'You'll let the fire in! We should get damp towels from the bathroom and roll them up to block the gap under the door.' I start towards the bathroom, but Daniel blocks my way.

'Wait—'

'Why?'

'Listen, babe, listen.'

'What do you mean?' The only sound I can hear is blood throbbing in my ears. 'I can't hear anything.'

'Exactly.' He takes hold of both my wrists and makes me meet his gaze. 'Exactly. If it was a big fire there would be lots of noise, right? Flames and people shouting?' He sounds like he's talking to a child.

'I guess…'

'So it must be a small fire, right?'

I nod slowly.

'So I'm going to open the door.'

I don't say anything, but when he lets go of my wrists and turns away I make no attempt to stop him.

'Christ!' he says, as the door appears to open to nothing, no blaze of red and orange or fume-clogged stairwell.

I come up beside him. Lying behind the door are what appear to be the remains of a soft knitted garment, a cardigan or a jumper perhaps, although it is barely recognisable since a large section of the wool is blackened and charred while the rest is burning with a bright, carroty glow. Although the flames are modest there are scorch marks on the back of the door where they have begun to experiment with the paintwork.

It takes me a split second to process what I'm looking at, then I rush to the bathroom, grab a bath towel off the floor and stuff it in the washbasin to make it as wet as I can. When I return Daniel hasn't moved from the doorway, he is still staring at the sorry inferno with a blank expression.

'Take this.' I pass him a corner of the sodden towel and together we drop it over the blaze, which capitulates with a final burst of black smoke.

I lean against Daniel, light-headed with relief. 'What the fuck?'

He doesn't reply. Instead, after a moment, he lifts the edge of the ruined towel with his foot. Stretching towards us are the remnants of a pale blue mohair sleeve, the stitched cuff still visible, the arm bending in a beckoning gesture, like an invitation or even a summons. As we both gaze, speechless, at the wool, I remember the last time I saw it – flecked with vomit, pressed against Daniel's door – and I am saturated with a cold, dreadful unease.

'You need to talk to her.' My voice is alien with fear. 'She needs to understand how serious this is. And then you need to go to the police.'

# CHAPTER ELEVEN
## *Now*

On my way home in the taxi I position the bag on my lap rather than risk it lurching around the floor of the cab. Although Mark said the gun was a fake I realise I have no exact idea what this means, whether it shoots blanks or doesn't shoot bullets at all. How authentic is a dummy gun anyway? Would it be obvious to a casual observer, Angus say, if he were to stumble across it, that the gun isn't actually the bona fide genuine article? Not that the presence of a fake firearm in the bosom of our marital home would be a great deal easier to explain than a real one.

As I cuddle the leather close to my chest, curiosity drags on my fingers akin to the pull of a Tolkien ring. The possibility of easing back the zip, of reaching inside, is like holding an invitation to a wildly inappropriate party, a car crash in waiting that you know is bad news but are powerless to resist. With an immense effort, I fix my gaze on the ordinary day outside the window – shops, pedestrians, the occasional leaf-bereft tree – resolving to hide the gun as soon as I get home and forget about it completely, unless the guy with the white ponytail and his mate really do make an unscheduled appearance.

Angus and I have placed the Victorian chest beside one arm of the sofa to provide a surface for wine glasses or, assuming one day we actually have a social life, bowls of upmarket crisps and those odd little Japanese crackers. The key is small and tarnished and slots snugly into the lock. As the lid swings upwards I wonder if the box might conceal some other Mark-related memorabilia, but the interior is disappointingly bare and smells only of sap and dust and the camphor-like prick of mothballs. Carefully, I extract the gun from the briefcase and lay it inside. Considering the weapon, stark and black against the yellow of the timber, it occurs to me that if someone were to kick the trunk, knock against the wood, perhaps with a shoe, the impact would betray the fact that the interior is not as empty as Angus believes.

After a moment's thought I go upstairs. It takes me a while to locate what I am looking for but eventually I find the object of my search, a blanket, an item Angus has never seen and will never miss, folded tenderly inside an old suitcase. Returning to the chest, I squat down, and retrieve the gun as gently as if I am lifting an infant out of its crib before swaddling the weapon within folds of white wool. I begin to squish the bundle back inside the box, however, very soon my hands fall still. For a second or two I stare, undecided, at the package, and then I unravel the blanket again.

The casing appears to be made out of some kind of plastic with 'Glock 17 Gen 5 AUSTRIA 9 x 19' stamped at intervals along the barrel. At first glance it looks pretty real, but I reason there isn't much point in making a replica that can't act the part, not unless all you want to do is play cops and robbers in the playground. Straightening up I curl my right hand around the grip and raise the gun to shoulder height. It's a nice weight, not too heavy; it feels like an extension of my arm, something I could become used to rather easily. I let my forefinger settle momentarily on the tab that protrudes from the trigger, imagine yelling at ponytail man to fuck off and leave me alone. It must be so easy to get what you want with a gun. I wonder if it would have helped me five years ago, whether it would have stopped Daniel, prevented him from hurting me, before it was too late.

Eventually I drop my arm and turn the casing over. Surprisingly, the grip has been worn quite smooth and on close scrutiny I see the barrel is pockmarked with dents and nicks. As I absorb the implications of this, a prickle of anxiety ripples through my bones. How the hell does a dummy gun get this much attrition? Waving a replica in someone's face to frighten them off is one thing but it doesn't inflict wear and tear. This particular fashion accessory appears to have had a whole unsavoury life of its own. I wonder if there's a way to know for certain whether or not it really is a fake, other than actually firing it.

Slowly and uneasily I wrap the gun back inside the blanket. Careful not to leave an ivory silk-bound edge trailing over the side, I place them deep inside the box and turn the lock. Once the chest is secure, I use copious amounts of tape to make certain the key is stuck firmly to the underside of the mirror frame, just as Mark directed, and then I am done. For a while I sit on the sofa, automatically choosing the end furthest from the scene of my endeavours. My head is dense with the throb of an afternoon hangover and my palms are tacky with sweat. I am horrified and enthralled – and both emotions seem unnervingly interchangeable, it feels like losing the ability to differentiate hot from cold, or up from down. Or possibly, and perhaps more appositely, right from wrong. Maybe I am particularly susceptible to that type of confusion.

At last I get up and go to the kitchen for a glass of water. I let the tap run until the flow is practically glacial and then drink to the point my throat aches with the chill of it. I tell myself the gun is a replica and there for my protection; that it is capable only of frightening somebody, not of doing actual damage. I tell myself I did not have sex with Mark today and that is a good thing; the fact I may have wanted to is a lot less admirable, but generally on this side of the pearly gates we are judged on our actions and not on our desires. I tell myself I am getting married and that I had better start behaving that way.

I chuck the last dregs of the water down the sink, rinse the glass and head upstairs with a renewed sense of purpose. It is Wednesday, not a Viktoria day, so our bedroom is exactly as we left it this morning: the half-pulled curtains reveal a slice of pebble-dashed sky above the roofline, the duvet is tossed and rumpled, and the wardrobe spills a scuffed pair of my ankle boots and a couple of fallen coat hangers onto the carpet. I make the bed the way Angus likes it, tightening the bottom sheet with proper hospital corners and plumping the pillows. I tidy away the abandoned clothes and clear the bedside tables of mugs and the tangle of dirty tissues, crumpled receipts and spare chargers, which has been accumulating for weeks and Viktoria has obviously not dared to touch. After that, I turn my attention to the washing basket. It is a wicker affair and lacquered white, suggestive both of cleanliness and, so far as is possible with such an item, sophistication, and it lives in the corner of our bathroom.

I am on my knees sorting the darks from the whites in true housewife style, seriously debating – believe it or not – whether a blue-and-white striped shirt belonging to Angus could be put on an existing heap or requires me to begin a third pile, when I glimpse a piece of black fabric lodged deep into the space between the basket and the wall. I guess it is a stray sock belonging to Angus, the sober tone consistent with his equally sober suits, but my assumption turns out to be misplaced. On extraction from the hidey-hole, it is immediately apparent that the item does not belong to Angus or, for that matter, to me. What there is of it – which frankly is not much at all – consists of black nylon: a tiny, stretchy crotch backed by the equivalent of a shoelace that appears to be designed with the main aim of shearing apart the wearer's bum, and is now coated with grime from the length of time it has spent wedged on the skirting board. I am holding it up to the light, my stomach churning, wondering if a fully-grown woman could actually fit inside it, when the telephone rings.

I get up slowly and go to the extension in the bedroom.

'Hello,' Angus says. And then, with remarkable, if misplaced, relevance, 'How are you feeling?'

I glance at the thong, still in my hand, blink back the final flicker of the arak. 'I'm fine,' I say, automatically. Oddly, in an empty, disengaged sort of way, I do feel fine.

'Really?' Angus sounds surprised too. 'I thought you left work because you weren't feeling well?'

*Did I?* It seems such a long time ago I almost struggle to remember my departure but I'm pretty sure I told Agatha I was taking an early lunch. I hesitate, uncertain what to say. Luckily, Angus fills the gaps.

'I couldn't get hold of you on your mobile this afternoon and so I called the office number. Agatha told me you had to go home because you had one of your headaches.'

I remember switching my phone to silent on my way to meet Mark, which was probably the last time I thought about communicating with the outside world. I offer a silent prayer of thanks to Agatha. 'Yes,' I say quickly. 'I did have a headache. I've taken a couple of tablets and I feel OK now, although it's probably too late to go back into work.' My voice trails away and I feel Angus processing my explanation, sifting through the words and the tone as if he knows there is something amiss but he can't quite identify the flaw in my explanation.

After a moment he says, 'Well, I was phoning to say I'm going to be late home again tonight. I'm Skyping New York at eight. We're thinking of buying a property in Brooklyn. Don't bother to wait up, the call could drag on a while.' Recently Angus's work has become more demanding – apparently there is an international market for small, edge-of-town hotels – which has meant an escalation of these inconveniently timed meetings. Now I am wondering if this change of routine has any connection with the revelations of the laundry hamper.

Stabs of angry hurt begin to penetrate the anaesthetic of shock. I scrunch the pants, the *lingerie*, into a ball, a very small ball indeed.

'Are you sure you're OK, Claire?'

'Angus, what would you say if I were to tell you that I'd found a black thong in the bathroom?'

A fragment of a pause.

'What on earth are you talking about?'

'I've found a thong, some knickers, behind the washing basket.' The tips of my knuckles are little icebergs in a sea of blotched pink.

'For God's sake, Claire, I really don't have time to talk about the washing. You probably dropped them—'

'They're not my pants.'

This time there is a full second of silence.

'What are you saying? They must be yours.' Angus speaks very deliberately. His voice has become weighty, like a cloud burdened with rain.

'They aren't mine, Angus. I don't own anything like that, and besides they're far too small for me.'

'They must be an old pair, you must have forgotten—'

'They don't belong to me!'

There is silence again. Then, 'Surely, you can't think I have anything to do with them?'

'Well, I doubt complete strangers are breaking into our house simply to use the laundry basket, so by a process of elimination I guess you must have some idea where they came from.'

'Jesus, Claire! You think I fucked some little tart and brought her knickers back home?'

'Well, no… I don't know…' The fury in his voice rocks me backwards but is reassuring all the same. 'Where can they have come from?' I add, lamely.

'Maybe they belong to Viktoria?'

'Viktoria? Why would her underwear be in our bathroom?' As I speak, I wonder if Angus could be right. I know that Viktoria makes herself coffee, sometimes a sandwich; maybe she takes a shower too, in our beautiful marble bathroom? I picture her large, sad, uncertain eyes – it doesn't seem very likely.

Angus sighs. 'Look, Claire' – his tone is suddenly rich with patience, and something else, the satisfaction, perhaps, of the problem-solver – 'I expect it was from my trip to Frankfurt. I got some laundry done while I was at the hotel. The knickers, thong, whatever it is, were probably in someone else's load and got mixed up with my stuff. I must have packed them without noticing.'

I don't say anything.

'OK?' he prompts.

'OK,' I say eventually.

'So, I'll see you later.'

'Right.'

I wait for him to hang up first, which he does after a moment, as if he has first counted steadily to three in his head.

I put back the handset and uncurl my fingers holding the thong. It sits limply in the palm of my hand like a dead tarantula. If Angus is right, if he is telling the truth, then the knickers should be clean: dusty, of course, but still lightly fragrant with anonymous beach-fresh perfumes. Tentatively, I raise the spider to my face, I hesitate for only a second before I bury my nose deep into the gusset and inhale. The smell is rancid and stale and overpoweringly familiar, the lived-in stench of skin and sweat and sex.

I transport the thong downstairs, holding it at arm's length between my thumb and forefinger and release it into the kitchen bin. My hands are shaking and all the nerve ends on my scalp are screaming, as if somebody is yanking hard on my hair. I would love to call up Angus and explain to him the flaw in his Frankfurt explanation, the trouble is I am so very far below the moral high ground myself that my accusations would probably morph into a stream of teary confessions. As I stare into the bin the black nylon puddle gazes back from the slime and stain of eggshells and teabags. Although I am living in the most fragile of glass houses, I wonder if I should hang on to the evidence of Angus's infidelity, just in case, after all, I decide to lob a little stone, and I go in search of a plastic bag.

To my annoyance, the kitchen drawer where we keep those sorts of bit and pieces is stuck and I have to wrench it hard. When the runners finally glide free the culprit becomes obvious, a creased and torn piece of correspondence that was caught down the back of the panelling. The letter is from the Post Office to Mark, confirming the redirection of his mail. As communications go, this one is not terribly exciting. However it does at least reveal Mark's new address – in Newham, E12. I fold the page in half and tuck it thoughtfully into the pocket of my jeans before turning my attention back to the task in hand.

Removing the knickers from the waste, I drop them into a plastic bag, extract the key from underneath the Spanish mirror and unfasten the chest. The blanket is still there, pure and white, the Glock tucked safely inside. My fingers wriggle under the wool and rest for a moment on the reassuring flank of the barrel before I fetch the carrier, lock it inside the trunk beneath the blanket, and return the key to its hiding place.

Once that job is done, I haul a bucket of soapy water and a scrubbing brush up to the bathroom and wash the floor, lifting the laundry basket clear of the slopping suds and scouring with particular diligence in the vacated space that Viktoria's efforts have obviously missed. When I am finished I take a shower and clean myself, tipping my face under the jet and bathing away the last contagion of Mark, the impress of his lips, the texture of his tongue. They say that two wrongs don't make a right, but maybe in this instance they can neutralise each other, combine like matter and anti-matter to annihilate the guilt and leave nothing in their wake save a last gasp of energy. I have strayed and it appears that Angus has strayed. And now we have both tumbled down the neck of the snake, back to square one.

I deliberately stay awake, reading rather absently, until at about eleven thirty I hear the rattle of Angus's key in the lock. At that point I turn off the light and roll onto my side. I am curious to see whether the state in which Angus has returned home is consistent with a late-night, transatlantic business call, but I have a better chance of sticking to my plan if I feign sleep, rather than risk picking up the thread of our earlier conversation with the reek of black nylon lingering in my nostrils. I hear Angus's tread on the stairs and, despite my closed eyes, become aware of him standing in the doorway. I sense his gaze on the coffin-shaped mound of my body and the rearrangement of the air that signals the arrival of another person, a second breathing chest. After a moment the darkness shifts once more and I listen to him move towards the bathroom. It is then that he trips. Somewhere near the top of the stairs, I think, the sudden weight of him causing the floor to reverberate in alarm.

'Fuck! What the hell…?' His howl would have woken me however deeply I had been slumbering.

'What's happened? Are you all right?' I sit up and switch the bedside lamp on.

'Yeah.' He limps back into the bedroom and slumps down heavily on the edge of the bed. 'The bloody washing basket is on the landing. I walked straight into it.'

'Oh, my God!' There is an explanation for that, of course, but it is not one I want to volunteer. I slip my arms around his shoulders. 'Did you hurt yourself?'

'I don't think so. It was a shock more than anything.' He eases off his shoes, examines his left ankle, and then stands up to take off his trousers. I see from the buttery glow of the single bulb how tired he looks. Lit from the side his profile is preoccupied and pale. He yawns, as if confirming my assessment.

'You're back very late.'

'Jesus, you're telling me. I thought the lot in New York would never get off the phone.' Pulling back the duvet he climbs into bed. 'Sorry I woke you up. That bloody basket nearly had me down the stairs.' He leans close and kisses me lightly. His breath is sour, laced with coffee and possibly nicotine but not, I think, with alcohol, and while the shadow of tomorrow's stubble is rough against my cheek I can only detect a ghost-like trace of aftershave, no female scent. 'Go back to sleep, babe,' he murmurs.

Under the covers my skin smarts like a cat whose fur has just been stroked the wrong way. Angus has never called me babe before; it's at least five years since anyone has called me that.

# CHAPTER TWELVE

The next day at work Maggie intercepts me on my way to my desk. She is wearing a red silk shirt and a navy skirt, a rather striking combination that shouts competence and ambition, unlike my could-do-with-a-clean beige suit that I'm quite certain doesn't shout anything at all but might murmur something less complimentary if anyone cared to listen carefully enough.

'Can I have a quick word, Claire?'

Like all of the offices on this floor Maggie's bureau consists of a transparent box, although since she has added an assortment of pot plants it has the feel of a conservatory or greenhouse.

I perch on a chair on the opposite side of her desk. 'About yesterday afternoon, I'm really sorry I missed the Wednesday meeting. I'd be happy for it to count as part of my annual leave, or work some extra hours to make up the time.'

Maggie frowns, brows knitting together in genuine confusion. 'There's no need for that, Claire. I don't expect my team members to work when they're ill.'

I try not to let the surprise show on my face.

Something must reveal itself because Maggie adds, 'Agatha was very worried you had come down with another migraine and wanted me to know. I understand you tried to find me, but as I explained to Agatha I had a meeting before lunch and went straight out for a sandwich afterwards.' She smiles apologetically. 'Sorry about that. Hopefully you didn't wait around too long. I expect you were desperate to get home?'

'That's OK,' I manage weakly. Agatha seems to have covered my absence pretty comprehensively and rather convincingly. I wonder if a request for a return favour is waiting in the wings.

'Anyway,' Maggie says, 'the reason I wanted a word, is, well, these headaches…' She stops and glances down at the pristine arrangement of pens and post-it notes before continuing, 'I'm aware they can sometimes be a sign of stress, and I wanted to check you weren't feeling too overloaded or overwhelmed by the work?'

'There are a lot of cases—'

'Yes.'

'And sometimes it can be difficult preparing them all in time for the hearing—'

'Of course…' Maggie cocks her head on one side, giving the impression of a concerned robin.

'But I don't think that's the problem.'

'No?'

'The headaches started a long while before I began working for the department, nearly five years ago now.'

'Right.'

My boss's relief is evident. Her mouth opens and although her lipstick is a similar shade to the colour of her shirt, the harshness of the light reveals it to be very slightly more orange. I know she wants to ask what caused my headaches to start but is unsure on which side of the caring or blatantly curious line such an enquiry would fall.

'It was an accident,' I say, to resolve her dilemma. 'An accident at university seemed to trigger them.' I don't add that I wasn't the victim of the particular accident in question.

'Oh,' Maggie says, 'I see.' Her conflicted expression suggests I have raised more questions than have been answered. 'Well' – her tone becomes more businesslike – 'I hope you know you can come and talk to me at any time. About anything at all that might be affecting your work.'

I wonder if hiding a replica gun for a man who resembles my dead boyfriend falls into this category. At least it would give her a break from discussing the falling levels of highly skilled migrants. 'Yes,' I say. 'Thank you.'

'And if you are ill, then of course you must go home. Though hopefully' – she cocks an eyebrow – 'that won't be too often.'

'Of course. I mean, no. Thank you.' I push back the chair and escape.

I have barely taken two steps out of the office before Agatha appears at my side, I have the strong impression she has been watching the door to Maggie's office.

'Is everything all right?'

I nod, walking briskly towards my desk. Agatha trots by my ankles as if she is a terrier on a very short lead.

'I was worried you might say the wrong thing to Maggie. Since you didn't know what I had told her. When you didn't come back from lunch I wasn't sure what to do, and as Maggie wanted to find out why you weren't at the team meeting—'

'It's OK.' I cut across her chatter to shut her up. Agatha's cheeks are flushed with the excitement of the subterfuge and she is speaking louder than I think she realises. Although it is not yet nine o'clock various work stations are filling up with people unzipping coats and moaning about the tube or the weather, I don't want to give them something less banal to talk about.

When I reach my desk, Agatha is still beside me. She hasn't said another word, but her face is fixed anxiously on mine. 'Look,' I whisper at last, 'thanks so much for covering for me yesterday, I really appreciate it.'

I hope this is enough to placate her and I switch my attention to my files, open at the pages where they were abandoned yesterday morning. I need to get back to the claim of an adult son who wants to leave Nepal and join his elderly Gurkha father who is resident in the UK. The hearing is tomorrow and I have another three cases to prepare plus a load of admin to get through.

Agatha, however, keeps hovering. She clearly expects some kind of an explanation for my daring to go AWOL during the sacrosanct occasion of a team briefing and a thank you, it appears, isn't quite sufficient to tick the box.

'The thing is Agatha,' I say finally, 'nothing much happened.' Other than getting pissed on arak, being given a gun and finding out my fiancé has probably slept with a woman who wears string for underwear and has the bum size of a twelve-year-old. 'My lunch went on longer than it should have done and afterwards I wasn't really in much of a state to come back to the office. You know how these things can happen.'

She nods, although she looks a little blank.

'Anyway,' I say, because she still hasn't moved, and I feel it might be useful to remind her why we are both here, 'what are you working on at the moment?'

'Oh!' She blinks, as if she's just woken up. 'The usual statistics report, Maggie wants to have it at the next team meeting.' Agatha means a report setting out the percentage of the cases – the appeals – that succeeded at the tribunal during the last month. This regular, tedious task inevitably falls to Agatha, probably because out of all of us she's the one least likely to complain about having to do it.

'OK, well, lucky you…' I gesture at my papers in a need-to-get-on way and sit down. After a moment Agatha does the same, but before I have read more than two or three lines of text she taps on the low Perspex screen separating our desks. Lifting my head, I see she is holding out a page of single-spaced type.

'These are the minutes I made at the briefing yesterday afternoon. I thought you might like a copy to keep up to speed with what we discussed.'

'Oh. Well, brilliant. Thanks.' I take hold of the sheet over the top of the divide.

Before she has quite let go of the paper, Agatha says all in a rush, 'Claire, actually it's my birthday tomorrow and some of us are going out for a few drinks. Would you like to come along?'

Her pale, needy gaze latches on to mine. I realise I have no idea who Agatha is friendly with at work, who the *some of us* might comprise, and whether they are likely to dilute or exacerbate the strangeness of an evening out together. However, with my hand clutching the fruits of her diligence it feels as though I have no choice.

'OK, thanks,' I say. 'That would be great. What time are you going?'

She smiles broadly. 'About five thirty. Since it's Friday.'

'Sounds good.' And then, because I can't quite help myself, 'Who else is joining us?'

There's a small pause before she replies, 'Jane is definitely coming, and Nigel said he could probably make it although he may not be able to stay long.' Jane is Maggie's secretary and Nigel, my companion at the immigration conference, is one of the dullest men I have ever met; the fact that even he appears to have a competing engagement says more than I want to know about the allure of Agatha's birthday drinks. I wait for further additions to the list, but that seems to be the lot.

'Right,' I say, 'fine.' I know that if I'm going to back out I need to do so this very second, remember a theatre booking or a weekend away. Or that I want to wash my hair or have plans for a vital supermarket trip. 'Agatha?' I catch her attention just at the second she lowers her head and I see the panic bloom on her face. 'Just a thought,' I say, 'shall I speak to a few of the others about tomorrow? See if I can boost the numbers a bit.'

Agatha looks like she can't believe her ears. 'Would you really do that, Claire?'

I shrug. 'Sure,' I say. 'Why not? You had my back yesterday.'

She beams so intensely I have to look away.

*

Walking home from the tube I stop off at an M&S Simply Food. Normally I'm a Tesco girl: '*Every Little Helps*' and all that jazz. It certainly did in our house when I was growing up. Although my stepfather's modest terrace was a significant improvement on the flat above the newsagent, stretching his salary to cover a family of four must have been like trying to make a double bed with a single sheet. My mother measured her housekeeping to the last silvery five pence so she could budget small treats into the weekly schedule: chips after swimming, cinema trips on two-for-one Mondays and, most thrilling of all, visits to Pizza Hut as a reward-come-bribe for suitably shiny school reports. You could probably plot my academic trajectory between the ages of six and sixteen in servings of pizza dough, ice cream and coke, all consumed in the alcove of our local high street branch, with Rob beside me taking full advantage of his sister's unexpected talent for nailing A grades.

Tonight, however, Tesco won't quite cut it – for our evening meal I want indulgence and sophistication on a plate, and with minimal effort. For once I'm feeling pleased with myself and in a mood to splash out because I've already managed to convince another ten people to join in the wild fiesta that is Agatha's birthday tomorrow evening. To be honest, as soon as a couple more from the department agreed to come out it was easy to persuade the others, since I could sell the event as a simple Friday night piss-up rather than anything to do with Agatha. However, to make sure her part in the festivities is not entirely overlooked I have at least organised a collection; at the last count I now have about thirty quid to buy a card and a couple of vanilla-scented candles or something equally safe.

Before I go inside the store I message Angus: *OK 4 2nite?* My question is followed by a heart and three kisses. I am being ultra-cautious, since I already texted him earlier to check he wouldn't be home late. To my relief he responds straight away with a jaunty thumbs-up sign and the exact same composition of hearts and kisses. Affection by emoji. Say that in the right way and it sounds like a perfume instead of a substitute for real communication, but at least his reply means my plan is still on course. I intend to cook us a nice meal – or, more accurately, heat one up, since it hardly seems worth the bother of preparing one from scratch when M&S is several culinary leagues ahead of me – open at least one bottle of good wine, and make good my ambition to move on both from Mark and the absurdity of having a gun in my living room by having wonderful, relationship-restoring sex with my fiancé. Didn't the Red Queen tell Alice to believe six impossible things before breakfast? Apparently, it's just a matter of practice. Well, taking a leaf out of the good book of the Red Queen, I intend to practice forgetting about Mark.

I lay the table with great care, or *properly* as Angus would describe it, searching out butter knives and dessert forks despite the fact there is no accompaniment of bread and the dessert is lemon posset. I even fold real napkins beside each plate rather than simply using torn-off squares of kitchen towel. The food looks pretty impressive too: a large piece of salmon topped by latticed pastry and served with crushed parsley sauce; a tub of layered and shredded vegetables in a cheery mix of colours; and a bag of new potatoes that I gambled on being able to boil without the assistance of either Mr Marks or Mr Spencer.

By the time the front door opens an open bottle of wine is chilling in a cooler and a selection of tea lights are throwing a dancing, flickering light around the walls that sings of romance and reconciliation. I've even found time to change out of my suit into velvet jeans and a low-cut black top, twisting my hair into a ponytail that hangs over my right shoulder. It's a while since I've made this much effort with my appearance at home and flexed the beauty muscle – I've been a little lazy.

'Wow,' Angus says, putting down his briefcase. 'Is it a special occasion? Did I forget something? An anniversary?'

'Nope.' I go right up to him and loop my arms around his back. 'I just thought we've both been working so hard that we don't seem to have much time for each other at the moment. So tonight we're going to change that.'

Angus's gaze skates around the room, takes in the table and the lights before settling back on me. I've made up my lashes with black mascara and wetted my lips with scarlet gloss; I imagine I look rather different from the beige woman to whom he said goodbye this morning, barely bothering to make eye contact.

'Sounds good to me.'

His voice is hoarse with surprise, but he adjusts pretty speedily. One of his hands slides into my hair, while the other pushes between our bodies, settling on the rise of my breasts under my T-shirt. We kiss – properly – and I realise I can't remember the last time our embrace seemed this natural or this greedy. I feel his fingers prise my top from under the belt-loop of my jeans and find my bare skin.

I squirm in his grip, taking a step backwards. 'Dinner first.'

Angus shrugs off his jacket in one quick movement and eases the knot in his tie. 'Is that really necessary? Won't it keep?' The muted glimmer of shadow and flame soften his starched good looks, turning his features less prim and more unbuttoned.

For a moment I'm tempted to postpone dinner, but I know the tiny potatoes, the artful, polychromatic vegetables and the tender pink of the salmon, all of them waiting in the oven, need to be appreciated right now. They are cooked to perfection and I've never produced a perfect meal before.

'No,' I take his wrist and tug gently. 'Come and eat, or else it will spoil.'

Angus sighs in a mock-tragic sort of a way. However, he lets me lead him to the table and sits down while I fetch the food. Before I pour the French Chablis that was nearly twenty pounds a bottle, I drape a tea towel over my forearm. 'Would Sir like to taste it?'

'Yes,' he says, 'Sir would very much like to taste it!' But instead of raising his glass he pulls me towards him and kisses me again. When the wine splashes my arm he licks it off, holding my gaze as he does so, and I think we might not make it through dinner after all until he glances at his plate and says with real relish, 'This looks wonderful, Claire.'

Dinner progresses just as I hoped it would. At one point the candle I have placed in the middle of the table goes out and Angus insists on fetching matches from the kitchen to relight it. 'You look so good tonight, Claire. I don't want to miss a second.'

When the spark is restored we laugh for no reason, and toast each other with extravagant, happy gestures.

As we chat, I tell him about my Gurkha case. I don't, of course, stray into the problematic territory of my meeting with Maggie or my absence from work the afternoon before, which is beginning to seem like the plot of a film I watched a long time ago, rather than a day, the previous day in fact, of my own life. Angus discusses the American acquisition that has been taking so much of his time, a bargain location called Ditmas Park, where property is much cheaper than the trendier areas. Wanting to sound intelligent and interested – the paradigm young professional – I ask about the staffing costs in New York as compared to London. However, to my surprise, Angus shrugs off the query. Apparently, that type of cost is not a big consideration, since it turns out his hotels don't need as many staff as he had thought. Although his answer strikes me as odd, the mood is too good to spoil by posing difficult questions, so I change the subject.

Angus distributes the remaining wine between our glasses. Our plates are empty and I'm about to go and collect the posset from the kitchen, and perhaps another bottle, but there's no hurry, like the song says, it feels as if we have all the time in the world.

'By the way,' Angus says, leaning back in his chair, 'you know we're having dinner with friends of mine on Friday? The good news is I've managed to get us a table at The Ivy.'

'Wow, that's fantastic,' I say, meaning it. I've never been to The Ivy, and probably never would if I wasn't with Angus. I beam at him, taking a sip of the Chablis.

I am trying to remember if I put another bottle of white in the fridge when a thought arrives like a fire engine screaming on to the scene with lights flashing and siren blaring. In that instant I feel the evening, *my* evening, hang for one moment in the balance before plummeting off the edge of my beautifully constructed rails.

'Wait,' I say slowly. 'Friday? Isn't it Friday tomorrow?'

'Is it?' Angus frowns and then chuckles. 'Yes, you're right. God, I can't believe how quickly this week has gone. I must have lost track with all those late-night calls to America.'

'Which means the dinner is actually tomorrow night?' Inside my stomach the salmon and potatoes is rapidly congealing into a rancid pink lump.

'I suppose if tomorrow is Friday then it must be. Why?' Angus's tone lifts, 'That's not a problem, is it?'

*Oh shit.* I close my eyes and pause a second before I open them again. 'Yes, I'm afraid it is. I completely forgot about the dinner and now I've agreed to go out with some people at work.'

Angus blinks at me. 'Well, tell them you can't make it after all. If you've only just made the arrangements it shouldn't be difficult to alter them.'

'It's not that easy…' I recall Agatha's expression during that split second when she thought I might change my mind, when *I* thought I might change my mind. 'It's somebody's birthday—'

'There must be others going, surely?'

'Yes, about ten, but—'

'In that case one less won't matter.'

'It will matter because I'm the person who arranged it. If I don't go, I'm not even certain it will go ahead.'

Angus puts down his wine glass and then adjusts its position, as if the precise distance between his drink and his plate is a matter of significance. 'I told you about this dinner three weeks ago.'

'I know—'

'So how could you not remember?'

I don't reply, although several possible reasons spring to mind, given the events of the week so far.

'Look, Claire, you'll just have to cancel. I really don't see why it's such a problem.' Angus's features have acquired a watchful intensity.

'It's very hard to explain.' I drop my eyes to avoid his gaze, twiddling the stem of my glass between my fingers. I can't tell him that Agatha covered for me, since I can't tell him *why* she had to cover for me, and I don't feel able to communicate the complexities of precisely why she needs me to support her birthday drinks – without actually meeting Agatha, which Angus has never done, it would be impossible to understand.

When I dare to lift my head I find Angus glaring at me as if he is trying to bore into the wall directly behind my chair and realise that this is what it must feel like to be a witness on a stand. I think, I'll remember this the next time I'm in the Immigration Tribunal, though I can't tell whether it will make me more sympathetic or actually more persistent – knowing how *naked* it feels sitting there, with truths so close to the surface that the right line of questioning could reveal them in a moment.

Eventually I say, 'Is there any possibility of changing the date for dinner? Could we go on Saturday instead?'

'You're suggesting I just call up The Ivy and get them to switch the reservation to Saturday? Do you have *any* idea how difficult it is to get a table at that restaurant?' His sarcasm is metres deep.

'No,' I murmur. 'I'm sorry—'

'And you want me to ask my friends to change their plans for the weekend because my fiancé forgot about our dinner engagement and made alternative plans she's not willing to change!'

'Angus, I'm sorry!'

Having risen to a crescendo Angus's voice drops suddenly, like a pianist drawing a recital to a close with a final, definitive chord. 'You can't go to the birthday party, Claire. That's all there is to it!' He picks up his glass again and drains it.

I run my tongue over my lips. Inhale. Make myself meet his eyes and say firmly, 'I can't back out of the birthday plans, Angus. I'm really sorry, but I simply can't do it.'

For a while neither of us speak. The evening is lying at our feet beyond recovery, like an animal that has been felled by a stray bullet. After a minute or two, Angus gets up, dish in hand. I jump to my feet and indicate at the smeared traces of salmon flesh and peas, 'I can take that into the kitchen, I need to fetch the dessert anyway.'

Angus doesn't move a muscle. 'I'll take it. I don't want dessert.'

'For heaven's sake, Angus!' As I lean forward he elevates his hand, raising the plate out of my reach. My heart is scudding inside my T-shirt, bleating with distress. 'Angus, this is ridiculous! Please sit down. Let me get the lemon posset.'

I see him lower his arm and for a split second I think he is going to sit down but then his mouth curves into a smile that my gut registers as bad news before my brain does.

'I already told you I don't want any dessert, Claire! Didn't you hear me? No fucking dessert! And if you want my dinner plate, well you can certainly have it!' He slams the china back onto the table with such force it skims over the cloth and smashes onto the floor together with a wine glass and the carefully re-lit candle.

There is a moment of unblemished silence before he turns and starts to walk upstairs, the back of his neck rigid. Halfway up he stops.

'It was a nice meal, Claire, but you didn't actually cook anything, did you?' he says without turning around. 'All you did was open some packets. I saw them in the kitchen when I went to fetch the matches.'

After Angus has gone, I begin to pick the broken shards of porcelain and crystal off the carpet, kneeling on the floor and piling the fragments onto the unbroken plate. I hear him pacing overhead in our bedroom and wonder if he will come back downstairs again when he has calmed down, knowing I would prefer that he didn't. I realise I am not particularly surprised at how the evening has turned out, although whether that is because I never really believed I could make a success of it, or because I never really believed I could make a success of Angus, I can't tell. The Red Queen, I think, needs to be told her advice is actually shit.

I see that a piece of glass I'm holding is glossed with red and assume it's from my lipstick until a bead of blood drops lazily onto my lap followed in quick succession by another. Grabbing one of the napkins, I bind my finger with it, lean back against the wall and close my eyes. The last time I sat like this, on the floor of my sitting room, was just after the white-haired guy and his mate came to call for Mark. I remember how I sank to the ground after slamming the door. How Mark came and sat beside me. And I remember what happened next.

I don't know how long I stay there, folded against the skirting board, but the next thing I am aware of is my hand, the wounded, wrapped hand, being held gently by somebody else.

'Good God, Claire, you've cut yourself!'

I open my eyes and see Angus on his knees in front of me. His eyes are puffed and bloodshot and I realise with slow astonishment that he has been crying.

'It's OK,' I say, 'it's just a scratch.' I begin to struggle to my feet until Angus puts his free hand on my shoulder.

'No, stay sitting down until I've checked out the damage.'

'There's no need. Really, I'm fine—'

'Stay where you are, Claire!' There is an echo of his earlier tone that makes me freeze. However, almost instantaneously he smiles. The steady, expansive way it moves first his lips, and then his cheeks and then his irises, is like a dimmer switch gradually turning the light to maximum. He says softly, 'I'm so sorry for spoiling the evening. I'm going to make everything better but first I'm going to take a look at your hand.'

I wait by the wall and a moment later he comes back with a tray bearing a small bowl of water, some cotton wool, antiseptic cream and a box of plasters.

'Now then…' He peels back the napkin and proceeds to bathe and dress the rather unimpressive cut on the second finger of my right hand with painstaking care. 'Shall I get you some Nurofen?' he asks once the plaster is in place and it is obvious there is no more possible first aid to perform.

'No, Angus, it's really not necessary.'

He keeps hold of my wrist as if I might get up and sprint out of the door if he let it go. 'I was out of order, Claire, for reacting the way I did to the fiasco about tomorrow. I'm sorry.'

'That's OK,' I say, knowing it wasn't OK at all but aware that perspectives can change; that what may not seem OK at the time it happens may come to seem really quite OK later. And vice versa. I touch his cheek, 'I'm sorry for forgetting about the dinner.'

'I only behaved the way I did' – he continues – 'because I was disappointed. I wanted you to meet my friends and I expected you to be so pleased about going to The Ivy.'

I groan. 'It's such a shame the reservation clashes with Agatha's birthday.'

'Who's Agatha?'

'She's a…' – I don't quite know what label to give our relationship – 'a colleague, we work together in the same team.'

'She's not a very close friend, then?' Angus lets go of my wrist and pushes a stray lock of hair away from my eyes, tucking it behind my left ear.

'No, but—'

'Are you sure you can't cancel?' His hand stops moving and settles on the bell-pull of my ponytail.

'Angus!' I take my hand from his face.

'I'm sorry! Forget I said anything.' He returns his hand to his lap and we sit in silence.

'Look,' I say eventually, 'the birthday drinks start about five thirty. They may not go on too long. I could probably get to The Ivy for about eight o'clock.'

'That would be perfect!' Angus kisses my cheek as if he were congratulating me. 'We'll wait for you in the bar.'

'You don't want to wait at the table?'

'Not without the star of the show! Now,' he stands up, 'how about that dessert?'

I follow him into the kitchen and take the lemon posset out of the fridge. Instinctively, it seems, both of us avoid going back to the table and the shattered remains of the meal; we eat standing up by the countertop instead. At least Angus eats; he makes a point of finishing the entire thing, complimenting me on my choice of dessert and observing how well it goes with the salmon. I find I have lost my appetite and end up tipping most of my bowl into the sink where it drains down the plughole in a canary-coloured swirl of sugar.

I offer Angus a coffee, but he declines, as I knew he would, saying it will keep him awake and he needs an early night because he has an eight o'clock meeting the next day. However, it gives me reason to boil the kettle, to delay downstairs while he heads to bed. I carry a cup to the sofa and curl into one of the corners. I shouldn't have forgotten about the dinner and Angus shouldn't have lost his temper. But how do you identify the point where one wrong ends and another wrong begins?

I find I have chosen the end with the trunk and I place the mug carefully upon it. I imagine what might have happened if I had opened the box earlier this evening, how easy it would have been to change the dynamics of the argument.

One of the tea lights I lit earlier is still burning and there is a faint glow of borrowed light from upstairs where Angus is probably getting ready for bed. In the almost dark the furniture in the room makes anonymous shapes while the elegant decor and bespoke shelving is invisible. Without these superficial distractions I can feel the age of the building as if it is a pulse throbbing through the paintwork. Like an audience settled in for a show, the trophy house is digesting the first act, sufficiently interested, I think, to keep watching: waiting to see what will happen next.

# CHAPTER THIRTEEN
## *Five years earlier*

When Daniel walks in the door of the Railway Tavern it takes me a split second to recognise him, although actually he's dressed no differently from when I said goodbye to him six hours earlier. I am struggling to adjust to this reinvented Daniel, the one who looks absurdly old in his budget suit, lace-up shoes and a haircut so severe the felted planes of his skull are visible like the contour lines on a map. He arrives at my table, where I have been waiting with growing frustration for nearly an hour, and dumps his laptop bag by the chair opposite mine.

'How did it go?' I ask.

'I don't know,' he says. 'Hard to tell. I guess they were pretty nice, but they could have been nice because they were interested or nice because they're not interested so they couldn't be bothered to ask me anything difficult.' As he speaks his eyes rove about the room, as if surveying the smattering of drinkers and lingerers who seem to be the backbone of the clientele; the occupants of the saloon are mainly commuters stopping for a shot or three to sweeten their re-engagement with family life, or loners settling down to a long, liquid dinner. I didn't look out of place sitting on my own for so long; now that Daniel has arrived he and I are the only couple here.

'Hey' – I touch his hand – 'I expect they were nice because you were brilliant. If they weren't interested they wouldn't have asked you to go for an interview, right?'

'Maybe…' He turns to me at last and I see how exhausted he is. 'There were so many applicants for only four spaces. They were interviewing for the whole of today in thirty-minute slots, and apparently yesterday was exactly the same.'

I sigh in sympathy.

He gestures at the empty glass that was actually my second. 'Drink?'

I nod and he heads to the bar.

About six weeks ago Daniel announced that he didn't want to be a lawyer after all, despite the fact that out of our crowd Daniel is the one most likely to bag a first. Instead, motivated, it seemed, by the constant news reports of refugees packing themselves into over-crowded boats and airless trucks, he wanted to work as a strategist for one of the international organisations that are trying to put systems in place for the homeless and displaced. Once the wave of post-exam partying had ebbed he began to apply for jobs, real jobs with job descriptions, contractual hours and annual salaries boasting of alien concepts such as pay progression and pensions. Most of the other law graduates, me included, have signed up for law school, the medics and vets still have years of debt accumulation ahead and everyone else either plans to travel or do a succession of unpaid internships, arranged and funded by their freely educated, home-owning parents. We all know the real world is rushing fast towards us, but so far only Daniel has dared to step into its path.

While he waits to be served, I watch him pull out his mobile, glance at the screen and put it back in his pocket. I promise myself not to ask him about today's tally of messages. Whenever I do he assures me it's been better – '*much better*' – lately and always insists so forcibly that there's no need to get the police involved I've stopped asking him to call them. All the more annoyingly, I'm starting to suspect he is concealing his phone from me, tucking it away in drawers and bags, so I have no easy way of checking the real volume of traffic on his mobile or even of monitoring the drip-drip of pings and buzzes; it's not that I don't trust him, I just want to know what's going on. Surely that's not unreasonable?

Anyhow, this evening, I want to talk to Daniel about something other than his bonkers ex-girlfriend; I've discovered he has a surprise up his sleeve, a nice surprise, and I'm impatient to tell him that I know all about it, to save him the bother of keeping the secret any longer. Besides, it will be a welcome distraction from the dying embers of our student days. I touch the shoulder bag hooked onto the back of my chair for reassurance; it's just a matter of choosing the perfect moment.

Daniel returns carrying a pint and a large glass of white wine while gripping a packet of salt and vinegar crisps between his teeth. The Tavern is a scruffy, unfashionable place, its dark tables pocked with water rings and its carpets and curtains so old that the place reeks of cigarettes although smoking in pubs has been banned for years. The only reason we're here rather than one of our old haunts is because of its location, which is right next to the station. When Daniel had his first interview in London a couple of weeks ago I arranged to meet him on the platform so we could wander into town and get something to eat. Since his train was running late he suggested I wait in the Tavern; we adopted the same routine when the same thing happened a few days later and, well, here we are again.

Daniel sits down and rips open the middle of the crisp packet.

'So tell me how it went,' I say. 'What did they ask you?'

He shrugs and takes a long pull on his pint before speaking. 'I already told you I don't know how it went. I'll find out in a few days.'

'Well, could you answer their questions?'

His glance is withering. 'Of course I could answer the questions. It wasn't bloody *Mastermind*. But what matters is whether I gave answers they liked and how my answers compared to those of the other candidates. And I have no way of knowing that myself, so I'm afraid I can't tell you.' He drinks again, like somebody necking water after a long, hot run.

I sit up in surprise and consider him more closely. The shadows staining his eye sockets, the ridge-like prominence of his cheek-bones and his pale complexion have become such permanent features that I realise I had stopped noticing them. I wonder if this is the stress of job-hunting, toing and froing to London on trains that never seem to run to timetable, or whether he has been lying to me about the volume of messages and calls. Perhaps the numbers haven't actually eased off at all.

'Daniel?' I begin, but he interjects before I can get further.

'Hey' – his foot finds mine under the table – 'I'm sorry for snapping. I'm just tired, you know? It's been a long day.'

'Sure,' I say. 'Of course. I understand.' I smile and press back against his leg.

He inspects his near-empty glass. 'I'm going to get another pint. Do you want anything?'

'No, thanks.' I have barely touched the first drink he bought me, but as he gets up I catch his sleeve. 'OK, I'll have another to keep you company.'

While he waits at the bar I see him take off his jacket and throw it across his arm. The evening is sultry; although the weeks of glorious sunshine have finally dwindled a persistent heat lingers, like dulled beauty on an older woman's face. I consider my shoulder bag, the *contents* of my shoulder bag. This, I decide, is the ta-da moment: the perfect antidote to the chronic flatness of this evening's mood.

As Daniel places his order I fish into my bag and pull out a large glossy travel brochure, unable to resist a quick, tantalising flick through its pages before I set it down. The title is *City Breaks*, with listings for hotels and flights, and even suggested itineraries in all the usual places: Paris, Rome, Venice, Madrid, Prague. I have my eye on Venice; who wouldn't die for a weekend of gondolas, art and gift shops bursting with masks and glass bottles? But if Daniel has set his heart on somewhere else – even, I barely dare to hope, already booked tickets, chosen a hotel – possibly a charming little bed and breakfast run by a silver-haired landlady – I won't mind at all. Anywhere we can be together, undisturbed, with nothing to focus on but each other, is more than fine by me.

I found the brochure in the drawer of Daniel's desk about ten days ago, when I was searching for his phone. It was hidden beneath a stack of publications from the United Nations on the refugee crisis, together with a couple of similar magazines from different travel companies. The other brochures contained trips to more exotic destinations like India, Thailand and Vietnam. I'm not an idiot, however. I know locations like those are way too ambitious for our poor crippled credit cards, although I don't blame Daniel for picking them up and fingering their seductive pages even if he finally settled – as I know he must have done – on the more modest *City Breaks* option.

I place the brochure in the middle of the table. The photo on the cover shows a couple, hand in hand, gazing dreamily up at the Eiffel Tower. The picture has been taken from behind so you can't see their expressions, yet anyone can tell from the coordinated, upward tilt of their heads and their interlocked fingers what a wonderful time they are having.

'Look what I found!' I say as Daniel approaches with two fresh drinks; it's hard to keep the note of triumph out of my voice.

His movements slow and he puts the glasses down on top of the happy couple, which prevents me from picking it up and pointing out the pages of Venetian hotels as I intended.

'So I see,' he says. Then he adds carefully, 'What were you doing in my desk drawer?'

'Just tidying,' I lie.

Daniel sits down without saying anything.

'When were you going to tell me?' I prompt, after a moment. He takes a sip of beer. 'About what?'

'About this!' I jab at the Eiffel Tower picture impatiently. 'Our trip.'

'*Our* trip?' He holds his pint motionless in mid-air. 'What trip?'

A nub of doubt rolls into my stomach. 'A city break, or'– I hesitate – 'maybe somewhere further afield?'

He stares, as if I've suddenly started speaking in Mandarin or grown horns, which makes me blurt out far too quickly, 'Isn't that why you've got so many travel brochures, because you're planning a holiday for us?' As I say the words out loud and watch the expression on his face change incrementally through confused to incredulous, I see how wrong, how ridiculously way off beam I am, and immediately I can't understand why I ever believed such a thing in the first place.

Although I have ground to a halt, my insides icing up, Daniel still says nothing. After a second or two he puts down his glass. 'I haven't been planning anything. Not for us, anyway.'

'What do you mean, *not for us?*'

'It's my parents' silver wedding anniversary next month. My brother and I want to surprise them with a weekend trip some-where.' His words sound carefully picked and his gaze drops from mine, which suggests this is not actually the full story.

'OK,' I say slowly. 'That explains the *City Breaks* brochure, but what about the ones to India and Asia? Vietnam isn't exactly a weekend destination.'

He throws a glance at the wall. 'I just picked them up with the others when I went to the travel agent.'

'But why, Daniel? Why would you do that?' I am pretty sure I already know the answer and my mouthful of wine is already beginning to taste as cheap as it costs.

He takes a breath. 'Because I might go abroad for a few weeks, before I start working.'

'You mean on your own. Not with me?'

'Yes, but not for very long. I just want to have some time out before I get stuck with an employment contract and hardly any holidays. This could be the last opportunity I'll ever get to do something like that.' He drinks again, a swift businesslike slurp. 'After all the work and pressure of exams I thought it would be good to get away for a little while, without—'

'... without me.' I finish bitterly. 'I can see why you didn't want to tell me. Here I was under the blissful illusion you were planning to take me away, whereas in actual fact you were plotting to get as far away from me as possible!'

'*Plotting*? I was considering taking a short break! And yes, this is why I didn't want to tell you, because I knew you would overreact, make it about us, when all I want to do is have a few weeks with a backpack and only myself to think about before coming back home and signing up to the rest of my life!'

As we glare at each other, I gradually realise that we have become the central feature of the room. Nobody is looking at us directly, but each punter's head is now angled slightly in our direction.

At last I say more quietly, 'It's because of her, isn't it, your nutty ex-girlfriend? She's driving you to do this. She's driving you away from me.'

Although his pint is half-full and I haven't yet touched my most recent glass of wine, Daniel begins to stand up, as if he's about to go back to the bar, or anywhere else that might offer an alternative topic of conversation. After a second he slumps down again. 'It's got nothing to do with her. I can handle her. I *am* handling her.' He pauses; for a moment I think he's about to add something, but he doesn't elaborate. Instead he glimpses over his shoulder at our audience and lowers his voice to match mine. 'Look – I just want a couple of weeks in the sun, roughing it a bit and going where the mood takes me. You probably wouldn't enjoy that kind of travelling anyway...' He reaches for my hand, which is lying limply on top of the Eiffel Tower.

'Yeah, I'd probably hate it. I'm way too fragile to be able to cope with foreign towns and exotic beaches.' Although my tone is sarcastic I let him mould my fingers to fit within his own.

'We can go away together another time. But we can't live in each other's pockets, however much we love each other.'

When I don't respond he shakes my arm to get me to look at him.

'Do you love me?' I whisper at last, beyond pathetic, unable to stop myself from extracting meaningless promises with which to build a fantasy future.

'More than you know, babe.' He leans across the top of the table and kisses me. I inhale his warm breath and run my tongue over his lower lip, chapped from his daily cycle trips and wet with beer, then make myself break the contact. I lift our glasses off the brochure and scoop it back inside my bag, my irises welling with humiliation and self-pity that Daniel pretends not to see. In actual fact, I want to rip the cover from the spine and tear the smug, happy, Paris-loving couple into shreds, however my dignity is hanging by a spider's thread as it is. I am an idiot, my head is yelling, and I will lose him. I will lose him soon, unless I remind him why I am both hot and cool and the best option he will ever have.

I take my time stowing the brochure out of sight to give my tears a chance to dry, before reaching for one of my hardly touched glasses of wine. Thinking fast, I make myself smile as I raise the rim to my lips.

Daniel watches as if asking a question, as if he knows the evening is being recalibrated but is unsure what direction it is taking. At last he says guardedly, 'Come on, tell me about your day?'

'Never mind my day' – I gesture at his pint – 'drink up. You might not have a surprise for me but I've got one for you instead.'

His hands stay motionless on the table. 'What kind of surprise?'

'A crazy one.' I widen my eyes and make them shine with possibilities.

'Crazy?' He blinks. 'What kind of crazy?'
'Fun-crazy,' I promise.


Sometime later we are hovering beside a hedge that runs behind the bus stop on Hills Road, close to my student house. Daniel believes, I think, that we are about to take a ride, but it is actually the hedge I am interested in and what is behind it. Not that long ago I noticed a handful of withering bushes amongst the healthy ones: a pocket of susceptibility within the dense armour of green. I soon discovered that standing at a particular angle revealed a sweep of lawn, a children's climbing frame and further beyond a large rectangular swimming pool. As temperatures soared and exams loomed, I used to gaze at that water, cursing the buses – or lack of them – and knowing my day held only hours of study bent over a desk in a stifling library.

I wait until the public transport system finally does its stuff, scooping up and out of the way a granny and a spotty teenager, and then begin to push through the weakened patch of foliage. Immediately Daniel grabs the back of my flimsy shirt. 'What the hell are you doing?'

'You'll see,' I hiss. 'Come on.'

As we step onto the grass, Daniel peers towards the distant trees that are fast disappearing into the night. 'Isn't this somebody's house?'

I don't reply.

He groans. 'Tell me we haven't just broken into someone's home!'

I pull his arm. 'It doesn't matter. Nobody will see. The windows don't overlook this part of the grounds.' It's true, even in daylight it's hard enough to spot the bricks of the Victorian building that appears to be located somewhere behind a further orchard or vegetable patch and now the summer dusk is rubbing out the shapes and details of the garden, turning us invisible.

I head towards the pool, a darkened oblong barely distinguishable from the lawn. The covers are heaped at one end, as they have been since the heatwave first began, and on the side furthest from us is a wrought-iron table with an umbrella stuck mast-like through the middle of it. Although Daniel is hanging back I am confident he will follow me. We are both a little drunk, blunt around the edges, and ready to believe a reckless idea is actually a fantastically good one. Sure enough, after a second or two I hear his footsteps behind me. When they stop abruptly, I guess he has just spied the water.

'You're not…' he says, sounding amazed and also, I think – *I hope* – a tiny bit impressed. In answer, I turn around and slowly take off my watch and put it in my pocket. Next, I kick off my flip-flops, yank my shirt over my head and unzip my shorts, all the while keeping my eyes on his face.

'We won't do any harm,' I say. 'And nobody will ever find out.' I like this version of me, the fearless, feckless, good-time girl, and I know how much Daniel likes it too. I slip out of my pants and bra so that I am standing naked in front of him.

'For God's sake!' he says, but a smile is expanding over his face and a second later he drops his jacket on the ground and starts to unbutton his shirt.

Without waiting for him to finish undressing I hurry towards the dim glow of water where I drop onto the side, my calves and feet dangling over the edge and the stonework cold under my bum. A second later I slip silently into the pool. The water is warm and so incredibly soft it's like sliding between bed sheets of the purest cotton.

I swim a careful breaststroke to the far end, the deep end, the ripples rhythmic and feather-light about my arms, and I hold on to the edge while I watch Daniel emerge from the gloom. For a moment he looks as though he's about to launch himself at the water and I brace myself for the harkening splash that will broadcast our presence to the world, but at the last instant he thinks better of it and crouches down before easing himself into the shallow end. A few more moments and he is beside me. One of his hands reaches for the side of the pool and the other pulls me close, twisting into the tendrils of my hair, and searching out my face and my bare, wet skin. As we kiss, his legs coil around mine so tightly they feel like seaweed, or octopus tentacles, dragging me down under the surface. If I were to let go of the edge I think I might drown.

Since we don't have a towel we use Daniel's shirt to dry ourselves off as best we can, shivering in the mauve night air. Sober now, both of us are keen to leave before our luck runs out. Daniel puts his jacket back on over his bare chest and we jog towards the hedge and the distant beacon of the bus shelter roof, emerging through the foliage damp and disheveled like Narnia returnees stepping back through the wardrobe.

On the way home to Daniel's room we stop for shots at a bar, clinking glasses, euphoric with success and laughing at the strange looks being thrown at Daniel in his shirtless suit. Later we buy chips from a kebab shop, eating them straight from the packet and licking the salt off our fingers as we wander the last streets home. We are high on life and love and oblivious to anything but each other until we round the last bend and discover the pavement is pulsing red and blue as if we have just stepped under an old-fashioned disco ball.

The police car is parked outside the entrance to Daniel's building, the beacon on the roof swirling lazy circles, the rear lights flashing crimson.

'Jesus!' I drop the last of my chips, clapping a hand to my mouth and glancing at Daniel who looks like somebody winded, as if he needs to lean against a wall. I know we are thinking the same obvious thing: *his fucking crazy ex, what has she done now?*

'It may be nothing to do with her,' I say desperately, although most of the other students have already packed up their rooms and gone home. We are both aware that there is only one potential source of trouble: the only question is how bad it is. And then, as the answer comes to me, I am flooded with relief. Daniel has contacted the police; he has finally told them about the harassment, about the fire; he has finally taken a stand, and now they have come to ask him about the incidents formally, to take statements, probably from both of us.

I walk swiftly across the road, pulling Daniel with me, as a policeman comes out of the main door. Watching us approach, his impassive gaze flickers briefly over me before settling on the face of my boyfriend. If he notices our unconventional attire and wet hair he doesn't say anything. 'Daniel Herron?' is all he asks.

Daniel nods briefly.

'I'll wait for you upstairs,' I tell Daniel. 'I've brought my key with me.' I squeeze his fingers and deliver a radiant smile. The timing may not be great but I am so glad he is finally sorting this out. With luck, it will bring the whole of this horrible sorry episode to an end. I add, quietly but not so quietly that the policeman couldn't hear if he wanted to, 'This is your chance, Daniel. You mustn't hold back, you must tell them everything.'

The policeman steps towards us and there is just time enough to note the stern opaqueness of his gaze, to register the odd, rather stricken expression on Daniel's face, and time for the slightest tremor of doubt to shudder through the depths of my gut, before he addresses us again.

'Daniel Herron,' the policeman says, placing his right hand on Daniel's left forearm as he speaks. 'You are under arrest on suspicion of rape. You do not have to say anything but it may harm your defence…'

I don't hear the rest of the caution because at that moment the tremor explodes into a full-blown earthquake, demolishing the pavement under my feet. 'No!' I shout, as the policeman leads

Daniel to the passenger door of the police car. 'What are you doing? There's been a mistake!'

Both Daniel and the policeman pause, glancing in my direction. For an instant, the policeman's guard slips to reveal a glimmer of sympathy.

'Stop!' I yell. 'Wait!' Then, 'Daniel?'

I watch with disbelief as instead of speaking to me, instead of speaking up, Daniel turns his head towards the interior of the car.

'You're making a mistake,' I yell. 'A terrible mistake! She's lying! She's making it up because she can't bear that he loves me and not her.' I must be crying because my voice is choking while my cheeks are wet with tears and snot. There is the sound of slamming doors, the efficient cough of the engine leaping into action, the dying drone as they drive away, and then the street is empty, the lightshow over, and I am left behind, hating his wicked bitch of an ex more than I have ever hated anyone before in my life.

# CHAPTER FOURTEEN

## Now

The next day, Friday, my Gurkha case is depressingly straight-forward. The Gurkha, or ex-Gurkha – as he is now quite elderly – beams at the judge with such gentle sincerity I think he can have no idea how weak his case is. Despite his age, he is seated at the table as if a broom handle has been stuck up the back of his shirt, the palms of his hands resting lightly on each knee. Just looking at him makes me sit a little straighter myself.

'You want your son to come and live with you?' I ask, although I already know the answer to that question, since it is the only reason we are all here.

'Yes,' he says through an interpreter, nodding vigorously. 'My wife and I are old now and we want our family to be together while there is still time.'

'Your son is an adult,' I say, 'and he has a job in Nepal. He isn't dependent on you for money, is he?'

'Not at all,' his smile intensifies. 'My son has done very well.'

'And' – I continue – 'your son has lived on his own for several years now, without any problems?'

'That is correct.'

I try to catch the judge's eye to see how quickly he wants to wrap this up, but he avoids my gaze and pushes his glasses further up his nose. Although he is a youngish man, he appears older; his hair is already thinning and he wears wire-framed spectacles that remind me of the kind worn by owls in children's stories. He fiddles with them frequently – and unnecessarily – which is probably a sign that he knows the appeal is hopeless and wishes he could do something about it.

'Is there anything else you would like to tell me about your son?' he prompts, after a moment.

A veil of panic passes across the Gurkha's face before he finds the words he wants to say. 'We are still his family. Without a wife and children of his own my son's place is with his parents. You see, although my wife misses her child very much she is too scared and old to take the aeroplane to Nepal.' He glances briefly behind him at a heavy woman with a stick, who is craning forwards as though being 50 cm closer to her husband might make all the difference to their case.

'Can your son travel?' the judge asks.

'Yes.' The Gurkha is nodding again. 'For some years he worked abroad.'

'Was he living with you at the time?'

'No, he was living on his own in Dubai.' The Gurkha's chest expands with pride, although his wife is blinking rapidly, and I suspect she sees the writing manifesting itself on the UK border wall.

At the end of the hearing the Gurkha's representative hands in a written submission which, from its jumble of different fonts and irregular line spacing, is plainly just a cut-and-paste job from other similar cases. Going through the motions, he makes the usual noises about his client giving the best years of his life to fight for our country and the historic injustices that have separated Gurkha parents from their children. It is easy, uncomplicated money – since the Gurkha's son is now an adult, and clearly not dependent on his parents for money or anything else, he simply doesn't fall within the scope of the immigration rules, and his representative knows it.

Once the appeal is over we all troop out of court rather dismally, except for the Gurkha who is still wearing the same expression of sunny hopefulness and stops in the doorway to thank the judge in broken English for doing his job – my words, of course, not his.

I am back at the department shortly after lunch. Agatha looks so relieved to see me I guess she has been worrying I might have forgotten about her birthday and gone straight home from the tribunal.

'Still all right for tonight, Claire?' she says, even before my bum makes contact with the chair.

'Of course,' I say, brightly. My finger is throbbing under its waterproof plaster. A small reminder of yesterday evening's entertainment. Little does Agatha know how close to the wind the birthday ship has actually sailed.

We spend the rest of the afternoon working, or I do, at least. I'm busy ploughing through my first case for Monday, trying to get my head around the different factions hell-bent on destroying Syria, while Agatha consults her watch every two minutes and trots back and forth to the drinking fountain. She appears so tense I start to question whether I've actually done her a favour by making the birthday drinks bigger than she intended. Maybe she would have been happier with only Jane and Nigel and me? However, it's too late to do anything about it now.

By five o'clock the office is fragmenting towards Friday night meltdown. Several people have already left, ostentatiously lugging bags bulging with papers as their justification for an early getaway. The noise level is ramping up, nobody is bothering to keep their voices at the normal library-like hush while some colleagues are openly chatting or messaging on their phones.

'Can I get you some water, Claire?' Agatha is standing by my desk, clutching a plastic cup with such force that the side of it has buckled. She must have asked if I want a drink at least four times during the course of the afternoon.

'No, honestly, I'm fine. I really need…' I gesture at my papers.

'Sorry.' Just as her pale-blue gaze drops to her shoes there is a short blast of music from the other side of the room followed by gales of guilty laughter.

With an exaggerated sigh I close my file. The intricacies of the relationship between Hezbollah and President Assad will have to wait until after the demands of my hedonistic weekend. Long live democracy and a country where the worst its leaders do is make errors of judgment and occasionally have sex with unsuitable people.

'Shall we go and get ready?' I ask Agatha.

'Get ready?' Quickly lifting her head, she gives me a half-smile that seems more like a panic reaction.

'Yeah, I was going to change a bit, before we go out.'

'Right.' There is a small pause before her hand flaps uncertainly at her trouser suit. 'Actually, I haven't brought anything else to wear.' She sounds like she is confessing to a crime.

'OK. Well it doesn't matter.' To be honest, I don't suppose I would be bothering to make an effort either were it not for my engagement at The Ivy. I haven't mentioned the dinner to Agatha; the right moment never materialised during the course of the day. The only moments were ones when I could all too easily imagine her face cracking open with disappointment at the prospect I might abandon her before the evening was over.

Inside one of the cubicles in the ladies' toilets I wriggle out of my dress. The garment is a tight-fitting, scooped-neck, sleeveless design, and when I take off the shirt underneath, add a necklace and some stilettos, the ensemble transforms from everyday office worker into sexy sophisticate. I am happily familiar with this particular transformation because I wore the exact same thing on my first weekday date with Angus, measuring the scale of his appreciation by the length of time his eyes lingered on my hips as I entered the bar. I am hoping the outfit might rekindle the electricity of that night, the conviction I saw him form in the three seconds it took me to cross the gap between the door and his bar stool that I was worth hanging on to. The final step in the process requires only the usual artwork with standard-issue face paint from Boots and shaking my hair into a caramel cloud, which is achieved by pulling off my scrunchie and holding my head upside down as I brush out the tresses.

Outside the loo I am surprised to see Agatha. She is standing with her back to the cubicle, facing the row of sinks, and in the mirror above the taps I am almost certain I see her drop something inside her handbag and shut it with a snap before she swings around to face me. 'Wow, Claire! You look so different! I mean,' she stumbles awkwardly over this potential gaffe, 'that is, I think you look great!'

'I'm not finished yet.' I get out my make-up bag and prop it on the ledge above the taps. As I begin my normal routine with foundation and lipstick, Agatha washes her hands very slowly. Her reflection reminds me of a small, docile animal. A lamb waiting for the slaughter. Or the snowy-white animal that followed Mary around, until it probably drove the poor woman completely bonkers and forced her to kill it.

'Agatha?' I say.

Her gaze shoots up with quick expectation. 'How about we use my hairband to tie up your hair?'

'Do you think that's a good idea?' She looks like I've suggested she take off her knickers.

'Sure.' I put down my mascara and move behind her, gathering the lank tresses away from her cheekbones and twisting them into a high braid. All the while I feel the tension in her shoulders, the temptation to run. When I'm finished I pat her shoulder. 'There. Look!' The hair is not a complete fix, but it is an improvement.

Agatha studies herself in the mirror, and I do the same. A work in progress. As I wonder what other enhancements might be possible, I become aware of a smell. Faintly alpine, I assume it's a cleaning product.

'Here,' I say after a moment, 'try taking off your jacket.'

The plain white shirt she is wearing makes an ungainly cushion in the top of her waistband, however when we untuck the cotton to hang over her trousers and turn the sleeves halfway up her forearms the appearance is actually quite bohemian. Possibly the beginnings of cool.

'Wait...' On a roll, I raise my hand towards Agatha's throat in order to undo the top two buttons. Her wrist flies towards mine as if to stop the intrusion, however it draws to a halt about an inch from my own, hovering uncertainly. Easing the cotton open, I catch another gust of that same sharpish, pine-like odour. Agatha's mouth is slightly open, her breath is heavy with self-consciousness and her cheeks are pink. Her cheeks are *pink*, I realise, despite the fact it is November and nobody could possibly describe the departmental ladies' toilets as cosy. All at once I understand that what I am smelling is gin: cheap gin. Although the situation is really quite obvious, I've come to the party late because I never had Agatha down as the type who would swig from a bottle in secret – it shows how wrong most of us are about people most of the time.

I glance towards her handbag and, following the direction of my gaze, her face floods crimson.

'Dutch courage?'

She gives a brittle little nod.

'No harm in that. Although' – I try a smile – 'you're not supposed to be terrified by the prospect of your own birthday drinks!'

She doesn't smile back. Instead her eyes are bright with embarrassment, and also possibly the gin. 'It's different for you, Claire,' she murmurs.

I could tell her that in fact it's not so very different for me, only these days I'm able maintain the illusion, the necessary facade, the holy trinity of confidence, competence, and belonging, better than most. It's an art we all have to cultivate. Sink or swim, and sometimes you only find your water wings at the point when sinking becomes a real possibility.

The moment is interrupted by the peal of my mobile. For a second we both regard my bag like it is a child tugging on a sleeve at a particularly inopportune time. When I finally dig out the phone, assuming it will be Angus, or bloody Vodafone again, my hand freezes. I am almost certain that the number displayed on the screen belongs to Mark.

I glance at Agatha, who is doing a very bad job of pretending not to watch me, and then back at the phone – the treacherous, temptress snake in the dubious Eden of the women's toilets. Unlike Eve, however, I have to be concerned about appearances and regardless of the obvious question as to whether I should be speaking to Mark at all, I clearly can't speak to him in Agatha's earshot. Besides, I have arrived at a crossroads. A junction at which Angus points one way, together with hard-won respectability and a beautiful house, while Mark and the complicated ghost of Daniel points towards a dark and twisted trail in the opposite direction. The decision ought to be easy. I thought I had already made up my mind. And, after all, Mark is not here to look at or touch, to dizzy me with want by the pressure of a single finger on the inside of my wrist. The trouble is, since the fiasco of yesterday evening and the ruined meal I haven't been able to stop worrying that not only do I not know Mark, I barely know Angus either. And, despite what they may believe, neither of them actually knows the first thing about me.

Whilst I am still prevaricating there is an abrupt return to silence as the ringtone expires mid-trill. I return the phone to my bag without comment and pass Agatha my favourite lipstick. 'In for a penny…'

She hesitates before taking it, as if I'm a favourite aunt who is passing her a sweetie that she daren't refuse for fear of seeming rude.

*

When we return to the office Jane, Nigel and a handful of others are gathered around my desk. Even if a couple of those I spoke to yesterday seem to have dropped by the wayside, I am pleased to see there is still a respectable number. A few actually appear to have smartened themselves up, although, it has to be said, not quite as dramatically as Agatha and I have done.

'We were about to give up on you,' Jane calls as we approach. 'We thought you must have gone ahead.' She looks to Nigel for confirmation of their recent dilemma, but he is too busy staring at Agatha. The red lipstick was the best and final touch, as it often is. I feel quite proud of myself. I see her return his gaze with a brief, self-conscious smile, before her head drops. A question flickers across my brain: the obvious question.

We are downstairs in the foyer when I remember that I've left the candles I bought the birthday girl in a carrier bag under my desk. 'I won't be a minute,' I say. 'I have to go back for something.' There is a collective groan at the prospect of further delay while Agatha shoots me a look of alarm, as if she thinks that even now, on the cusp of battle, I might desert her. 'Don't wait,' I tell the assembled audience. 'I won't be long.'

However, the weekend exodus means I have to wait ages for one of the lifts. They are too busy on the upper floors, collecting loads of eager bodies and pouring them into the foyer like migrating wildebeest in search of spring grass, except that in this case the lure is liquid and very rarely green. Once I do finally manage to retrace my steps, I find our level is practically deserted. A couple of stalwarts are still beavering away – you have to be a particular kind of loveless saddo to be working late on a Friday – otherwise the office is settling into its weekend slumber.

I try not to think about the missed call from Mark. How easy it would have been, in retrospect, to speak to him, to say to

Agatha, 'I'm just going to step outside for a moment and take this in private.' I should be pleased I resisted, smug perhaps, yet the stronger emotions, needling beneath the fabric of my sexy dress, are regret and curiosity. And plain-old lust. It seems that doing the right thing can feel just as unsettling and unsatisfactory as doing the wrong thing, and can be a hell of a lot more boring.

I retrieve Agatha's present from under the desk, where it is languishing with my discarded work shoes. The candles have been folded in yellow tissue, and with Sellotape from the stationery cupboard I am able to create a reasonable-looking package. After that, I sign the card simply *from all of us*, adding lots of jolly kisses.

Hurrying back to the lifts, I reach for my phone. It's such an instinctive reflex to check for texts and notifications, to generate that little starburst of endorphins, I can even kid myself my actions are nothing to do with Mark. The self-deception lasts just as long as it takes to see the record of his missed call plastered like a reprimand across the screen, at which point I immediately start to hunt for a voice message.

'Claire! Heavens!'

'God! Sorry.' I've walked straight into Maggie. She looks first at my face, and then my outfit, and I see the reassessment happening behind her eyes like a satnav system recalculating a route after a missed turning.

'Off out, are you?'

I haul my thoughts away from Mark. 'It's Agatha's birthday. Some of us are going to Kelly's.'

'I see. Good.' I can tell Maggie is wondering if Kelly is a place or a person, her gaze darts about my dress, as if unsure of the safest place to land. 'In fact, I did want to have a word… perhaps now isn't the best time?'

'The others are waiting for me,' I say apologetically. I've been gone at least fifteen minutes already and Agatha will probably be in a blue funk. Besides the last thing I want right now is a conversation with Maggie about work, or my headaches, or whatever else she has in mind.

Either Maggie doesn't notice, or she deliberately ignores the hint. 'I suppose you've heard about the High Court case that's been brought against the Home Office?' she says. 'For taking too long with asylum claims.'

Yes, I have. I'd be hard-pressed to have missed it, given all the recent media coverage and political handwringing, and I'm not sure what to make of it. Grim for the asylum seekers to have to live with an uncertain future, but it's not as if the caseworkers spend all day with their legs on the desk drinking coffee or filing their nails. The world is fucked up and everyone wants to come to the UK. It's bound to mean there's a bit of a queue. 'Um… yes,' I say vaguely. I take a small, rather pointed, step towards the lift.

'So, I was wondering if you might want to get involved. Be part of the in-house defence team?'

I swing back towards Maggie. 'Really?'

'Well, with a degree from Cambridge you have excellent academic qualifications. Better than most of your colleagues.'

I blink at her directness, and the fact I wasn't expecting to have to talk about my Oxbridge credentials on a Friday evening. 'I suppose so.'

There's a small pause while Maggie waits for me to continue, to add something more positive, no doubt.

When I don't elaborate, she says finally, 'Let's discuss it further on Monday,' and starts to walk away. After a few paces she stops and turns around. 'Everything all right, Claire?'

'Yes, fine,' I say, because we all say that all the time, since the alternative is far too complicated.

# CHAPTER FIFTEEN

Kelly's resonates with low-level amber light from the ochre paint-work, the golden upholstery and the bulbous lamps hanging low over the bar, while black-marble partitions create intimate squares of seating. It's rather like walking into the centre of a honeycomb. I have been wanting to come to this particular drinking hole since it opened a couple of weeks ago, and it would seem that a lot of other people feel the same way too because it's heaving. The tables have all been taken – probably since mid-afternoon – so most of the clientele are thronged in a loud, amorphous mass running the length of the bar.

I finally spy Agatha and the others at the far end of the room. Nigel is leaning over the top of the counter trying to attract the attention of one of the harassed guys hard at work behind it. From the fact that Nigel is brandishing an empty glass in each hand, I'm guessing the first round has already happened without me.

'Sorry, that took me longer than I expected,' I say into Agatha's ear, after weaving a path through the jam of bodies to reach them. She is wedged into a tiny space right beside Nigel and appears slightly taken aback by my apology. It occurs to me she might not have been watching the clock as closely as I thought. Before I can say anything else Nigel turns around with two large glasses of white wine, one of which he passes to Jane and the other to Agatha.

'Claire,' he says, 'what can I get you?' He has to shout above the din.

I tell him I'll have a white wine too, although actually I'm more interested in the fact that Agatha is following Nigel's every movement as attentively as if she were trying to spot the sleight of hand in a magician's trick. They couldn't be any closer without actually standing on top of each other. The answer to my earlier question is pretty obvious and it provokes in me an immediate, visceral unease, the sense that it – whatever *it* is – will end badly. For Agatha, that is, not, of course, for Nigel.

I accept my drink and tell myself not to be unduly pessimistic. There is no reason why tonight might not initiate a wonderful romance for them both, except that I am an expert at lopsided relationships. I know first-hand the different variations their dark, unhappy paths may take, and this particular imbalance stands out a proverbial mile. A moment later I realise Agatha is laughing at something Nigel has said, a witticism I couldn't hear because the cacophony is too loud to make normal conversation possible. I also see she has nearly emptied her glass. I reduce the pace of my own sipping, as if, via some subconscious reflex, this might slow her down too. The effort is wasted, however, since tonight Agatha's powers of devotion are concentrated entirely on Nigel.

About an hour later I decide the time has come to give Agatha her present. In the meantime Jane has bought a round and now my turn has arrived. As I distribute the fresh booze I figure the little celebration might lessen the speed of the impending car crash that is apparent from Agatha's increasingly pie-eyed glaze, and at least when I've performed both my birthday and drink-buying duties I will be free to leave. I might even get to The Ivy early, and at this rate Agatha won't even notice I've gone.

Once everyone has a full glass, I yell above the racket to get their attention. Then I take the botched yellow packet out of my handbag and mumble a sentence or two about it being Agatha's birthday and the gift being from all of us. From a few of the slightly startled looks which accompany this announcement, it's clear several people have completely forgotten about this side of the evening altogether. 'Happy birthday,' I say with a flourish, and together we manage a ragged, collective toast.

Passing her glass to Nigel, Agatha takes delivery of the parcel. She's wearing an expression of such rapturous anticipation I think she's bound to be disappointed when she pulls back the paper, because how excited can anyone really get about a couple of wax tapers scented with a fragrance as banal as vanilla? I'm wrong, however. She lifts the candles from the tissue with such genuine delight that it's actually rather sad. There's a second when the momentum flags, the objects suddenly awkward in her grip as she wonders what to do next, before Nigel suddenly dips forward and kisses her cheek. 'Happy birthday, birthday girl,' he says.

Agatha's hand flies to her face and the moment is so perfect, so golden, that instead of feeling sorry for her I am pierced by an unexpected shaft of envy and have to look away.

An instant later Nigel plunges into the crowd. Our joint gaze watches in bewilderment as he vanishes, but a few seconds later a hand appears triumphantly over the top of the sea of heads, beckoning us to an empty table. As we gather up our bags and coats I take my chance to shout, 'I may head off in a moment. I really ought to go and meet Angus.'

Agatha grabs my wrist as if I'm about to sprint for the door, almost dropping the candles in the process. 'Don't go, Claire. Not yet. We're having such a lovely time.' The pressure of her fingers on my forearm fluctuates lightly and I see she is weaving from side to side. I hesitate, and that moment of indecision is enough to find myself propelled towards the table, squeezed onto a padded bench between Agatha and another girl from the office called Katy. Immediately, Agatha twists to look over her shoulder, searching for Nigel, I imagine, who has disappeared again. I assume he's gone to the loo, however a few minutes later he emerges from the masses bearing a tray of shot glasses and a bottle of Smirnoff.

*Shit*, I think, although nobody else seems very surprised.

'OK, everyone,' Nigel settles himself opposite Agatha and starts to pour out the vodka, 'we're going to play Medusa. Now can everyone remember the rules?'

He sounds like a stand-in for Ant or Dec, oozing exuberance like a puppy on Red Bull. There is a wave of giggling around the table and a few people roll their eyes. Although I've never heard of Medusa, I've played enough drinking games to know how exactly they work, and the type of people who always come off the worst. Beside me, Agatha has gone very still indeed. I risk a glance and see nervous bemusement. I would be willing to bet my newly acquired house that not only does she have no idea how to play Medusa, she has never experienced the joy of shots before either.

'Listen up' – Nigel takes off his tie, stuffing it inside the pocket of his jacket that is already hooked, businesslike, over the back of his chair – 'I'm going to explain how the game works so that nobody can complain afterwards that they didn't know the rules…' He is looking directly at Agatha as he speaks and it dawns on me there is more to Nigel than his arse-numbingly tedious contributions to team meetings suggest. It is possible he fancies Agatha and this performance is an elaborate means to get her pissed, so they can ride off together into the sunset with all their awkward inhibitions in tatters. However, I'm fast coming around to the suspicion that Nigel is actually a little shit, that he has never grown out of the mindset that believes the pinnacle of a good night out, the greatest hilarity known to man, is the total humiliation of the most vulnerable member of the group.

'It's very simple,' Nigel is continuing, 'I say, "one, two, three, *Medusa*," and we all have to stare at somebody like this…' He goggles with a theatrical flourish at Jane. Then, pivoting back to Agatha, 'Now, if you pick somebody who doesn't pick you, that's fine, but if two people choose each other they both have to drink a shot.' He raises his eyebrows. 'Got that?'

Agatha nods, a rabbit snared in laser-sharp headlights.

Of course, the inevitable happens. A tale that barely needs telling. Nigel yells, 'Medusa!' and immediately Agatha's eyes meet his ready gaze over the tray of glasses. Nigel chucks the alcohol down his throat like a veteran while Agatha gags as she makes a game attempt to swallow in one. Exactly the same thing happens the second time, and the time after that. The hungry ripples of laughter now emanating from our party make me suspect that the others might have been tipped off about the entertainment in advance, that Nigel planned this piece of theatre like a game of cockfighting or dog-baiting, or other blood sports that were banned decades ago on grounds of cruelty, and I am so fucking angry I want to tip the remains of the Red Label over his smug fat head.

'For Christ's sake,' I hiss in Agatha's ear, as Nigel refills their glasses for the fourth time, 'look at me instead!'

'Now now, Claire! No cheating!' Nigel wags a finger at me as Agatha manages to wrench her eyes away from him to try and make sense of what I've said. She is too hammered to see straight, let alone think straight, and I'm thinking I simply have to get her out when all at once her face erupts with visible panic. Clapping a hand over her mouth, she staggers to her feet and pushes past the obstacle course of knees and bags. After a moment I get up to follow, because I have to, because nobody else is going to do so. As I step away, I see Nigel lean back in his chair, laugh and then throw his arm around Jane and they begin to kiss, in a casual, we've done this before sort of a way. At first I'm surprised and a second later I'm not surprised at all. And then that snap inside my brain happens and I think that actually there is nothing to stop me doing precisely as I want.

I stop and turn back to the table. I pick up the bottle of Red Label and I empty the remains of it all over Nigel. I shake it over his thighs and his hair and while that hand is dousing every part I can reach, my other hand is reaching for the shot glasses, the

ones that are still conveniently full because nobody other than
Nigel and Agatha has touched a drop of vodka, and I throw their
contents into Nigel's lap and, when he pulls away from Jane in
astonishment, straight towards his baby-blue irises.

'Fuck, Claire! What the fuck?' Nigel holds his arm across his face
as Jane dabs manically but ineffectually at his sodden trousers with
a tissue. The others appear too shocked to speak. 'Thank Christ I
won't be seeing you again, you're a fucking maniac!'

Although I don't understand this last comment, I don't bother
to reply. I'm breathing hard. I need to go and find Agatha but
actually I'm enjoying the moment too much to leave.

When Nigel's eyes emerge from behind his sleeve, I'm pleased
to see they are red and smarting. 'It was just a bit of fun. Everyone
gets pissed on their birthday.' His tone is a combination of anger
and self-justification. I am familiar with that particular voice, the
pitch that says I can't be blamed for not drawing the line where
you would draw it, the tactic of self-delusion, the excuse that the
problem is somebody else's fault. I have heard it all before. There
is only one glass of vodka remaining on the table. I pick it up
and pour it slowly over Nigel's crotch. And then I go in search
of Agatha.

I find her in the loos, at least I assume she is the person vomiting behind the closed door of the first cubicle. I consider asking
whether she wants me to come in, however I have no desire to get
that close to her – in either sense of the word. After a few minutes
I knock on the next-door partition and ask if she's OK, but the
only reply is more retching. I think it's lucky we tied her hair
back and then I think I'd better let Angus know what's going on.

According to my phone it's nearly eight o'clock already.
Although the thought of leaving Agatha to fend for herself is
tempting, the act of desertion would be tantamount to dumping
a puppy by the side of the road. Reluctantly I send Angus a text
to say I've been delayed by an ill friend – truer than it probably

sounds – and I should make The Ivy by 8.30 p.m. at the latest. As I press send, the toilet bolt crunches into the casing and Agatha emerges looking truly awful. Her mouth is surrounded by a scarlet haze – smirched lipstick, I presume – her face is the greenish-grey of old taps and there are stains down the front of her once-white shirt.

'Come here,' I say, because she is swaying like a rudderless boat. At the sink I splash water on her cheeks and use a paper towel to rub off the red stain. I worry how she will react when she sees Nigel with Jane, however by the time we venture back into the bar an entirely different lot have settled at our table and the happy troop of birthday revellers are nowhere to be seen. As I steer Agatha towards the exit, odd pockets of hush travel with us through the crowd, as well as looks that range from the wary to the downright scandalised. I'm guessing my little performance didn't go entirely unnoticed.

I am hoping to discharge my responsibilities at the door of the taxi, but my optimism is misplaced. As I lean into the cab to say goodbye, Agatha makes a grab for my hand. 'I'm going to be sick again.'

'You won't,' I say, hopefully. 'You'll be fine.' However, this is highly optimistic, plainly she is not fine, and I can't kid myself that she is – I've been in this sort of position enough times myself to know the difference between fine and in need of assistance. I check my phone. There is no reply from Angus. I try calling but he doesn't pick up. When the taxi-driver begins to make impatient-sounding noises, I hesitate one further moment before climbing in and slamming the door behind me.

Agatha lives in Hanwell. Although she doesn't offer up further details, the taxi driver must deem the information good enough to be going on with because he sets off pretty smartly towards West London. Hanwell is some distance beyond Ealing, and Ealing is not exactly around the corner from either the Immigration Tribunal or Kelly's. I realise with dismay that the journey is going to be long and bloody expensive and it's probably going to be me who has to pay for it – in a myriad of different ways. A few moments later the temperature of the interior plummets as November air floods into the cab like a burst water main. Agatha has opened the window to its maximum and is lolling against the door, her face turned towards the rushing night. I expect the cabby to complain, but his only reaction is to pull a pair of green woollen gloves out of his pocket when he stops at the next lights. I imagine he considers the freezing conditions preferable to his taxi stinking of puke.

As we make our way onto the Westway, the intended-to-be super-fast transit between Paddington and Kensington that is invariably snarled to a standstill, I ring Angus. He doesn't pick up my first call and my next attempt goes straight to voicemail. It is very nearly nine o'clock, despite the pleasant distractions of The Ivy he must be wondering where the hell I am and what has happened to make me so late. He must surely be expecting me to phone. If our roles were reversed I would be checking for some type of communication every few minutes. I would be calling him. I would probably even be slightly worried. I compose a carefully worded text, explaining I have had to take the ill friend home, offer profuse and grovelling apologies, and promise to explain the full awfulness of the evening as soon as I see him. Yet when I press send I sense the message falling hard and flat onto the road beneath our spinning wheels.

It takes several lifetimes to reach Hanwell and by the time we get there Agatha is slumped in her seat, eyes half-closed and skin like alabaster. As we approach the town centre I touch her arm, her flesh is cold and unresponsive. She looks like someone who has been frozen in the name of science: an experiment in cryogenics. However, just as I am wondering about the practicalities of extracting an address, the sight of a man stacking crates by the entrance to an Asian supermarket seems to rouse her. She struggles up and tells the cabby to stop next to a bus stop. We are still on the Uxbridge road, I can see shops, an off-licence and a Polish café, but there is no sign of residential flats. Nevertheless, as soon as the taxi pulls over Agatha opens the door and stumbles onto the pavement. I follow, once I have paid the fare, which is ninety fucking quid for the privilege of sitting in an icebox for an hour and a quarter. I decide to ask Nigel to reimburse me on Monday, it will be worth doing just to see his look of incredulity at the notion anyone might expect him to help to clear up his own mess.

Agatha heads to a door next to the Polish café. Beside it an entry-box system is set into the wall, the type with a keypad and intercom. To my relief she presses the buttons without hesitation, exposing a staircase covered in a blue nylon carpet that ascends directly before us like the side of Ben Nevis. I wonder if she will have to crawl up the steps, however with one hand on the bannister and the other around my shoulders we actually manage a slow, steady progression. The apartment at the top requires a single key and then we are inside the welcome warmth of Agatha's abode.

Her flat is not what I anticipated. Even if I would have been hard-pressed to describe my expectations, I certainly wouldn't have predicted cute or sweet, an environment over which somebody has clearly taken a good deal of trouble. The main room is a kitchen, sitting room and diner combined, the centerpiece of which is a small, comfortably scuffed leather sofa that probably came from a flea market and is now adorned by handmade cushions embroidered with complex floral designs. For a moment I picture Agatha scouring stalls, holding earnest, anxious discussions about price, and later threading needles with silky cottons while heating a ready meal for one. This little imaginary tableau of solitude makes me shiver in a *there but for the grace of God* kind of way, although I am quite aware that God is unlikely to be the engineer of my good fortune. No doubt if the matter could be resolved by a simple bolt of lightning, or a command from the clouds, the relative prosperity of Agatha and I would be switched pretty pronto.

Through a short process of elimination – via the discovery of a tiny bathroom – I locate the bedroom and leave Agatha slumped on the bed while I search out the largest glass I can find in the kitchen and fill it with water. By the time I come back she is lying down and appears to have fallen asleep. I leave the water on the bedside table for when she wakes, contemplating whether my guardian-like duties require me to actually undress her and tuck her under the covers. In the end I simply take off her shoes and glasses and roll her onto one side. Just in case she vomits again I prop her into position with a line of pillows.

I am on my way out of the room when her voice makes me leap out of my skin.

'Claire?' Agatha's eyes open. To my horror they resemble miniature paddling pools.

'Don't think about this evening,' I instruct from the doorway. 'It will seem better in the morning.' It will almost certainly seem one hell of a lot worse in the morning, as she tries to piece together the parts of the evening she can remember with the parts she can't, however I have more than done my bit and I badly want to go home.

This seems to do the trick, until she suddenly struggles into a sitting position. 'What about the candles?' she says urgently. 'Have you got them?'

'The candles?'

'My present,' a tear hovers on the edge of her lid before rolling through the barrier of her eyelash and splashing onto her cheek, 'I think I left them in the bar.'

# CHAPTER SIXTEEN

I take a train back to Ealing. I've already spent far too much money I have no prospect of recouping from Nigel and in any case there are no black cabs cruising the less-than-metropolitan strip of downtown Hanwell. After waiting thirty minutes at a station, as far away as possible from an elderly person who is busy shouting obscenities at the invisible man, it is a little after eleven before I am eventually standing outside the empty darkness of my own house.

As the door shuts behind me I flick a lamp switch and stand for a moment absorbing the simple but acute pleasure of being in my own sitting room. I check my mobile for any sign that Angus is still alive. There isn't even a missed call. To make sure I would notice the ringtone, instead of putting the phone back in my bag I prop it on the radiator ledge that runs beneath the Spanish mirror. I am just on the point of removing my hand when a metallic glint on the carpet snares my eye. Bending down, I see that the key to the wooden chest is lying on the floor close to the skirting board, presumably having fallen from its hiding place on the underside of the walnut frame. Absurdly, I glance over my shoulder before picking it up, as if Angus might silently have materialised in the doorway and be witnessing my every move.

I soon find my problem is more practical than the imaginary presence of my fiancé. The tongues of tape that held the iron to the wood are furred and bald and now incapable of attaching the key securely. Although it is easy to fetch more Sellotape from the kitchen, the implications of the discovery are less straightforward.

Has Mark returned to the house? Or has somebody else unpicked the tape, prized the strips from the wood and smoothed them back into place, having had a good hunt through the contents of the chest?

As I tear fresh Sellotape with my teeth, my thoughts resemble a pack of braying hounds falling over themselves to detect the right scent. Nevertheless, the job is done, and I am halfway up the staircase before it occurs to me that I ought to have checked that the Glock itself is still inside the chest, wrapped snugly in the blanket. I could go back down, of course, look in the box and run through the tedious business of securing the key all over again. However, it is late, I am tired, and if Angus were to come home and discover me inspecting a firearm in the living room our missed date at The Ivy would be the least of my problems.

Upstairs I go into the bathroom, and when I come out I turn off both the bathroom and the landing light, engulfing the house in the never-quite-dark of the London night. A moment later I reach for the switch on our bedroom wall. Then immediately, instinctively, I scream. The illuminated space reveals Angus, who is sitting bolt upright in bed and staring at the door.

'Jesus, Claire,' he says quietly, 'don't you recognise your own fiancé?'

My heart is pounding in my ears like hooves on a tarmac road. 'I didn't realise you were home,' I manage.

'I got back about half an hour ago.' Then he says, almost as if it's an afterthought, 'Where were you? We waited so long for you in the bar we nearly lost the table.'

I shake my head, trying to collect my thoughts. My pulse won't slow down, the shock has thrown it into flight mode and it appears to be not yet convinced the danger is past. 'Agatha, the girl... the birthday girl... she got drunk, very drunk. I had to take her home...' I watch Angus as I speak, trying to gauge his reaction, but his face is waxy with impassiveness. 'I sent you messages, I tried to call—'

'My phone ran out of charge.'

A silence, as if we are both waiting for the other to speak first. It occurs to me that he probably heard me downstairs and has been wondering what on earth I was doing.

Eventually he says, 'Are you coming to bed or are you going to stand there all night?'

While I was changing in the ladies' loos I imagined Angus enjoying this dress, anticipated the sense of luminosity that comes from being the object of an admiring gaze, however now that I undoubtedly have his attention the spotlight feels uncomfortable. Extinguishing the bedroom lamp, I shed my clothes as quickly as possible and slide between the covers. For some reason I am careful not to touch him.

'Why were you sitting up in bed,' I ask, 'in the dark?' The enquiry slips out before I am conscious of formulating it, as if it's the product of a deeper instinct than logic or intellect.

'I was about to go to sleep,' Angus says, 'but then I thought I should wait, to check you got back safely. I sat up to keep myself awake.' He sounds slightly offended by my question.

'Oh.' There is a pause. I dip my head and kiss his shoulder. 'Thank you. I'm so sorry I missed the dinner.'

Angus grunts and rolls over, presenting me with the neutrality of his back.

For a while I lie on my back, staring into the dusky grey. I am pretty certain there is an elephant in the room, however try as I might I can't see where it is standing – or who is standing behind it.

The next day we wake late. Angus fetches tea. As he goes through his ritual with a teapot and a strainer, I listen to the scraps of noise emanating from the kitchen, expecting him to revisit the issue of The Ivy and the spoiled dinner with his friends as soon as he returns to the bedroom. To my surprise he doesn't mention the previous evening at all. Instead he hands me my usual mug, we drink the tea and then we have sex. Until the moment his hand settles on my left thigh, I assume we are being careful, stepping into the morning the way, without shoes, you might pick your path across a floor littered with broken glass. However, Angus's touch is both assertive and assuming, the way I have always known it to be, less of an offer and more an acknowledgement of a gift, as if he is claiming something he already knows to be his. Sliding deep into the den of the bed, the strangeness of the previous evening feels like a figment of my overzealous imagination, an eerie, ephemeral mist that rises from the pages of a storybook and is easily dispersed by the morning sun – or, in this case, the heat of coupling bodies.

The rest of the day is normal, even nice. After a late breakfast we choose a film to watch later, and then Angus says he has to do a couple of hours of work, which gives me an opportunity to mooch around the shops and spend a little money. I wonder how Agatha is faring, but since I don't have her mobile number the best I can do is send an email to her work address, writing, rather blandly, that I hope she's feeling OK. It's a pretty pointless gesture since she probably won't read it until she gets to the office on Monday.

I'm so relieved to spend a happy day doing exactly the kind of stuff other young professional couples do at the weekend that I even come up with an explanation for the disturbed Sellotape and fallen key. I decide Mark must have removed the Glock while Angus and I were out of the house. Pondering the matter during daylight hours, it suddenly seems to be the obvious solution. Neither the guy with the white ponytail nor his mate has paid me a visit, and if Mark has been watching the house he is likely to know this. Surely the most likely scenario is that Mark telephoned me yesterday evening to say he wanted the gun back, and since I didn't answer he took advantage of an empty house to let himself in and take it? The only obstacle to verifying this theory is the presence of Angus, who spends the day either with me, or sitting at our dining table with his briefcase and a pile of papers.

In the evening we see the film – each clutching a plastic tumbler of wine, with a bucket of popcorn lodged between us – and then we go for an Indian. It's not until halfway through the meal, when the chicken *bhuna* and lamb *jalfrezi* are steaming nicely on burners heated by tea lights, that Angus says, as he helps himself from the oval dish, 'I did tell you, didn't I, that I have to go away tomorrow for a few days?'

'*Tomorrow?* No' – my fork drips onion and coriander sauce onto my plate as it dangles in mid-air – 'you haven't mentioned it before.'

'Oh,' – Angus doesn't pause, tipping a fluffy pile of rice onto his plate – 'I thought we'd already discussed it. I'm flying to New York. I need to have a face-to-face meeting with the real-estate guys.'

'Right.' I haven't moved a muscle. It crosses my mind that the unexpected trip might be my punishment for missing The Ivy, but the notion is so outlandish, so childish, I let it go. 'Angus, tomorrow is Sunday.' My voice comes out sadder and smaller than I intended.

'I have to be in New York first thing Monday morning, and if I arrive in good time tomorrow I can visit the location myself prior to the meeting.'

I nod; his logic is unimpeachable, although absurdly my throat is choking up.

My fiancé, busy with popadoms and chutneys, finally pauses to meet my gaze. 'You don't mind, do you?'

'No… well, a little.' I pull an exaggerated rueful face, let him see my disappointment. 'I'll miss you. It rather spoils the weekend.'

I suppose subconsciously I'm expecting him to apologise, say that he will miss me too, or even reach for my hand. Instead, the muscles around his eyes contract fractionally; there is a triumphant narrowing of his irises.

'Good,' he says, 'I like it when you miss me.' And he begins to eat again.

It turns out the flight is an early one. By 5.00 a.m. I'm sitting in bed with my arms curled round my knees and a cardigan across my shoulders. The heating has not yet kicked into action and although I've pushed back the curtains the glass remains black and empty.

'You're not taking much,' I say, watching Angus fold a polo-neck shirt and some underwear into a carry-on bag. 'Don't you need a suit?' He is dressed in dark denim jeans and a grey Armani sweatshirt.

'The meetings will be very casual, and I'll be back by Wednesday.' He drops a washbag into the case and zips it up with an air of purpose that feels incompatible with both the day and the hour. As if waiting in the wings for that particular cue, the husky rumble of an engine gathers volume and then treads water immediately outside our window.

'That's my cab.' Angus grabs his sheepskin coat from the back of the bedroom chair before kissing me briefly with cool lips. 'I'll see you soon.' Picking up the case he hurries out the bedroom. In quick succession I hear the thump of the front door and the lighter slam of a car door, followed a moment later by the tapering drone of the departing taxi.

The sudden wash of silence leaves me feeling both alone and wrong-footed, the same jarring feeling as when you misjudge a flight of stairs and take a step downwards only to find you have reached the bottom already. I make a half-hearted effort to go back to sleep but within minutes I've given up and I'm in the sitting room contemplating the wooden chest. Although I'm still wearing the cardigan over my nightdress and have added a pair of fluffy socks to the fetching ensemble, I'm still shivering. A part of me doesn't want to look inside the box, the part that is happy to proceed with the comforting hypothesis that Mark has reclaimed his property. Nevertheless, I know I have to find out for certain

– face the proverbial music – even if my record of facing up to unpalatable truths has left something to be desired in the past.

I wait for ten more minutes, on the off-chance Angus returns in a panic for a forgotten passport or lost papers, and then I go through the fiddle of the previous evening in reverse to extract the key from its new bed of tape. When I open the lid the only visible item inside the chest is the crumpled white blanket. I lift out the bundle and sit down on the sofa before unpacking the wool a fold at a time, like a game of pass the parcel in which I control when and if the music stops. There is nothing there. I even stand up and shake the blanket as if it were a sand-infused picnic rug, but there is no sudden thump of a falling firearm, no ricochet across the carpet, and the lack of noise is louder than the sound of any dropped gun. It shouts to the watching house that my dark little adventure, my unfortunate escapade, is over and, rather piously, that there is no need for me to ever have contact with Mark again.

For want of a better plan of action at 6 a.m. on a Sunday morning I wrap myself in the blanket and put on Netflix. I picture Angus checking in at Heathrow, the weary clamour of travelling people who have been up for hours and are quickly losing track of time and place. I decide that I miss him and then, a moment later, a little renegade thought that has misread the script entirely pokes its head into my woollen cocoon to murmur that Angus being away presents the perfect opportunity to see Mark. I distract myself by watching a series that features numerous no-doubt fictional adventures in the life of Mary, Queen of Scots, which rather comfortingly make my own exploits seem pretty tame.

Eventually I must fall asleep because when I am next aware of thinking anything the room is light, I am too hot, and Mary is in the arms of yet another nobleman. I pull myself free of the blanket and double it into ever-decreasing squares. I decide to stow it back in the chest, and this is what I am doing, stooping forward with the soft block of wool, when I see the Glock winking up at me from the depths of the trunk like a bad joke, like treasure on the bottom of the seabed.

I dump the blanket onto the sofa, lean into the chest and touch the black-resin casing as if I don't quite trust my eyes. It is possible, I suppose, that the gun detached itself from the cover, but I know how snugly the package was wrapped and the chances of it burrowing free are even less likely than those of the key detaching itself from the mirror.

I turn off Mary and her antics with her latest lover and take the Glock out of the chest. Although its presence is a shock, my right hand is already flickering over the barrel as if acquainting itself with the contours of an unfamiliar but intriguing face. I decide, quite consciously, that I should put the gun away while I make myself some breakfast and work out what to do, yet instead I find myself wandering around the room, not pacing exactly, more exploring how it feels to go walk about with a gun in my hand.

It fires without warning. My arm jerks upwards with the recoil, throwing me off balance and causing me to stumble into the staircase. The sound is so ear-splitting that for a moment I mistake it for pain and think I have shot myself. My heart and throat pulse together as I sweep the floor at my feet, expecting to see the blood pooling around my lovely fluffy bedsocks, staining the cream cashmere with scarlet paint. To my relief the carpet is clean and bare, apart from the pair of heels I was wearing the night before and probably discarded en route upstairs. Tripping over them must have caused my grip on the butt to tighten automatically, my finger to press the trigger. It is the obvious explanation, it accounts very well for what has just happened, except, of course, that part of the story in which the gun is supposed to be a fake.

As the final laps of noise recede, I stare at the deceitful Glock before transporting it very slowly to the dining room table and placing it next to the fruit dish – still life, but with a twist. For a moment I stop, poised for the arrival of a concerned neighbour, but this is London and it probably takes more than one gunshot to get somebody out of bed on a Sunday morning. When it is clear no one is coming I hunt around for the damage. Eventually I find evidence of the bullet's impact just above the shelf next to the television. Our beautiful bespoke joinery has a hole in the back of the cabinet, a scar, like an eye gouged out that is about the size of a ten-pence piece. It is lucky the trajectory wasn't six inches further to the left or else it would have shattered the TV screen. Nevertheless, I don't fancy explaining to Angus the reason why the paintwork is no longer in the same pristine condition it was when he left for the States.

After rummaging around in the kitchen cupboards for a minute or two, I find the object of my search, a large china bowl that Angus and I bought on a short trip to Lisbon; the same weekend he proposed. Perhaps I should have marked the occasion with a more significant purchase than a piece of pottery decorated with azaleas, however once it's perched on the shelf next to the television the bowl does a fine job of concealing the bullet hole.

I manage to hold off about half an hour before I finally succumb to the peculiarity of the morning and phone Mark. I try to guess what he might be doing on a Sunday and realise I have absolutely no notion at all. I have no clear idea of how he spends even his working days, but my sense of his leisure time, his home life, is vague to the point of being a blank page.

He picks up after only two or three rings, breathing heavily. 'Claire?' he says quickly. 'Thanks for getting back to me but I can't speak right now.'

'Wait!' I say, because he sounds like he is about to hang up. His call to me on Friday evening seems so long ago that I'm momentarily taken aback he assumes that is why I have contacted him. 'I need to speak to you.'

I hear a muffled, barked instruction, as though he has spoken to someone with his hand over the phone. Then, 'What is it?' His tone suggests I might have a second or two of his attention at most.

'Did you take the gun out of the chest?'

'What?' Another inaudible comment to a third party, then a pause as if he is walking into another room, before he says more softly, 'Christ! Is it missing?'

'No, not missing, but I think the trunk has been unlocked. And when I looked this morning the gun had fallen out of the blanket I used to wrap it up.'

His sigh is one of relief tinged with annoyance. 'You're being paranoid. Nobody else knows about the gun.'

'You haven't moved it, then?' I've drifted over to the table and find myself lifting up the Glock, slotting the butt into my palm. I think of it lying in the chest, *under* the blanket. I don't understand how it could have tunnelled free all by itself.

'Me? No, of course I haven't.' In a much louder voice to someone else, he says, 'I'm coming. I'll just be a couple of seconds.' His voice drops into the receiver again. 'I have to go.'

'I need to speak to you properly,' I say, firmly, insistently. My assertiveness surprises me. I add my pièce de resistance, sounding, I think, impressively casual. 'By the way, the gun – the Glock – is not a dummy. I know it's real because I've just shot a hole in the wall of the living room.'

There is a silence in which all I can hear is a hollow rattling, as if somebody is wheeling a supermarket trolley along the pavement directly outside the window. Finally, Mark says, speaking quickly, 'OK, meet me this afternoon. Come to Tottenham Court Road tube station at four o'clock.'

Before I can ask any questions, he cuts off the call.

# CHAPTER SEVENTEEN

After a small detour, I arrive at the station slightly after four. Although I travel through this space every day on my way to work, there is a subtle change to the vibe on a Sunday afternoon. On reaching ground level the same stew of noise hits you in the face but there are fewer suits and more tourists, less the smell of money, more the stink of fast food, while the cranes and diggers renovating Centre Point have fallen still behind the forests of mesh fencing and orange-striped cones. My vibe is different too. I'm wearing a grey wool coat belonging to Angus that is long enough to brush my ankles and I've pinned my hair into a loose bun on top of my head. If I had used a pale lipstick, the style would be straight from the sixties, the sex-kitten look of Brigitte Bardot. Instead, however, I've chosen a hungry, bright coral. All kittens grow into cats.

Mark isn't waiting for me and as the numbers on my watch flick to five- and then ten-past four there is still no sign of him. I glance across the street at the other entrance to the tube station but the only figure of note is a small black Lab hunched dismally beside the paper coffee cup that his owner is using as a begging bowl. Above the Centre Point tower the sky is slowly turning winter pink, which I dimly remember might be good news for London's shepherds. Crossing my arms to stop the cold from seeping between the folds of wool, I try to make myself concentrate on counting the endless floors of concrete.

A second later there is a hand on my shoulder.

'Thirty-three.'

I pivot round into the bulk of Mark and the lanolin smell of a leather coat. Long and chocolate-brown, it's the kind of thing Daniel would wear. *Would have worn.*

'What?'

'Centre Point, it has thirty-three storeys.'

I am about to berate him for being late, but the fact of his presence is already diluting my resolve. His breath grazes my face, warm and sweet and smelling of wine, the full-bodied kind of red that accompanies a good joint of roast beef. My Sunday lunch was tuna forked straight from the tin, as the Glock and I considered each other across the top of the Ikea dining table.

Mark leans forward, and my skin quivers, anticipating the kiss. Instead he says, 'Come on, let's get out of the cold.'

I assume he means a coffee shop or a bar, but we bypass several of those, march beyond the Dominion Theatre and turn down a side alley. A moment later I am following him into an apartment building. We cross the deserted foyer and head into a lift that judders upwards, pauses rather alarmingly and then begins to climb again. At the top is a hallway of doors. Mark rummages in a briefcase before extracting an oddly large bunch of keys. It takes him several attempts to find the right one and then we are inside a small apartment, the only redeeming feature of which is the view; in the dusk the lights from the city bedazzle like ships on an ocean that is stippled with fluorescence.

I am so mesmerised it is a while before I can tear my gaze away. By the time I do, Mark is coming out of another door – to the bedroom, I assume – minus his coat and briefcase, and he walks towards the kitchen cabinets that occupy the far side of the modest living room.

For a moment or two I watch him open and shut the cupboard doors. He appears to be hunting for something, although most of the shelves are empty or populated by an occasional mug or glass, or a solitary, random grocery item.

'Does this flat belong to you?' I ask at last. They are the first words either of us has spoken since we arrived and my voice sounds unusually loud.

For an answer – which isn't an answer at all – Mark deposits a half-empty jar of Nescafé and a liqueur bottle on top of the counter, pushing each of them slightly towards me as if he is making a chess move. Then he says, 'Take your pick. This is the best I can offer.'

When I gesture at the bottle he sloshes a generous slug of an amber liquid into two thick tumblers and passes one to me.

I perch on the edge of the sofa, which is black, shiny imitation leather. I'm still wearing my coat – rather, Angus's coat – and I'm reluctant to take it off. The bones of the flat radiate cold as if the heating has not been turned on for some time. The unwelcome chill is exacerbated by the severity of the bare white walls, the lack of curtains and the laminate wood floor. The only sign of human habitation is a pair of brown suede loafers by the door, which look expensive and too big to belong to Mark. I find I am shivering and I don't think it's just because of the temperature.

Mark sits down and positions himself so close to me that our legs are pressed together; even through the barriers of wool and denim I am electrifyingly aware of the bulk of his thigh. '*Saluti!*' he says, clinking his glass with mine. The sweet, tawny concoction tastes of almonds and plump golden apricots. He reaches for a tendril of my hair that has escaped from its pins and is lying on my cheek. 'Tell me, what's the problem, Claire?'

I recount the story of the key on the carpet; the curling, ineffective Sellotape; the care with which I had enfolded the Glock within the cream blanket and its unexplained escape. All the while I'm talking, Mark plays with my hair, spiralling it around his forefinger and letting it go before immediately starting the process again. I catch his hand in exasperation. 'You're not listening!'

'I'm distracted. You're looking good tonight.' He cocks his head to one side, as if conducting an appraisal of a younger colleague who is beginning to make good after a disappointing start. 'Now we've injected a bit of excitement into your life, I'm coming to the view that deviating from the rules might suit you rather well.'

The casual superiority that infuses this announcement makes me flinch, but I guess he can't be expected to know I've managed to generate my own excitement perfectly well in the past.

He tips forward to kiss me.

I move my head just enough to avoid the contact. 'Wait, Mark. This is important.'

'It can't be that important.'

His mouth is poised above mine and instinctively I run my tongue over my bottom lip. He isn't Daniel, but my body is on autopilot, reacting as though he is, as if every time I have sex with Mark we rewrite history and Daniel becomes the person who chose me over her, who didn't crush my heart underfoot by pretending to want me but actually loving somebody else instead. I put my free hand onto Mark's shoulder, managing – more or less – to keep him at bay.

He sighs at my intransigence. 'Look, I told you on the phone. You're being paranoid. The key must have fallen because you didn't use enough tape to hold it up. Nobody can have taken it because nobody else knows it's there. Unless you've told them?' At this last possibility his voice hardens briefly.

I frown at him. 'Of course not.'

'So, there's nothing to worry about.' He holds up his glass, his focus switching very deliberately, very theatrically, between its alcoholic content and my head. 'Do you realise that in this light the Amaretto is exactly the same colour as your hair?'

'Mark—'

'Claire, we're wasting time. There are so many better things we could be doing—'

'Why did you tell me the gun was a fake?'

At this, his hand falls from my face and he straightens. Before he speaks there is a hesitation so small I might not have noticed the gap if I hadn't been listening for it. 'I didn't want to frighten you. To shock you.'

'I might have hurt myself – shot myself. And if those men had come to the house I would have shot them. I could easily have killed one of them.' I say this carefully, matter-of-factly, without melodrama.

Mark doesn't reply. It is enough to confirm what I suspected, that he has thought of this possibility already. That he probably gave me the Glock with that very intention. As outcomes go, what could be more convenient than having your creditor taken out in a random shooting by an unhinged female? I let the silence settle, moulding itself around the prospect of the white-haired man lying dead on the doorstep, to make him aware that I know just how much he was hoping this would happen.

'Why did you want to see me?' I ask eventually.

'Hey, you were the one who wanted to meet!' His eyes are a little too wide; the crease between his eyebrows is a little too deep. I can tell the surprise is feigned.

'I said that I needed to talk to you. We could have spoken about the gun on the phone some other time. Instead, you told me to come here.'

I hold his gaze with mine. There is an invisible thread between us, our eyes conducting a miniature tug of war. For the first time since we met the torque, the tension, feels quite evenly matched.

'I suppose I must have been keen to see you. I can't imagine why…' He puts his glass on the floor and then his right hand slides between the pleats of Angus's coat. Underneath I am wearing a red silk blouse. Mark's hand settles on my breast, just above the cup of my bra, and begins to stroke the flesh through the flimsy muslin of the shirt.

'What else, Mark? There's another reason too, isn't there?' Although I am able to keep my voice level, my skin is tingling with static, not merely the place where his fingers are in contact, but across the entire surface of my body.

It is evident my questions surprise him. I watch him digest the revelation that I have guessed more than he expected; I see him weigh up the pros and cons of coming clean now, at an earlier, more sober stage in the evening than I imagine he planned. A second or two passes before he says, 'As a matter of fact something *has* come up. I could do with your help.' He pauses, although his hand keeps up its steady rhythmic caress.

We are still staring at each other, eyes locked. It's a struggle not to reveal the effect he is creating, how close I am to dropping backwards on the sofa, putting an arm around his neck, pulling him on top of me.

'I need some information about the immigration appeals during the last six months, a list of the unsuccessful ones and the names and addresses of the people who brought them,' he says eventually. 'Is that possible?'

I blink, not because it isn't possible. The success or failure of each appeal to the tribunal is a matter of record. Not only is it possible, Agatha's careful compilation of the monthly statistics means it is not even difficult, most of the data is already sitting in tabular form on her computer and the rest can be lifted from the witness statements. However, whatever request I might have anticipated Mark would make of me, it certainly wasn't anything to do with the immigration process.

'Why do you want to know that?'

'It's for my work, Claire. That's all the information you need.'

'I don't have any idea what you do, other than develop houses.'

'Recruitment. I run a recruitment company for website designers. Place them with different companies.'

I feel my eyebrows arch at the unlikelihood of that scenario. 'Then why the hell are you interested in unsuccessful immigration appeals?'

'There might be some website designers amongst them, people who need a job to make another visa application. Possible new business for me.'

This explanation is so ridiculously thin I half expect him to look away in embarrassment, but he doesn't, although his fingers fall still.

At last I say, 'That's not the real reason you want the information, is it?'

'I think it's a good enough reason to be going on with.'

'Supposing I don't want to help you anymore?'

He smiles, removing his hand from my breast and placing it very deliberately on my leg.

The new interaction pulses through me, hard and warm.

'I think you will.'

I let his mouth find my mouth and his fingers release the buttons on my blouse, while my own hands unfasten his shirt. Freed from the barriers of wool and silk and cotton he presses his naked chest against mine. Yet even as I sense my body dissolving, something feels wrong in a way it should have done but never did before, and I am struck by the conviction that this will be – must be – the very last time.

All at once there are footsteps in the corridor, voices that get louder before stopping immediately outside the apartment. To listen, I wrestle my face away from Mark and as I do so he hears what I am hearing. Suddenly he stands up, doing up his flies with one hand and his shirt with the other.

'Shit. Fuck. They're early! Get in the bedroom!'

Confused, I roll off the sofa. 'Who is it?'

The metallic rustling of keys sounds on the other side of the door. Mark gives me a small push towards the room where he left his coat and briefcase and I am inside it with the door closed behind me before I have had time to formulate a single coherent thought.

I sit on the bed and slowly do up my blouse. Beside me the curtain-less window is filled with the same extraordinary vista of

London, the night illumination of the city tempering the dark to a soft, plum-coloured hue. Gradually, my breathing steadies. It's even colder in here than in the sitting room and I've left Angus's coat languishing somewhere in the vicinity of the sofa – I can't remember the exact moment when we parted company. I rub my arms. Since I daren't turn on a light to find Mark's jacket, I consider the possibilities of the bedspread. It appears to be thin, cheap cotton, but it is better than nothing.

As I yank the cover free of the mattress something substantial slides onto the floor at my feet. Bending down, I realise the object is Mark's briefcase. From the other room, I can just about make out the low lilt of conversation. Tracking the pitch and flow of dialogue as best I can, I am fairly certain there are two male voices, one of which must belong to Mark, interspersed with the occasional higher tone of a female. From the volume – or lack of it – I guess they must still be standing in the entrance to the corridor.

The briefcase rests tantalisingly on my lap. Now I'm holding it, I can see it's more of a manuscript wallet: leather, slim, the type designed to carry only a few crucial documents. The table next to the bed hosts an old-fashioned anglepoise lamp. After a tiny hesitation, I pull down the arm to its full extension and position the bulb so that a small cone of light shines directly onto the pillow, and then I slide open the wallet's brass catch.

Inside there are three pieces of paper, the lined A4 kind that comes in bulky, tear-off pads I haven't seen since my note-taking university days. Holding the pages under the tight glow of the lamp reveals each sheet contains a separate handwritten list, all inscribed in the same bright navy ink that Mark used when he gave me his telephone number in the desolate scrap of river wasteland.

The first list appears to be a catalogue of companies, stacked neatly underneath each other and in no obvious order. I run my eye over the names. It is possible, of course, that they are simply Mark's clients, businesses that require website designers, but nobody in their right mind would put money on that particular scenario. As I stare at the writing, one of the companies seems familiar to me. I am sure I have come across it somewhere before but the context and the details elude me.

The second page contains names and addresses, about ten in total. As far as I can tell the names are female and they are all what the *Daily Mail* would describe as 'foreign sounding' – no Sarahs, Janes, Helens or Jessicas. Instead, among others, we have a Prisha and a Dhriti, an Abebi and a Madu. Although I can't identify with precision what is so disturbing about the list, as I read a sense of trepidation creeps like floodwater over my ankles, and crawls its way with icy fingers up my calves, my knees, my thighs...

The timbre of the voices in the other room lifts slightly, the way it does when a discussion is drawing to a close. In haste, I look at the last page. The layout is the same as the second page, except that unlike either of the other two sheets this one has a heading: *Tier 2 Visas*. A Tier 2 visa is the main route into the UK for skilled immigrants; to get a visa of that quality you not only need a job offer but also a certificate of sponsorship from a UK employer with a sponsorship licence.

For all I know the women included on this list might have Tier 2 visas and they might be about to take up well-paid jobs in website design or other skilled work, except that I know this is not the case for at least one member of the group. It was the spelling that jumped out at me. The unexpected k in place of the c. Viktoria is the fourth name down. *Our cleaner.* I recognise her surname from the references she gave me, and I am quite certain that if she was a skilled immigrant with qualifications in website design, or anything else for that matter, she wouldn't be earning a pittance cleaning up the crap in our house.

The conversational background music stops, but there is no thud of a shutting door, no signal of departure. Instead, footsteps approach. I stuff the pages back into the briefcase and switch off the anglepoise just as Mark appears in the entrance. He comes over to the bed and takes the wallet from me wordlessly. The semi-dark cloaks the doubt in his eyes and the questions on his face, although I know the suspicion must be there. He disappears, shutting me back in the gloom, only to return a matter of moments later.

'You can come out now,' he says, and I emerge into the temporary dazzle of artificial light.

While I stand, uncertain what to do next, Mark picks up his tumbler from the carpet and heads towards the kitchen counter. I spot the briefcase lying on a coffee table, now empty, I imagine. The beauty of old-fashioned handwriting is that it can be destroyed without a trace, it leaves no digital imprint, no telltale file on a hard drive; the letters are footsteps in the sand waiting to be expunged by the incoming tide.

Mark pours himself another measure of Amaretto and holds the bottle out to me.

I shake my head. 'I think I should be going.'

'Already?'

'I ought to get home to Angus,' I lie, knowing full well that Angus has probably just cleared customs at JFK. Mark flashes me a look of surprise, probably at my belated demonstration of nuptial fidelity.

I lift Angus's coat from the back of the sofa and shrug my arms into the lining while Mark watches.

'You won't forget the information I asked for, will you?' His tone is stern, poised to sharpen further should it be necessary. 'Call me as soon as you have it.'

'OK,' I say. 'It will probably take me a couple of days.'

Mark nods. He seems relieved and a little surprised at my easy cooperation. However, I have no intention of forgetting about the list of the names and addresses. For the moment I can't think of any better way to determine the exact nature of Mark's grubby little game than to keep on playing it. What's the old adage? Keep your friends close and your enemies closer. And if you can't tell the difference, then it seems to me that the only option is to learn how to manoeuvre in a very small space.

Besides, what hasn't yet been mentioned is the Glock. I checked the minimum sentence for unlawful possession of a firearm before I left home and it is five years. If anyone were to ask I would say that Mark would not stoop that low, that he would never blackmail me, but to get what they want people go further than they would ever have believed. They surprise themselves. I suspect there is actually no easy alternative to doing what Mark wants me to do – for now at least.

I say goodbye from the entrance – a quick, sterile wave of my hand – and step into the hallway. Just as the door is closing I peer around the edge of it.

'By the way' – I watch Mark jump in surprise – 'just so you know, I've thrown the gun away.'

'What?'

'Earlier this afternoon, on my way to meet you, I chucked it into the Thames. I couldn't take the risk of having a real firearm in the house. That would be against the law.' As I speak, I visualise the barrel sinking into the folds of the peat-coloured water, the river sealing over the deadly plastic without a trace.

Mark's expression clouds with anger and shock. I shut the door before he can reply. Then I am back in the lift, down to the foyer, and stepping out into the electric hustle of Tottenham Court Road.

It is clear now that my premonition on the sofa was wrong. It turns out I had already had sex with Mark for the last time before I got anywhere near him today, even if I failed to register the significance of the encounter when it happened. That's not unusual, I suppose. Some 'last-ever' events we know about, we prepare for, we may even celebrate: our final day at school, for instance, or the farewell concert of a rock legend. Mainly, however, we drift along with no conception that the thing we assume is going to be there for as long as we want it has actually just occurred for the very last time. By way of example – and this is a good one – the last ever time that a person says they love you.

# CHAPTER EIGHTEEN

*Five years earlier*

The tail lights of the police car disappear around the corner and leave the street shadowy and quiet. Wiping the back of my arm over my face, I transfer a mixture of snivel and snot onto my shirtsleeve and trudge up the staircase to Daniel's room. For a while I sit on the bed – his bed – not bothering to switch on a light and watching the dark denim of the night outside the window. My knees are tucked up to my chin and my wet hair is hanging loosely either side of my knees. I notice I'm cold, but it's the kind of chill that accompanies a fever, nothing to do with the outside temperature, rather my body reacting to an inner sense of damage and attack; the swim in the pool, the silky caress of the water, the long, lingering kiss with Daniel, they feel like they happened years ago or even to someone else, somebody whose boyfriend has not been arrested on suspicion of rape.

When a clock begins to chime, I realise my watch is still in the pocket of my shorts and I have no idea how late it is. I count twelve strikes. Midnight: the tipping point, the witching hour, the end and the beginning rolled into one collective instant. I don't bother to undress. I lie down. I tell myself Daniel will be back first thing in the morning; as soon as the police start to interview him they are bound to see what a colossal mistake they've made. Surely they won't progress a rape complaint without some evidence – physical evidence? If Daniel kicks up enough fuss perhaps we can even turn the tables? Her texts, the little bonfire on our landing and making such a serious, unfounded allegation must be enough to charge the crazy bitch with something. The image of her outside Daniel's door comes to mind, vomiting into the wool of her cardigan and cradling a bottle of gin. Although Daniel said I should have been more sympathetic, shown some understanding, I hated her from the start, she was pathetic and, worse than pathetic I knew she was trouble, possibly dangerous. And I was one hundred per cent right.

I must sleep because the next time I'm aware of anything at all, the square of sky in the window has lightened to the fragile blue of a bird's egg. For a split second I forget what's happened. I register, *Daniel's room*, reach my hand towards the comforting bulk of his shoulder and only remember where he is when my fingers graze the cotton of the empty pillow. I try to nap again, but my mind is whirring, as if it has been busy all night scanning recent memories, creating theories and drawing conclusions, even while I slumbered. Unwelcome thoughts are swirling around my brain, jabbing at me through the achy fog of last night's alcohol like peas beneath the pile of mattresses that belonged to the fairytale princess.

Number one: it's blindingly obvious that for the last few weeks, Daniel has been deliberately and conscientiously concealing his phone from me, these days he never so much as glances at the screen in my presence. I assumed he was being discreet, that he didn't want me to worry about the steady accumulation of bonkers texts and missed calls, or have me hassle him about going to the police, but maybe discretion wasn't Daniel's primary motivation after all?

Number two: every time Daniel has been to an interview during the last few weeks he has ended up leaving London a long while after he planned or the train home has not, apparently, run to schedule. Either way, I have spent a lot of time waiting for him in the Railway Tavern and on each occasion he has not got back until much later than he said he would.

Number three: if I make myself relive the moment of the arrest, picture Daniel's face, freeze the frame and scrutinise those liquid-brown eyes, I see an expression of shock, certainly, but not – if I'm really and brutally honest, if I manage not to flinch and turn away – surprise.

All of which means, *could* mean, there might be something going on between them – Daniel and his ex. Not that he would rape her, that idea is preposterous, of course, but if he has been seeing her again, if they have had sex, then how would the police be able to tell who is telling the truth?

I find I am shivering. I swing my legs off the bed and gaze around the room. I feel as if I ought to be hunting for clues, however the only item with anything useful to tell me is likely to be Daniel's phone, which he will have with him – which the police are probably checking this very moment. I open the drawers of his desk and rummage through some papers. I did this before, of course, when I was searching for his mobile and came across the travel brochures, so I already know the bureau contains nothing of interest. Yet that doesn't stop me from emptying the compartments, stacking various publications from the Red Cross and United Nations onto the floor, before returning them again in tidy, sharp-edged piles, as if by putting a load of pamphlets in order I can somehow thwart the sense of unravelling that is happening inside my head.

Afterwards I examine Daniel's clothes, all his jeans and jackets, turning the lining of the pockets inside out and brushing all the flaky, crummy bits of debris onto the floor. Here I discover nothing more illuminating than a couple of pound coins, scraps of silver gum foil and a scribbled revision timetable for the week beginning 14 April, written on a folded piece of A4.

Feeling suddenly small and very grubby, I retreat to the bed and sit with my back against the headboard. Do I really believe that Daniel might have gone back to her, that he might have slept with her? How could he even consider such a thing after her dreadful behaviour, having seen her so wretched, so pitiful? How could he possibly want her, in that state, more than me? I try to confront the absurd idea head-on, stare down the fear and make it disappear, but although the notion cowers and backs away it stays in the corner snarling at me, refusing to actually lay down and die. And then the hurt swells and swells in my throat like an over-pumped balloon until at last I burst into a storm of splashy, self-indulgent tears.

Sometime later, maybe half an hour, maybe an hour, I am drying myself in the shower, when I think I hear the click of the door into the bedroom.

I stand very still holding my breath, however the only audible sound is the mono-tonal drip of the showerhead into the tray.

'Daniel?'

There is no reply. I manage to wait just another moment before my patience snaps. Tucking the towel around my chest I hurry out of the bathroom.

Daniel is taking off his jacket. As I watch he spends a moment settling the tailored cloth very carefully over the back of the chair by his desk. There is tightness in his movements, a tension to the angle of his neck. Finally, as if he has run out of other options, he turns around.

'Hey!' I fling myself at his torso. 'Oh my God! I've been so worried. What a fucking bitch! I can't believe she did that, to accuse you of...' I can't bring myself to use the word rape, as if saying it would make the allegation credible, respectable, so I nuzzle into the shirt he must have put back on in the police station – I wonder if anyone asked him why he wasn't wearing one, if he had to mention our illicit swim. 'Thank God they saw through her so quickly.'

Daniel doesn't say anything, however his arms eventually, lightly, encircle my back.

I inhale the smell of him, his aroma is as good as alcohol, the way it seeps into my bloodstream, untangles the knots in my muscles, banishes the ridiculous, irrational thoughts in my brain. I raise my face, tip back my mouth and wait. I am rewarded with the brush of his lips and a brief taste of dense, hung-over breath, before he breaks the contact.

I gesture with my head towards the bed.

Daniel's feet remain rooted to the carpet. 'I need to clean up. I've spent the whole night in a police station. I probably stink.'

'I don't care.' I tug his shirt impatiently. 'I've just had a shower. I'm all squeaky clean and' – moving his hand from the small of my back to the flimsy join of the towel at the front, I drop my voice to a stagey whisper – 'completely naked.'

Still he doesn't shift. 'I'm also tired, babe, and hungry. The only food I've eaten since yesterday lunchtime is those chips. And if I don't get a coffee soon, I'll be asleep on my feet.'

'OK.' A thousand tiny pins prick my eyes. I hold the lids open, willing the tears not to spill. 'I understand.'

I receive another fleeting kiss, before Daniel gently shakes his wrist free of my grip and steps backwards. As he moves away, I glimpse a mark on his shirt. 'What's that?' I say, pointing, glad of the opportunity to change the subject.

'What do you mean?' His fingers dart to his neck.

'There's a stain on your collar. A red streak.'

'Really?' He swings to one side, so the crimson smudge is no longer visible, and begins to undo the buttons. 'Don't worry it's probably nothing. I need to change my top anyway, put on something fresh which doesn't reek as badly as I do.' Pulling off the shirt, he screws the material into a ball that he lobs into the corner behind the door. He strides to his wardrobe and takes a faded orange T-shirt from a hanger. Just as he is about to drag the fabric over his head, he stops and looks at me with sudden impatience. 'Hurry up, babe. Go and get dressed. I'm bloody famished.'


Not many restaurants are open at 6.30 a.m. Even the pre-office latte brigade with their suits and wheelie briefcases are not yet on the scene. We end up going all the way into the centre of town, heading by unspoken agreement to the McDonalds close to the market place, which never seems to close. Dropping down to Trumpington Street, we brush past the walled precincts of Pembroke and Corpus Christi, before coming on to King's Parade and the gothic colossus of King's Chapel itself. With the students gone and most of the tourists asleep, the city is the emptiest I have ever seen it. Slanting sunlight illuminates the aged beauty of the buildings: the spires, the turrets and the gold-tipped railings with snatched glimpses of the manicured lawns beyond.

Daniel and I don't talk. I take his hand and I'm relieved to feel his fingers curl around my own. Our footsteps slap steadily on the pavement, there is something peaceful about this walk, a healing quality drawn from the earliness of the hour and the antiquity of our surroundings. By the time we arrive on Rose Crescent I have convinced myself our problems with Daniel's screwed-up ex are over. She has tried her best to destroy us with her evil lies, but here he is with me, in one of the loveliest cities in the world, and we have our whole future together.

I touch Daniel's arm. 'You must be shattered. Go and find us a seat, I'll fetch coffee and something to eat.'

Five minutes later I'm clutching a plastic tray laden with two breakfast wraps, a serving of pancakes and syrup and a couple of flat whites. Although nearly all of the tables are vacant, Daniel is sitting at the counter that runs the length of the window, staring through the glass. He jumps when I plonk the bounty in front of his nose.

'Food,' I say. 'Time for you to recharge.' Perching next to him I reach for one of the wraps. Although the smell of the sausage and brown sauce is vaguely nauseating, my stomach automatically growls in eager anticipation of what will probably do it no good at all.

After a second Daniel lifts up a coffee and cradles the paper cup between his palms. I begin to eat, feeling vaguely self-conscious of the noise I am making, which all at once seems intrusively loud in the near-empty restaurant.

'What happened?' I say between mouthfuls. 'Did it take them long to realise the complaint was malicious?'

Daniel shrugs and sips the layer of milky froth. 'I don't know.'

'What do you mean, you don't know? The police must have decided there was nothing in it or else they wouldn't have dealt with it so quickly.'

'I guess.' He doesn't look at me, his focus anchored to the rim of his McCafé beaker.

'When did she claim you raped her?' I try to sound matter-of-fact, as if this is a perfectly normal topic of conversation to be having during breakfast.

At first Daniel doesn't reply but as I open my mouth to prompt him, he finally says, 'Yesterday.'

'What!' I choke on a combination of hash brown and bacon. 'That's so stupid,' I say, when I finally manage to swallow. 'You were either in London or with me, you didn't even see her. The police must be furious she wasted their time like that. No wonder they released you.' I feel light with a heady, helium euphoria. I think that when we're done here we'll go back to Daniel's flat and spend the rest of the day in bed. I wave my half-finished wrap towards the tray. 'Come on. You haven't eaten anything yet.'

Daniel pokes a plastic fork into the pancakes that are starting to congeal into fatty, yellowish mounds. He breaks off a portion but instead of picking it up wipes the piece round and round the plate.

A frozen sliver of night punctures my chest. 'The police, they have let you go?'

Daniel inhales and exhales, the surface of his coffee rippling with his breath like an inland sea dragged by the gravity of the moon. 'I've been released pending further investigations.'

'What! That's fucking ridiculous!' The only other diner, a woman in a long green dress, turns around and frowns at me. I lower my voice. 'Why is there anything to investigate? They don't have any evidence you've even slept with her since Easter. They can't keep you under suspicion just because some sicko ex-girlfriend screams rape!'

Daniel doesn't say anything.

After a second or two I realise I have stopped eating. My wrap is dangling in mid-air, I see, as if from a distance, that sauce is oozing from the folds of bread and dribbling onto my jeans.

'Daniel?' I touch his arm. 'Daniel, please tell me that they don't have any evidence.'

He puts down his cup and lifts his gaze. His eyes are empty, expressionless holes. 'Babe…'

The word, the inflection, is enough.

'No!' My life is a tea tray that tips at that moment, all of the crockery sliding off the edge and smashing into a spoiled, un-mendable heap. 'No!' I stand up, making the legs of the stool scrape loudly along the floor.

'Wait!' Daniel throws out an arm to restrain me. '*Babe*, it was just the once, I promise. It didn't mean anything. It was just to keep her quiet—'

'*Keep her quiet?*' I am practically spitting.

'I was desperate to stop the calls, the texts. Only she thought it meant I wanted to get back with her, and when I told her that it didn't, that I didn't, that I still love you' – he gives me a little shake – 'that's when she must have gone to the police and claimed I raped her.'

'You fucking idiot!' I stare at him. My blood is coursing with emotion like a pack of dogs or a forest fire, wild and out of control. The pain is acute and physical, as if he has just ripped off one of my limbs. Him, her, me – in this moment I could happily annihilate us all. 'How could you possibly imagine that sleeping with her would make things better?!'

I wrench myself free of him and push through the chairs towards the door. Through a screen of tears I am vaguely aware of the woman in the green dress watching, her expression both horrified and rapt. Near the door, I stop. I realise I am still holding the remains of the crappy breakfast wrap. 'Your shirt,' I say loudly, 'that mark on your collar, was lipstick, wasn't it? Her lipstick.'

'Babe, I love you...' Daniel stretches out a pathetic, hopeless arm.

Yellow and blue makes green. What does love and hate make? What is the correct label for that particular concoction of emotions? I may not be able to name the word, but I know exactly how it feels. I hurl the sandwich at his face, those strong, even features I expected to adore forever, however I am too far away, my aim isn't strong enough, and my would-be missile splatters harmlessly by the feet of our green-skirted audience.

It strikes me that if I actually want to hurt Daniel, I'll need to do a whole lot better than that.

# CHAPTER NINETEEN

## Now

On Monday morning I go straight to the tribunal. I am expecting to be there for most of the day, but the barrister for the asylum seeker in my Syria case asks for the hearing to be adjourned because his client overdosed on paracetamol while he was on the Circle line at the weekend. Apparently the only reason he didn't manage to kill himself was because a doctor got on at Baker Street and noticed there was no reaction when she stood on the man's foot. The young male judge deals with the rest of the list so perfunctorily I suspect his thoughts remain stuck, circumnavigating the London underground system.

Although I stop en route to pick up a coffee and sandwich at Starbucks I am back at the department a little after two o'clock. Coming out of the lift I run into Jane and a guy I vaguely recognise from the asylum-support team, both of them saddled with armfuls of papers. On seeing me, Jane's face blackens into a scowl and she murmurs something to her companion that makes him glance in my direction with interest. Before I can decide whether or not to cut them dead, the doors close and they are whisked to the safety of another floor.

At my desk there is no sign of Agatha. Her computer is lifeless, there is no bag slung over the back of the chair or even a clutter of dirty coffee mugs, the normal footprint of an industrious morning.

'Anyone seen Agatha today?' My enquiry, addressed to the half-dozen or so workstations nearest to ours, is met only with shrugs and barely detectable shakes of the head. It is obvious that nobody wants to engage with Agatha's absence, or with me. I imagine Jane has had a productive morning filling in the details of Friday evening for those who weren't there to experience the entertainment on offer at Kelly's for themselves.

Once I've unloaded my files I send an email to Agatha's work address, which is the only contact for her I have. *Just back from the tribunal and it looks like you've not made it in today. Are you OK?* As an afterthought, I add my mobile number underneath. Although I'm not really expecting her to respond, my phone rings even before I've even checked the tribunal case list for the following day.

'Hello, Claire...' Agatha stops after this opening gambit, as if at a loss for what to say next.

'How are you feeling?' I prompt.

'I feel terrible.'

She sounds terrible too, as if she is curled into a small, tight ball on a bed or sofa.

'What, two days later?' I try to adopt the wasn't-it-a-laugh inflection that I would use in any other case of birthday party excess.

'I mean I feel terrible about what happened. I can't even remember most of it.' There is an audible intake of breath. Her voice falls to a whisper. 'I made such an idiot of myself.'

'Hey, we've all been there. I bet everyone has forgotten about it already.' This is a tad optimistic, given my recent encounter with Jane and the general mood music of the office.

'Do you really think so?'

'Sure—'

'Even Nigel?'

'Nigel?' For a split second I am dumbfounded that Agatha continues to have any interest in Nigel's views about anything, then I realise she probably has no idea of his hand in Friday's debacle. Nor was she privy to the touching little vignette of him snogging Jane. She is probably still under the illusion he might fancy her. 'To be honest, I haven't seen Nigel today,' I say flatly. This is true – I've been in the tribunal – and when I crane my neck to glimpse his normal abode on other side of the room it has the same abandoned look as Agatha's desk. 'I'm not even sure he's come into the office.'

'Oh.' She sounds a bit put out, and I wonder if the prospect of facing Nigel was actually the main reason she stayed away. With a noticeably huge effort to change the subject, she says, 'You must have finished your cases quickly?'

'Yup, makes a change to have an easy session. Back nice and early and I'm not in the tribunal again for a few days so I'll actually have the chance to prepare the next ones properly for once.'

An email from Maggie lands in my inbox with a tinny ping. I open it while Agatha prattles on for a minute about caseloads and backlogs, and I discover that our mid-week team meeting has been rearranged for tomorrow because Maggie's six-year-old daughter has a ballet recital on Wednesday.

I glance across at Agatha's computer.

'How are you getting on with the monthly statistics?' I ask. 'Did Maggie say she wanted the report in time for the team meeting?'

'The statistics report?' Agatha sounds a little bemused. 'It's not complete yet, but I should have time to finish it before Wednesday.'

'Well, that's just it, Maggie has brought the meeting forward to 11 a.m. tomorrow.' I squint at the conveniently timed missive.

'What? Really?' There is a panicked pause, presumably while Agatha checks her own inbox. Then, 'Oh God! I see what you mean.'

For a second or two, I let her anxiety expand into the silence until I say slowly, as if it is an afterthought, 'I don't suppose you would like me to spend an hour or two working on the report for you? Since I've got some free time this afternoon.'

'Oh, Claire!' There is a relieved whoosh of air down the line. 'That would be fantastic. I was just thinking I would have to come in really, really early and even so it would be a push to get it done by eleven.'

'No problem,' I say. 'All I need is your password to log on to your desktop.'

'Of course.' Immediately, she begins to trill a complicated sequence of letters and numbers. I grab a pen from my drawer and start to scribble.

Like taking candy from a baby.

Once the call is done I rise from my seat to fetch myself a caffeine hit before I embark on my homework for Mark. By the time I get back – a whole three minutes later – there are five missed calls from Agatha on my phone, while a text is pasted across the screen the first few words of which read, *On second thoughts please don't...*

My ringtone bursts into life again.

Before I can even say hello, Agatha blurts, 'Actually, Claire, I honestly don't need you to help with the report after all. I don't mind coming in early—'

'Right—'

'I wasn't really thinking straight. If I get to the office by seven o'clock, I'll have four whole hours to finish it. I'm incredibly grateful for the offer but I don't want you to spend time on my work when you must have your own to do.' She draws to a ragged halt. I can practically visualise the steam puffing out of her ears.

'OK. That's fine.' Although my tone is relaxed my brain is scrabbling frantically, trying to work out what the hell is going on.

'You don't mind?'

'Why would I mind? I was only doing it to help you out.'

'And you'll tear up my password?'

'Of course.'

And I will, just not quite yet.

It takes me a matter of seconds to locate the statistics folder on Agatha's computer. For the last six months she has set out in neat, tabular form the case numbers, the names and nationalities of the corresponding appellants, the type of appeal and whether each one succeeded or failed. The information has obviously been trawled from the computerised history reports of the case handlers, which record all the key dates and actions in every claim. The statistics for October are still incomplete, of course, but I decide it is better to take what I can get now, rather than rely on another opportunity to access Agatha's work later in the week.

I am just about to dispatch the files to my personal email address when I become aware of someone approaching.

'Hi, Claire.'

I look up to see Katy standing beside me.

'Isn't that Agatha's computer?'

'Yeah, Maggie asked her to do a report for the Wednesday briefing and she's panicking because the meeting has been rescheduled for tomorrow. I'm emailing her the document to work on at home.' I press send, rather theatrically, praying that Katy won't have a chance to clock the recipient. When she doesn't say anything, I add, pulling a sad face. 'Agatha couldn't handle coming in today. Not after what happened on Friday. I feel so bad for her.'

Katy has the grace to blush. 'Right. Well, actually I was just bringing this back to her.' She lifts up a package crudely covered in torn yellow tissue and lays it gently on the desk. 'I guessed she wouldn't remember to pick up the candles and so I took them with us when we left.' The pink in her cheeks intensifies, probably at the recollection of the group of them doing a runner before Agatha could make it out of the ladies.

'Great,' I say, 'Agatha will be really pleased. Thanks.' I get the strong sense Katy is trying to take a peek at Agatha's screen and see what I am doing. I hang on to her gaze so there is nowhere else for her eyes to roam, even when the silence frays from the merely awkward to the unambiguously painful.

'I guess I'd better get on with some work,' she says, eventually capitulating, and walks slowly back across the office.

Once she has gone I contemplate Agatha's screen again. There was nothing remotely unusual about the statistics files, as far as I could tell, no smoking gun, no reason at all why she might not have wanted me to view them, so the obvious question is why did she suddenly change her mind? What on earth did she worry I might stumble across?

I scroll down her list of directories. They all have eminently sensible tags – notes of team meetings, Home Office policy updates, key guidance from the higher courts – and even if one of them did contain some peculiar buried secret, Agatha could hardly believe I would be likely to discover it while finishing off the October statistics. Her inbox is merely a testament to the dreary tedium of office life. The only non-work-related messages I can see are both from me, the one I sent her on Saturday and the other from this afternoon.

I decide to forget about Agatha's strange behaviour and focus on the job in hand – Mark. I close down her documents and email account and I'm about to log out when I spot the polychromatic icon at the bottom of the screen, the flower-like symbol with its multitude of coloured petals. The shortcut for photos is only conspicuous because there's no similar icon on my own home screen; the need to store images not being an obvious feature of my job – or of Agatha's.

Naturally I click on the link. I am expecting to find a harmless, if mildly embarrassing, collage of Agatha's life. Holiday snaps in somewhere like the Cotswolds or Devon, a house with aging parents and equally ancient dog. Recipes or embroidery patterns, perhaps, or images of second hand furniture, for the next haberdashery or homeware project. An intimate insight into the domestic minutiae of a humdrum life that Agatha would rather keep to herself.

What I actually see, blazing from the screen in full resplendent masculine glory, is Nigel. Nigel is everywhere, staring back at me like an animal trapped by the bars of a virtual zoo. Various pictures show him at an early, relatively sober stage of last year's Christmas party, a glass in one hand and a cutting of mistletoe in the other; addressing an earnest group of visiting students in the lecture room; and at his desk, lost in concentration and chewing on a pencil. He has also been captured in action outside of office hours, the images obviously snapped by Agatha from a distance: Nigel striding across a park, Nigel outside a pub with a couple of mates, and even Nigel coming out of a purpose-built apartment block, possibly his own home, looking, it has to be said, pretty rough.

There is no prize for guessing why Agatha was so anxious to keep this little album private – it makes her seem like a demented stalker. In normal circumstances I might be prepared to admit that it takes one wayward individual to recognise another, however given the amount of photographic evidence on display here I would say that anyone at all would reach exactly the same conclusion as me.

I am gawping, slack-jawed, at the photographs, wondering if there is a way of talking to Agatha about Nigel without actually revealing I've been snooping around on her computer, when my gaze spirals into the image of Nigel and his friends drinking beer in the sunshine. Nigel occupies the right-hand side of the picture, the bloke in the middle I am confident I have never before seen in my life, but the woman on the left – slight and blonde – is considerably more familiar. She is angled away from the camera, towards the white sleeve of the waiter, which is protruding into the frame with a tray of drinks. Nevertheless, I am virtually certain I am staring at our recently hired cleaner, Viktoria. There is no reason why Nigel and Viktoria shouldn't know each other, of course, and it's impossible to tell from the picture whether they are friends or lovers, or merely happened to find themselves sharing a table – it can happen when the sun is shining and everyone wants to sit outside. Nevertheless, it's an odd sort of coincidence.

I turn off Agatha's computer with a queasy, unsettled feeling, and open one of my own files. I am reading the first page of an asylum decision letter for the third time, trying to muster some concentration, when Maggie appears at my elbow and indicates with a minute jerk of her chin that I am to follow her.

In the sanctuary of her conservatory office, she revisits the matter of the High Court claim she spoke to me about on Friday, explaining who will be working on the case and outlining the timetable for getting instructions to the barrister representing the Home Office. I am still making notes, bent diligently over a pad with a black biro in hand, when she says out of the blue, 'I was just leafing through the personnel files the other day – I already knew you went to Cambridge, Claire, but I couldn't find many details about your time there.'

Raising my head, I see that this is intended to be a question. I shrug, hoping to come across as nonchalant rather than difficult. I can't argue with the accuracy of the observation.

'What college did you go to? Your CV doesn't specify.'

'Trinity,' I lie. Although Maggie is hardly likely to phone up the admissions office, if the opportunity arose for her to ask any contacts she might have I would rather she drew a confusing blank than discovered the ignominy of those awful last weeks.

'I was at Queens.' She throws me a warm smile, like an invitation to a club.

It is tempting to reciprocate. Instead I give her a half-smile, enough to acknowledge the offer, slot the lid on my pen and stand up.

Maggie's face stiffens fractionally. 'It must have been a good night on Friday,' she says, just as I am approaching the door. It is another statement-come-question, a bowling ball pitched towards a set of skittles.

'Oh,' I say carefully. 'Why do you say that?' I stop beside a tall plant with thick foliage. I touch one of the leaves, but it is impossible to tell whether the rubbery surface is real or artificial.

'Agatha hasn't come in today. I've never known her call in sick before.'

'I don't imagine that's because of Friday. Probably a bad cold or she's picked up a virus.' Two lies in less than two minutes. I move my hand onto the door handle.

'And Nigel isn't here either.'

'Really?' I try to sound surprised.

'There's no sign of him. He hasn't telephoned Jane to say that he's ill. It's actually rather annoying because both he and Agatha are supposed to be producing reports for the meeting. Any idea where he is?'

'None at all, I'm afraid.' I could suggest that Nigel might have walked under a bus or suffered some other kind of freak accident, however I don't think I would be able to suppress a note of optimism from my voice. Instead I say, 'Agatha is aware the meeting has been moved to tomorrow. I know she's intending to come into work very early.'

'Oh. Well…' Maggie seems partly pacified. 'Perhaps Nigel has written his report already. I'll ask Jane to see if she can find any sign of a printout on his desk.'

I wait a respectful couple of seconds before closing my fingers around the lever and escaping.


Much later in the afternoon, once most of my colleagues have left for the day, I move on to the second part of Mark's little task. I delete the details of the successful appeals from Agatha's inventory, so the list comprises only the failures, those who will be desperate for the chance of another ticket in the great immigration lottery. After that I fetch a selection of the original files from storage.

Amongst all the papers each dossier inevitably contains a witness statement from the individual bringing the case, or a family member living in the UK – if the individual lives *outside* the UK and is relying on a family member for their golden passport entry – and each witness statement contains the address of the person making it.

I add those contact details in a separate column beside the name of the corresponding appeal, just like Mark instructed.

Well, almost like he instructed.

By way of a small departure, I make up addresses for those appeals where I don't have the dossier because it's not amongst the pile I collected from storage. Sometimes instead I tweak a name or change a sex. I am banking on the assumption this strategy will give Mark enough information to persuade him I did what he asked and that he will put the errors, the gaps, down to lying claimants or poor administration. Nevertheless, it feels as if I am inventing my own kind of lottery, exposing a few of these people to God knows what, while hiding, protecting others for no reason save that their files are located further away from the storage room door.

At one point I hear a 'Goodnight, Claire.' When I look up, Maggie raises her hand from the other side of the office. 'Don't stay too late.' The instruction is mellow with approval, the assumption that my industry is well-directed. She probably imagines I am starting the research for the claim in the High Court.

In the wake of Maggie's departure I reconsider the list. I think about meeting Mark for the first time, curled on his sofa with a glass of red wine, how I happily mistook his questions about my work for an interest in me. If he was looking for ways to get inside information about vulnerable immigrants then our encounter must have seemed like a perfectly ripe apple dropping straight into his lap. Before my resolve can weaken I remove *every* genuine address that I have taken from the files and replace them all with fictitious ones, inventing road names and flat numbers and adding convincing-sounding postcodes. I reassure myself that since it will take Mark a while to realise the full extent of what I've done, I'll still have a chance to get to the bottom of what he's up to. And when the moment of discovery comes I will simply have to face up to the consequences of not being the quite-so-perfect stooge after all.

By the time I'm ready to print out the finished product the cleaners have arrived, hoovering the carpet, emptying the bins and shouting snatches of conversation to each other over the noise of the machines. As I watch the printer cough the final page onto the tray, I tell myself the statistics I am disclosing are not really confidential. Anyone can sit in the tribunal, and assuming the weight of misery and desperation didn't send them straight to the distraction of the nearest bar they could compile their own set of data, their own tally of failure, very easily. Besides, I have the greater good in mind. The means justifies the ends, and all that. Sometimes our notion of right and wrong needs finer calibration, more nuance than the one-size-fits-all approach we normally abide by.

# CHAPTER TWENTY

I call Mark on the way home. It's barely twenty-four hours since he asked me for this information and, like a student returning an assignment ahead of schedule, I am proud of my efficiency – even if my competence comprises a certain creative element. There is no reply, only an automatic answer message in a stilted electronic voice. Later in the evening, I try twice more, still with no success. Leaving a message feels too risky, too exposed, so eventually I give up and go to bed accompanied only by an acute sense of anticlimax.

Tuesday unfolds in an equally uneventful manner. I arrive to find Agatha beavering away at her desk. Immediately she says, 'You did destroy my password, didn't you, Claire?'

'Yes,' I say. 'Of course.' I offer up a little prayer that Katy doesn't mention seeing me on Agatha's computer.

Seemingly satisfied, Agatha returns to her statistics report, which she manages to finish by 10.30 a.m. The team meeting passes without Maggie making any comment on the continued absence of Nigel, and in the middle of the afternoon Jane wanders over to Agatha and me with two mugs of coffee. I am so blindsided by this unexpected gesture of friendship that Agatha jumps in before I manage to say anything.

'Do you know where Nigel is?' she asks. 'It looks like he's still not come in.'

Jane blinks rapidly. I see her thoughts follow the track mine took the previous day and reach the same swift conclusion that Agatha has no idea what happened on Saturday night, or the part

Nigel played in it. 'I'm not sure,' she says. And then, unexpectedly, more quietly she adds, 'Although I think Maggie might know something.'

'Really?' I consider Jane with surprise. Maggie didn't appear to be aware of what had happened to Nigel when I saw her yesterday. However, if she's since found out something, Jane is bound to be in the picture too.

Jane puts a mug down next to Agatha's computer, her features perfectly composed. I imagine this is the real reason she came over to our desk, to dangle her superior knowledge in front of us both like a ball of wool, then whip it away the moment one of us reaches out an enquiring paw.

'I'm not allowed to say anything.'

'He's not in any trouble, is he?' Agatha is staring at Jane with worried eyes.

Jane avoids her gaze and hands me my coffee. 'Not at the moment.' Dipping her head she hurries away with small smug steps.

As soon as Jane is out of earshot Agatha explodes. 'God, Claire! What on earth do you think has happened to Nigel? I hope he's all right.'

I shrug. 'I have no idea.' I couldn't care less about Nigel. Agatha seems frantic, however. 'Look,' I say, at last, 'maybe Maggie's just pissed off because he hasn't reported in sick properly. It could be as simple as that.'

'Do you think so?'

'It's possible.'

Possible, but not, I would say, terribly likely.

At various points of the day I try to get hold of Mark. He still doesn't pick up. Eventually I leave a message, keeping it brief and neutral, merely asking him to call, 'so that I can update him on the project I have been working on.'

*

By Wednesday it feels as though a board of film censors have combed through my life and painstakingly airbrushed out any aspect that might require an 18+ certificate. Mark still doesn't return my call, my day in the office is sweetly uneventful and at 9.00 p.m. Angus returns home brandishing a Jo Malone carrier bag that is fastened at the top with a glossy black ribbon.

I get up from the sofa and circle my arms around his back. 'How was your trip?' We are standing beside the Spanish mirror; in the glass we look quite cool, quite hip – Angus, tired and slightly dishevelled, and me, bath-fresh wearing a pink cami and pyjama bottoms.

'Oh, you know…' he says vaguely, 'delays, meetings, terrible airline food.'

'What time did your flight get in? I thought most of them from New York were overnight?'

Stepping free of our embrace, Angus starts to take off his jacket. 'Like I said, there were delays. Take-off was put back because the pilot fell ill and they had to find another.' He checks his watch. 'To answer your question I guess the plane landed about two hours ago. Here,' to slip his second arm clear of his sheepskin he passes me the Jo Malone package, 'I bought this for you.'

He watches while I extract a bottle of perfume from its abundance of extravagant packaging and spray a little on my wrist and neck. The smell is ruby-rich and spiced with clove and musk.

I hold out my forearm to Angus, twisting it to offer the paler underside. 'What do you think?' I have never managed to find Jo Malone for sale in any airport and consider his present a triumph.

Obligingly he dips his head and inhales. 'Very nice.' Instead of straightening up, his lips graze a trail along the length of my arm. They settle briefly on the soft, fragranced skin at the base of my throat and then move to my mouth.

My mother provides the greatest excitement of the week so far by telephoning on Thursday evening, inevitably just as Angus and I are about to sit down and eat.

'You haven't forgotten it's Rob's birthday on Saturday?' she asks, as soon as we've trotted through the basics.

'No,' I say – truthfully, as it happens, because my phone pinged that afternoon to remind me of the impending landmark.

'You normally come home for the weekend closest to his birthday, so we can all go out together.' My mother trails the statement like fishing bait, the spaces between each word increasing very slightly.

'Mum, it's really busy at the moment. I'm not sure I can get away.' Angus glances up from his plate of risotto as he begins to comprehend the gist of the conversation.

'That's a shame, darling. You haven't been home recently. I know how much Rob would love to see you.'

There is a silence, which I know my mother is quite capable of extending indefinitely. She is a master in the art of keeping quiet to get her own way – regrettably I don't appear to have inherited the same trait. After somewhere between ten and fifteen seconds of listening to Angus eat, I sigh and say, 'I suppose I could get a train after work on Friday.' Seeing Angus frown, I add, 'Although I might need to get back on Saturday.'

Once the exchange is over I say to Angus, 'I have to go and visit my family this weekend. It's my brother's birthday.'

'So I gathered.'

'You were away last weekend,' I counter.

'That was work.' Angus's face has folded into itself with annoyance. 'And I didn't leave until Sunday.'

'Well, this is family. My family. I haven't seen them for a while.' Angus doesn't say anything and I realise I have been quite tactless, given his lack of contact with his own parents.

'You could always come with me,' I say, more gently.

He shakes his head with a lopsided smile. 'I daresay I'll find something to do to pass the time.'

I half expect him to say more, to mention the gym or tennis or a pub lunch with friends. When he doesn't elaborate I am suddenly glad to be heading home, back to the familiar territory of unspectacular, predictable Ipswich, and my equally unspectacular, predictable family.


The Friday evening train is packed. Despite my best efforts to get away in good time it was five when I left the office, which means I am faced with the happy trilogy of peak fares, no seats and a buffet trolley that has run out of hot water for tea and coffee long before it finally reaches me. At least it's a good excuse for an early gin and tonic, which I drink lodged in the gap between the luggage rack and the loo.

At Colchester there is a general spewing out of passengers onto the platform and the rest of us, bound for the watery rural plains of Suffolk and Norfolk, dive towards vacated chairs with the reactions of sprint runners. I find myself next to the window, the seat cushion warm and adorned with a confetti of crisps.

Although it is too dark to see much at all, the exterior of flat unbroken grey suggests we are passing fields, trees and hedges, the kind of lightless countryside it is easy to forget exists when you live and work in central London. The lack of space means my handbag is on my lap and a small overnight bag is wedged between my feet. Every so often the woman who is half-asleep in the space opposite murmurs an apology when she crosses or uncrosses her legs, kicks the bag and mistakes it for my foot. After a while, I check my phone, because that's the obvious thing to do on a train when the only possible source of an endorphin rush is an electronic device. There is a text from Angus, sent only a minute earlier.

*R u back tmrw or Sunday?*

I consider my ghost-faint reflection in the glass for a moment before replying. It doesn't seem worth spoiling the relative tranquility of recent days for the sake of another night in Ipswich.

*Tmrw* ☺, I type.

Immediately my mobile pings again. I am smiling as I look down, anticipating Angus's reaction, but the grin dies on my face.

For the first few seconds the shock of the words displayed on the screen is too great for me to make any sense of them. They jump and pop in random patterns, emitting fireworks of alarm even though I can't actually manage to read the complete message. Even when the letters finally settle into sentences – three quite short sentences – I still have to study them to lift any meaning from the WhatsApp message.

*Playing about again? You've gone too far this time. Stop right now if you want past mistakes to stay in the past.*

I let my hand fall to my lap and stare at the black blanket of nothing sweeping past the window. My heart is pounding in time with the roll of the train, as if they are racing in tandem down the track.

I try to reason rationally and ignore the freezing sensation in my stomach. It is clear the sender of this message has discovered my relationship with Mark, but who – apart from Angus – would care enough about it to threaten me? And surely Angus wouldn't react by writing like a backstreet gangster seconds after asking when I was coming home? Besides, all he knows about Daniel is the newspaper report of the cycling accident that I showed him ages ago. The only person I can think of who understands the past, and its dirty, sordid complexity, is Julia. Yet I am quite certain Julia is the last person who would want to rake all that up again and poison the air of whatever new little world she has managed to create for herself.

I make myself study the screen again. The phone number of the sender rings no bells whatsoever.

I wonder, suddenly, if Mark has a girlfriend. There is a child, I remember, from the first time I viewed the house, and – he said – an ex-wife. It is possible he is now with somebody else, a partner who has reason to mistrust him, who has studied his phone and has found his calls to me. She might have confronted Mark, she may have demanded my name. She would have had to dig very deep to unearth anything of interest, anything suspicious, about Daniel; she would need to have been extremely motivated indeed. However, it's possible that a girlfriend who has been cheated on, who has been lied to, who can't bear to lose, could fit that particular bill very well.

I run my tongue over my dry lips. The woman opposite has begun to snore, gentle little hiccups, her head resting against the glass. On the table in front of her is an open bottle of Evian. I contemplate reaching forward and taking a mouthful of water. Although I am sorely tempted, I know I won't help myself to her drink because it seems way too forward, far too rude. Funny, how we baulk at taking little liberties, how much it is easier to take the bigger, more dramatic steps.

*Who is this?* I type. *What do you want?* I chuck the mobile into my bag, then I change my mind and slip it into my trouser pocket for quicker, easier access when the response arrives.

The train is slowing down, the journey time between Colchester and Ipswich is barely twenty minutes and already we are pulling into the station. Standing up, I catch a brief glimpse of my stepfather waiting patiently by a closed coffee kiosk before the carriage jerks forward another few metres and instead the window exposes a couple of lads larking around with cans of lager.

'I've brought the Fiesta,' my stepfather says when we embrace on the platform. 'I didn't know how much luggage you would have.'

I hold up my small bag. 'I can only stay one night.'

'Oh well.' He shrugs, although I don't expect my mother to take the disappointment of the curtailed visit quite as easily. 'It would have been a cold night to walk.'

My parents live about a mile from the station – it probably takes as long to get out of the car park and battle the Friday night traffic as it would have done to cover the distance on foot. Still, the journey gives me an opportunity to check my phone, the light flaring briefly in the darkness of the car.

My stepfather half-turns from the steering wheel. 'Angus missing you already?'

I smile and make a movement with my head that is neither a nod nor a shake.

The screen is blank.

My mother and Rob appear in the hallway as soon as we arrive, it's entirely possible that they have been hovering in the vicinity of the front door since the moment my stepfather left to collect me. My mother hugs me, before holding me out at arm's-length, like an item of clothing she has just taken off the rack in a shop. 'You're looking thinner, Claire, too thin. Don't you think she looks thin, Andy?'

Before my stepfather can speak, my brother comes to the rescue by squeezing past my mother in the narrow hallway and wrapping his arms around me. He is wearing an old navy-blue T-shirt with a Star Wars motif. The cotton smells of homework on the kitchen table, of TV dinners on our laps, of walking to the newsagents every Saturday to spend our pocket money. My brother smells of memories I didn't even know I had. He smells of my childhood.

'Hey, sis, good to see you.'

I remember that my younger sibling is very soon going to be a father. 'Congratulations,' I say, and when he looks at me blankly – the pregnancy was announced some time ago, after all – I add, 'about the baby.'

'Right. Thanks.'

I examine his face, trying to detect any sign of reticence about the impending responsibility, but the only trace of anxiety I can see is a warm, outward kind of concern. Directed at me, I think.

'I'll just take my bag upstairs,' I say, to extract myself from the excess of affection clogging up the hallway.

Upstairs my room is practically the same as when I left to go to university: a single bed by the window, a bookshelf with a complete set of A-level revision guides and a DIY Formica desk that bridges the small space between my wardrobe and the outside wall. The only concession to the passage of time is the duvet cover. I realise that my mother has finally switched a close-up photograph of the members of Take That – minus Robbie – for sprigs of blue flowers against a cream background.

I perch on the bed, compelled to consult my mobile again. There is no further communication from my mystery correspondent. I compose a text to Angus to say that I've arrived safely, more to test the water than because either of us regards the journey between Liverpool Street and my parents' front door as particularly hazardous. A perfectly pleasant if short reply zips back immediately.

I pull up the message from the train. Reading it again provokes the same cloud of nauseous confusion, the same complex, unforgettable thoughts about Daniel.

'Claire, whatever are you doing up there?' There is a surprising edge to my mother's voice.

'I'm just coming down.' As I switch off the light, our garden becomes visible in the window, tinted vaguely orange in the borrowed glow of the street lamps. Rob and I used to play there for hours when we were little. He was so young when my father left us he had no notion there might be anything bigger or better beyond the boundary of its wooden fence. I, on the other hand, had glimpsed the possibilities that were there for the taking. To my horror, staring at the defunct swing, the listing bird table, a lump the size of a tennis ball appears in my throat. If I had hoped that by coming home I might rediscover the person I used to be when I lived here, the person I was before I met Mark, before I met Daniel, it's obvious I've been wasting my time. That person checked out and did a runner quite some time ago.

'Andy says that you're staying just the one night! We're all supposed to be going out tomorrow to Pizza Express. For Rob's birthday.' My mother is standing at the bottom of the staircase and has started speaking before I am even halfway down the steps.

'I'm sorry. I really need to get back to London. What with my government work at the department, and the wedding to organise…' I play these two trump cards, dangle them like flags, while we walk to the kitchen where Elsa is sitting at our scrubbed pine table. I had forgotten she would be here or, to be more accurate, I had hoped I would have Rob to myself for the evening. When she gets up to greet me the bump under her dress makes her look like a snake that has swallowed a golf ball.

'Claire is only here for tonight,' my mother announces, although I'm pretty sure the others must be well aware of this already. 'We'll just have to make the most of her while we can.' As we all shuffle into places around the table, she extracts an enormous shepherd's pie from the oven and proceeds to dole out equally enormous portions.

I find I can barely eat, although the scrutiny of my mother's gaze makes me shovel a few forkfuls down my throat. After about ten minutes, when I am fielding questions on the tribunal, on Angus, on our plans for the Big Day, I feel my mobile twang in my pocket. Something in my expression must change because the conversation suddenly dies.

'Everything all right?' my stepfather asks.

I nod, before realising that I can't possibly sit through the meal without checking my inbox. 'Actually, sorry, but I'd better…' I am getting up, pulling out the phone and holding it aloft like a piece of vital evidence in a court trial while the others regard me with astonishment over the top of their knives and forks. 'I won't be a moment.' I dive into the hallway and consult the screen. Nothing but an email from booking.com promising me a fifteen-percent discount on any reservation made before midnight on Sunday.

I creep back into the kitchen rather sheepishly. 'There's a bit of a crisis in the office at the moment,' I proffer by way of explanation. 'I just needed to check if that was a message from my boss.'

My stepfather raises his eyebrows. 'On a Friday evening?'

My mother gives my stepfather her withering look, 'Claire's job isn't like yours, Andy. The government doesn't stop because of the weekend. It's twenty-four hours a day, seven days a week. Isn't that right, dear?' Naturally, my mother has never witnessed the haemorrhaging of civil servants out of the door at 4.30 p.m. on a Friday.

I reward her with a smile and take the chance to start asking Elsa about the pregnancy – anything to change the subject. Elsa immediately launches into a willing account of ultrasounds and birthing plans and the benefits of breastfeeding a baby until it is practically a teenager. My parents and Rob all trade anxious glances, but when they see I am not going to start weeping or rush out of the room again everyone relaxes and for the next half an hour I forget about the sinister message and I forget about Mark. I probably even forget about Daniel.

Afterwards we clear the dishes. Once the kitchen is tidy I decide to empty the bin and carry the rubbish out through the back door. I take my time with this manoeuver, wondering if Rob will pick up on the old clues, our secret sign language. Although I'm aware he is watching me, I'm not convinced he will actually respond until I hear his footsteps on the path behind me as I am dumping the black bag into the dustbin.

'Hey!' His voice is soft in the orange-infused dark.

When I turn around I see that he is clutching a packet of Bensons. He holds the box out towards me.

I shake my head. 'Still smoking? I thought you gave that up years ago.'

He considers the cigarettes, a mixture of guilt and affection written across his face. 'Hardly ever these days. And I'll have to stop completely soon because of the baby…'

The dustbins live on a cement base at the bottom of the garden, screened by a low brick wall that is topped with a trellis. This is the place Rob and I would sneak out to smoke when we were kids, hidden from sight of the house, sheltered from the wind. The stench from the rubbish wasn't great, particularly in the summer, but a lot of the stuff we were smoking back then had a strong enough smell to counteract that particular problem.

We crouch with our backs against the brick. I balance on my heels to avoid the chill of the concrete while Rob sits with his legs outstretched and crosses his ankles. He strikes a match, cupping his fingers around the flame as he lifts it towards his mouth. I tuck my hands as far into the sleeve of the opposite arm of my jumper as they can reach. It seems I've become a London softy – I'm cold already – but this is my only opportunity in a long time to have my brother to myself.

'Won't Elsa wonder where you are?'

Rob slots the matches back into the pocket of his old parka jacket – at least one of us had the foresight to put on a coat. 'She was calling a friend. She won't even notice I've gone.'

'What about Mum and Andy?'

'They know where I am.'

'Did you tell them?'

'I didn't need to tell them. They realised exactly what I was doing when they saw me follow you out the door. It probably made them get all nostalgic for our teenage years.' Seeing my expression, he snorts. 'Come on, Claire. They've always known we used to hang out here.'

'Really?'

By way of reply Rob merely blows a perfect smoke ring, his party trick, though it seems rather less impressive now than when he was sixteen. We watch the silvery strands wobble and dissolve, before he says, 'So, fill me in on your perfect job, your perfect man, your perfect life…'

He sounds neither sarcastic nor jealous, merely interested. This is typical of my brother. While I was always striving to reach that must-be-emerald grass on the other side of the garden fence, Rob was quite content with the exact shade of green right under his feet.

I peek sideways; he is staring straight ahead, following the long trail of smoke as it drifts over the panelling that divides our modest estate from the garden of the house beyond. 'Come on, Claire, spill the beans. Tell me how the other half live. Is it all government deadlines and cocktail bars?'

I think of Maggie and the countless stacks of immigration files falling apart from age and the effort of holding together so many sad stories; the slow grinding of the judicial machine, the fraught individuals waiting for their turn in the mincer. I think of Kelly's, of Nigel, his forearm over his eyes, his crotch drenched with vodka, and the long taxi-ride home with a semi-comatose Agatha. I imagine Rob, shaking his head, even laughing, when I confess the unholy mess of last Friday night and let him see the first, tiniest glimmer that his image of my life is so wide of the mark he might as well be mistaking me for a different person entirely.

As I open my mouth Rob turns to catch my gaze. To my horror he's smiling expectantly, his face coated with that same mixture of awe and anticipation my parents have adopted like a family dress code. It looks for all the world as if he's about to join the chorus and announce how proud of me he is.

I stare at the ground. 'I suppose so,' I say. 'There are a lot of deadlines and the work feels important. I'm in the tribunal about three days a week presenting cases and because there's not nearly enough time to prepare them properly we're working under constant pressure. And I guess we go to some OK bars. Last week was somebody's birthday so we tried a new place that has just opened. Amazing decor with a kind of nightclub vibe.'

'Step up from The Bull then?'

'Yeah, a little bit different…' The Bull was where we both had our first legal drink, preceded by a good many illegal ones. I try to imagine Angus or Mark in The Bull, perched on a sticky seat with a pint and a packet of pork scratchings, and fail dismally.

Right on cue, Rob says, 'Tell me about Angus. I feel as if I hardly know the guy.'

'Well,' I say, and stop. Absurdly, my mind has gone blank. I blink into the dark, waiting for inspiration but the dustbins are not the most stimulating backdrop. I am saved, temporarily, by the distant sound of a train, the soft swell of noise occupying the space my reply should fit, but when the roar recedes and I still don't reply Rob raises his eyebrows with theatrical exaggeration and laughs.

'Come on, Claire. It's not a fucking exam question.' He lifts up his left wrist, consulting his watch. 'Fifteen seconds to describe your beloved.'

*My beloved?* I stare at him. From nowhere, as if a window has just been opened, my mind fills with a memory of Daniel and me crossing King's Parade in the lemon sunshine of mid-spring. Daniel, slightly ahead of me, holds out his hand, trailing it behind his back, knowing without question, without needing to look around, that I would take it. I close my eyes. I open them again and consider the black-and-grey planes of concrete and bin. With an effort I focus on Angus. I can picture him, of course, but Rob isn't after a physical description. He wants to understand what it will be like to hang out with his brother-in-law, go to the footy or the pub together, and I can't really help him with that. The idea of Angus in the stands at Portman Road is as absurd to me as the notion of him drinking in The Bull.

After a few moments, Rob lowers his arm. 'I can't see the second hand in this light anyway.'

He takes the cigarette out of his mouth and taps the ash onto the ground with a concise, deliberate movement. For a while neither of us speaks. Then he says slowly, 'So, what's going on?'

'Nothing,' I snap, not because I am cross with him but because I suddenly can't bear the fact he understands so little about me when he used to know everything. And what he didn't know, he could guess instinctively, like he had a sixth sense, like we owned a shared wavelength, our own private channel of communication. Now he doesn't have the first clue. We have ten or fifteen minutes before we freeze our balls off, and I have no idea where to even begin.

Rob offers me the cigarette and I take a long pull on it. I feel the passage of the nicotine crawling into my blood, firing my neurons like low-level voltage. 'Angus runs a hotel business, boutique hotels,' I say finally. 'He works hard and he has to travel a lot. He's quite a serious person, precise and well spoken, and he wants his surroundings, his home, to be smart and tidy. He likes Indian food, fishing, Scandi box sets and French film stars – the female ones of course, all black bobs and pert boobs.'

I hold the smoke tight inside my throat before exhaling it in a ghost-grey bubble that collapses immediately – my smoke rings were never as good as Rob's. I could add one further, more interesting, fact about my beloved: that, by our standards, Angus is rich, and the house we have just acquired in West London would probably buy our family home three times over – aka security for life.

Naturally, I don't say this. Rob and Elsa are living with my parents while they save for a deposit to put on a flat. They moved back nearly a year ago and not only has there been no mention of when the situation might change but they all appear to be getting on just famously. I don't think Rob would appreciate how I could find the prize of my own foothold in the property market so compelling, so powerful. Or perhaps, the opposite is the case, knowing me like he does, like he used to do, maybe I am concerned he would understand the attraction only too well.

Rob is nodding seriously, as if the complexities of his prospective bother-in-law have been fully illuminated by my desultory sketch. 'Have you been to stay in one of Angus's hotels?'

I glance at him. Surprised by both the question and the fact the idea had never occurred to me before. 'Not yet,' I say. 'I expect we will soon.' I make a mental note to suggest to Angus we have a weekend away, perhaps to do some early Christmas shopping. It suddenly strikes me as crazy that Angus should have easy access to a whole series of city breaks and we never take advantage of them.

I shift on my heels in an attempt to pacify my calves, which are violently protesting at the squatting position I have adopted. I really need to stretch but standing up might guillotine our conversation once and for all. 'Is work going OK?' I ask, instead.

Rob shrugs. 'It's fine. Same as usual.' Rob fits kitchens for a specialist company in Ipswich: one van, two blokes and numerous slabs of carefully crafted oak and pine. My industrious brother was employed within about a month of leaving school and as far as I know his role has barely changed in the last six years.

'How's Barry?' I say, referring to the other occupant of Rob's van.

'Barry had to leave, he developed back problems. There's a new man now called Steve.'

'How is he doing?'

'He's all right, quite bit younger than Barry with a complicated love life.' All at once Rob grins. 'Spices up the day a bit, hearing what he's been up to. Monday mornings fly by!'

It's my turn to nod, as if it is possible I would find driving around all day while listening to lurid accounts of Steve's sex exploits even remotely bearable. 'So, you're not too bored then?'

Rob squints up at my face before looking down and grinding out the stub of his cigarette, crushing the tip into the concrete.

'Of course I'm bored, but being bored is one hell of a lot better than being out of work. Or being hungry or being ill. I'm lucky; it's a decent job, a decent employer and I've got Elsa to think of and a baby on the way.' He pauses, and then adds more quietly, 'We can't all be like you, Claire.'

I want to tell him that not being like me is a good thing, possibly a very good thing indeed, but Rob is already getting up, slapping the dust from the back of his coat. After a moment he offers his hand and as I grasp it he yanks me to my feet. There is a split second when I am on the point of saying something real. We are so close it feels as if it might be possible to find the words, to create a lever to prise open a crack of proper communication.

'It's bloody freezing out here.' As Rob takes a step away from me a barrier drops between us, like the toughened window in a prison visiting room. Thin and invisible but nonetheless making actual contact impossible. Walking back towards the glow of the kitchen window I can't help but wonder whether it is Rob or myself who is trapped on the wrong side of the glass.

Later, I am sitting under my blue-and-white duvet, the cotton starched and packet-stiff, speaking to Angus before I go to sleep. My single bed is flush against the wall that divides my room with Rob's – or Rob and Elsa's, I should say. After a brief synopsis of the day, the journey, being home, I say carefully, 'I'm thinking about staying here another night.'

There is a surprised pause. Then Angus says, 'You told me you would come back tomorrow.'

'I know, but I'll miss Rob's birthday celebration. Everyone is going out for a meal.'

'Won't you see Rob in the morning?'

'Yes, but—'

'We don't spend enough time together as it is, Claire. You're always so busy—'

'… *I'm* so busy!'

Angus ignores the interruption. 'Don't forget we have a wedding to plan. If I don't see you until Sunday that's another whole weekend wasted.' Although polite, his voice sounds taut with self-control.

I capitulate with grace and change the subject. In many ways one day at home is actually quite enough.

Once the call finishes I become aware of Rob and Elsa talking next door. I had forgotten the modest size of the house, the slimness of the walls that used to enable Rob and me to have a conversation without either of us needing to get up. Now I can hear the rumble of their words, the higher, upward inflection of Elsa's questions and the deeper, shorter response of Rob's answers. Although they are talking too quietly to make out what they are saying, every so often I think I catch my name, spoken by Elsa, her voice sharpened by either concern or curiosity.

Eventually they fall quiet. I imagine them drifting to sleep, Rob's hand resting lightly on Elsa's belly, on the baby that is growing, that is becoming, inside it. *My little brother: a father.*

After a moment I open the drawer of my bedside table. The contents haven't changed since I was last home, or probably at any time during the previous fifteen years: a selection of hairbands, a stack of cards from my 18th birthday, an ancient eye-shadow palette in lurid blues – and the address book I used when I was a teenager. Tucked into the pointless, empty 'z' section is a photograph, a little faded now, but still with the same old power to make my head and heart pound that it has always possessed.

I hold up the image and my youthful father grins back at me through liquid-brown eyes. His right arm is raised, as if to shield his lean, tanned face from the sun or run a hand through his crop of dark wavy hair. I have always hated how he looks in this picture, so carefree, so *happy*, the embodiment of the contented family man, although the shot was taken only days before his great escape. I suppose he must have been thinking about his one-way ticket at the time. At least his expression won't be quite so blithe now – my father fell off a mountain in Canada some years ago, a careless, fatal slip, apparently, from an over-ambitious walking trail.

My phone dings from the bedside table.

*OK to book film 20.15 tomorrow?*

It seems Angus is taking no chances. I look around at the walls of the space I grew up in. The light is switched off, but I prefer it this way; I can see the teenage posters, the long-defunct revision schedules, the schoolgirl montage of now-dispersed friends, better in the dark. As soon as the room illuminates I have to inhabit the present again. What do they say about travelling hopefully?

*Fine*, I type, *Home mid-afternoon.*

I still haven't heard from Mark. After a second's deference to the lateness of the hour, I call him. The line hesitates, before connecting and then rings, once, twice, before suddenly cutting off. I am still holding the phone in my hand when a message lands on my screen.

*Don't call me*

Is the instruction intended to be temporary or permanent? The tone is hardly that of somebody who last time he saw me appeared desperate to get his hands in my knickers and has requested a not-inconsiderable favour. Besides, who, in the history of the world, has ever not immediately called someone who told them not to call?

Straight away I text, *I have what you want.* Which is pleasingly enigmatic, even though the meaning should be clear enough to Mark. I wait impatiently, certain his next response will soon be winging its way to land on my imaginary doormat. There is nothing. After five minutes I phone his number and I'm taken straight to voicemail.

Just below my exchange with Angus glowers the WhatsApp message I received in the train:

*Playing about again? You've gone too far this time. Stop right now if you want past mistakes to stay in the past.*

If Mark has a girlfriend who has found out about the affair, this would not only explain the threatening WhatsApp message, but also his behaviour tonight, his entreaty not to call.

It seems I have an attraction for this sort of man, the kind who expect their girlfriends to share, to be grateful for what they can get, even if this particular girlfriend appears to be unwilling to play ball. I wonder how much digging around about me she has done, whether she is merely bluffing, faking it, when she says she is aware of my mistakes.

Whatever she might think she knows she is bound to be wrong. The past is the greatest optical illusion; one time you look you see the beautiful young woman, and the next, the same facts, the identical snip of the continuum, reveals the wicked witch. It just depends on the mindset in which you approach matters.

# CHAPTER TWENTY-ONE

I arrive home shortly before three o'clock. As I step through the front door there is the crackle of paper under my feet – mail on the mat, a sure sign that Angus is not here. A scribbled note taped on the glass of the Spanish mirror confirms his absence: *Had to go into office. Back about 7 xx*

Angus rarely uses kisses and I suspect their presence is his tacit recognition that I have every right to feel pissed off at his absence, given the fuss he made about me being away and his determination to get me back as soon as possible. My wave of annoyance dissipates pretty quickly, however; having spent the first half of the weekend fending off an excess of parental attention and readjusting to the tedium of having to wait for the bathroom, a period of time to myself feels almost luxurious. I kick off my shoes, change into a pair of slouchy tracksuit bottoms and put on the kettle.

I am about to retire to the sofa, mug in hand, to resume my acquaintance with Mary, Queen of Scots when I notice the post still scattered by the door. There is a flyer from a new local sushi company, a bank statement addressed to Angus, a couple of charity circulars, and a crisp white envelope with the HSBC logo and, more eye-catchingly, the word *URGENT* stamped in conspicuously large red letters. Although my stomach automatically jumps in anticipation of the reprimand, some failed deadline, or missed payment, I soon spot that this last letter is in fact addressed to Mark. Since it's the first piece of his correspondence we have received, presumably the redirection service he set up when he moved out has now expired.

After barely a second's hesitation I rip open the envelope.

The prose is courteous yet quietly venomous. After '*a recent review*' HSBC has apparently decided that it no longer wishes to provide Mark with banking facilities and is giving him thirty days' notice of its intention to close his accounts. Not only will the debit balance require immediate repayment on the date of closure, but also Mark's credit-card limit has been reduced to a derisory £300 with immediate effect.

*Jesus.*

I perch on the edge of the sofa, the sheet of paper in my hand. Somewhere or other I still have the redirection confirmation from the Post Office, so it would be perfectly possible for me to forward the bank's bombshell to Mark myself. However, it occurs to me that there is a more attractive alternative: I have four whole hours to kill before Angus is due home; what better way to spend it than delivering the letter by hand and checking out the candidacy of Mark's girlfriend for the role of my mystery message sender?

Before I leave the house I swap the tracksuit bottoms for a pair of leather leggings, add an oversized jumper and a gilet, and pile my hair into a sexy mess on top of my head. Adding, naturally, the obligatory coat of red lipstick – from my previous experience of encounters with the official girlfriend I have learned not to underestimate the benefit of proper preparation.

As Mark's flat is located in Newham I have to take the Central line all the way from Ealing to Stratford and then switch on to the Docklands Light Railway. However, at least the long journey is an opportunity to decide how to play the situation. The girlfriend may deny all knowledge of the message, of course, but I think that's unlikely, given the pugnacious overtones. More likely she will go on the attack. Actually, I have no problem with that. I have no intention of fighting my corner for Mark; for once – believe it or not – I am content to play the role of the magnanimous loser. My sole objective is to find out what she has guessed about me, about my past – and to persuade her to keep those suspicions to herself.

The train breathes in as it moves across London, sucking up a human soup of race and language into its small, dense space and spilling most of it out at familiar landmarks such as Oxford Circus and St Paul's, so that by the time I reach Stratford, just beyond Liverpool Street, the carriage is practically empty again. When I get off at Canning Town the only person who alights is a thin bearded guy wearing a beanie and accompanied by a greyhound.

The station is open-air with automatic, unstaffed ticket machines and now the train has borne away the beanie guy the platform is entirely empty. If the sun were shining, it is just possible the vista might possess some kind of bleak, post-apocalyptic beauty. However, today the sky is the same shade as the cement infrastructure, only without the beautification of the graffiti that has been sprayed in red-and-black paint above the plastic seats: the most attention-grabbing example of which informs a waiting world that '*Callum has herpes.*'

Google Maps tells me it's a ten-minute walk to Mark's abode. The roads appear to be identical, long and straight and bordered on both sides by terraced houses that look as though a builder has simply pressed copy and paste down the entire length: a door, an adjacent window, two windows upstairs and nowhere for the bins to sit other than the sliver of space between the pavement and the front wall. Mark's house is distinguishable from its neighbours only because of a 'To Let' sign, which judging by the pristine state of the board appears to be a recent addition.

Since the front door doesn't have a bell, or actually any kind of knocker at all, the only option is to rap the shabby paintwork with my knuckles, which I do, perhaps more loudly than I intend.

There is no response.

It is probable, of course, nobody is home but just as I am adjusting to this outcome I hear a telltale scratching on the other side of the lock. There is barely enough time to adopt my best scarlet smile before I find myself gazing straight into the pupils of a girl. She appears to be Thai or Vietnamese and it takes me a moment to realise that she is not, as was my first impression, a child, but is actually a young woman of around nineteen or twenty.

'Can I help you?' She is regarding me with curiosity that borders on fear, the surprise in her voice is submissive, the inflection of somebody who has learned to be wary of strangers.

'Mark lives here, doesn't he?' I say, with more confidence than I am feeling. 'Are you his girlfriend?'

She blinks twice in quick succession and looks at the floor. 'No.'

I note the tatty jumper under her dungarees, the belt cinched tight around a tiny frame. Long dark hair hangs limply either side of cheeks that are sallow from lack of sleep. Or sunshine. Or joy. Or very possibly all three. It is similar to gazing at a photograph of somebody who might be beautiful but the picture is now too faded to tell one way or the other.

'I'm guessing you *are* his girlfriend.'

Behind her, at the back of the hallway, I spot two packing cases that have been stacked one on top of the other, presumably to minimise their footprint in the narrow space.

'Mark moved out. He doesn't live here any more.'

I remember saying that too. Perhaps we should start a club.

'I think he does.' I take a small step towards the door and the woman shrinks backwards.

Before I can say anything else, a child arrives – a boy, only three or four years old, with dirty bare feet and rich sooty curls. The woman grabs his hand and either the simple fact of his presence or the pressure of his small fist seems to embolden her. 'There is nobody here called Mark,' she says more firmly. 'You must have the wrong house.'

I try switching tacks. 'Did you send me a message?' I ask. 'A nasty WhatsApp message?'

The shock of this suggestion makes her lift her head. She meets my gaze with big dark eyes and her irises glimmer with incredulity – and honesty. 'I've never met you before,' she stammers. 'Why would I send…?'

'… It's all right, Malee. I'll deal with this.'

Mark is standing at the top of the staircase. Although he's dressed in jeans the usual flawless white shirt has been supplanted by a plain fawn T-shirt, which is splattered with something red – presumably ketchup rather than blood, given the domesticity of the scene before me. When he starts to descend the steps I see that his stay-at-home outfit is completed by a pair of old-man tartan slippers. It's as much as I can do not to point at them and laugh.

The woman's glance switches rapidly between Mark and me. She must see something revealing, read, perhaps, the distant echo of attraction, of sex, on our faces, because all at once her posture sags slightly. I recognise that feeling, the desperation to avoid what is right in front of your nose. I remember myself five years ago, when I too was ignorant of my beloved's infidelity, the depths of his deception. I wonder how she would respond if push should come to shove. If she would react the same way that I did.

'So you know her, do you Mark?' Her tone is ripe with fear and suspicion. Another emotion too – scorn, I think. Perhaps this is not a novel situation for either of them. I suppose there's no *ex*-wife.

'Go and wait in the kitchen.'

The woman hesitates for several seconds before moving away, tugging the child with her.

Mark steps in front of both of them. 'What do you want?' he asks me.

The alarm in his eyes is plain. The way his gaze flicks, instinctively or deliberately perhaps, towards the head of his departing child and the tangle of his soft ebony curls.

How quickly, how surreptitiously, the tables can turn and the pendulum can swing. I like power, I understand the pull of it, the desire we have for control, the way we strive for it, consciously or subconsciously, and the way we never quite know what we will do with it – what it will do with us – until we have it within our grasp.

'I've brought you this.' I take the bank letter from my coat pocket and hold it out as if presenting a carrot to a pony. 'I'm sorry I opened it. I didn't realise it was addressed to you until it was too late.' I don't bother to try to sound convincing.

After a moment Mark comes forward and takes the torn envelope. I can tell that he badly wants to know if I have anything else for him, something more useful, while at the same time he is willing me not to say more in earshot of the kitchen.

I shake my head very slowly. When – *if* – I give him those names and addresses, it will be on my terms – and once I am more confident of the return part of the bargain.

He is starting to close the door when I say rather loudly, 'Actually I really came here because I was looking for someone else, not you at all. I wanted somebody called Daniel.'

Mark freezes, staring at me in astonishment.

I am directing my voice through the open gap, letting it float towards the kitchen – a belated, pathetic offering to Malee. 'I thought you could help me find him but I must have been mistaken. I was probably wrong about that right from the beginning.'


On the way home, I sense the approach of one of my migraines. Like noticing storm clouds bunched on the horizon, or the air acquire that greenish, pre-thunder hue, I feel the tension mounting at the base of my skull. When the headaches have happened before, I've always thought of them as an echo of the past, the wash of pain as the lap of waves still spreading outwards from that shock point five years earlier. Now, I'm not so certain. Today, the gentle throbbing seems closer to a premonition, a warning of what is to come, a church bell tolling in a distant valley.

An alarm.

I break my journey, disembarking the Central line at Chancery Lane in order to get some air and quell the nausea that is stirring, animal-like, in the pit of my stomach. For twenty minutes or so I sit on a bench in the gardens of Lincoln's Inn and let the facts buzz loosely around my brain. I think about the lists of names in Mark's briefcase and the information that he wants from me concerning the tribunal. I consider how odd it is – how lucky for him – that someone like me, working in the immigration service, happened to buy his house. I recall how confident Angus was that our offer would be accepted, how familiar he seemed with the financial affairs of our prospective seller. I think about meeting Angus at the immigration conference, his interest in my work. And then I think about Angus's business, how I've never visited any of his hotels; I've never even seen a picture of one.

The trees are winter-bare and the flower beds are dormant, yet nevertheless the bookish quiet is calming. While I sit there an earnest-looking young woman hurries past and disappears into one of the lamp-lit barristers' chambers. I imagine her bent over a desk, trying to shoehorn the details of her case into a structure for the courtroom, a narrative that allows for a binary outcome, a 'yes' or 'no', a 'guilty' or 'not guilty', rather than facts that splinter into a labyrinth of possibilities, a thousand different nuances of blame.

By the time I get home it is close to half-past six and my head is lighter, my vision clearer. I have about an hour before Angus is expected back. I fetch myself a large tumbler of water and sip it while I consider the contents of the fridge; the half-eaten carcass of a roast chicken, a block of dried-out cheese and components for a salad that are limp and soft and already beginning to rot. More temptingly, there is also an open bottle of Sauvignon Blanc.

Flouting the threatened migraine, I abandon the water, pour myself a glass of wine and sit down with my laptop. The company that Angus runs, his chain of boutique B & B's, is called MPC Hotels, which, if you think about it – and until this afternoon I hadn't considered it at all – is not the most evocative label for a destination business, a provider of escapes.

I tap the name into Google, wishing I had done this months ago. Still, despite my wriggly little misgivings, I am hoping to find a reasonably sophisticated website; images of European cities, iconic landmarks of towers, castles and ancient forums, or at the very least couples strolling hand-in-hand or sipping drinks in charming, flower-bedecked town squares. Instead the results appear to be links to composite sites such as Booking.com, TravelRepublic and TripAdvisor, all of which suggest at first glance that the average rating for a stay in an MPC boutique hotel is a desultory one – or, if the reviewer is particularly generous of heart, two – stars.

At random I pick out MPC's offering at a place called Green-aways in Nottingham for consideration. Booking.com describes the hotel as being less than a ten-minute walk from the city's sights, situated in two acres of Victorian gardens and with compact but well-designed accommodation, a reception and a vending machine for drinks and snacks. Although the place sounds quite pleasant and is a steal for such a central location, the customer feedback is less than pleasing. Put it this way, the quotes are not the kind to plaster across any promotional material, unless you happened to be experimenting with a weirdly perverse type of marketing strategy:

*Filthy stains on carpet… Hair on sheets… Light hanging off wall… When I telephoned to ask for a refund the MPC representative hung up.*

I try The Grange instead, depicted as being a stone's throw from Marble Arch and the perfect budget option for a break in the nation's capital. Gheorghe from Romania, however, does not share this opinion, with an impressively evocative turn of phrase he calls it '*a dirty horse stable that smelled of drugs.*'

I take a slug of wine, determined to find more flattering feedback, different comments that will stop the escalation of mathematics happening inside my head, the two plus twos that are snowballing down the side of the hill, making four, then six, then eight…

'They all expect too much.'

The sentence, low and toneless is delivered close to my left ear. My posture snaps upright.

Angus is beside me, his head hovering near my own. He is positioned so close that the breath of his voice is warm on my neck. I can smell coffee and a warm hint of peat from something like brandy or whisky. I suppose I must have been lost in concentration, but I am surprised nonetheless that I didn't notice him come in, that I didn't hear the scrape of his key, the thunk of the shutting door. Unless, of course, he got home earlier and has been upstairs all the time.

Angus leans forward, puts his finger on the mouse and scrolls quickly down the stack of reviews. 'Thirty quid a night, the middle of London, and they want a room like the Ritz.' His lips curl down with distaste, or maybe his reaction is just plain disappointment. 'Here' – he stops abruptly at an unexpected four-star review – '*Good value as a place to crash after a piss-up,*' he reads out loud. 'Finally, somebody who understands that in this world you get what you pay for. There's nowhere else as cheap to stay in London. It's a fucking bargain.'

'I thought you said they were boutique hotels,' I say quietly.

'Boutique was your word, Claire, not mine.' Angus lifts his hand from the keyboard, returns it to his side as if he is standing sentry. 'I simply told you the hotels were small and located in city centres. *You* called them boutique, *you* added the gloss.'

I can't now remember if this is true or not. Even if Angus is right I could point out that he has never once corrected my impression; informed me that the real nature of his business is running a string of inner-city shitholes.

'Besides,' Angus says, with a kind of belligerence that is almost pride, 'what does it matter as long as they make money? I found a gap in the market, and I filled it. The big hotels might provide posh sheets and room service, but it doesn't stop them paying their workers a fucking pittance. Why is that any better than what I do?'

As if this is the final word on the issue he moves away from me, heading towards the kitchen and as he leaves I feel myself expanding, relaxing into the space he just vacated, although I wasn't actually aware of how tense I had become. I hear the sound of the fridge being opened, then a cupboard, the clink of moving bottles. A few moments later, Angus emerges from the archway that separates the kitchen from the sitting room. He is holding a glass of the Sauvignon, knuckles bleached from the intensity of his grip.

He watches me watching the screen, although I'm only pretending to look at it now, regarding him from the corner of my eye instead. I'm certain Google has more secrets to spill but I'm not going to unpack the clues in front of Angus, lay them out as if I am emptying the contents of a picnic basket onto a rug.

'Shall we go out, now you're home?' he says. The rapid change of subject is clearly deliberate, while his turn of phrase increases my suspicion that he might already have been waiting upstairs when I returned from my adventures in Newham.

Before I can reply my mobile begins to buzz. It is resting, face-up, beside my computer. I must have switched off the ringtone on my way to visit Mark, not wanting to be interrupted by Pink's jaunty lyrics while encountering his girlfriend. Now my mobile is flailing on the table top, the collision of the soundwaves against the polished wood causing it to spin and buck like an insect stranded on its back.

I stare at the screen. I am sure the number plastered across it belongs to Mark. Angus follows my gaze. In my head the noise of the phone becomes louder, more desperate. In other circumstances I might have taken a perverse pleasure in ignoring Mark's summons, the discovery of new will-power, the flexing of recently acquired muscle. Although, of course, my restraint is not actually will-power at all, just the benefit of more facts. And the presence of my fiancé.

I glance at Angus whose face is impassive, inscrutable. Eventually, as it must, the insect dies. Neither Angus nor I speak, although the air is so thick with questions I think there ought to be a chemical symbol for them, like oxygen or carbon dioxide. I wait for him to ask the obvious one:

*Who was it, Claire? Why didn't you pick up?*

Instead he drains his wine. 'Are you ready?' he says and turns on his heel. 'I'll fetch your coat.'

An hour later, Angus and I are seated side by side in the cinema. Angus takes my hand into his lap; his grip is gentle but firm, as if he is holding a small furry creature such as a hamster or a guinea pig that might escape at any moment. He has picked a supernatural thriller, which strikes me as the kind of choice a teenager might make on a first date, an excuse to huddle close in the dark. I find it hard to believe that Angus shares this motivation, although during the last sixty minutes he has been unusually attentive, particularly affectionate, complimenting my hair and offering profuse and grateful thanks for my early return from Ipswich. I wonder if now that I have discovered the grubby nature of the MPC offering he feels his cover has been blown. To be honest I don't think it has been – not completely, not just yet.

Although quite recent, the film is actually a rerun of pretty much all the supernatural thrillers in the history of the world; a house built on a burial site and lots of angry dead people overreacting. There is scary music to hype up the tension and careful camera action to keep the real source of danger just out of sight. I am probably too distracted, too busy with the implications of the MPC website and my earlier arithmetic, to appreciate the subtleties of the film, the plot twists and the special effects, but the result appears to be crass and rather childish. It seems to me that the only ghosts worth worrying about are those who distort the view of the present; the ones who just like the clever cameraman prevent you from noticing the menace sitting right under your nose.

# CHAPTER TWENTY-TWO

I expect Mark to phone again during the weekend and am careful to keep my mobile switched off whenever I am with Angus. However, when I check at surreptitious moments there are no missed calls or texts.

By Sunday evening I am considering my next move, whether to contact Mark myself. I am even creating an absurd kind of 'for and against' list in my head, as though contemplating a strategic career change. This particular inventory of pros and cons involves weighing up the considerable attraction of not disclosing my immigration information against the questionable disadvantage of never – and I presume this would be the case – seeing Mark again. Even now, when my only interest should be getting to the truth behind his sleazy line of work, I am shocked to realise that I am not entirely immune, not completely invulnerable, to the recollection of his fingers on my skin, the sensation of his mouth inches from my own.

My deliberations are a complete waste of time. When I approach the departmental building on Monday morning, Mark is standing on the left-hand side of the glass-plate door. He is glancing between his wristwatch and the tide of office workers sweeping from the tube station to their high-rise desks, creating a convincing impression of someone with a pre-arranged meeting, a good reason to be there. He only fixes on the crowd – on me – as I draw near.

I half expect him to tell me I'm late, to complain that I've kept him waiting, but instead he takes hold of my elbow. 'We have to talk.' Close up his features are bruised with fatigue, his eyes threaded with spider veins.

'What about?' I say.

He steers me along the pavement and into a side alley where there is an old inn with black timbers and hanging baskets. Naturally the pub is closed, the passageway empty, the baskets devoid of flowers.

'Don't play games with me, Claire. You know what about. Have you managed to get the information I asked for?'

The pressure on my arm reminds me of coming home to find him in my kitchen, the shock of finding the white-haired man and his mate on the front step, the slam of the door. The way Mark looked at me, like Daniel used to do, before he led me upstairs.

I nod, briefly, let his grip relax, before I add, 'But I don't have it with me.'

'Where is it then?'

'At home,' I lie. 'How was I to know,' I say, watching his face tighten, 'that you would come here today?'

'I need those names. I need them very quickly.' His voice is a mixture of distinct emotions. I can hear fear, desperation and menace – there is definitely the sense of threat a fraction below the surface.

'Why?' I ask.

The question must catch him off guard because he retracts very slightly.

'Why,' I persist, 'is it so important to have them right now?'

'I told you before, it's how I earn my living.'

'Recruiting website designers? These placements you need to make must be very urgent—'

'You saw the letter from the bank.' His gaze has drifted to the wall behind my shoulder.

For a moment neither of us speak, then I say, 'Did you send me a WhatsApp message?'

Mark's attention snaps back to me. 'What kind of message?'

'An unpleasant one,' I say curtly.

He shakes his head slowly. 'Nothing to do with me.' He looks at me curiously, eyes narrowed. 'Poking around in matters that don't concern you can be dangerous, Claire. Best to steer clear.'

I jiggle my elbow loose, wait for him to release it completely, before saying, 'I'll let you know a time and place to meet.'

'When?'

Already, I can tell he is anxious to reinstate his grip, to resort to a physical form of power. His signet ring is practically twitching with impatience.

'Soon.' I start to walk briskly towards the normality of the main road.

The game – *his* game – is becoming clearer. A skilled job – in website design, to take a random example – can get you a UK visa. And if you have the right to stay and want to bring your family here too, all you have to demonstrate is a high enough salary. So if you're not actually a website designer what you need is somebody to give you a nice pretend job, along with some convincing fake pay slips and bank details. Who would take such a risk? Probably quite a lot of people, particularly someone who has lost their case and is desperate to make another application to the Home Office, to have a second bite at the cherry. They would probably pay every penny they could lay their hands on for one last chance to stay in the grey, rainy UK. The question is, what happens to them after the lies have been told, after they've used the false documents in their applications, or in court? When the fraud being found out would mean them losing absolutely everything.

At the corner I stop and gaze back over my shoulder. Mark is slumped against the facade of the old pub, texting fiercely. 'By the way…'

His head lifts; face open with surprise.

I pause, arch my brows. 'Nice choice of slippers.'

*

I can tell something is up the moment the lift opens. The door to Maggie's office is closed and instead of sitting at their desks or gathering in the kitchen my colleagues are cloistered in groups of three or four and whispering urgently. Only Agatha is sitting down, alone, and she gets up as soon as she sees me, beckoning me across the room with all the subtlety of a newly promoted traffic cop.

'Claire, come here! Something awful has happened!' she says as soon as I reach the vicinity of her desk.

'Really?' I say warily. Agatha's cheeks are blotched pink and she is clutching a balled-up tissue. My first thought is that Maggie or Katy has had some horrible accident and then the obvious occurs to me, that the individual most likely to elicit Agatha's tears is the very same person who has not been at work during the last week. As Agatha opens her mouth to reply, I say, 'Is it Nigel?'

She nods vigorously. 'How did you know?'

Ignoring the question, I start to unfasten my mac. 'What's happened?' I say matter-of-factly. 'Is he dead?'

Agatha's cheeks drain white like a plug has been pulled. 'What?' she says in shocked tones. 'No, he's not dead!' She pauses and plucks my sleeve, as if to reboot the dramatic narrative. 'He's been suspended!'

'Oh?'

'Actually, it's worse than that! Apparently the police want to question him but they can't find him and he's not returning anyone's calls!'

'Didn't Maggie have a meeting with him? When she suspended him?'

'No! She sent him a letter. Although his desk has been cleared of personal stuff he hasn't been in work at all. Not since the Friday of my birthday.' Agatha stops suddenly and blushes at the memory.

I think about the evening at Kelly's too, but not for the same reasons. I'm recalling Nigel's odd comment when I was dousing him with vodka. *How glad he was that he wouldn't see me again.* He must have known then that he wasn't coming back. At least not during office hours.

'What do the police want to ask him about?'

'I'm not sure,' Agatha draws a jagged breath. After a second, she says in a quiet voice, even though Nigel is all anyone is talking about, 'I think Jane has an idea. She said that when Maggie was searching for the report Nigel was supposed to have done for the team meeting last week she found something in one of his desk drawers.'

'What kind of thing? Do you mean a weapon?' I imagine Maggie opening Nigel's bottom drawer and discovering a Glock 17 nestling amongst the printouts of case reports from the Upper Tribunal.

Agatha shakes her head. 'No, it was nothing like that. Apparently, Maggie found these strange lists.'

Like a slamming door I remember that it was Nigel who introduced me to Angus at the immigration conference. 'Lists of what?' I say carefully. My fingers have come to a halt on my final coat button.

'Names. Names and addresses. And you'll never guess the weirdest thing—'

Actually, I think I might.

'… Jane says they all seem to be connected with people who have lost their appeals in the tribunal.'

For the next hour or two I make sure to appear absorbed by the preparation for my next batch of cases. Every so often I am aware of Agatha lifting her gaze, watching, waiting to see if I do the same, before returning to her own work with a sigh. Eventually, at about eleven o'clock, she pushes back her chair.

'I'm going to get a coffee. Do you want one?'

Before I can reply she hurries towards the kitchen and I see that the timing is deliberate, to coincide with Jane, who appears to be taking roughly her eleventh break of the morning, each time accompanied by a different collection of groupies.

I could tell them they are focusing on the wrong person, that I very much doubt Nigel will ever read Maggie's suspension letter or answer the police's questions. My guess is that he has already left the country. I suspect I could also provide Jane's eager entourage with a much fuller account of Nigel's transgressions than she can, set them in their proper context. Not that I could yet quite provide chapter and verse, but like one of those quiz games in which the image fills in progressively, telltale pixel by telltale pixel, little by little the picture is coming into view.

While Agatha is hovering around Jane, I reflect on the contents of my own desk drawer, the lists of names and addresses for Mark that, unlike Nigel, I have had the sense to keep safely under lock and key. If I were determined to maximise the commercial potential of that material, to exploit its revenue-making capacity, I consider where a suitable location might be to make that happen, to put the show on the road – so to speak.

And then I text Mark.

# CHAPTER TWENTY-THREE

The young woman in my case the following day comes from China. Slight and dark, she is in her twenties and was recently arrested for being an illegal immigrant. However, oddly, she now appears to be saying that in fact she arrived in the UK more than six years ago.

'What have you been doing since then?' I ask.

'Working,' she replies. She is giving her evidence in Cantonese with the aid of an interpreter since she doesn't appear to have picked up any English during her extended stay.

'Doing what?'

'I lived with a family. I looked after the children and the house.'

'How did you find the job?'

She blinks at me as if she doesn't understand the question.

'Did you have to apply for it? Was it advertised?'

'I had a telephone number.'

'Who gave you that number?'

'The people who brought me to the UK, they gave me the number and told me to call it.'

'How much did you pay these people?'

There is more blinking. I repeat the question. 'How much did your family pay the people who brought you to this country?'

The young woman says something to the interpreter who replies in Cantonese.

'Don't talk amongst yourselves,' the judge says, sounding slightly tetchy. 'If you've something to say you must tell the court.'

She speaks again, looking at the interpreter throughout. 'My family didn't pay anything. The people took me because my uncle owed them money.'

Nobody says a word. Outside, surly grey rain is dripping down the windows, and the courtroom lights are blazing although it is 11.00 a.m.

After a second or two the judge clears his throat. 'Do you mean,' he says, 'that your uncle *gave* you to these people instead of money, as a way to settle his debt?'

There is a fractional pause.

'Yes.'

'And did the family you worked for in this country pay you anything?' the judge asks, rather pointlessly, because now we all see the nature of the beast that has entered the courtroom.

The young woman naturally shakes her head.

'You must talk out loud,' the judge says, although his voice is much gentler, 'for the court record.'

'I didn't get paid any money, but I was given food.'

The judge sighs sadly, and nods at me to continue my interrogation.

'Why didn't you leave or call the police?'

The woman answers rapidly, her intonation rising, as if she can't believe the stupidity of my questions. 'The family had my passport and I couldn't call the police because I was not allowed to be in this country.'

'So how *did* you come to leave the family?'

'One day they asked me to go to the shop. Instead of going to the shop I kept walking.'

'Without your passport?'

'Yes.'

There is another small silence while, I think, we are all imagining walking into a foreign, friendless town, probably with no more money in our pocket than the cost of a pint of milk or a loaf of bread.

The judge leans forwards. 'Where did you live? What did you do?'

'I earned money from different jobs. They weren't very nice.'

We wait for her to elaborate, but she doesn't. Instead her eyes fog as if she is no longer seeing us or the courtroom, but a more horrific scene altogether. Whatever line of work she was driven to pursue I suspect it was not an improvement on her years of domestic servitude.

Clearly troubled, the judge turns to me in exasperation. 'Why hasn't there been a referral in this case?' He means a referral under the national mechanism for identifying victims of modern-day slavery. The answer is because as far as I know this is the first time the background to the case has ever been revealed. I glare at the young woman's representative who really should have found this out, but strangely he has become too preoccupied with his files to notice.

I tell the judge I need to call the office, knowing full well what Maggie will say and sure enough within ten minutes the case has been adjourned so that the proper procedures can be followed. When the judge explains what is happening the young woman barely reacts. Although she must be relieved that the day of reckoning has been postponed, that finally she might get some sort of help, her expression is blank. Years of practice, I suspect.

The weather doesn't let up all day and by 7.00 p.m. a steady downpour is hammering the outside of my raincoat, pinpointing the gap between collar and neck with the accuracy of miniature Exocet missiles. I could pull up my hood, but I'm rather enjoying the sensation of rain on my face, turning my hair into slick, dark ropes. It suits my mood.

At the top end of Oxford Street the retail carnival of Christmas is fully underway, lights and lanterns strung high across the traffic and the pavements packed with shoppers clamouring for cabs. However, as I venture further north the roads soon become quiet, with firmly closed doors and drawn curtains. According to the reservation website, The Grange is supposed to be a ten-minute stroll from Marble Arch, however it takes at least twenty minutes of fast walking before the building finally emerges out of the gloom close to the Marylebone Flyover.

I spot Mark before he sees me. He is waiting, shoulders hunched, staring directly into the rain from the protection of a small, dimly lit porch. As I approach he straightens and takes his hands from his pocket.

'Why the hell did you want to meet me here?'

I shrug and step into the entrance. 'It seemed as good a place as any.'

Mark blinks. For a second, I think he is about to ask me something searching, but all he says is, 'Have you got the lists?'

The doorway is so small we are standing close together, the rain inches from our faces, smacking into the tarmac with a hypnotic rattle. It is almost like being beside a waterfall, in other circumstances it might be quite romantic.

'Do you want to go inside?' I say.

'Why would I want to do that?' He looks at me quizzically. The shadows gouging the hollows of his eyes and cheeks seem further pronounced than before, the whites of his eyes more compromised, the face of someone on the run, or at least with his back to the wall.

I touch his shoulder through the sodden fabric of his mac. 'It's a hotel. There must be rooms. I thought you might, you know' – I gesture with my head towards the interior – 'want to find somewhere?'

He stares at me as if I have physically shoved him off-balance, all sense of orientation gone. I watch him attempt to read my expression in the half-light of a low-energy bulb and I smile encouragingly. Inch by inch he leans forward, tilting his head, directing his mouth towards mine.

See how easy it is?

I wait until I can smell his breath, the point at which his lips are on the point of skimming mine before I step backwards. 'For Christ's sake, I was joking!'

He gapes at me with a bemused kind of anger.

'I thought you might be keen to see the place. Check it over.' My tone is light and sarcastic. 'Make sure it's fit for purpose. Your purpose and Angus's purpose. Whatever it is, you're obviously in this together.' My heart is beating faster than I would like. To my surprise, moving away, rejecting his kiss, still requires a small effort of will.

'Whatever you think you know,' Mark says slowly, 'you're wrong.'

'I'm guessing you asked me for this list of names the moment you realised that Nigel had scarpered. You had to turn to me because I was the only person, the only goose, left in the department who could possibly lay the golden eggs for whatever blackmail racket you're involved in.'

Mark looks briefly into the rain, as if to check we are still alone. Or maybe there is something about the rain and the sense of obliteration it offers that is appealing. 'I have no idea what you're talking about. Who the hell is Nigel?' The ice in his voice matches his expression.

I don't reply. I never have played poker. Bluffs and counter-bluffs are not my strongest suit. Besides, I'm too busy absorbing the fact that Mark didn't deny knowing Angus.

While the silence expands a phone begins to trill from somewhere deep within Mark's coat. He hesitates before belatedly moving his hand towards the lining just as the ringing stops. I wonder if the caller was Malee, waiting amongst the packing cases for Mark to come back and take her and their child God knows where.

As if confirming my theory, Mark says, 'I have to go. Give me the information you promised. That's the reason we're here.'

I reach into my handbag. At first the papers elude me amongst the rest of the junk. As I root around, Mark explodes, the panicked reaction of a man who sees I am no longer his easy pushover. 'If you're pissing me about, Claire…?'

'I'm not.' I finally pull out the clip with a flourish. 'Here.' I pass the pages to him with as much nonchalance as I can muster.

Mark's face is black with anticipated fury, however his scowl lightens as he glances down the list of names and addresses. After a moment he folds the sheets in half and stuffs them into the right-hand pocket of his coat. 'Right.' He looks at me a long moment before suddenly leaning forward and cupping his hand around the back of my skull.

I feel the pressure of his fingers hard against the bone, holding it still. Then he lowers his head and pushes his mouth against mine. His lips are firm and dry and smell of alcohol. I keep my own lips closed and my eyes open. As farewell kisses go, it wouldn't make one of the top-ten movie greats.

As soon as he stands up, I ostentatiously wipe the back of my hand across my face. 'Are you off?' My voice is intentionally casual.

He nods.

I half-pivot towards the entrance into the building. 'Not coming with me, then?'

He frowns. 'Why are you going in there?'

'Thought I'd have a look around.'

'There's no public access.' He motions at the keypad on the wall.

'I know the code.'

Stepping out of the porch, he shrugs. 'You're crazy.' Already the rain is running in rivulets over his forehead and cheeks. He lifts up a hand. 'Goodbye, Claire,' he says, and walks away into the dark.

I wait for his outline to blur and then vanish completely before I open my handbag again. My phone contains a note of the four-digit entrance code that was emailed to me when I made my reservation earlier today. A night in The Grange, an investment of thirty quid just to get in the door and see what I can find – give the roulette wheel a good old spin.

As if I might want to change my mind, place a wiser bet perhaps, the entry mechanism doesn't work until my third attempt and once I step inside the tiled hallway reeks of cigarettes and weed. I fumble on the wall to find a light but pressing the switch has no impact on the blanket of dark. Using the torch on my mobile I make my way slowly down the corridor, illuminating the plastic numbering that is stuck at drunken angles on the doors. The only sound is the ringing stamp of my footsteps, the hotel itself appears empty – a hollow, filthy shell. Or perhaps I've arrived earlier than most of the normal clientele.

Although my booking is for room 9 I reach a dead end and the opposite side of the building without getting any further than room 6. Retracing my steps, however, reveals a narrow staircase that bends in a right-angled corkscrew to an upper floor. At the top, I spot the first hint of life – a thin bead of light is leaking from under the door to room 7. Stopping outside, I listen, but there is no sign of an occupant, no chatter from a television or the rustle of somebody moving around. No trace of even the small murmurs of sleep or sighs or breath. After a few moments I give up.

Room 9 is not locked, however there is a key on the inside of the door, which suggests, rather worryingly, that the priority of most of the hotel's clients is locking themselves in, rather than securing the place when they leave. I also find a lamp on a bedside table. To my relief this bulb is not broken and a weak flush of yellow reveals the full extent of my surroundings. It's safe to say the decor is not the work of an expert. The walls are the colour of sludge, while the window is curtain-less, boasting an array of dead insects scattered over the sill. Although the floor is covered by thin carpet the yarn is pockmarked with burn marks, and an ancient, ugly radiator appears to be smeared with a brown substance that doesn't bear close examination. At least, from the icy temperature of the room, it's apparent that nobody has turned on the heating.

I perch on the edge of the mattress. The duvet is grubby and doubled back on itself as though untouched since the last occupant climbed out of bed. I wouldn't spend the night here if somebody paid me to and I don't imagine that anyone else would either. However Angus makes his money it can't possibly be from repeat business. Instinctively I gather up the cover and straighten the edge over the rank-looking pillow. As I conduct my housekeeping service, a scrap of fabric, a tail of something black falls from the folds of the cheap polyester.

Picking up the item between my thumb and forefinger, I realise the article is not unfamiliar. Small, stretchy and made of nylon, the thong bears a striking similarity to the piece of underwear I found in our bathroom. I stare at the knickers, mind and stomach heaving. Angus obviously has no need to venture to Germany to acquire such an item after all – he clearly has the same opportunities from business trips much closer to home, an explanation that is frankly far more plausible than a mix-up by the laundry service in a Frankfurt hotel.

After a moment or two I toss the thong across the room where it tumbles into a little black puddle beside the radiator. Then I get up and go to the window. Although the glow from the lamp restricts my vision I can tell the view is of a yard with a handful of parking bays and a gate that leads to a pedestrian walkway. As I watch, the interior lights from the closest car go out. Two men are walking away from the vehicle and they disappear around the edge of the building towards the entrance.

I move to the bedroom door, open it a few inches and peer through the gap into the corridor. Muffled voices float indistinctly from the floor beneath, as well as something else – I think I can make out the broken sobs of someone crying, but the weeping is so fragile and my ears so full of my own heartbeat that the distress might simply be my imagination. The conversation below peters out. Instead I hear the clump of boots or heavy shoes begin to echo on the stairs.

I shut the door, turning the key as quietly as possible. The footsteps become louder and more certain and then stop directly outside my room. I watch with horrified fascination as the china knob rotates fractionally before being halted by the lock. The grip is released, another futile effort attempted and then the door judders violently as somebody shakes the handle.

'It won't fucking open! Here' – fists pound on the wood – 'what the fuck are you playing at?'

I tiptoe back to the bed and sit on my hands. The panelling trembles again, a well-aimed foot this time, I think. Just as I am wondering if my visitors actually intend to kick down the barrier, a different male voice says, 'Is this the right room?'

'The fucking light is on—'

'Yeah, but…'

Someone takes a few paces and stops a short distance away.

A pause.

The rap of knuckles followed by the snap of a catch opening. Then, 'It's in here, dickhead.'

More footsteps, the clunk of a closing door.

The new tranquillity lasts less than a second. A song blares suddenly through the walls followed on its heels by the chummy tone of a DJ. Unbelievably it sounds very much like Radio 2, with the volume turned so high the presenter could be sitting next to me on the bed. I study an oval stain on the duvet, a grey lump of gum stuck on the headboard. Ed Sheeran is singing now, melodic and mild, but we've all seen the films, we know the ruse, a blackboard duster of music to rub out – annihilate – less lyrical noises. It doesn't take a brain surgeon to work out what's going on, and I don't think it's a meeting of the Ed Sheeran fan club.

I get up. I find I am shivering, although that might simply be my damp coat and the lack of heating. The key turns with a soft click and I consider the empty passageway. A pale flood of light is spilling from the entrance to room 7 where, to my surprise, the door is standing ajar. I listen, ears straining, but I can't hear anything apart from the racket of the radio – Coldplay, now – that fills the landing as effectively as sand. I take off my shoes – black, court, the trappings of a uniform from another universe – and creep slowly along the landing, carrying them by their straps.

Outside room 7, I halt and peek through the space between the wall and the edge of the door. Oddly, I can smell something sweet, possibly floral, like fruit or flowers, but all I can see is the end of a bed, a duvet half-crumpled on the floor, and beyond the mattress a window, part of which has been boarded up. And still the only audible voice belongs to Chris Martin.

I wait, breathing quietly and trying not to shift position. Nothing – nobody – in the room is moving. After a moment I push the door lightly to make it swing slowly on its hinges, which it does with a long and ghost-worthy creak.

For two, possibly three, seconds I think the woman on the bed is dead. Lying corpse-like on her back, she is wearing a translucent baby-doll nightdress rucked high around her thighs while chunks of dark hair are clumped around her head. She looks as if she has drowned, been pulled, too late, from a river full of pondweed and then abandoned on the bank.

All at once she sits bolt upright and stares at me with a bright, unfocused gaze. For a moment or two we simply gape at each other and then she opens her mouth and says something I can't hear because of the song that is screaming from the radio beside the bed.

I gesture towards the noise. She follows the direction of my hand and after a moment of indecision reaches out her arm to switch off the machine. Silence arrives like a double-decker bus, its presence as loud as the music had been.

'Who are you?' she says and swings her legs to the floor as if she thinks she might soon need to run. Her voice has an accent, but I can't identify it.

'Claire,' I say. 'My name is Claire.' The words sound brash and naked in the sudden vacuum.

Her head tilts to one side as she examines me through huge pupils, her eyes flicking to the shoes dangling from my hand and back to my face. I spot a bruise, a purple handprint spreading across her left cheek.

'Why are you here? What do you want?'

'I've come' – I pause – 'I've come to help.'

She laughs, although the actual noise that comes out of her mouth is devoid of humour. 'Do I know you? Have we met before?'

I realise the reason I am struggling to decipher her accent is because her speech is slurred, the questions sound as if they are being dragged across the floor.

I shake my head. In actual fact, there is something hazily familiar about her face, but the notion is too elusive, too uncertain to trust.

'Then go away.'

'I—'

'I don't need your help.' She drops her gaze to the scrub of carpet under her feet.

For a while neither of us speak. Then I say, 'Who are they? Who are the people making you do this?'

She doesn't reply. Instead she closes her eyes. Her forehead gleams with perspiration, dark skin turned the colour of putty by the glare of the overhead light. 'You can't help,' she says quietly. 'Nobody can.'

'I could go to the police.'

'No!' Her eyelids fly open. 'No police.' She levers herself up from the mattress and begins to stagger towards me. 'You mustn't tell the police. Promise me…' She stops, swaying slightly in the middle of the room. Her breasts and nipples, the tight whorl of curls at the top of her legs, are all visible through the inadequate nightdress.

'OK,' I say. 'It's OK. I won't call the police.'

The smell of flowers seems stronger, although I doubt there is anything genuinely floral for miles.

I hold out my hand. 'Why don't you come with me?' The offer is sincere even if the idea of my beautiful home as a place of refuge, a sanctuary from the world, seems to be fast disintegrating.

She studies me, head on one side as if there might be something she recognises about me too. Then she takes a step, a hesitant, shaky step closer.

Voices and footsteps surge suddenly from the corridor.

'I told you it was in the car. You're fucking paranoid. She's probably scarpered by now.'

'She won't have gone anywhere. She's knows what will happen if she does.'

'Get out.' The woman makes an urgent flapping motion with her wrist.

I glance behind me.

'Go!' Her eyes are saucers of fear, fixed now on the open door. 'Go!'

As I slip into the hallway two male figures emerge from the top of the staircase. Putting my head down, I walk quickly.

We are about to pass each other when one of the men steps directly in front of me. He is squat and stocky with a small red tattoo on the side of his neck, something like a scorpion or a spider that quivers in time with his pulse. His mate is taller and either has terrible acne or a skin disfigurement, it's hard to tell since the only illumination is the wedge of light oozing from room 7.

'Hey!' Spiderman stabs his finger into my chest. 'Who the fuck are you?'

I imagine the woman in her baby-doll nightie waiting on the bed for the pair of them. Anger shifts under my skin like water trapped under ice.

'Who the fuck wants to know?'

Spiderman raises his eyebrows with theatrical exaggeration and leers at his mate. 'Feisty, isn't she?' Then his expression changes, becomes – astoundingly – even uglier, and he thrusts his face right into mine. 'Watch yourself. Nice girls like you need to be careful.'

I drop my gaze.

Timing is everything. I count to three. 'Right,' I say. 'Sorry. May I get past?'

'Say fucking *please*.' Spiderman is so close his breath is tickling the inner skin of my ear and the reek of beer is overwhelming. It's as much as I can do not to jerk away my head.

'Please,' I repeat. Obediently. Demurely.

A good girl.

He nods at me slowly, approvingly, a smug little smirk contorting his lips. I wait for him to stick his hands in his pockets and shift himself sideways, until he is off guard entirely, before I draw back my knee and drive the bone hard and fast into his groin.

There is an animal-like scream that is white with pain as he doubles over, clutching his crotch.

'Jesus! Fucking bitch!' His mate, Scarface, makes a grab for my hair, but I've already dropped my shoes and I'm pitching forwards, aiming for the stairwell.

It's supposed to be easy. I am young and pretty fast, and Scarface is pretty pissed and several beats behind the music. However, without shoes my feet have no purchase on the shiny surface of the tiled floor. Instead of sprinting, I have to half-run and half-skate in order not to lose my footing. My handbag thumps against my chest as I reach the stairs first, but Scarface is close and getting closer.

Throwing myself down the dark steps, I hear Scarface crashing into the corners and swearing behind me. I trail one hand along the wall for balance, praying I won't slip, that those grasping arms won't haul me backwards. I reach the bottom and the front door beckons at the end of the corridor, the outline glimmering from the beam of the porch bulb through a small high window. I race forwards and feel my left ankle slide from underneath me. For an instant the hallway hangs off kilter, listing like a ship, before the floor rises up to whack my knees and elbow. I don't notice the pain. I am too aware of Scarface, his proximity, his hands that are stretching, desperate for some part of me to grab.

As I haul myself upright and lunge towards the exit, I suddenly panic that the entry system might be the kind that requires a code to get out of, as well as into, the building. If it doesn't I should make the door slightly ahead of my pursuer. If I have to stop and punch in those four little numbers, well, then I am in serious trouble.

I reach out one arm; clasp my fingers around the cold metallic handle, and pull. When I meet resistance, when for that first split second the door doesn't move, won't budge on its hinge, fear slices through me like a blade even as the catch begins to give and then all at once releases.

Head down, I sprint – properly now, on the sweet, sticky gravel – towards the road. The rain is coming down faster than ever. For some reason I think of stair rods. My mother describing a deluge as '*coming down like stair rods*'. No idea what stair rods are, but the water is falling continuously, being blown at me sideways in furious squalls.

Scarface bellows behind me, his voice rough with fury. 'Stop that fucking bitch!'

I hear the injunction, register the meaning, the implication of the entreaty almost too late and look up to see a man in a raincoat standing directly in my path, ten or fifteen metres away. For a fraction of a second the connection between my powers of observation and my brain breaks down. I clock the height, the shape of the man, the way he is standing with his chin jutting forwards, his collar lifted, yet I am unable to connect together the pieces, to recognise my fiancé, until Angus opens his arms and calls my name.

'Claire!'

I am not aware of making the decision – of processing thoughts – at least with my head. My body, my instinct, does it for me, before I am even conscious of trying to decipher the complicated expression burning in Angus's eyes.

I pivot on my heels and race away from him, darting around a couple of old conifer trees towards the back of the hotel where the cars are parked in the yard. I can hear him yelling after me, shouting to come back, but already he seems far away, his voice drowned by the rush of the November rain and wind.

When I reach the pedestrian gate I glance, briefly, over my shoulder. There is no sign of Scarface, or Angus either. Yet still I keep running, following the tarmacked path on sodden feet, dodging the dog turds and mushed piles of cardboard packaging. I don't stop until I reach a main thoroughfare where traffic is cruising up and down, spraying pedestrians with the water glazing the road.

I jog over to a bus shelter and tuck myself against the inside frame. Leaning forward, I press my palms on my thighs and gulp the damp London air that tastes almost fresh after the rancid atmosphere of The Grange. My chest is raw and aching. Too many days sitting at a desk – I'm obviously not as fit as I thought. Angus's face floats in front of my eyes, unreadable, inscrutable. Even though I am hot and sweating, I shiver at the memory, and as I tremble a little piece of memory shakes into place. Perhaps, I had already made the connection, somewhere in the deeper levels of my conscience, when I swerved around Angus and those deceptive, welcoming, outstretched arms.

I know now why the woman in the room was familiar. I remember where we have seen each other before. She was the Indian woman with the too-bright, over-eager smile. The one who lied to the Immigration Tribunal about her job and salary, whose deceit was unpicked by the judge scrolling so carefully, so smugly, through her WhatsApp messages. I picture the mask of hopelessness on her face, the panic when I suggested calling the police. I don't think she was all dressed up in her baby-doll nightdress for the money. I'm guessing she was there because she had no choice. Because somebody has convinced her if she doesn't play ball, she and her family will be in very deep shit indeed.

Mucus, the gummy embodiment of disgust, swells in my throat and I spit onto the asphalt. If my stomach was not empty I could vomit properly, try to purge myself of the contamination.

I notice that I'm being watched. Out of the corner of my eye I see a middle-aged woman rooted wisely at the opposite end of the shelter from me. Tired and bedraggled and weighed down with two Iceland carrier bags she nevertheless appears mesmerised by my appearance on the scene. I assume she is examining with disapproval the yellow lump of gob I regurgitated a moment ago. Then I understand she is actually fixing on the place where my shoes would be if I happened to be wearing them.

I track her gaze. A pinkish puddle is forming around my left heel where the blood from a scrape is being diluted by my sodden tights. Otherwise my feet are black, the tideline of dirt rising above my ankle. They are also very wet, very sore and beginning to feel very cold.

The woman shifts her interest to my face then quickly drags her attention away. Nobody in London puts a difficult question to a stranger. They might get an answer that requires them to do something to help.

'I dropped my shoes,' I volunteer, which is true, but hardly a comprehensive explanation.

'Oh.' Since I have spoken, the Iceland woman is obliged to notice me again. Her gaze flicks momentarily, unwittingly, to my feet once more before she quickly immerses herself in the timetable attached to the back wall.

A minute or two later a bus arrives. I get on without bothering to check the destination. Any port in a storm. The Iceland woman appears about to follow me aboard but changes her mind – another ten-minute wait at a freezing shelter is obviously preferable to travelling alongside a shoeless madwoman. The driver huffs impatiently while I dig my Oyster card out of my handbag, however at least he doesn't look at me, let alone my feet. He stares vacantly at his windscreen wipers, which are trying valiantly but unsuccessfully to keep the rain at bay.

I move towards an empty seat, ducking the gaze of other passengers. Not that avoidance is difficult, since they are all immersed in their phones or some other solitary world. I hear the engine engage into gear, the tick of the indicator, the steady beat sounding like the second hand of a clock, a countdown. As the bus pulls out into the traffic, I see a man emerge from the footpath. Ignoring the rain he begins to walk one way before changing his mind and heading towards the shelter. He looks towards the bus as it passes him, his focus vague, preoccupied, then all at once bitingly sharp.

Fleetingly, Angus and I lock eyes through the moving window. I see a stranger. I wonder if he sees a stranger too.

Sinking onto the grubby cushion I rest my head against the glass. My skull is thumping, my body losing adrenaline like blood pumping from an artery and filling instead with a smouldering kind of exhaustion. I close my eyes, but although I can block out the filthy night outside I can't prevent the final pieces of the puzzle assembling inside my head. However many times I prize the pieces apart and attempt to fashion a different picture, the end result is always the same.

After a while I draw my phone out of my pocket. Out of curiosity more than anything else. There are three missed calls from Angus and an urgent flurry of texts, the general gist of which professes bewilderment and concern at my actions.

While I am staring at his messages my ringtone jumps to life. *Mark.*

I hesitate, and then answer.

'Where are you? Are you in the hotel?'

'No. I'm on a bus.' I squint outside but there is nothing except traffic and rain, no way to distinguish my precise location.

'Did you tell Angus you were going to The Grange?'

I don't reply. The answer to the question is no, but either Angus found out or he happened to be there. It probably makes no difference one way or the other.

'Look, I think I saw him in the car park. And if he finds you there… if he thinks you know what goes on there…' Mark's voice dies away as he seems at a loss for what to say. All I can hear is the sound of his footsteps, fast on the road.

'What?' I prompt.

'I'm warning you, Claire. Don't go home.'

He hangs up before I have a chance to respond. That's my lot. I suppose I ought to be touched at his concern.

I put my phone back in my bag. I have no intention of going home. However, I probably ought to find out where the hell I *am* going.

I make my way down the gangway to the driver. I get as far as, 'Excuse me, where…' before he points with a scowl of satisfaction at a small square notice pinned on the Perspex divider.

*Don't speak to the driver when the bus is in motion.*

Obviously formulating a sentence and navigating the London traffic is a form of multitasking frowned upon by Transport for London.

'Uxbridge,' says a voice behind me. 'It's number 207 and it's going to Uxbridge.'

I turn around. The words belong to a bearded man whose trousers and long beige tunic are plainly visible under his open coat.

'Thanks,' I say. Sitting down I Google the route of the number 207 and am rewarded with the first piece of luck I've received in quite a while – it goes straight through Hanwell. I am just returning my phone to my bag when I feel a tap on my arm. The bearded man is holding out something small and dazzlingly white.

'Take this,' he says, handing me a handkerchief. He nods at the blood smears on the floor of the bus. 'For your foot.'

About an hour later we reach Hanwell Broadway. As soon as I see the Asian supermarket, the bustle of business behind the plate-glass windows, I stop the bus and a minute later I'm standing outside the entrance to Agatha's flat. Although the deluge has reduced to a drizzle the pavement is awash with puddles. My feet are newly soaked and the cold has slunk up my calves and thighs, inhabiting the whole of my body. When I press the intercom buzzer I find my right hand is shaking so violently I have to steady my wrist with my other hand.

'Claire?' Agatha sounds incredulous, as well she might. '*Of course* you can come in.'

The door buzzes open and I meet her halfway up the steep staircase, as she is hurrying down. At the sight of me, her eyes become wide as a rabbit's. 'Oh my God, Claire. What's going on? What on earth happened to you?'

'It's a long story,' I say.

Agatha nods once, a single deliberate movement. Questions are bursting from the pores of her skin, I can practically see them written in cartoon-like bubbles around her head. However she manages not to ask any more until I'm sitting on her sofa with a cushion embroidered with a country cottage behind my back and my feet immersed inside a washing-up bowl of hot water and bath gel.

Handing me a small glass of something tawny, she hovers expectantly.

'Sit down,' I say.

She plops onto the sofa beside me.

'So' – I take a swig of the drink, and taste brandy that is surprisingly smooth – 'I know why Nigel had a list of names and addresses in his desk at work.'

Agatha's cheeks pale in shock. I suspect that despite all those eager, hushed conversations in the kitchen at work, given a choice right now, she would actually rather not know and keep the mystique intact.

'He's been selling them.'

'Selling them? Who to? Who on earth would want to buy them?'

I have another gulp of brandy. Feel the burn of the alcohol in my gullet. I remember the arak. Mark. Standing in the godforsaken spot by the river. Wanting to climb into his coat, inside his skin.

I glance at Agatha who is waiting, open-mouthed. 'Well, eventually to some kind of syndicate.'

'But why…?'

'So they can blackmail the women.' I drain my glass and then say, rather quickly, 'I think that syndicate includes and might even be run by my fiancé.'

Agatha blinks. 'Angus?'

'Yeah, Angus.' I am slightly surprised she remembers his name.

Agatha stares at me. She is sitting so still I can see her ribcage rising and falling with each breath. 'What do you mean?'

'Nigel has been passing the names and addresses of people who lose their case in the tribunal to someone called Mark – I imagine he's being doing it for a while. Mark then tries to sell fake jobs and paperwork to the really desperate ones, so that they can make another application to stay in the UK. But it gets worse. Afterwards the names and addresses get sold on to Angus and his syndicate.'

Agatha's eyes remain puzzled.

'You see,' I say, 'people, particularly women, who have incriminated themselves, lied to the government and the courts by using false documents, can be blackmailed to do pretty much anything.' I think of my encounter in room 7. 'No doubt with the threat of the police and deportation. And Angus's hotels are the perfect cover for running all kinds of disgusting exploitation and blackmail operations.'

Agatha doesn't respond but her irises gradually clear and a moment or two later her voice coasts from above my head.

'Claire?' She is standing over me with the brandy bottle and sloshes another generous measure into my glass.

'I imagine,' I say slowly, 'that the real reason Angus wanted to go out with me, to marry me, was my job in the immigration service. He obviously knew Mark long before we bought the house, and when Nigel introduced us at the conference Angus probably decided it would be useful for him to have another inside contact. Someone who might provide Mark with more information for his grubby little business and so provide extra fodder for his own. I expect he was aware about Mark and me all along. God' – the brandy acidifies in my mouth – 'maybe it was Angus's idea? He probably didn't care whether Mark and I slept together – just so long as I would produce the goods if Nigel didn't.' I put my glass down carefully next to the washing-up bowl. Slosh the water around a bit and gaze at its oily, opaque surface.

'I don't think so.'

I look up.

'That can't be right, Claire.' To my surprise, Agatha is shaking her head.

'Why not?'

'Well, I don't know who Mark is,' Agatha gives me a quick, almost disapproving glance, 'but Angus is always so attentive. The way he always looks at you, like you're the only person in the room. Although he might get jealous I'm sure he loves you and that he would hate to think of you with somebody…' She stops abruptly as her face floods crimson.

For a second, neither of us speak. Agatha switches her focus to a point beyond my left shoulder, blinking rapidly.

'Agatha' – I am talking slowly, reluctant to voice the obvious – 'You haven't met Angus. You've never seen us together.'

There's no reply.

'*Have* you seen us together?'

She glances at me. Looks away again. 'Yes.'

'How?'

Agatha swallows, and all at once I anticipate exactly what she's going to say. 'I've got some photographs – just a few.'

'Of me and Angus?'

She nods unhappily. 'I saw you one Saturday, just by chance near Oxford Circus. You didn't spot me because you were too busy chatting. Angus put his arm around you. I snapped a couple of photos without even thinking. And then another time you told me you were going to a hotel the next morning before work, to discuss your wedding. I… I was in the area quite early myself,' the crimson shade of her complexion deepens, 'and as I watched you go in I took another picture.'

'OK,' I say slowly. I don't know whether to feel angry or not. The water in the washing-up bowl has cooled, my feet are beginning to chill all over again. I take them out and tuck them under me on the sofa. If I had a blanket I would wrap that round me too, nice and tight. Anything to create an illusion of security. 'Have you still got the photos? Can I see them?'

Agatha fetches her mobile and without a word taps in her code. When she passes me the phone, her demeanour is like a criminal handing in a weapon to the police. I sift through the images until I find the ones of Angus and me. A few unguarded instances caught and kept indefinitely. Agatha is right. We appear more together than I would ever have expected; we look like a regular couple. Real affection is splattered all over Angus's face. But what is a camera? An objective, insightful observer able to reveal the truth, or the easy fool of a skin-deep sham?

Preoccupied, I scroll through the gallery. Soon I reach the pictures of Nigel, the same ones I saw on Agatha's computer. I stop at the photograph of Nigel sitting outside a pub with Viktoria. Now I consider it closely I see that Viktoria doesn't appear too happy, and expanding the image actually reveals a chilled expression, a frozen combination of fear and horror. I wonder if she has just been warned about the true price she will have to pay for her nice fake visa as a skilled migrant.

'I've stopped taking pictures now.'

I raise my head.

Agatha is watching me. Her left hand is resting on her forehead and she is peering between her fingers as if she can barely look. 'I don't know why I did it. I suppose it made me feel closer to people I like…'

I nod. I guess we all want the same thing, to be close to the people we like; the trouble is sometimes we all want to be close to the same person.

I lift the screen nearer to my face. Examine the enlarged image. I have the strong impression it has more to tell me than I'm seeing right now. There is something about the photograph that unsettles me, even if I haven't understood the full import of it yet.

A ringtone interrupts my concentration. The trill from my bag is loud and urgent and when I fish out my phone I see that Angus is once again trying to get in contact with me. The call ends before I can decide whether to answer it or not. In the silent wake of the sound waves I think about Agatha's photos, the ones of me and Angus – the warmth in his eyes, his arm around my shoulder – and I wonder if, perhaps, the time has come to find out who Angus really is.

'I need to borrow some shoes,' I say to Agatha.

'What?'

Uncurling myself from the sofa, I pass her the phone. 'I have to go home.'

# CHAPTER TWENTY-FOUR

## *Five years earlier*

It is Saturday again, a whole week later.

I don't remember much about how I got home from McDonalds. I must have walked, maybe even run some of the way. I have a vague memory of Daniel following, calling my name, and me, out of breath, crying, stumbling, and a stranger catching my arm, female, concerned: *'Is everything all right? Can I help?'* I recall reaching my halls, my room, and the tiny, temporary sense of release, of sanctuary, when I climbed into bed and dragged the duvet over my head, longing to hide, wanting to disappear, needing oblivion.

For the rest of the day and most of the next I either drank or slept, steadily working through my remaining supply of room-temperature party wine. At some point I became aware of banging on my locked door, of Daniel pleading through the thin wood veneer. The sound of his voice made me want to scream – craving him and hating him at the same time for what he'd done to me, *to us*, felt like being strapped onto one of those medieval racks, a slow, inexorable ripping apart of my soul. In a strange way the agony seemed both inevitable and unreal, as if some part of me had always been expecting this nightmare, and yet as if I must – eventually – wake up. I guzzled wine until I was sick, to the point where I couldn't tell whether the words spinning in my head actually were from Daniel or the product of my frenzied imagination.

The following afternoon a bunch of red roses arrived, lustrous and velvet to the touch. Since the delivery guy refused to return them to his van I carted the bouquet into the back yard where the dustbins are kept and abandoned the long, elegant stems to rot amongst the stinking bin bags.

The next day, roses again, these ones yellow as Spanish lemons. Although I took them straight outside, this time I had a better idea than simply dumping them with the rubbish. Once it became dark I carried them to the house with the swimming pool and propped them by the front door. An apology to the owners, if you like, or maybe the gesture was more akin to a memorial wreath, marking the spot of the last evening that Daniel and I had spent together. Before leaving the flowers on the step, I removed the notecard, reckoning that whoever found them would be confused enough without the added complication of his contrite, concise message:

*'Please forgive me, I can't bear to lose you.'*

On Wednesday, it was sunflowers. That's when I started to crack. The armful of bobbing blooms made it over the threshold into my room and after watching the golden petals wilting on the table for an hour or so, I finally succumbed and stuck them into a jug of water. Thursday brought a posy of wildflowers, and Friday some large, rather posh-looking buttercups. Without a vase (no student I know owns anything quite so mumsy), my only option was to use a couple of pint mugs that were too small for the job and made the arrangements top-heavy and precarious.

Now I am holding Daniel's latest offering, delivered only a few minutes ago – a cellophane-encased spray of peonies with heavy lilac heads that are just on the point of blossoming. Since there are no more suitable receptacles I half-fill the washbasin and shove them in there.

Apart from the floral embellishments, it has to be said that my room is looking pretty rank. I guess that's what comes of spending 168 consecutive hours crying, drinking and eating crap. In addition to the unmade bed, the undrawn curtains and the distribution of clothes across the room, I can count four drained wine bottles – although there may be more – two tubs of Ben and Jerry's – again, possibly the tip of the iceberg – and God knows how many empty crisp and biscuit packets.

I open the window to let in air and sunlight and then I go in search of a bin liner. This new sense of purpose, of capability, is possible only because I am on the verge of forgiving Daniel. I have rationalised my thinking; I've convinced myself that I am acting out of compassion not weakness; understanding, not insecurity. I tell myself the constant texts and calls, the hounding, must have driven him to the edge of madness. Maybe she persuaded him that *one last time* would be all it took to make her disappear. Last night, as I lay wretched and sleepless in the pre-dawn gloom, I could almost hear her begging him to sleep with her, '*Say goodbye to me properly, Daniel, and then I'll let you go.*' He would have been horrified of course, but desperate as well – anything to get rid of her and keep us together. How could he possibly know the little witch would take the chance to accuse him of rape? The longer the scenario plays in my mind, the more certain I become that Daniel has actually been the victim in this, a foolish dupe who loves me, and needs my support now more than ever.

The small white envelope that accompanied the peonies is still sitting on my desk. After a moment's hesitation I tear it open and extract the card from inside which has written on it, simply:

'*Missing you*'

There is something else too. A note has also been stuffed in the envelope as if by way of breaking news, an update after the card had been penned. Unfolding the scrap of paper, I read:

*'Police investigation dropped. Please come back!!'*

It is enough. The creaking camel's back of my self-control shatters under the weight of this final straw. I grab an old sweatshirt and some trainers. I am already wearing jeans and a T-shirt, the same clothes I have been pulling on and off all week. There is a stain on the thigh of the jeans, which is probably wine – hopefully nothing more gross – and when I take a quick peek in the mirror above the basin I'm rather taken aback at the sight that greets me. Without make-up there's nothing to disguise the effects of a week of too much booze and sugar. My face is bloated and pasty and framed by what resembles a lank and greasy floor mop. With a twinge of disgust, I realise that I haven't bothered to wash my hair since I was in Daniel's room last Saturday morning.

I consider stopping to take a shower. However, now I have decided to go back to him, now I can see how selfish and thoughtless I've been, I literally can't wait a single moment longer. The rape complaint is not being pursued, surely that is a signal that everything will – must – return to normal? My hands are shaking as I find my bag and key, and my pulse is galloping. I am practically bursting out of my skin with excitement and euphoria. *How could I have been stupid enough to put us both through this long and dreadful week?* I very nearly let Daniel's insane ex ruin his amazing relationship with me, his actual girlfriend.

I am so beside myself with impatience that I drag my bicycle from the store at the back of the halls. Everyone in Cambridge has a bike, but I've barely cycled anywhere since I started going out with Daniel, my slightly rusty second-hand contraption isn't remotely compatible with his sleek racer, and besides, I much prefer walking, particularly beside him, hand in hand, able to chat and joke and kiss. Remembering that now, I laugh out loud at the thought that we'll soon be doing that again. Probably this afternoon. Then I brush a coating of grime from the seat and clamber aboard.

My route takes me the length of never-ending Hills Road, past the Botanic Garden on my left, and eventually to Gonville Place which runs alongside the open space of Parker's Piece. Daniel lives on a side road between the edge of the park and the nearby sports ground. The traffic is heavy with afternoon commuters and school-run mummies, but today I barely notice the four-by-fours crowding inches from my leg or smell the soup of diesel fumes because my head is so full of him. I wonder how he will react when he sees me. I picture his face breaking into sunshine, his arms held wide. I imagine stepping into his embrace, the whispered sorries that will quickly turn to kisses, the warmth and wetness of his mouth.

I reach the corner of Hills Road and stop at the junction. As I'm waiting for the lights to change a man on a road bike crosses the intersection ahead of me, moving fast towards the cycle path that heads through the middle of Parker's Piece. It takes a second for my brain to process the image, to assess the outline of the figure bent low over the handlebars, the rigid set of mouth and eyes, the starkly shorn skull, and to identify the vision as none other than my darling love himself.

With disbelief I watch Daniel's retreating rear wheel until a horn hoots from behind and I have to scramble across the road and onto the side of the park to allow the cars to flow past. *Where on earth can Daniel be going?* Not the railway station, which is in the opposite direction, or my halls, which are behind me. And he wasn't wearing his normal cycling gear, the uniform of Lycra shorts and top that denotes one of his training sessions. Rather his lack of helmet and breakneck speed suggest some kind of emergency. I gaze pointlessly at the path he took towards the north of the city, but all I can see are shoppers, dog-walkers and groups of carefree teenagers settled on the grass with beer bottles and music.

*North.* A note chimes in my head, something that Daniel said after we heard his fucked-up ex had actually dropped out of university, that she wasn't even going to take her final exams. When I asked him whether she was going home – willing him to say yes, that he would probably never see her again – he actually replied, no, that she had moved to into a room north of the centre, close to Midsummer Common. If past history is anything to go by then the most likely explanation for Daniel's wretched expression, the most glaringly obvious candidate for some new calamity, is her. Fear soaks through me like ink on blotting paper. Slowly, I swing my handlebars onto the same cycle track Daniel took a moment ago and follow in his wake.

The river hugs the farthest, most northerly border of the common, while a number of residential streets snake around the southern edge, so it is here that I concentrate my search. The houses are mainly fashionable terraces, and with a location so close to such a lovely, grassy expanse I dread to think what they might cost. It seems quite likely that some of these homeowners would be only too glad to offset their enormous mortgage costs by renting out a spare room. While a tiny part of me is clinging to the hope I am wrong, that Daniel was going somewhere else entirely, I know with the certainty of basic arithmetic that I am not wrong at all.

Barely containing my mounting anger I trawl up and down the tarmac, my eyes peeled for any sign of him. I can't believe she has ruined this moment as well, changed what would have been a sweet reunion into another ex-infused drama.

I almost don't see his bike at all. At first I pass straight by the wooden fence, it is only as I am looping back along the same stretch of road that I spot in the panelling the gate that is standing slightly ajar and, through the opening, Daniel's smart silver frame propped against the back of the house.

Leaving my own set of wheels on the pavement, I slip through the gap. The narrow yard beyond the gate seems to have been partitioned off from the main part of the house, containing only paving stones riddled with hungry-looking weeds and a rotary washing line pegged with a shirt and a couple of pairs of female pants. At the far end, there is door with a dirty, opaque windowpane. With my ear to the glass I can pick out the lilt of conversation inside, but I can't make out what is being said, I can't even be sure who is speaking.

After a moment I ease the handle very gently and step inside. Straight ahead of me the wall is blank, but on my right a staircase rises steeply to the floor above. For a moment or two there is silence and I am beginning to think I was mistaken, that nobody is here after all, when all at once I hear, very clearly, 'I'm not lying, Daniel. I'm telling you the truth.'

The tone is so strong and calm that for a bewildering instant I wonder if the person talking is Daniel's ex after all.

'You still don't believe me, do you?' she says in her new voice. 'Come into the bathroom, if you like. You can watch me pee on the stick. And don't' – there is instant venom, as if she is holding up a hand to silence Daniel's open mouth – 'don't you dare to suggest that it might not be yours!'

As I realise what she's saying I slip momentarily out of time, falling between the seconds, and then the world lurches sideways and my gut spasms with the suddenness of a running stitch. I double over with my arms wrapped around my stomach. I want to yell, to shout out, but I have no breath and there is nothing, absolutely nothing, I can think of to say.

'Why do you think' – she continues – 'I dropped the charges? I have the baby now – a part of you. Whatever you do, wherever you go, a part of you will always be with me.'

I am staring at the floor, at the unswept, unwashed terracotta tiles. *If Daniel slept with her last Saturday how can she know? How can she possibly be certain so soon?* The question pounds urgently and the answer, the all-too-obvious response, rises immediately in my throat, sour and gagging.

Daniel's voice now. 'The rape allegation was blackmail, was it? Come back to me, darling, and I'll stop the prosecution? You're sick! A complete bloody psycho.'

As I straighten up and make myself look to the top of the stairs, Daniel appears, stepping backwards out of a room, right hand scrabbling frantically at his non-existent hair.

'But you did come back to me. Whenever it suited you. Which actually seemed to be pretty bloody often! You even spoke about us going away together, taking a holiday, to make a fresh start once and for all.'

She emerges from the doorway, following Daniel, both of them oblivious to their audience below. To my astonishment she is transformed. Dressed in a long, floaty summer dress, with tresses piled into a gleaming, sexy heap and red lipstick, she looks magnificent, practically regal.

'Don't you remember?' she says. 'What you used to say to me?' She pauses before her voice becomes the parody of a whiney little boy. '*I'm so confused. I don't know what I want. I miss you so much. I miss*' – stepping into his chest, she grasps his T-shirt – '*the sex.* And then' – her inflection snaps back to normal – 'last Saturday, suddenly you weren't quite so confused any more. You decided I should fuck off nice and quietly, so you could carry on the perfect life with your new girlfriend, without her being any the wiser. Well, I had a different idea, Daniel,' she tips back her face, scarlet lips hovering just below his own, 'I reckoned she needed to know how *indecisive* you are. And that given the right circumstances you might even tell her yourself.'

Daniel doesn't speak, he is gaping at her transfixed.

She watches him carefully. 'I'm right, aren't I? You did tell her? And I'm guessing she ditched you. Well, that's OK, because, here's the thing' – suddenly her voice cracks, she swallows, and when she speaks the words are rent with emotion – 'nobody else will ever love you nearly as much as I do.'

Mouths inches apart, neither of them moves. She is panting, her ribs are swelling and falling. I see the candy-floss tip of her tongue graze her upper lip. Daniel closes his eyes. He places his hands on her shoulders. They're about to kiss, I know he's going to kiss her. My heart is crumbling, disintegrating into ruined, useless fragments, yet I can't tear away my eyes. This is the end of the show. *Daniel loves her. He doesn't love me.* The curtain swoops across the stage in one tumultuous avalanche. Perhaps I should applaud? From my position in the stalls I am perfectly placed to give them a standing ovation; me, *Julia*, Daniel's throwaway, temporary girlfriend bowing to the victory of his triumphant, twisted ex – *Claire*.

From everywhere at once there is a scream. For a tick of the second hand, the thud of a pulse, I think it is my voice that is being ripped from my throat and is shredding the walls. Until, that is, the moment I see Claire fall. No matter how often I replay the scene, willing the frame to freeze at the moment of impact, I can never be certain how hard he pushed. All I know is she staggers to one side, stumbles, and the gauze of her beautiful dress entraps her foot, sending her crashing and rolling the entire length of the staircase.

She finally comes to rest in twisted heap at the foot of the bannister. For an instant I am stone, immobile and petrified, and then her low wail of pain breaks the spell.

'Claire! Claire! Oh my God! Are you all right?' I rush to where my nemesis, the person who has caused me and Daniel so much grief, is sprawled, arms and legs bent like a puppet. I kneel beside her and to my relief, she raises her head a little, propping herself onto one elbow.

'Julia?' She sounds groggy with shock. 'What are you doing here?'

'Don't move,' I tell her. 'Not until we can be sure you're OK.' I lift my gaze to the landing where Daniel is surveying the scene, his face is waxen and unreadable. Eventually he begins to descend the stairs, moving slowly as if to check that every tread will bear his weight.

'She tripped,' he says. 'It wasn't my fault. And anyway, she's obviously fine.'

I can't tell if he means to speak to me or merely to himself.

At the bottom of the steps he stops, but rather than Claire, rather than the woman lying injured on the floor, his attention appears to be entirely focused on me. As he stares at me intently, his brow furrows while his features distort with revulsion. All at once I realise I how angry he is. How angry he has been for some time.

I touch my hair, the matted, greasy crow's nest.

'Julia! Christ – what the hell happened to you?' he says.

Absurdly I feel my cheeks starting to burn. I open my mouth, but the words have all vanished.

Daniel looks across at Claire and back at me and then he walks past us both and out of the door. Within moments I hear the ratcheting clink of his bike being wheeled away followed by the loud bang of the gate.

I glance at Claire. Her eyes are fixed on the space Daniel has just vacated; she has the appearance of somebody who can't believe what she's witnessed.

'We were meant to be together,' she whispers.

She means Daniel of course, her and Daniel. Her features are knotted with bewilderment. Bewilderment and also, unbelievably, determination. She hasn't given up, I realise, she hasn't finished with him just yet. It hits me that Daniel was never mine, even when I believed he loved me. He was always hers and somehow, I know, he always will be. My chest begins to quiver with pitiful little sobs.

After a while Claire's fingers press my arm. 'Julia?'

Gazing down, I notice with a shock how white she is and then I feel the wetness soaking through the knees of my jeans. I sit back on my heels. A sticky red puddle is forming beneath her crumpled body. The fabric at the top of her legs is filling with blood, crimson waves saturating the flimsy, pretty cotton.

'Do something, Julia,' she whispers. 'Make it stop. Please make it stop. I'm going to lose the baby.'

I consider how much I hated her because of Daniel, how much we hated each other and how, for this moment at least, we are the ones together instead. I take off my sweatshirt and roll it into a ball. I am about to place it between her thighs but I don't because it is pointless. Anyone can see from the sopping floor how utterly pointless it is. 'I can't stop the bleeding,' I say, shakily. 'I don't know how. I don't know what to do.' I wrap the sweatshirt over her shoulders, her skin is cold and little beads of dew are appearing on her forehead. 'Help!' I shout into the empty stairwell. 'Somebody help us! Please!'

# CHAPTER TWENTY-FIVE

## *Now*

As I approach from the tube station I see the house is dark, the empty bones of its interior visible through the undrawn curtains to anyone who happens to be passing. The rain has returned, repellent and relentless, and by the time I reach our front step the drops are sliding from my hair like glass beads tumbling from a broken abacus.

Inside, I realise the blackness is not complete after all, a faint glow is trickling from the kitchen, a thin, half-hearted kind of luminosity that might emanate from one of the small bulbs under the kitchen cabinets. A light that could easily have been left on by mistake.

'Hello?' I push my voice into the gloom while I stay, dripping, by the entrance. 'Angus, are you there?' The only reply is the zip of tyres spraying water on the tarmac behind me. Reaching for the light switch, I remember six months earlier, leaving the team meeting, coming home, my head bursting and suddenly hearing Mark's voice: '*Don't Claire!*' For a second, the clarity of the memory causes my fingers to flutter indecisively in mid-air before they find the brass casing and flood the room in yellow.

To my relief the surroundings appear unchanged, untouched. The sofa, the neatly filled bookcase, the Spanish mirror, the muted tones of the cream-and-taupe colour scheme, all suggest an ordered life troubled by only ordinary complications that have been forgotten about by the following week. My cereal bowl is sitting in the middle of the table, where I must have abandoned it this morning before I took the tube to work, to my nice, respectable civil service job.

Shutting the door, I note the quiet thunk of the returning latch, the sense of being severed from the world outside. I wonder how long I will have to wait for someone to arrive and keep me company; I contemplate who that someone will be. I lay my coat, the wet, sodden weight of it, over the bannister, and after a second's hesitation decide to check out the stray light – just in case he has arrived already but is keeping his presence quiet.

From the archway into the kitchen I see Viktoria hasn't been in to clean today because the countertop still bears a jar of peanut butter and a plastic tub of a butter substitute that should have been put in the fridge, while the dim arc of a downlighter illuminates the chopping board and the sludgy remains of a melon. At least, however, no one is standing beside the counter; there is no sign of either Angus or Mark.

In the sitting room I pace around the furniture. I am wearing Agatha's trainers, which are a size too small, but although they are rubbing my sore feet I don't intend to take them off in case a pair of running shoes turns out to be exactly what I need.

I check my phone.

Nothing.

I brush a film of dust from the top of the TV. Turn it on. Catch a few unbearable seconds of a late-night chat show and immediately switch it off. I fiddle with the few possessions we've bothered to display on the shelves: a silver fish-shaped trophy that Angus won in some angling competition, a Bluetooth speaker – a practical, rather than aesthetic addition – and my Portuguese bowl, the one painted so beautifully with azaleas.

Finally, a key rustles in the lock. My stomach clenches like a fist preparing to land a punch as the door is flung back and

Angus staggers across the threshold. With his clothes plastered to his body and his blonde hair dark with rain, he resembles a man who has been shipwrecked, who is lurching on to the sand of an unknown shore.

He gapes at me with wide, wild, astonished eyes. 'You came back.'
'Yes.'

For a long moment we simply stare at each other, and then he moves towards me. Although my instincts are telling me to back away, into the kitchen, the garden – a different life perhaps – I make myself hold my ground, refusing to flinch as the distance between us narrows to less than grabbing distance.

He stops about a metre away. I search his face, it should be utterly familiar, however I am struck by the same sensation I felt in the bus, that I am looking at a stranger. He stretches out a hand, not to grab me – it turns out – to touch my face, but he is too far away to reach.

'You slept with him, didn't you?'

The accusation, the surprise of it, rocks me onto my heels. 'Who?' I say lamely. *Lamely and too late.*

'Mark, of course. You slept with Mark! You booked a room. I found your reservation on the system and I went to see what the hell you were up to. You were both there together. I saw you kissing in the porch.'

Although there is rage in his voice, to my astonishment I realise he also sounds distraught. I gape at him in disbelief. 'No! It wasn't what it looked like.' *Not that time, anyway.* The sentence, my denial, flounders on the jagged rocks of guilt.

Angus steps forwards and takes hold of my forearms, squeezing the muscles made feeble by the endless hours I spend sitting at a desk. 'I should have guessed that Mark would try to involve you in his crappy business. Such an easy way to get back at me for making him sell his precious house.' He inhales, pauses, exhales, his breaths ragged with distress. 'I need to tell you something.

There was a gun in that chest Mark gave you. He had hidden the key under the mirror, stuck it with tape, but it fell, I found it—'

The pressure of his grip intensifies. He is hurting me but I don't – I can't – reply.

Angus tilts his head. Watching my face he misreads my silence. 'It doesn't matter. Not now. The gun has gone. It disappeared some time ago, I think Mark must have collected it.' His pupils bore into mine like tiny drills and his expression gradually changes. 'Jesus Christ, Claire! You knew about the gun.'

Still, I don't react.

'You knew because he asked you to hide it, and you did what he said, because,' he lets go of my arms, 'because you were already sleeping with him.' He gazes at me; the raw and naked gaze of the dispossessed, the abandoned. The gaze that I am so familiar with myself.

Regret, sadness, all those toothless, belated emotions swell in my throat. I swallow them down; I remind myself that Angus has hardly been the devoted, faithful fiancé himself.

'You never told me that you and Mark are friends.'

Angus curls his lip. 'We're not friends.'

'Business partners, then.'

He doesn't reply.

I raise the stakes.

'And *you* slept with somebody else too.'

At this, Angus shakes his head vigorously. 'Of course I didn't.' There is an empty beat, then, 'I love you.'

'What about the thong I found in the bathroom?' I persist. 'The one you said had been mixed in with the laundry in a Frankfurt hotel. It was dirty, Angus. Disgusting. The fabric stank. And not of washing powder. Besides, I found another just like it tonight in my room at The Grange' – I shiver involuntarily, as if a ghost has walked in – 'so I know exactly where you got it from, what you were up to.'

The expression on Angus's face changes, not to one of culpability, exactly, more as if he is computing a difficult exam question. There is a flat second of confused silence before the impasse is interrupted by a different voice.

'I imagine it belonged to Viktoria.'

Slowly, we both turn our heads. A figure is standing in the shadows of the landing. A man who could, in the half-light, be Daniel. Except, of course, that Daniel is dead. And the person who is starting to come down the staircase – steadily and with purpose – is Mark.

'Viktoria probably came straight here after her night shift at The Grange. I expect she needed a shower after all that hard work.' Mark's tone is conversational, as if he is discussing any old diary schedule. However, all at once it tightens. 'I would move away from Angus, if I were you, Claire. He's a very dangerous man. You've seen for yourself the kind of business he runs, what goes on in those shitty little rooms. And you nearly married him, how fucking careless is that?'

Angus turns to him, ashen and snarling, 'You lying bastard! That's your filthy set-up, not mine. I didn't want any part of it. I told you to stop. I was making enough from the paperwork but you always need more money, you always go too far!'

Descending into the sitting room Mark halts beside the Spanish mirror. The crummy T-shirt with the ketchup stain is gone; he is back in one of his blindingly white shirts and a pair of jeans. 'You need to step away, Claire. This is a man who blackmails vulnerable women, who has no conscience. My only crime is giving a few hopeless sods a ticket to ride, the chance to make something of their lives in the land of milk and honey when they have no hope of getting here any other way. A few fake jobs, a few false visas, where's the harm in that? They drew the short straw in the great postcode lottery of life. I'm just adjusting the balance a bit.'

My gaze switches between Mark and Angus. Only one of them is telling the truth. Without making any conscious decision, I have already edged slightly further from Angus. We are like three points of a triangle, although Mark is closer to the front door than I am, Angus is closer to the arch into the kitchen and the route to the garden. Bet on the wrong horse and my exit is blocked.

'*You* were the one who wanted the lists of names and addresses,' I say to Mark.

'To give to Angus—'

'That's a fucking lie!'

Mark pays no attention to Angus. His focus is entirely on me. 'I needed some money quickly. I was desperate – you saw the letter from the bank. And Angus was willing to pay a lot for that information. Not surprising, I suppose. You've seen what he does with it. How enterprising he is.'

I don't say anything. I know there are clues I'm not quite piecing together. I will myself to concentrate, to factor, to rationalise, but there is too much adrenaline coursing through my veins to think straight or quickly. It's like a light being shone directly into my eyes – similar, in fact to the blinding effect of low winter sun.

'Come here, Claire. Come to me.'

The way Mark is positioned with his back to the staircase I can just about see the reflection of his profile in the polished glass. If I half-close my eyes, squint through the dusk of lowered lids, he could be Daniel. Daniel, when he loved me. When I thought he loved me. When I wanted to believe he loved me more than anything else in the world.

'*Come here, Claire.*'

I take one pace, two paces towards the Spanish mirror.

Something glimmers; something flickers in the reflection; an unexplained needle of light that appears and is gone before I can work out where it came from. I pause, but Mark doesn't notice my hesitation. His attention has already swivelled to Angus, his features dressed in a sneer of triumph. 'You might have taken my house, my one fucking chance to get my head above water, but I took your girlfriend. Right here, in fact,' he gestures upstairs, 'and again in my car. She was very keen. Up for it any—'

The crack of bone on bone splits the air. Blood spurts in a bright, crimson arc. Mark clutches his face, howling. As Angus lowers his fist he throws himself at Mark's chest. Arms locked around Mark's waist, he drives Mark backwards, until they fall on the coffee table and crash to the ground with Angus pressing his fingers into the base of Mark's throat.

Mark gags. He is choking from lack of air and the red liquid smeared over his face and hands, running into his mouth and drenching the pristine cotton of his shirt. Grabbing Angus's hair in both of his fists, he hauls on Angus's skull until Angus is forced to raise his head, and then in one slick movement Mark releases the hair and jams his bloody thumbs into Angus's eye sockets. For a second or two Angus maintains the pressure on Mark's neck, but the gouging fingers force him backwards and all at once his grip slackens.

Mark begins to sit up and his arms drop from Angus's face, I assume he is going to push Angus away, I think he will stand up, they will both get up, that the fighting, the violence, will be over. That perhaps it is all a dream, a nightmare: Mark, The Grange, the woman in the baby-doll nightdress, even Daniel, the brilliance of the sun and the too-fast car. For an infinitesimal moment I am back in my childhood bedroom, safe amongst my A-level textbooks and my Take That duvet cover.

Then I see Mark reach his right hand towards the back pocket of his jeans. There is a spark, a flash of metal jabbing upwards so quickly I am not certain anything has happened until Angus gasps, a surprised, outraged groan, and I see the handle of our kitchen knife protruding from his ribs like the arm of a slot machine in a tacky seaside arcade.

Mark shoves Angus sideways into a crumpled heap on the floor and staggers to his feet. It is suddenly very quiet. I hadn't noticed the grunting and the heaving until the screaming absence of it now. I can't even hear any traffic. It seems as though everything has stopped.

'What have you done?' I whisper. I am on my knees beside Angus; blood is pooling on his chest around the hilt, amassing in a dark disc the shape of a saucepan lid. The flow is smooth and steady, like an underground spring seeping unstoppably to the surface. Angus is staring at me. His gaze is rigid with shock but the intensity is fading, his complexion bleaching from white to grey.

I gape up at Mark. 'What have you done?' I repeat. Now I am shouting.

He wipes his face with his forearm, smearing a crimson stain across his sleeve and doesn't reply.

Something brushes my left hand. Angus's fingers are flickering against my own in small, jerky, uncontrolled strokes. A thin trickle of plasma runs from the corner of his mouth over his chin and down his neck. His hand flutters again and his lips move. He is trying to speak, although his lungs are filling with blood, his body is drowning. I bend low over his chest.

'Claire…' His voice is transparent, a ghost. 'Be…' – he tries to breathe and exhales red bubbles – 'careful.' His lips are turning blue. A horrible brackish shade of blue. I lean closer and the ends of my hair drag through the bloody pond of his chest. 'It was meant for Mark.' The words are an almighty effort, tossed to me beyond the suction of gravity. 'The message… meant for Mark.' His eyes hang on to mine, but their grip is sliding, slipping away from me.

'Angus!' I shake his shoulder. 'Angus!' I realise that I am crying but my tears are useless and too late.

For a moment he looks at me, suspended over the abyss, holding me within his gaze. And then the connection breaks, his pupils freeze and I know he has plummeted, that he is seeing nothing at all.

I haul myself upright to face Mark, who is watching, his expression impassive.

'You killed him,' I yell. 'Why did you kill him?' I am shaking, and my head is swimming in confusion. I don't know whether to be very afraid or if the danger has passed and my biggest threat is lying dead on the beige carpet.

Mark's expression doesn't alter. 'He was an animal, Claire. You saw for yourself the kind of things that went on in that hotel.'

'What did Angus mean about a message? That it was meant for you?'

Mark shrugs. Stretching his right hand up towards his head, he runs his fingers through his hair in the standard gesture of mystification and on his little finger I glimpse his signet ring. The chunky silver band embossed with black lettering.

Watching him, I suddenly understand why Agatha's image of Nigel caught my attention; I decipher the clue that it held as the blindingly obvious giveaway clunks into place. The hand holding the tray of drinks also wears a ring, a signet ring. The extended forearm protruding into the frame, the white sleeve, didn't belong to a waiter at all. *It was Mark. Of course it was Mark.*

'You told me that you didn't know Nigel,' I say slowly.

'Did I?' Mark drops his arm to his side.

'You said, "Who the hell is Nigel?" when we were outside The Grange.'

'So?'

'I've seen a photograph of you and Nigel, together with Viktoria.'

His glance is sharp and surprised, but he recovers quickly. 'Come on, Claire. What does that matter? I was protecting Nigel. I didn't want you to find out he was involved in any of this.'

'You lied.'

'Yeah. So what? I told you, I had my reasons.'

'No—'

My brain is buzzing as the final dots now join up. As soon as you can prove one simple deceit, all the rest of someone's story crumbles like sand. Every lawyer knows that. A lie could be a single, solitary mistake, a one-off, an aberration, but believe me that's never the case. A liar never tells one lie, if he is lying about one thing then he's lying about everything else: like the identity, for example, of the person who is really responsible for turning vulnerable immigrants into drugged-up hookers.

'Although Angus was part of the fake visa set-up he had nothing to do with the blackmail, did he? And when he found out you were using his hotels he told you to stop.'

'I don't know what you're talking about.' Mark's tone is dismissive, but I see a muscle twitch in his neck, his gaze travel briefly towards me and then to the door. I wonder if he is about to make a run for it. However, to my surprise he walks over to Angus instead, to his body, squats down and picks up the wrist as if checking for a pulse.

'I saw his WhatsApp message,' I continue, '*Playing about again? You've gone too far this time. Stop right now if you want past mistakes to stay in the past.*' I have recounted those sentences so many times I can recite them word for word. 'You've been involved in the same thing before, or something like it, and the message from Angus made you think that this time he would go to the police. Only he sent the message to me first, from his business mobile, before he sent it to you, probably because we'd just exchanged texts on his personal phone.' I remember the packed train to Ipswich, full of sleeping commuters, the sudden disorientating fear that someone had found out about Daniel, but it was nothing to do with Daniel at all. 'Angus must have realised his mistake as soon as I replied.'

Mark drops his head. As though he has stopped listening, almost as if he is bored. His grasp moves suddenly from Angus's arm to the handle of the knife, which he hauls from Angus's ribcage in one swift movement. A rush of liquid wells from the wound but it's not the bloody mess of Angus's chest that has my attention; Mark is on his feet and brandishing our chef's knife like a dagger, red raindrops dripping from the blade and onto the carpet.

'You and me now, Claire. All alone. Just how we've always liked it.' The casual menace alters his voice like a change of key. Major to minor, smooth to rough, phoney to real.

I retreat towards the opposite side of the room, the wall with the television and the shelving units. The place is beginning to stink, my nostrils are filled with the salty, sulphurous stench of an abattoir and my stomach is pitching as if I am at sea. I badly want to throw up, but I make myself swallow, force the vomit down into my throat.

'I suppose,' I say, conversationally, 'you were hoping to find the Glock. Did you check the wooden chest to see if it was still there?' Although Mark doesn't answer, his glance at the box tells me I'm right. I picture him opening the lid and finding nothing but a Tesco carrier bag containing a black thong. 'I told you I threw the gun in the river. Didn't you believe me?'

Mark's grip on the knife tightens, as though he is psyching himself up for what must happen next. 'This is your fault, Claire. I told you to stay away. It was only supposed to be Angus, but you had to come and get involved.' His eyes flash with frustration; I realise he is genuinely annoyed his plans have been thwarted.

He moves forward and I back further into the corner that houses the television. Both my routes of escape, the front door and the kitchen, are less than ten metres away but if I were to try to make a run for either of them I would have no chance at all.

'What do you want from me?' I say, although the answer to that question is pretty obvious. I am merely buying myself some time.

'Nothing. I've already got what I wanted. You've served your purpose. The trouble is that now you know far too much. You're too clever for your own good.' Mark's face and shirt are caked with blood and his nose is slanting at an ugly, unnatural angle, yet he is only one throw of the dice away from the person who captivated me the first time we met. The person who made me believe I could have Daniel after all.

'You mean the list of names?' My back is flush against the painted woodwork, there is nowhere else to go, but I can't resist the chance to shatter his vile illusions.

He raises his eyebrows in a *doh* sort of way. 'Selling fake documents to those losers will probably make me ten grand which will be enough to keep the bank happy. The real money will start after that.'

'If you can find them,' I say quietly.

He pushes his temple closer to mine; all the colours of his skin – the grey, the ashen and the red-stained pores – exposed. 'What do you mean, *if I can find them?* You gave me their addresses, some will have moved on, but most will be traceable.'

'I gave you *addresses*. I might not have checked as carefully as I should they were the *right* addresses, or even actual addresses at all.' I'm looking straight into his eyes and so I get the satisfaction of seeing the flash of fury cross his face, but I don't spot his left hand, the one without the knife, fly up and smack into the side of my head. A white, scalding stripe of pain bursts inside my skull as I crash into the shelves. The floor tilts. I grab hold of a shelf to stop myself from falling. I have to stay upright. I have to reach the third shelf. That's the whole reason I lead him to this part of the room.

Mark grabs a fistful of my hair and yanks, the way he did with Angus. 'You imbecile, you've ruined everything.' He hauls me upright so that I am hanging in his grip like a rag doll. 'Look at me! Look at me! I want to see you. And I want you to see the knife!'

Slowly, I lift my face. I can feel my sight fading, the bruised and swollen skin is closing my right eye. A dribble of something warm runs down my cheek.

For a moment Mark's expression freezes. 'I liked you, Claire, I really did. You can look fucking amazing at times.' He pauses, tilting his head to one side. 'I warned you not to come here, remember. Really, you've only yourself to blame.'

While he's talking I extend my right arm behind me, stretch up one shelf, two shelves, and then to the ledge where I made sure the Portuguese bowl was sitting less than an hour earlier. My shoulder is twisting in its socket, the sinews straining to snapping point as my fingers crawl upwards.

Mark's right hand twitches and draws back slightly, the slick blade is gleaming red. He is considering the knife a little sadly. 'I hope you realise that I don't have any choice about this?'

I find the edge of the dish, tip the bowl onto its side.

His mouth twists in anticipation as my fingers grope the interior and enclose around the smooth black barrel of the Glock 17.

My first shot misses. I fire too quickly, too wildly, over Mark's shoulder and hit the Spanish mirror instead. A storm of glass erupts in a deafening crack; jagged fragments explode across the room, a rain of lethal darts fired from the bow of the wooden frame. My flesh stings as if I have been bitten and I watch the crimson tributary curl around my forearm as it holds the firearm steady, pointing it at Mark's chest.

Mark's hand is pressed to his left cheek, blood is seeping between the gaps. His eyes are blown wide with shock. 'You told me you got rid of the gun.'

'I lied.'

Mark opens his mouth but no words come out, at least none I can hear above the roaring in my own head. Like I say, if somebody is lying about one element of their story the chances are the rest is made-up too. Like the visibility of a lone cyclist when the winter sun is low on the horizon. Like how much time is needed to stop a car.

Daniel is dead because I killed him, because I ran him over with the light in my eyes and my face full of tears. Split-second decisions are the most interesting ones, they come from somewhere deep within; the part we do our best to hide, even from ourselves.

I become aware of an urgent, screaming noise. The wail of a siren rents the air and blue light pulses beyond the window. Someone – the neighbours, I imagine – must have called the police, which means I have, at a conservative guess, about five seconds to make up my mind before the matter is out of my hands. Almost immediately a car door slams, footsteps slap on the tarmac.

'Don't do this, Claire! There's no need now. You're a nice girl.' Mark's voice is wheedling, pleading.

How fucking satisfying is that?

I could tell him that people are never what you think – Mark wasn't Daniel and he never could be – but I don't waste my breath.

Very gently, I squeeze the trigger.

# CHAPTER TWENTY-SIX

Once the police finish their questions I go and stay with my parents. Within twenty-four hours of being treated like a patient on the critical list I am practically climbing the walls, nevertheless it takes another excruciating ten days to convince everyone to let me return to London.

My first engagement is a back-to-work meeting with Maggie in her office – the department's answer to Kew Gardens. A tray containing biscuits, a tall dark flask and two white china cups are positioned between her computer and a potted aspidistra. Maggie seems uncharacteristically nervous, a worried frown folding the flesh between her eyebrows into an exclamation mark.

'Do sit down, Claire,' she says, gesturing at a chair and settling herself on the opposite side of the desk. The moment I am seated she bends forwards, leaning on the bridge of her interlaced fingers, 'I just want to say,' – she pauses – 'I just want to say that none of us can imagine what you've been through and we all think you've been incredibly brave. If you find you need any more time away from the office, for stress or… um… anything else, I want you to tell me straight away.'

There is something slightly hollow, rather forced, about her little speech. I can imagine her standing in front of the mirror practising, to get the sincere yet non-melodramatic inflection right. I wonder if she suspects I might take advantage of her offer to catch up on my Christmas shopping.

'Right then, let's talk about the High Court case,' is her response to my murmured thank you. Although she sounds relieved to be switching to a more normal topic of conversation, her features don't relax. Instead she picks up a pen and pulls a pad of A4 towards herself in an overly obvious down-to-business sort of way. 'I don't know if you remember me mentioning the case to you before,' she clears her throat with a little hiccup, 'before you went away?'

I nod encouragingly.

'Well, there's been a development. Of course, you're still part of the team but I've assigned someone else to assist you. I needed to start the ball rolling in your absence, and I wasn't sure what the police... if you...' Her voice trails waywardly before regathering momentum. 'Anyway, his name is Jamie and I'm sure you'll get on very well together.' Then she adds, 'He went to Cambridge as well. Trinity like you, I believe.' She glances at me and then immediately down at her blank sheet of paper and I know for a fact she has found out that I never set foot in Trinity College, she may even have discovered that I never completed my degree. Her problem is that now she can't say anything to undermine my status as the tragic heroine in case the stress is too much for my fragile health and she has to sign me off sick for six weeks.

'That's fine,' I say smoothly. 'I don't mind working with Jamie.'

'Good.' She takes off the lid of the pen as if to start writing but then puts it down. I wonder if she is about to offer me some coffee, however she seems to have forgotten all about the presence of the thermos and the custard creams. 'Claire, I hope you don't mind me asking,' another hesitation, 'I was wondering whereabouts you're staying? I mean, I imagine you're not still living at—'

'Agatha,' I say, to spare her agony. 'I'm sleeping on Agatha's sofa.' Actually, my sitting room already has a new carpet and the walls have been repainted, just to make sure there are no pesky bloodstains to put off any prospective buyers. As a precaution the estate agent has suggested keeping the house off the market for a couple of months, until the story dies down, however they don't expect its current notoriety to dent the price in the long-term. Apparently, a couple of gory deaths might even generate a bit of extra interest, an additional premium. People can be strange, but I can't pretend I don't like the idea of the extra money.

'And the… er… police. Have they finished asking you questions?' Although Maggie's tone is light there is a filament of wire running through the centre of it. This, I think, this is the heart of the matter, the reason why Maggie has been acting like a cat traversing a bed of hot coals.

'Yes,' I say, looking her straight in the eyes. 'I only fired the gun in self-defence. The police know that.'

To be honest it wasn't very difficult to convince them. Although Mark had a knife and I had a gun, and in the Top Trumps game of deadly weapons there could only ever be one winner, there was no getting around the fact that my fiancé was lying slaughtered on the floor. I was bound to be feeling rather nervous, a little trigger-happy, and from Mark's point of view it was simply a matter of bad timing that the police arrived just seconds too late. As I explained when I was questioned, my one piece of luck was the Glock 17, which Mark had left in the wooden box. Angus had found the key to the chest – taped under the mirror, would you believe – and he told me about the gun before Mark appeared on the stairs. I was able to open the box while Mark and Angus were fighting – though sadly it was too late to save Angus. He was a hero, really. Mark killed him because he threatened to go to the police.

The almost-truth can be very plausible indeed.

*No, I didn't see the cyclist. Yes, I have to admit that I had been following Daniel. I just wanted to look at him, you see, catch a glimpse – I suppose it's true that I hadn't come to terms with the break-up. He was cycling far too fast, all the witnesses say so, and at the junction I couldn't see a thing. The sun was very low, shining straight into my face, and of course the frost didn't help. The field beyond the road was dancing with a million tiny diamonds. It was mesmerising, the last thing I noticed before the impact.*

The trick – I'll tell this for nothing – is not to cry. Much better to be struggling for control, searching for composure. Gaze out of the window and rummage up your sleeve for a tissue. Then look back, just for a moment. A small, brave smile. Say, '*I don't think I'll ever get over what happened.*'

The trick is to believe the story yourself.

Maggie is watching me. Her pad of paper is still untouched. 'Right, Claire. I don't think there's anything else.' She stands up, and so I do as well. The biscuits must catch her eye because she glances at them and colours slightly. 'I'm sorry, I didn't—'

'It doesn't matter, I had coffee before I came in.'

'Right. So – welcome back!' For an instant Maggie's right arm extends as if to shake my hand, but she thinks better of it and retracts her elbow almost before the movement becomes visible.

By the time I get to my floor everyone else is already working – at least the ones who aren't presenting in the tribunal today. I don't know what I'm expecting: a cake, a barrage of questions, a round of applause? However, to my surprise nobody says much when I arrive, they all appear engrossed in their files and hardly seem to notice me at all. As I slip into my seat, Agatha catches my eye over the top of our desktops and smiles. It's pretty obvious she has spoken to my colleagues while I was with Maggie. '*Claire won't want anyone to make fuss,*' I can hear her saying. '*She'd much prefer to carry on as normal.*' I suspect the word 'anticlimax' doesn't feature terribly strongly in Agatha's vocabulary.

I turn to the papers piled on my in-tray and open the first case. The appellant is an asylum seeker from Crimea who claims he was forced to deliver anti-Russian leaflets to pay for his mother's cancer treatment – some people get a really shitty deal. I manage to read about twenty pages of statements and interview notes before I decide to fetch the coffee that Maggie forgot to give me. Agatha must have done a pretty thorough job at discouraging any outward displays of curiosity because even when I go to the kitchen and hang around for a few minutes nobody bothers to join me.

I am on my way back to my desk when the sight of a coat slung over the back of Nigel's chair temporarily stops me in my tracks. I hurry over to Agatha. 'Nigel,' I say, pointing, 'when did he come back?' Agatha's expression lights up like a Christmas tree before deflating an instant later.

'No, Claire. That's not Nigel. I don't suppose he's ever coming back. A new guy sits there now, his name is Jamie. In fact,' she pokes my side unnecessarily, 'there he is now!'

As I turn around a man appears on the other side of the room, walking from the direction of the lifts. Mid-height with short dark hair, he must notice us staring in his direction because he stops and lifts his hand by way of greeting. Immediately, Agatha waves back enthusiastically.

My arm, however, remains pinned to my side. I can't move a muscle and my voice has vacated my throat. Really, it's as much as I can do to remember to breathe. I can hardly believe my luck. The man smiling at me across the wasteland of the office floor, the man who is about to become my colleague, my working partner no less, looks exactly like a professional, more sophisticated version of Daniel.

# A LETTER FROM SARAH

I want to say a huge thank you for choosing to read *The Couple*. There are so many books to pick from these days that I really appreciate the fact that you decided to read mine. If you did enjoy it and want to keep up-to-date with all my latest releases, just sign up at the following link. Your email address will never be shared and you can unsubscribe at any time.

*www.bookouture.com/sarah-mitchell*

The psychological thriller has become so popular in recent years and as I wrote *The Couple* it was easy to see why. As an author it is very liberating to have as a main character somebody with dark depths to her personality who is strong – or bad – enough to take matters into her own hands and seek revenge against those who have wronged her. Some readers may well find Claire a disturbed or evil character, while others may have a little more sympathy for the decisions she makes. A few may even wonder if, in the right set of circumstances, they could possibly be tempted to behave in a similarly shocking way themselves! I think a big part of the pleasure of books like this is the licence they give us to explore these shadowy yet tantalising boundaries within the safety of fiction.

Lots of psychological thrillers have a legal setting, and for most of them that setting is the criminal court. In *The Couple* I chose instead to use the backdrop of the Immigration Tribunal. Since so many recent news stories are about people fleeing from terrible situations in other countries I thought it might be interesting to tell you a little about what happens to their claims when they get to the UK. And also the particular kind of vulnerability faced by immigrants seemed to me to make a very good basis for a crime story. I ought to emphasise, however, that although the examples of cases referred to in *The Couple* are typical of the kind of work done by the immigration tribunals, of course none of them are based on real people.

I hope you loved *The Couple* and, if you did, I would be very grateful if you could write a review. I'd be so pleased to hear what you think, and it makes such a difference helping new readers to discover one of my books for the first time.

I also really appreciate hearing from my readers – you can get in touch on my Facebook page, through Twitter, Goodreads or my website. When I am beavering away at my desk it is always wonderful to get a message and realise that somewhere people are actually reading what I've written!

Thank you
Sarah

 @SarahM_writer

# ACKNOWLEDGEMENTS

The seedling for *The Couple* was planted in a crime-fiction class at UEA several years ago. I am greatly indebted to Professor Henry Sutton for believing in it from the very start and for his whole-hearted encouragement and guidance as the novel took root and began to blossom. I would also like to thank my lovely agent and editor – Veronique Baxter and Jenny Geras. I am incredibly lucky to have such expert and professional support, and their input has enabled the book to flourish and become the best version of itself that it can be. Another huge thank you is owed to my friend, Clare Barter, who manages to combine wonderful, insightful comments on the text with gentle corrections to my spelling and grammar! Finally, to my husband Peter – thank you for all the big and all the little things (and for solving my computer problems every single time…).

Lightning Source UK Ltd.
Milton Keynes UK
UKHW020344230819
348428UK00016B/312/P

9 781786 817907